Rona Randall

Dragonmede

A Troubadour Spectacular

Futura Publications Limited

A TROUBADOUR BOOK

First published in Great Britain by
William Collins Sons & Co Ltd in 1974

First issued by Fontana Books in 1975

First Futura Publications Revised edition in 1980

Copyright © Rona Randall 1974

ISBN 0 7088 1571 5
Printed by
William Collins Sons & Co Ltd
Glasgow

Futura Publications Limited,
110 Warner Road, Camberwell,
London SE5

Rona Randall was born in Cheshire, but brought up in London from childhood. Her first ambition was to become an artist. She won a three-year scholarship to a local college of art but circumstances prevented her from taking this up. She took a secretarial course, but hated it, and later became a drama student of the late Frank Forbes-Robertson; toured, played in rep, understudied and played 'bit' parts in London but didn't make the grade . . . 'Couldn't really act well enough!' . . . so fell back on a secretarial job in an editorial office, and loved every moment. She became a journalist, then a short-story writer, graduating to serials and novels. She is married to a chartered quantity surveyor, has one son, two grandchildren. She lives in Sussex. Her hobbies are making pottery, when time permits, collecting antiques, theatre, travelling and, of course, reading.

For my husband

One

BY MOST STANDARDS my upbringing was scandalous, although it was a long time before this fact was brought home to me. As a child I accepted without question the bohemian, rather shameful, but happy life I lived with my mother until I was old enough to learn that it was, to say the least, unconventional, and even then I continued to accept it because whatever her mode of living, her lack of morals, and her feckless attitude toward money, my mother had the rare ability to make life rich and full and warm. She lived generously and she loved generously, and more than all she loved me.

It wasn't surprising that visitors streamed to our tall terraced house in Bloomsbury. Her personality drew them like a magnet—and so did the gaming tables. The famous and the titled came nightly to our home, as well as the increasing number of freethinkers and intellectuals who claimed that it was unfashionable to respect aristocracy and tradition. There had been an industrial revolution and eventually, they said, there would be a social one too. But that was in some remote future which, mercifully, could not affect the present.

This was the middle of the eighteen-hundreds, with England at her golden age and the British Empire covering three-quarters of the world, so that it actually was a realm on which the sun never set. The nation accepted its power with the arrogance born of achievement—those who had not worked for it taking it for granted, never really dreaming that its superiority could ever decline.

This attitude was typical of the guests who came

to my mother's house. They regarded the middle-class Victorian virtues of sobriety and thrift with patronizing amusement, because they were wealthy enough to do so.

None of these guests was short of money; otherwise they would never have been there. They came to gamble, and gambling was a rich man's pastime—or a rich woman's. Most of them were married, but never to each other: rich women with their lovers and wealthy men with their mistresses; some extravagant young sons of noblemen who had been sent down from Oxford or Cambridge; and all with one dominant passion—gambling. Occasionally I wondered if their philosophizing about social equality and the emancipation of women was no more than a sop to their consciences, because once the cards were brought out they thought no more about either. Then the sparkle of anticipation would light my mother's eye and she would blow me a kiss in dismissal.

That was the signal for me to go upstairs to the rooms she had set aside for me and Michelle, for although some said she was without conscience, she was scrupulous in regard to me. Never would she allow me to enter the cardroom on the ground floor, even when I grew up.

"It is not for you, Eustacia. Remember that."

Actually, she had nothing to fear. Growing up in an atmosphere of gambling had inured me against it. Cards held no appeal, although I knew that but for my mother's skill with them, creditors would have been knocking loud and hard on our door. The excitement and challenge of gambling never infected me—perhaps because I sensed, at an early age, that it could become a fever in a person's blood, or because I also witnessed the tragedy and bitterness it could bring about.

Many were the times when I overheard quarrels and recriminations in the early hours of the morning, and I still carry childish memories of waking out of sleep to the sound of raised voices far below, of pattering barefoot from my bedroom and craning my neck over the banister to see down the well of the stairs to the ground floor, from where the voices came, and being puzzled and a little frightened because, earlier, those same voices had seemed friendly and it was hard to believe that they could become accusing and bitter.

Once I even thought I heard the shot of a gun, but when I wakened, crying out in fear, Michelle came running and, cradling me in her arms, told me it was nothing but the slamming of a door. "There is a wind tonight, *chérie*. It caught the front door as it opened and banged it loud . . ." And in the morning I had not breakfasted with my mother because, Michelle explained, she was sleeping late.

Long after, remembering the incident, I remembered something more: that for a household where the mistress was sleeping late there was a lot of activity that morning, a lot of coming and going; the clip-clop of horses as carriages arrived at our door; authoritative voices that seemed to be asking questions . . . and my mother's, strained but controlled, charming them into silence.

I listened from above while Michelle cleared away our breakfast things, and when she came back upstairs and discovered me there, she pulled me after her into the room we used by day and which I grew up to think of as "our" sitting room. Firmly, she closed the door.

After that the house was silent for many weeks. People stayed away, even my mother's most intimate friends, and although she was as warm and affectionate to me as ever, she was quieter, more withdrawn, with a tension about her which I put down to anxiety about money because during that period, when the card parties had ceased, bills accumulated and tradespeople became less affable. Some even called and refused to go away, like the loudmouthed man whose unyielding bulk seemed to block out the daylight, his many-tiered chin leaning over me like that of a great fat toad when I answered the door one day because old Bella didn't seem to hear the jangling bell.

I could have been no more than six at the time, although precocious for my years owing to my up-bringing, which had already taught me that bills should never be paid until the dunners were at the door. There was one there now. The enemy. I sensed it at once and tried to shut the door, and felt enraged because the toad's enormous foot got in the way, and again Michelle came to the rescue, whisking me away and calling imperatively to Bella, who came shambling up from the basement kitchen at once.

As long as I could remember, Bella had been with us, cooking and cleaning in her haphazard but loyal way. She was devoted to my mother and refused ever to leave her, even when her wages were overlooked.

One other thing about that day stands out in my memory like a vignette. It is the picture of my mother's hands feverishly searching through her bureau in the hope of finding some money with which to pacify the enemy, her long, carefully manicured fingers trembling a little as they flung aside papers and letters and a host of unpaid bills, then pouncing in relief on a little wad of banknotes.

"Thank God! I thought someone must have stolen them—I wouldn't put it past Hazel Courtland or Clive Danvers or any one of them!" She kissed the banknotes with a touch of her normal gaiety, and then kissed me too and said, "Let this be a lesson to you, Stacy: always keep a little something by."

"For a rainy day, Mamma?"

I'd heard Bella say that in the kitchen, and thought it very profound. "She oughta put something by for a rainy day, that she oughta. Gawd knows wot'll become of 'er if she don't."

But my mother wasn't impressed by my wisdom. She laughed instead and hugged me, enveloping me in perfume and affection.

"No, my darling, rain always goes away! But keep a little something hidden where your friends can't see it—and never let them know it's there."

And off she sailed to deal with the enemy, and because I loved to do things for her, but also because even at that age I knew she would bundle everything back untidily, and untidiness meant muddle and consequent scoldings from Bella, I began to pick up the scattered papers. I thought my beautiful mother would be pleased, but when she came back her glance went to my hands, and her face paled.

In one swift movement she snatched the papers away, and I stared in amazement, for I could see no reason why she should swoop so agitatedly upon a bundle of bills and some old picture tore from a periodical.

Some time after that the atmosphere in the house changed again.

It all started with a newsboy shouting in the street. My mother, who had been silent all day, sitting tautly behind the lace curtains of the first-floor drawing room but seeing nothing beyond them, suddenly leaped to her feet and called to Michelle to go quickly, *quickly*. Whereupon Michelle raced downstairs and out to the newsboy.

A moment later she was back, smiling and excited, and my mother, waiting rigid as a statue, came sharply to life and cried, "Acquitted? He's been *acquitted?*"

Michelle nodded and held out the paper. I saw bold headlines which I could not read, and a man's face which was familiar because I had often seen it right here in this house; I saw the newssheet go flying as with one triumphant sweep of her arm my mother hurled it aside, laughing and crying at the same time.

"He has been lucky, Madame, lucky. It could have been manslaughter—imprisonment—or worse."

"Never! Not for Lucky Jack! It was self-defense, anyway. What other verdict could there possibly be?"

She seized me then and danced me round the room, singing and laughing, wild with joy.

"We must celebrate! A champagne party! Tell Bella at once! And a new gown—I *must* have a new gown to welcome him back. I saw a divine thing in Bond Street the other day, pearl gray satin billowing over hoops, with tiers of lace in the softest Parma violet and a superb sash of deep purple velvet trailing to the floor at the back, and shoulder drapes falling from a deep, deep neckline, the kind he loves me to wear."

"And the price, Madame?" Michelle asked drily.

"Prices are never displayed on gowns like that—just one superb model in an exclusive modiste's window. It is probably outlandish, but who cares? This time tomorrow I shall be wearing it! This time tomorrow he will be here again!"

"And these?" With typical French practicality Michelle indicated the batch of unpaid bills. "*They* will still be here, Madame, and buying a costly gown won't help to settle them. Besides, at the moment your credit is not good."

"But the modiste in Bond Street doesn't know that. I have never dealt there before."

Laughter rippled through the room, and the unpaid bills were torn into shreds and thrown into the air like a cloud of snowflakes, and I laughed too, swept up on the tide of my mother's happiness.

She bought the gown. She gave the champagne party. People came back: all the old familiar faces. But his was not amongst them.

I did see him sometime later—again, in a newssheet. Bella had it in the kitchen and was trying to hide it.

"You can't," Michelle said. "She will have to know sometime. Better now, while she is alone, than when her friends can see her."

Bella handed over the paper reluctantly.

"What is it?" I demanded. "What are you going to show Mamma? Let me *see!*"

"Why shouldn't she?" shrugged Bella when Michelle tried to withhold it. "The mite's too young to understand."

It was a beautiful picture: the picture of a bride, dressed all in white. She stood within the entrance of a church, holding on to the arm of her bridegroom. I recognized him at once as the man called Lucky Jack—the man who had come regularly to our house for so long that even I guessed that it was not merely the gambling that drew him, but my mother. Sometimes I even wondered whether he would replace my father in her life, although secretly I believed no man ever really could.

I knew all about my father, of course. His name was Eustace Rochdale, which was why I was called Eustacia, and my mother had eloped with him at the age of seventeen. It was the sort of romantic thing my mother would do.

"Life in a country parsonage was too dull for me, darling, and your father was so handsome, so persuasive. It was love at first sight, I do assure you."

My father had been a soldier. Brave as well as handsome. He had died a soldier's death when I was little more than a babe in arms. This was the story my mother told me when childish curiosity made me wonder why I had no father as other children had. She told the story simply and without embellishments, and in so doing she gave me a hero forevermore—a father to be proud of, so that I felt superior to the other children who walked in Hyde Park after church on Sundays with their tightly laced mothers and stiff-collared fathers, tall-hatted, cravatted, bespatted men who worked at dull jobs in the City, unadventurous and unheroic. Spats! I would look at them contemptuously, mentally comparing them with a guardsman's military boots, for of course I knew without asking that my father had been in the Guards.

But my mother gave me something more than a hero for a father; she gave me a romantic love story to dream about and cherish. Eustace Rochdale had swept her off her feet, rescuing her from a life of imprisonment in a narrow-minded household with all the bravura of a knight rescuing a princess from a tower. No conventional wedding for them.

"My love, my father would never have consented! A sedate curate, yes—preferably well born and well connected, who might ultimately become a bishop; but a dashing soldier, never! So we eloped, and I've never regretted it."

How characteristic of my mother to do the unconventional thing and to take the consequences without complaint. Never did she bemoan her lot, although widowed when little more than twenty, with a baby to support and precious little to do it on.

"Never blame your father for leaving me unprovided for, Stacy. He died young and he did his best. He also . . . taught me a lot. And for that I am grateful."

As she said this, her long, tapering fingers flicked through a deck of cards with the rapidity of an expert. She used to practice daily, and I would watch fascinated as she cut the deck into two halves, then sent the gilt edges into a flying pattern of gold, interleaving them like a pair of fans until they were welded into one pack again. Over and over. Cut. Fan. Flick . . . *brrrrrr* . . . Shuffle. Weld. Deal All like lightning—faster and faster, until it was impossible to separate the motions of her supple fingers from the speed of the cards.

But she would never teach me. There were other things more enjoyable to do together. Walking in the park, for instance, be the weather wet or fine, warm or cold. My mother was fond of walking, perhaps because she had been brought up in the country, but also, she once told me, because it cleared away the cobwebs. I thought she meant the cobwebs which Bella ignored about the house and which she, who was so fastidious about her clothes and her toilet, surprisingly overlooked as well, but eventually I learned what the expression really meant and that this was the reason why she always went walking in Regent's Park the day following a particularly late night, returning refreshed and ready for another.

But also, she told me, walking preserved the figure. Without exercise a woman grew fat, and this she was determined never to be. So saying, she would look down at her flat stomach and slim hips with satisfaction, and walk along with the swinging step that drew men's eyes. She was tall, and her back was straight and slender, her waist so narrow that it scarcely needed lacing.

At home she frequently abandoned hoops; they were a nuisance, she said, and fashion must ultimately discard them for more practical skirts like those of the Regency—long, slim, and elegant. She wore house gowns on similar lines, softly outlining her figure. Some of her friends pretended to be shocked, but they copied her nevertheless. In these clinging gowns she would relax even to the extent of crossing her legs when lounging at ease in our drawing room. That was when I saw the eyes of men lingering on the outline of her thighs and upon the gentle swelling of her breasts above her low-cut bodice. It seemed then as if her whole body were laid bare, and at such moments something disturbed and vaguely frightened me. She became a woman I did not know. I wanted to shout at those men to turn their eyes away. Instead, I would slip quietly out of the room, aware that I was unnoticed.

But my mother had every reason to be proud of her figure, and I had every reason to be proud of her as we walked along together. She would hold my hand and I would dance along beside her, or she would let me run free across the grass, without even my bonnet or gloves on. I knew that other children, walking sedately with gray-uniformed nannies or quietly bowling hoops, envied me.

Sometimes my mother ran with me, pulling off her hat too and forgetting to be a lady. I adored her at those moments and would shout in delight when she swung me off my feet and whirled me around, not caring tuppence for the disapproving glances of sedate matrons.

But on wet days we kept to the paths; she was strict about that, as she was about my being well wrapped up in cold weather. Throughout my childhood I was aware of one dominant thing—my mother's protective feeling for me. It was as if everything she did, whatever she did, had one primary aim and purpose: to give me all the things that she considered best, and to shield me from others.

It was during one of our walks that Michelle came into our lives, and little did I dream how important she was to become to both of us, particularly to me. The rain was heavy, which meant that we had to keep to the paths and I had to be content with making squelchy sounds with my galoshes, my mother joining in the fun by making squelchy sounds with hers. She had a way of making a game of everything. She laughed at life. And laughed at it even more after she saw Lucky Jack's wedding picture; but it became hard, brittle laughter for the most part, except when she was alone with me.

But this particular day preceded that one by many

months, and the bitter note that I began to recognize in her laughter as I grew older was absent then. We ran head down against the rain in a wind driving too hard for umbrellas, which was why I stumbled over a park bench and the wet bundle of humanity lying upon it.

My mother stopped dead in her tracks, staring at the prostrate human being; then she sat down and lifted the rain-soaked head onto her lap, smoothing back the sodden hair and murmuring in concern. When my mother looked like that, full of pity and tenderness, she was at her most beautiful.

I knew that for the moment she had forgotten me, but I didn't mind. I too was staring at the ashen face, and I went on staring at it all the way home in the hansom cab which my mother went hurrying to fetch, leaving me beside the wet bundle as if mounting guard, then commanding a reluctant cabbie to lift the inert figure into his vehicle and into our house on arrival.

That was how Michelle came to our home, and stayed there, nursed back to health with warmth, good food, medicines, and kindness.

"There are workhouses for creatures like this," the doctor said. "The poor soul's not likely to recover from pneumonia. She can be taken there to die."

"And be buried in a pauper's grave?" my mother flung back as she snatched up her reticule and emptied out all the money she had. "Whoever she is, whatever she is, she's a hunan being. Do the best you possibly can for her, and if there isn't enough money there, I will find more."

"She needs constant nursing, Mrs. Rochdale."

"Tell me what to do, and I'll do it."

"Night and day."

"Bella and I will take turns."

"Do you know what you are undertaking, Mrs. Rochdale?"

"Yes. I am trying to save this poor girl's life—and I thought that was a doctor's mission too."

He had the grace to look embarrassed, but he picked up the money and pocketed it even so, saying it would be enough to go on with. For a long time afterward, until I met Nicholas Bligh, I thought that doctors assessed a human life in terms of money.

As he left the house that day, the doctor said to my mother somewhat apologetically, "You're a good woman, Mrs. Rochdale"—at which she laughed heartily, flinging back her dark head as she always did when amused, white teeth flashing.

"You're the first man who's ever said *that* to me!"

Michelle Dubois was a lady's maid, of no fixed abode, without a penny in her pocket. She had come from Clermont Ferrand to work in one of the fine Nash houses on the outer perimeter of Regent's Park. She had lost the job and couldn't get back to France.

"Why? Were you dismissed without wages?"

"Yes, Madame."

"That means you had committed some misdemeanor."

A questioning glance in the dark eyes, which now looked back from a pale but reviving face.

"You did something wrong," my mother explained.

"So they said, Madame."

"And were they right?"

Hesitation. A flicking glance at my mother's clear and knowledgeable eyes; the realization that to lie was useless; a reluctant nod.

"So the agency—I presume you came to this country through one of those new and dubious domestic agencies that bring girls over from the Continent?—would take no responsibility for you. Women come to this sort of pass all the time, in all sorts of ways, in this grand and glorious age of ours. The streets of London harbor them in their thousands, destitute and desperate; that is why it is known as the whore shop of the world." My mother touched the white cheek compassionately. "You have been with us for several weeks now. You're getting better every day. As soon as you are well enough to travel, I will pay your fare home."

"*Non,* Madame!"

There was terror now.

"So you're afraid to go back? Why? Would your family not accept you? What did you do, Mam'selle? Sleep with the master of the house? Or the son of the house? Are you going to have a child?"

An emphatic and confident denial.

"I can believe that. It was a stupid question because obviously, being so ill, you would have lost it. So it must have been something worse. Something for which you could have been convicted? Was it theft, perhaps."

Another denial, but less convincing. "I was—wrongly accused, Madame."

Silence. The small gilt clock on my mother's bedroom mantelpiece ticked busily. For someone who was ill, the best bed and the most comfortable room had been allocated as a matter of course.

"If you and I are to get along together," my mother said firmly, "we must understand each other, which means you must never lie to me, Mam'selle. *Were* you wrongly accused?"

The eyes in the pale face flickered again; looked down and then up; grew steady and honest.

"No, Madame."

"What did you steal?"

"A brooch, Madame. A small gilt brooch. Her Ladyship never wore it. It was there, tossed into a trinket box. She kept worthless things in that box, and when asked to give presents to charity she would take some out without even looking at them and have them parceled and sent away. So I thought she would never even miss it. It was such a little brooch. What I did was wrong, I know, but I could not stop myself. I never can."

"So you'd done it before?"

Silence again. Another nod.

"At home in France? Until you could no longer get work there, so came to England, where French maids are in demand? It is a familiar story, Mam'selle, and oh, so sad. And now you are afraid to go home because your family would have no sympathy . . ."

"I would be turned away, Madame. My mother is ashamed of me. She has kept house for the Curé since I was a baby. How could she expect a priest to open his doors to me again? He used to make me do penance, each time harder than before, right from the time I went to the convent to be educated. It was at the convent that I began taking things belonging to other girls. Just little things, Madame, so that I would feel the same as they. When I was expelled, Father Clément tried to help me. Six times a day he prayed with me, asking the Good Lord to drive out my wickedness and the Blessed Virgin to intercede for my soul. Also, when he rose at dawn for meditation, I had to rise too and go to church without first having food, and kneel on the stone floor with my feet and legs bare until he gave me permission to rise—sometimes for as long as two hours or more, if his holy thoughts absorbed him. Suffering, he said, would help to save me from perdition. He was very good to me."

"So it seems," my mother answered drily. "I don't wonder you are afraid to go back. And I though an English parsonage bad enought."

"A par-son-age, Madame? What is that?"

"Something not so bad as your noble Curé's house, you poor child. I, at least, never suffered physically. I merely stifled." The subject was changed quickly.

"So you like pretty things? Well, that's natural enough."

"But my premonitions are not natural, Madame. The things I see, the things I sense. For these too I was punished, and no one believed me when I swore they came to me like visions."

For a moment there seemed to be a stillness in the room, almost a sense of chill; then my mother said lightly, "Don't tell me you are psychic, Mam'selle. Do you foretell the future too? If so, spare me, for the future is something I never wish to think about. Live in the moment, forget the past, never worry about what is to come—that is my creed, and I advise you to share it."

Her petticoats rustled as she swept across the room, unlocked a drawer in her dressing table, and took out a jewel case. With her back to the bed, she unlocked it, then carried it across to the girl.

"These, Mademoiselle, are my jewels. I know each and every one of them. I wouldn't give one away to charity, becaue I consider that begins at home. I am showing them to you to prove that I trust you." She locked the case again. "And this is where I keep the key." She dropped it down the neckline of her gown, in the little valley between her breasts, and laughed. "You'd find it difficult to get hold of there, wouldn't you? And at night it is concealed in my room—this room, from which you will be moving shortly. I might mention, Mam'selle, that I am not always alone at night."

"Of course not," said the girl, understanding something I did not. "Madame is very beautiful. Naturally she would not be alone at night."

I was puzzled. What had beauty to do with it? When three people shared a house—Mamma, myself, and Bella—none of us was alone. Grown-up talk was often confusing.

But all my mother said was "Good. I think we understand each other. If you want pretty things, you must work for them. Work well and I will see that you have them."

The dark-ringed eyes looked enormous. "Work, Madame? You mean . . . ?"

"That you will be staying with us, of course. Do you imagine I would turn you out on the streets again? When I have money, which is when the cards go well, you will be paid good wages. At other times, you will be fed and have a home. In return . . ." My mother laughed gaily. "I have always wanted a French maid! It adds to one's social prestige, of which, alas, I have little. Besides, French lady's maids have talent with the needle and with the hair. That is so, is it not?"

"*Mais oui*, Madame! I am skilled as a dressmaker— the good sisters taught me well. They also taught me to speak English, although it was not so good when I first came to this country. And so that I should qualify as a really skilled lady's maid and obtain good employment, Maman sent me to be trained by a good coiffeuse. I can cut, style, do anything with the hair, Madame."

"Splendid. And don't worry about the times when your wages may not be paid. They will be few and far between, I promise, for I make sure the cards go well. I am a skilled player; I use my brains. Only sometimes it is tactful to let others win."

Michelle nodded solemnly. It was as if, right from the beginning, there were a rapport between those two which made explanations unnecessary.

"Who was your last employer, Michelle? You referred to her as Her Ladyship. She may be known to me."

"Lady Shalford, Madame." The words came a trifle apprehensively, as if Michelle were afraid that her Ladyship might be approached for a reference and this sudden good fortune come to an abrupt end—but my mother's explosive laughter chased away any lingering fear.

"Letitia Shalford, by all that's wonderful! Have no fear—she is no friend of mine. But her husband is. I know Lady Shalford by sight, of course. Everyone does. Good-looking, I grant you. She is famed for her clothes and her style and her hair, *and* for being the greatest snob in London. But now I know she is a fool as well. A good French maid is worth more than a paltry brooch. Here, take this."

Impulsively, my mother unpinned a small silver brooch from the wide lace collar at her shoulders and fastened it on Michelle's nightdress, brushing away the girl's incoherent thanks with the remark that it was of little value, otherwise she wouldn't be giving it away.

"Besides, you poor thing, you deserve some compensation for suffering destitution on the London streets. God knows what experiences you had before illness overtook you."

A thin hand came out from beneath the coverlet and seized my mother's. It was kissed with passionate gratitude.

"Don't, my dear, don't!"

"There is nothing in the world I would not do for you, Madame."

"All I ask is that you dress my hair as beautifully as you dressed Lady Shalford's, and that you teach my little Stacy to speak French as perfectly as you do. My parsonage instruction was woefully inadequate, but you speak your language as it should be spoken, I can tell. I suppose that is the result of being brought up in the Curé's house. Sadist and hypocrite he might be, but he must have been well educated and well spoken, and I've no doubt that the sisters at the convent were equally so. I am not ambitious myself, Michelle, nor am I a social climber, but for my daughter I want the best of everything."

And so Michelle became part of our household and my constant companion. She loved my mother, but as time passed perhaps she loved me more—at any rate, in a different way. She became protective, forever on guard for me. She gave her loyalty and gratitude to my mother and fulfilled every obligation to her. Since it was Madame's wish that her daughter should speak French fluently, Michelle made sure that I did. In time we talked to each other almost exclusively in that language.

It wasn't until I went to school that I realized why I had never really got to know the local children, and even then I didn't grasp the truth until it was unwittingly thrust into my face by a pupil who lived in one of the grander houses in Gordon Square. Her name was Prudence Holford.

The school was a private one, run by a couple of spinster ladies who knew more about good manners and deportment than about scholastic subjects. I think they accepted me as a pupil for two reasons: first, because they needed the fees, and second, because my French was so fluent that they would be able to pass me off as an example of their excellent tuition in that language, which I quickly recognized as being inferior.

The fact that I was brought to school each day by a French maid also impressed them, although I felt they looked askance at my beautiful mother, resplendent in dark green velvet and sables, the day she enrolled me. The poor things were both drab, bespectacled, and plain, so I knew they not only envied her but were awed by her until, with her devastating charm, she won them over. As we left, the interview finishing with many bobs and smiles as my mother counted out banknotes with a flourish (I learned later that fees paid in advance were almost unknown to them), I heard the elder Miss Mortimer whisper to her sister, "My dear, it *cannot* be true! She is so ladylike . . ."

But from Prudence Holford, who sat next to me in class, I learned the truth within a matter of weeks, for when her birthday came along I was not invited to her eagerly awaited party.

Pru was devastated. She wept copiously. "I don't *want* a party if you can't be there," she wailed.

"Don't be a goose," said I. "Of course I'll be there!"

We were alone in the Gordon Square gardens. People who lived in the square had keys to open the iron gate, which was kept locked to exclude outsiders, but after school Pru would steal her parents' key and we would spend long sessions there, giggling and exchanging confidences, mimicking the Misses Mortimer, sharing secrets—all the things that young girls do. But today Pru was in no mood for fun.

I was waiting, as usual, by the gate, and was puzzled because she didn't come racing out of her house as she always did, holding her skirts high above flounced petticoats. Instead, she dragged her feet, in their buttoned cloth-topped boots, slowly down the steps and across the road, kicking fallen leaves until they swirled around her ankles. She looked glum and unsmiling.

As soon as we were in the gardens, we went straight to what we called our secret place—a small grassy area hidden within a dusty shrubbery; whereupon she flung herself down and burst into tears. It was then she declared that she wanted no birthday party if I couldn't be there.

Because my answer seemed to pass unheeded, I shook her by the shoulder and repeated it.

"Of course I'll come. I've just told you."

She turned her head away, as if unable to look me in the eye, then blurted, "You can't. You're not invited."

It was like a slap in the face.

"But you promised!"

"I know I did. And I meant it. But Mamma says no."

Pru's tear-stained face and unhappy eyes suddenly made me feel more sorry for her than for myself, and since I was, on the whole, of a logical turn of mind, there seemed to me to be only one explanation.

"It must be because enough have been invited already," I said, swallowing my disappointment. "Bella always says she can cater for just so many and no more. I expect your mother thinks the same. I would be one too many."

"Oh, no, it isn't that," Pru answered with the brutal honesty of the young. "It's because of who you are. I mean your mother—what *she* is. Mamma says that none of the other girls would be allowed to come if it became known that Luella Rochdale's daughter had been invited, but I said you can't be blamed for what your mother does."

My body went taut.

"What do you mean?"

"Well, everybody knows, don't they? The whole neighborhood has known for years, Mamma says. About the gambling salon which the police pretend not to know about because, after all, it only seems as if she gives card parties."

"And why shouldn't she give card parties?"

"Oh, Stacy, it isn't only that! It's the men she entertains. And the things that happen. Like the time two men fought over her and one was shot. My mother says Luella Rochdale doesn't only make money by cheating at cards, but by taking men to bed with her."

I flung out my arm and struck Pru across the face, and then I was pelting toward the iron gate and out into the square. I didn't stop running until I reached home.

The front door was shut, and I didn't bother to

pull the iron bell, but raced down the area steps and into the basement kitchen. I heard Bella cry out in surprise, but on I went through the kitchen and up the stairs into the hall; up again to the drawing-room floor, where I halted briefly, glancing inside and finding the room empty. So was the little morning room behind it.

"Where is she?" I cried. "Where's my mother?"

"Come back 'ere, Miss Stacy! You come back 'ere!"

I heard the note of panic in Bella's voice, and that spurred me on. The bedroom. Her bedroom. I raced up the stairs again, and at the top Michelle appeared, took one look at me, and tried to block my way. I thrust her aside. I heard her cry out, *"Don't go in there*, chérie!" But it was too late. I had the door open.

My mother lay on a tumbled bed, relaxed and drowsy. She was half propped against pillows and was smiling sleepily at a man seated upon a window seat. He was wearing a robe, his back to the afternoon light. I couldn't see his face. I didn't want to. I stared only at my mother: at her full, round bare breasts and long, firm thighs, her flat belly and curving hips. Somewhere at the back of my shocked mind the thought registered that she looked like one of those naked women one saw in art galleries, painted on canvas or sculptured in marble, except that she was warm flesh. A drift of heat and perfume came to me from the bed—the perfume she always wore, but which she had applied more liberally than usual.

I was twelve and too innocent to realize the atmosphere in the room was of satiated sex. All I knew was that something had taken place between these two, something intimate and private which shut me out of her life.

I felt sickened and angry because I had been too blind to see what the whole neighborhood had guessed and talked about for years, but stronger still was the shock of discovering that there was a side to my mother about which I knew nothing.

The man drawled, "My dear Luella, how stupid of you not to lock the door."

My mother turned her head lazily, saying it was a nuisance having to get up to admit Bella with the tea, but she broke off abruptly at the sight of me. She covered her nakedness swiftly, but in that same moment I was out of the room and racing upstairs to my own, slamming the door and turning the key violently behind me.

Michelle kept knocking at my door, pleading to be let in, to let her talk to me. Bella also tried, ordering me to open up and stop sulking.

"You didn't oughta go barging into yer ma's room like that! C'mon now, ducks, unlock this 'ere door and let old Bella in. I gotta nice cuppa tea."

I remained silent and dry-eyed, sitting on the side of my bed, aware only of bewilderment and shock. I knew the shock to be unreasonable, because as long as I could remember I had seen men fall in love with my mother, and she with them; but her overprotective attitude toward me had kept me in blissful ignorance of anything more than that. It seemed incongruous now, because already I had heard sniggering schoolgirl remarks, when the Misses Mortimer were safely out of earshot, about what a man and woman did when they married.

"They take all their clothes off when they go to bed," Pru had whispered, which seemed shocking to me. I remembered feeling glad that my mother wasn't married, because these was no man to make her do such a thing. When my mother went to bed she wore beautiful nightdresses—I had seen them; but now I realized with a jolt that a woman could go to bed with a man even if she was not married, and disrobe for him, but what happened after that I refused to wonder about. I only knew, instinctively, that the man in the robe had been enjoying my mother's body in some way, and I hated him.

Memory pierced my mind with forgotten fragments: my mother's voice saying, "I might mention, Mam'selle, that I am not always alone at night," and Michelle nodding in understanding, saying that Madame was very beautiful, so naturally she would not be. But I had been—how old? Five, or less?—and the significance of the words had been beyond me.

I also remembered the long, meaningful, appraising glances of men as they eyed the curves of my mother's body, and my childish anger with them for doing so, and the total unawareness, on her part as well as theirs, when I quietly slipped away.

Now I crossed the gulf between childhood and young womanhood in one bound, bitterly resenting the fact that my mother had tried to present one picture of herself to me and hidden another. But dominant above all was the sickening thrust of Pru's words.

"My mother says Luella Rochdale doesn't only make money by cheating at cards, but by taking men to bed with her."

A chasm of unsuspected knowledge spread out before me, and as I recoiled from it I heard my mother's voice commanding me to open the door. It was calm and authoritative, and because I had always obeyed her, I did so automatically. I turned the key, then moved quickly away, leaving her to open the door for herself. That gave me time to reach the window and stare out across the rooftops, my back to her.

"So you don't want to look at me, Eustacia."

I made no answer. She closed the door.

"If you do, you will see no difference in me. I am still your mother. I love you as I have always loved you, and always will." She waited a moment, then said, "Please turn round, Eustacia," and although she put it as a request I knew it was really an order, and obeyed, wishing I had the courage to refuse.

There must have been something in my face which caused that sharp catch in her breath as she murmured, "You poor child. I should have spared you this."

"You should never have spared me, Mamma. If I had always known, if I had grown up being used to it, it wouldn't have mattered."

"You mean you would have accepted it as a part of life." Her shoulders rose and fell in a shrug which was half bewildered, half resigned. "Perhaps you are right. I am not a good mother, but I do try, and I've always thought that part of being a good mother was to protect a child from seeing or knowing things which you had no desire for them to see or know. But now I realize that the shock is greater when they find out."

"I know men fall in love with you, Mamma. I have always known it, because I've seen it happen. I have heard the way they speak to you and seen the way they look at you, and sometimes you have only seen them and not me, so I've guessed you loved them in return. I used to wonder if you would marry one of them, but was glad when you didn't. I like having you to myself."

"And now you feel you haven't?" She was no longer talking to me as if I were a child; nor was I talking to her *as* a child. Those days had gone abruptly.

"Believe me, Stacy, things are unchanged between us, but I should have prevented this afternoon."

"You mean prevented what happened when I was out, or prevented me from discovering? In that case, you should have locked the door, even if it meant the bother of letting Bella in with the tea!"

My voice cracked on a high note. I saw her flinch, and was glad. I saw her sit down slowly, a quiet, but elegant woman wearing a quiet but elegant dress, her lovely hair piled on top of her head, as regal as a queen. She was as remote from the naked woman upon that tumbled bed as I was remote from Pru's respectable world.

"Eustacia, I must make you understand. You are growing up."

"I am grown up."

"At twelve? That is still childhood."

"But not to me." The tears and the hysteria that I had held in check were threatening me now. "If I were a child, I wouldn't understand what it means when someone tells you that your mother not only makes money by cheating at cards, but by taking men to bed with her."

Color drained from her face so quickly that it no longer looked like her own.

"Who told you such a thing?"

I wouldn't, couldn't, give Pru away. I still remembered her crying with her face against the dusty grass.

My mother waited, and I remained silent. The silence seemed long and oppressive.

Then she said, "All right, Eustacia, I won't press you. Obviously, it was one of the girls at school, and obviously it is someone you want to protect, which means you must like her. I won't prize you away from your loyalty, but I will give you the truth. When I play cards, I know how to win. I have to. It is our sole means of support."

"Except my father's Army pension. Since he was an officer in the Guards, you'd be bound to get a pension when he was killed."

I thought she looked a bit startled, but she only said, "More schoolgirl knowledge, I suppose." Then she shrugged. "Pension or no pension, my dear, I couldn't run this house and take care of us all unless I won fairly regularly at cards. That is all I am prepared to say on that score. The other is more important. I have never in my life taken money from a man in return for my love. That is as true as the fact that I do fall in love, and men fall in love with me, and when you are older you will realize that when a man and woman love each other, everything becomes natural, and essential, and beautiful. Money can never enter into that, whether one's lover is rich or poor. And I have the perhaps unfortunate tendency to fall in love with men who are invariably poor, even when they are highborn and appear to be rich. But that doesn't matter. I give them happiness, and for a while they give it to me, but somehow I always seem to discover it was a mistake, or meet another man and fall headlong in love again. It is the way I am made."

She sighed in a way that seemed half resigned, half contemptuous.

"I am giving you the truth, Eustacia, because I realize now that you must have it, and accept it—just as you must accept the fact that in the whole world you come first with me. I hoped I would remain first with you until the day you marry and go away."

The thought of ever parting was so unbearable that I flung myself upon her, clinging tight, feeling oddly protective toward her and remembering innumerable examples of her devotion to me and her kindness and warmth toward others, and pitying poor Pru, who had a mean-spirited and spiteful mother; also all the other girls at school whose parents would have walked past a wet bundle of humanity lying on a park bench without lifting a finger to help it, let alone emptying their purses to bring it back to life.

After that incident, the relationship between my mother and me changed. On my side it was based on acceptance, although in some ways an uncomprehending acceptance, and on hers on a passionate desire that I should feel in no way different from other girls. That was why she sent me away to one of the new and fashionable schools for young ladies, choosing select Bedlington Grange in Kent.

Here no one knew of my background; my mother was the widow of a Guards officer (I believe at one stage I hinted at the Household Cavalry) and, as befitted the daughter of a deceased and distinguished soldier, I was carefully polished, mixed with daughters of the gentry, learned to ride—which I did with surprising ease considering that the nearest I had ever been to a horse was watching the riders in Rotten Row—and very quickly occupied a respected niche as a fluent linguist.

Speaking French like a native, I was allowed for that language to substitute German, which was much respected since it had been Prince Albert's own tongue. Languages came easily to me, but I discovered something for which I had a greater love, and that was art. Beside it, all other subjects paled.

The years at Bedlington were happy and ended all too soon. Not until I finally left at the age of seventeen did I realize that promises of lifelong friend-ship with school friends would be impossible to keep because invitations to their homes could never be reciprocated. I glimpsed those homes during holiday visits, and always they had one thing in common: respectable, united home life. The fact that my friends' parents were invariably wealthy and often titled was of less importance to me than that.

But in one way I scored: none of the girls had a mother as beautiful as mine. So much was evident on Parents' Days, when Luella attracted all eyes and charmed them into the bargain. But she was dutiful in more ways than attendance on visiting days; she fol-lowed my progress with greater conscientiousness than many parents, and when encouraged by the Headmis-tress to foster my talent for painting when I left, she made arrangements for me to study with a prominent Bloomsbury artist, Joseph Whitehead.

Nevertheless, I knew that my mother had only one real ambition for me: to marry well, and to marry soon. Without putting it into so many words, I knew she wanted me out of the setting in which she had reared me, and the thought made me pity her and love her more. I knew also she had hoped that sending me to Bedlington would lead to the kind of marriage she wanted for me—that I would meet some eligible and desirable brother of a rich and wellborn fellow pupil, thus justifying not only her choice of a finishing school but her struggle to maintain the fees.

On leaving, I felt that I had let her down because no such possibility was in view: I had met several eligible brothers and attracted some of them, only to terminate everything when I realized that to invite them to my unconventional home would mean one inevitable end. The gambling, the free-and-easy morals of my mother and her circle, the lax way of life which contrasted so sharply with the homes from which Bedlington girls were drawn set me apart from them.

I felt the sharpness of this contrast even more when I returned permanently to the Bloomsbury house. During my holidays my mother had been at pains to tone down the loose atmosphere for my benefit. After that unforgettable afternoon when I was twelve, she had kept her *amours* carefully guarded; when she took a lover, she was discreet. But when I returned home for good it was impossible not to realize that the atmosphere had worsened, that gambling was for higher stakes, and that patrons were less mannerly, less cultured.

When I said as much to Michelle, she sighed, raising her shoulders and letting them fall expressively.

"Alas, you are right, *chérie*. Your mother's salon is not so select as it once was. That is because the aristocracy is becoming poorer. It is the men in industry who have the money now, mostly from the Midlands and the North, where I believe they call it 'brass.' It is very sad. In the days of Lucky Jack, almost everyone who came here was titled."

"And was he?" Memory flashed back to the headlines which I had been too young to read, and the wedding picture which, in recollection, now told me so much. "What was his name, Michelle?"

She answered evasively, "I cannot remember, it was so long ago."

I said without thinking, "Can you remember someone being shot in this house?"

A shutter came down abruptly.

"Non!"

So it was true, I thought. I had never mentioned the thing Prudence Holford had told me, but I had remembered it, thought about it, and wondered.

Luella—as she now insisted upon my calling her, a practice considered by the conventionally minded as being overly familiar and disrespectful between mother and daughter—would still never allow me to enter the cardroom, and even tried to keep me away from the drawing room unless she considered her visitors respectable enough to meet me.

Between my home and Joseph Whitehead's studio my life took on a strange pattern, for in neither did I totally fit. At Bedlington I had acquired certain standards which my fellow art students viewed with some amusement, but when, because they were verging on the bohemian, I invited them to my home, Luella regarded them with undisguised distaste. This was not what she wanted for me; friendship with impecunious students offered no hope of the successful marriage that she so passionately desired.

On the other hand, neither did my home life, for this raffish establishment was the last place in which I was likely to find the kind of husband she had set her heart upon. As my twentieth birthday loomed up, I knew Luella was caught in a web of anxiety—torn between conflicting moods of remorse, thwarted ambition, and optimism. After all, twenty wasn't all that old, although marriage no later than eighteen was the expected thing. But after her careful planning, all that semed likely to be my fate was some dull occupation as a teacher of drawing or a life like her own, which was the last she desired for me and the last I desired for myself.

It was impossible not to see the effect this life had had upon her, the imprint it had left, the tight lines of anxiety about a mouth once soft and lovely, the reckless despair which she grew less able to hide. She seemed to trust no man now; only her skill at cards. She played longer and, I sensed, more recklessly, more desperately. Her slimness changed to thinness. She coughed a lot and grew impatient when old Bella clucked over her like a mother hen.

She also grew impatient with me.

"What is to become of you, Stacy, if you don't marry soon and marry well? What about Clarissa Mannering's brother? He was interested in you, you admitted this yourself, and when you returned from a visit there you also admitted that you found him attractive."

"I was a schoolgirl, Mamma, and he a student at Cambridge."

"You are not a schoolgirl now, and he will no longer be at Cambridge. And for goodness' sake, don't call me 'Mamma'! From a young woman of your age it makes me feel old. Write to Clarissa. Say you long to get out of London for a while. That will surely bring an invitation. And take Michelle with you. You know well enough that a French maid always creates a good impression."

"No, Luella."

"And why not, pray?"

"I won't run after people."

"Well, you may be sure they won't run after you!

No matter how lovely—and you are lovely, Eustacia—a girl in your position is never pursued."

"I won't cultivate people just because they might be useful," I insisted stubbornly.

"In heaven's name, why not? How else do you think I have filled the cardroom all these years? This attitude of yours will never get you a husband, and wasting your time with those art students won't either. They are penniless for the most part, and artists remain so until after they are dead. As for meeting the right type of man here, my love, even I have to admit there is no hope of that."

Which shows how wrong she was, for within a few days Julian Kershaw walked into our house—and into my life.

He was standing with his back to the drawing-room fire—a tall, blond young man of striking good looks and, I felt, a total lack of conceit. His handsomeness sat as naturally upon him as the well-tailored suit which my mother was covertly assessing.

I saw all this at a glance as I whirled into the room, flung down my portfolio, and, unpinning my bonnet, flung that down too. I had been praised by the critical Joseph Whitehead that day, and felt exhilarated.

"Ah, there you are, Stacy!"

There was satisfaction in Luella's voice, plus a kind of pleasurable anticipation which I was now well able to interpret. Money had entered the room with this young man. The thought, and the significance of it, chilled me somewhat. I had no desire for him to be welcomed here just for that reason; I wanted him to be welcomed for himself. I didn't pause to analyze my reaction. I was only aware of the impact he made upon me, which was one I had never felt before; not so immediately or so pleasurably.

My mother was making introductions. I heard his name, and that of another, and saw that a second man was seated nearby and that Julian was glancing at him expressively, as if to say, "Don't you know you should rise when a lady enters a room?"

Obviously, the second man didn't. He was older, thick-set, rather coarse-featured, and when he spoke it was with a strong Northern accent.

"Like mother like daughter, eh?" He eyed me boldly. "In looks, anyway."

Luella frowned slightly. "I can assure you, Mr. Crowther, that is the only way in which my daughter does resemble me."

"She'd do well to have your generous nature, Ma'am."

It might have been meant as a compliment; it might not. Luella let it pass, but not I.

"I agree, Mr. Crowther. My mother is the most generous woman alive. The number of needy people whom she has helped would surprise you."

He was not so thick-skinned as to miss the frosty note in my voice, but it left him unembarrassed. He went on lounging in his chair, and Julian frowned on him even more. I wondered how it came about that two such opposites should be here together.

My mother picked up the silver teapot and filled it from the matching kettle on the spirit stove beside her. Tea with honors, I thought. That meant that one or the other of these men was important. Or both. I feared it was the uncouth man, who loudly proclaimed what Michelle referred to so distastefully as "brass." And yet it was Julian Kershaw who had the cultured air and he, obviously, whom my mother wanted me to meet.

That meant she was accepting Crowther on sufferance or because she had to; otherwise she would have got rid of him before I returned. As it was, she was pouring tea for me, patting the sofa beside her, urging me to talk about what I had done today, although she had long ago ceased to be interested in my painting.

"My daughter is very talented," she declared with maternal pride, addressing the remark especially to Julian. "And in that, I can assure you, she does *not* take after her mother!"

The man named Crowther said drily, "A pity, if I may say so, Ma'am. I'm sure you have great talents, Mrs. Rochdale. Leastways, so I've heard."

I think it was the slow anger in Julian's eyes that endeared him to me. I knew that but for our presence, he would have taken his companion to task for being insulting. My mother caught his smoldering glance and smiled serenely.

"Alas, Mr. Crowther, the only talent I have is at cards, as you may find out this evening."

"No woman has ever beaten me at cards, Ma'am, and few men."

"I can believe it." Her tone was honeyed and her glance full of flattery. "But you are not going to refuse me the chance to try, I hope?"

He smiled indulgently.

"I shall be honored, Ma'am."

"And I," said Julian.

"Nay, lad, if you've any sense you'll keep out of the game. You know you always lose."

There was a note of contempt in the older man's voice, but Julian flashed a good-natured smile.

"Win or lose, what does it matter? It's only a game."

"That shows how little sense tha has, lad."

I felt a sharp concern. I didn't want this charming young man to become enmeshed in gambling. He caught my eye, and for a moment our glances held. I saw reassurance in his, as if he were saying, "Don't worry. I can take care of myself."

I hoped so indeed, but I had no trust in his companion, whom I judged to have a head on his shoulders, a scheming brain, and a certain ruthlessness. In broad, flat accents he asked, "And your daughter, Ma'am? Will she join us this evening?"

"No." Luella's voice was firm. "Eustacia does not play cards."

"She is wise, Ma'am. Or you are."

The shrewd eyes looked from one to the other of us, and slowly a kind of dawning comprehension crept into them, his glance finally settling on my mother for a long and thoughtful moment.

But Julian looked frankly disappointed, and before they left he said to me quietly, "I hope that when we return tonight, Miss Rochdale, I shall at least have the pleasure of seeing you, even if you don't join the game?"

I felt a swift elation coupled with an unaccountable shyness. My upbringing had taught me to mix with all sorts of people, so I had never suffered from self-consciousness, but now I was strangely tongue-tied, keenly aware both of myself and of him. The admiration and desire in his blue eyes disturbed me; the gentle smile of his beautifully shaped mouth disturbed me; everything about him disturbed me in a way that was both potent and important. I knew as well as he that we had to see each other again and that we would seize every opportunity to do so.

After the two men had gone, my mother was vibrant with excitement, calling imperatively to Bella to bring out the best wines tonight and plenty of food.

"That man Crowther has a hearty Northern appetite, I'll be bound. And as for you, Stacy my love, wear the sapphire velvet gown Michelle made for you. Blue is your color, particularly that shade. And see that she dresses your hair in that new style, coiled loosely on top of the head and puffed out at the sides; it makes your face look more heart-shaped than ever."

So she had noticed Julian Kershaw's admiration. This proof that I had not imagined it pleased me.

As I turned to go upstairs, Luella called softly, "He liked you, my darling."

I looked back with a little smile.

"Very much."

"Which means he is acceptable?"

"More that acceptable."

"Don't be too hopeful," I begged. "It might not last."

"But you want it to?"

I nodded, aware of the betraying color in my cheeks and an excitement equal to her own, but the thought of her disappointment if nothing came of this meeting distressed me. So did the thought of his losing money at her hands, and never coming back.

"Please, don't let him lose tonight."

"Rest assured that I shall not." Her hand came out and touched mine. "Trust me, Stacy. I know what I am about. He will return, I promise, and not merely for the thrill of the game."

I asked slowly, "Is he a gambler?"

She shrugged.

"Most men are."

"I would be happier if he were not."

"Then it is up to you to wean him away from it, and judging by the way he reacted to you, you should be able to do that easily enough. He is ready to be swayed by you."

"They seem ill-matched companions, he and that man."

"No two could be more different."

"Then how did they come here together?"

"Crowther came with an introduction from old Clive Danvers. You may remember him; he used to come here a lot when you were a child. Unfortunately, his wife found out and put a stop to it. Now I hear he has only an occasional flutter at his club, poor dear. It is an exclusive club, or was until it opened its doors to rich industrialists and merchants. It was there that

Crowther met him, and I suppose it was there that he met Julian Kershaw, for I cannot imagine them meeting socially. Kershaw is the son of Sir Vivian Kershaw. They are a well-known Sussex family. Crowther is a millowner from Lancashire. In every way they are poles apart, but I am glad Crowther brought Julian with him."

For once, I was in entire agreement with my mother. The only thing that mattered was that Julian had come into my life.

"Didn't you once tell me you came from Sussex?" I asked.

Luella nodded.

"From the same area as Julian?"

She answered indifferently, "I don't actually know where his home is. Sussex is a vast county, spreading all the way from Kent to Hampshire."

"Tell me about him," Michelle demanded as she dressed my hair. "He must have made an impact on you, this young man. I have never known you so anxious to look your best."

How could I describe him? Tall, handsome, blue-eyed, with a devastating charm? It sounded too much like a prince in a fairy story, and there was nothing so insubstantial about Julian. He was a man who made me aware of his masculinity and of my own femininity; he was intensely physical and made me conscious that I was too.

The strength of this physical appeal frightened me a little, but it also excited me. I remembered my mother lying nude before her lover and my cheeks flamed, for now I knew what desire was like and that I longed to be with Julian in such a way. But not illicitly. Not as a mistress to be visited secretly, like something of which to be ashamed.

Michelle's knowing eyes were upon me, and to cover

my confusion I glanced at the small gold fob watch
pinned at my breast, and urged her to hurry.

"Seven-thirty, Luella said, and it is almost that
now!"

"You must not be ready and waiting, *chérie*. That
would appear overeager, and deprive you of making
an entrance." She put the finishing touches to my hair
unhurriedly. "And unpin that fob watch; it ruins the
effect. You need no ornaments with that gown; just
your white skin to contrast with the deep blue.
There!"

She stood back and appraised her handiwork.

"The style suits you, but it is becoming com-
monplace these days. You need something more
striking, more unusual . . ."

Hairpins flew as her fingers pulled them out, and
at my cry of impatience she merely said, "Do you
or do you not want to win this young man? Pray do
not trouble to answer; I know it already. It is in your
face, and I am happy and hopeful for you. So have
a little patience, *chérie,* and I will do my best to
make your dreams come true."

"No premonitions?" I said with a laugh. "No secret
warnings that things may go wrong?"

"How can I experience such things without seeing
him?"

"That is easily rectified. Peep over the banister
tonight."

"I have every intention of doing so," she answered
blandly as she swept my hair from my brow, twisting
it into a chignon low at the back of my neck. With
my bare shoulders, the effect was striking. As always,
Michelle's taste was faultless, suiting the style of my
dress and to my looks, ignoring the dictates of
fashion.

She did more than peer over the banister that
evening. She opened the front door, forestalling Bella.
I stood on the landing, out of sight, listening to voices

from far below: the loud accents of the Lancashire man and the modulated tones of Julian. My blood raced. Even his voice could stir me.

Beneath my excitement I was aware that Michelle was not being her voluble French self, but silent and restrained, playing the superior servant, no doubt. She did that when she wanted to make the right impression, or to counteract the slovenly one that Bella often gave, especially if she had been too busy in the kitchen to whisk off her soiled apron. Michelle gave tone to our establishment, and I hoped that the uncouth Crowther was suitably impressed. I was also glad (and the realization shamed me) that it was Michelle who admitted them and not dear old Bella. I wanted Julian's approval of everything.

I heard Michelle show the guests upstairs to the drawing room, then the rustle of Luella's gown as she went to greet them. In a while I would go down and join them in a glass of wine, followed by supper with, perhaps, one or two other guests whom my mother considered worth entertaining and who would remain for the card party later while I went back to the drawing room and occupied myself for the evening. That meant I would be in Julian's company for, at the very least, two hours.

And after? That depended on how long play lasted. Meanwhile, I had to compose myself, still the wild beating of my heart, and quell the betraying color in my face. Michelle was right; to have been waiting downstairs would have appeared overeager. Even worse, it would have meant self-betrayal, for I could not have hidden this breathless excitement or my keen awareness of him.

Michelle's footsteps were returning. A moment later, she stood before me. Her face was white.

"Don't go down there, *chérie*. Don't go down there!"

I stared. I had never seen her look like this. Her

predictions and warnings were a familiar part of our lives—scarcely heeded, affectionately indulged; but now there was a tension about her which communicated sharply.

Momentarily, it frightened me. Then I asked briskly, "What ever are you talking about, Michelle?"

"You and that man. He spells danger, *chérie. Danger!*"

Two

I SWEPT PAST HER and down the stairs. She was referring to Crowther, of course, with his shrewd and calculating brain, his lack of sensitivity, his unscrupulousness. Her warning was needless; I had every intention of avoiding the man, and every confidence in my mother's ability to dispose of him should he prove troublesome. Many were the men to whom she had refused further admission. Carefulness was her watchword. I had nothing to fear.

My entrance was all that could be desired. Julian rose slowly to his feet, staring at me in obvious admiration, and my happiness because it was he who betrayed himself first was overwhelming. I made no attempt then to hide my own pleasure, and as he stooped over my hand and kissed it, I was wildly happy.

Everything happened so quickly after that. For the following week Julian came to the house every night, sometimes with Crowther, sometimes alone, making the card game the reason, but really coming to see me. This he admitted very soon.

"I'm not all that keen on gambling, but what a convenient excuse it makes. After an hour or two I can slip away to the drawing room to be alone with you."

I knew full well that my mother encouraged him in this, terminating any game in which he was playing as quickly as she could.

"It is simple, my love. A few hands for low stakes, and the others grow impatient for the high gambling to begin."

I was glad about this: she was being careful not to enmesh Julian in the real business of the evening. "He loses a little and he wins a little," she assured me when I expressed the slightest anxiety. I was glad about that too, because weaning him away from a game that was no more than a slightly unprofitable pastime was easy.

He assured me that he lost no more than he could afford, and invariably won it back again. "I'm not like Crowther. I don't make a business of it."

"You mean he is a professional gambler?" I felt apprehensive, anxious that my mother should not suffer at the hands of a skilled rival.

"By no means, but to a man of his nature, making money in any way is an essential in his life. He would be a bad loser, whereas I don't care tuppence whether I win or lose. I come here to see you, and you know it. I'm head over ears in love with you, Stacy."

"As I am with you," I admitted gladly.

All would have been perfection, but for Michelle. She went about the house looking troubled and uneasy, but I refused to heed her. For the first few days after Julian had declared his love, I could think of nothing and no one else. Michelle with her pessimistic brooding, Crowther with his cynical, watchful amusement, Luella with her suppressed eagerness, Bella with her curiosity agog—all meant nothing to me. The days began and ended with Julian's arrival and departure, and that Luella was being true to her promise was obvious, for he rarely spent more than half his time at the card table. Only once or twice, after he became an established visitor, did I have to wait overlong for him to join me, and when I did he was apologetic for keeping me waiting and kissed me even more passionately to make up for it.

It was at moments like this, when the sensual undercurrent to his nature became dominant, that the first seeds of uneasiness began to grow in my mind. He loved me, but he said nothing of marriage. Yet he pursued me with ever-increasing confidence and boldness. One night, after he had left the cardroom later than usual and my desire and impatience for his company had reached such a pitch that I was unable to hide it, he pulled me full length upon the drawing-room sofa and laid his body upon mine. Somehow my voluminous skirts were pushed aside. His breath was hot on my cheek, his mouth and hands searching. I felt them on my flesh and desire quickened within me, but simultaneously came fear. He was about to seduce me, and because I was my mother's daughter I knew what that would lead to: a passionate love affair, and then nothing. He would be the first of many lovers, and my life would follow Luella's unhappy and unsatisfactory pattern.

I didn't want it.

With one swift movement I was off the couch—restoring order to my disarranged skirts, smoothing my hair, turning my back upon him as I drew my opened bodice over my breasts and hid from him the tears that disillusionment brought. I heard his cry of protest, and then silence. I was trembling and knew he was too, but for a different reason. I shook because I was hurt, angry, and disappointed; he because he was physically rejected. Frustration of that kind displeases any man, but I thought indignantly that I had a right to be displeased too.

I had scarcely restored order to my appearance when the door clicked open and Luella stood there. It failed to occur to me that her entrance was timely. Her experienced glance assessed the situation at once, and although she sailed into the room quite calmly, giving Julian every chance to collect himself, he knew as well as I that she was angry. Luella as the outraged and dignified mother was extremely effective.

"Would you like me to accompany you downstairs, Mr. Kershaw?"

"No—no—I thank you, Ma'am."

"Then we will say good night, Mr. Kershaw."

Julian threw me one beseeching glance and walked from the room. Not until the closing of the front door echoed through the house did I break down.

Luella cradled me in her arms, rocking me as she had done when I was a child.

"He will come back, my love. He will come back."

I didn't believe her. Nor did I want him to come back solely because he desired my body.

"He will come back because he loves you, Stacy."

"As your lovers have loved you?"

"All men love women that way, but you have been cleverer than I. You were wise to resist him. It was a clever ploy."

"It was no ploy!" Indignation choked me. "I did it because that isn't what I want!"

"Every woman who is honest admits that she wants it. I know it is the fashion to feign distaste for physical love, but that is the fault of the well-bred gentleman, who keeps his wife as a symbol of respectability and his mistress for his delight. The men make the rules, and the hypocrisy of them is not our fault. A 'good' woman isn't supposed to enjoy sex. But as long as a man has money, he has only to stroll in the streets or parks around midnight to have his pick of thousands of prostitutes, ready and willing to give him any sexual diversion he wants. We live in an age of extremes— extremes of wealth and extremes of poverty, extremes of virtue and extremes of vice. This is why our menfolk like to imagine that their wives have such delicacy of feeling that submitting to their physical needs *is* mere submission. They want it that way, as proof of purity. If a wife enjoys the physical side of marriage, the inference is that she's on a par with the impure." Luella patted my hand approvingly. "Rejecting Kershaw, my love, was the wisest thing you could have done."

"But I've told you, I didn't do it because it was wise! I love him. I want him. But I didn't want to be taken like a slut on a couch, and I didn't think, when he first said he loved me, that that was what he intended."

"I don't suppose it was, but you can't blame a man for being carried away." She finished with a brisk, down-to-business air: "Do you wish to be his wife?"

I wanted nothing more passionately, and said so.

"Then you shall be. Now wipe your eyes, go to bed, and wait for tomorrow."

"Tomorrow won't bring him back," I said disconsolately. "He will never come back."

"I have already told you that he will; but you won't be here to receive him. Not at first. He must wait, grow impatient, believe you haven't forgiven him, that he has insulted you irremediably. That way he will want you more, and guilt will make him anxious to atone."

It all sounded very scheming to me, but when I said so, Luella laughed.

"And do you thnk men don't scheme when they want a woman?"

That was different, I argued. Man should be the hunter.

"Which is precisely what Julian Kershaw is going to be."

I went to bed unhappily, not really believing her. Michelle looked in to say good night, and regarded me with troubled eyes.

"He has hurt you," she stated in an I-told-you-so voice, which annoyed me so much that I was abrupt with her and then, of course, sorry, but by that time she had left the room, closing the door ominously behind her.

For the first time, I wondered if there might be something in Michelle's premonitions.

It was Luella I should have heeded, not Michelle, for everything worked out as she predicted. Julian began to woo me the very next day: first with flowers, accompanied by no message—lavish red roses which spoke for themselves. He kept away from the house for a week, and each day more red roses were delivered, until it was all I could do not to send a note round to his lodgings begging him to come to me. Had I know his address I am positive I would have done so, risking Luella's opposition, but it suddenly occurred to me that I had no notion of where he was staying, whether he had his own apartment in London or rooms in a hotel.

In all our hours together, he had talked little about himself—only about me, and our love, and his need and longing for me, and how he wanted to be with me always, which was why I had mistakenly assumed that marriage was his object, since "always" implied permanency.

When at last a note arrived, I fell upon it eagerly.

> Please forgive me, Eustacia. My behavior was unpardonable, but blame my love for you. It carried me away. I beg you to let me call.

It bore an address in Grosvenor Square, and Luella acted promptly: an invitation was dispatched for a card party two days later; but still the chance to see me was denied him.

"You stay out of sight," my mother insisted. "Go

upstairs to your studio and don't come down. Nothing will tantalize him more than to know you are in the house and yet unavailable to him."

I was aghast. The thought of being beneath the same roof yet barred from him was intolerable. Besides, I felt his punishment had gone on long enough and was not wholly fair. Julian had responded to my own impatience that night. I remembered rushing across the room to greet him, and being swept into his arms. My eagerness must have seemed like an open invitation.

I felt ashamed now for condemning his behavior, but when I said so, Luella pronounced firmly, "It is up to the man to exercise self-control where a young and inexperienced girl is concerned."

"And yet you said that night he was not to be blamed for being carried away!"

"That's as may be, but Kershaw must know well enough that you are a virgin, and yet he was ready to seduce you. Penitent he should well be, but don't go falling into his arms the moment he returns. Let him wait for that until after marriage, my dear."

She had wisdom for me, but not for herself, I thought, but said nothing.

I dined alone with Michelle that evening, then went upstairs to the attic, which I had turned into a studio. But now painting failed to absorb me, concentration was lacking, and several times I opened the door, straining my ears for the sound of his voice from far below. Long after midnight I went to bed, aware that the game had not yet broken up and hoping that he was lingering over it only because he might eventually be able to see me. Then something told me there was no hope of our meeting tonight—that Luella was determined to keep him in the cardroom for the sole purpose of depriving him of this hope and so frustrating him that the next time he came he would be determined to have me at all costs, and propose marriage without further delay.

The thought troubled me. I didn't want his hand to be forced. I wanted him to ask me to be his wife, but to ask of his own volition. I was also afraid he might take this deliberate avoidance as a rebuff, and never return. And so I lay sleepless, unhappy, tormented to such a degree that I rose and left my bedroom door ajar, listening for the sounds of departing guests. But not until the early hours of the morning did anyone leave: desultorily at first, in ones and twos, their voices from the distant hall indistinguishable, so that I had no knowledge of the precise hour at which Julian left. When I eventually heard Luella come upstairs to her room, it took all my self-control not to rush down to her, full of reproaches.

Next morning, at breakfast, I could feel Michelle's speculative glance upon me, and avoided it. I ate little, anxious to be gone, in no mood for conversation. A session with Joseph Whitehead was what I needed; he made his students work, and thus my mind would be taken off Julian and my frustrated longing for him.

"You are unhappy," Michelle commented as I pushed aside my chair; "but it will pass, my little Stacy, it will pass."

"Is that a prediction? If so, I prefer it to your warnings," I answered lightly.

"You do not heed my warnings, but you should. I knew when M'sieur Kershaw entered this house that it could mean only one thing."

"Danger!" I scoffed. "That was your prediction then. I am glad you have changed your mind."

"Who said I had changed my mind? Not I, *chérie*. All I say now is that your unhappiness will pass. It is a good thing that he is gone. For this reason you are unhappy just now, but I am glad, because with his going a terrible menace goes out of your life."

I flung myself out of the room impatiently. Michelle talked a lot of nonsense at times, and this was the biggest nonsense of all.

Then I realized that she must be unaware of Julian's presence in the house the night before. That surprised me, for Michelle missed little. This surprise was immediately followed by the depressing idea that perhaps she had known, which lent an ominous significance to her pronouncement that he had now gone for good.

I was depressed as I prepared to leave for Whitehead's studio. What if Michelle's intuition was right? What if Julian had departed in anger the night before, because he had come specifically to see me and been firmly denied? What if my mother's tactics had been wrong, after all?

I was suddenly angry with myself for heeding them. I should have followed my own instincts and hurried downstairs to see him. Now I had lost him irretrievably, I was sure of that, and my thoughts were despairing as I pushed sketches into a portfolio, aware that Joseph would be none too pleased with what I had achieved since my last session with him. My work reflected my restlessness and my inability to concentrate, but how could I explain to a man so old that I was too deeply and too unhappily in love to care about anything else?

For June, the morning was cold. From my studio window I could see London's dusty plane trees swirling in the wind. The skies were gray. The weather reflected my despondent mood and did nothing to lighten my aching loneliness. I fastened the portfolio listlessly and dragged myself down to my room, choosing a cloak at random. It hung in folds to the ground, covering the long straight dress that I wore when working because billowing skirts got in the way in Joseph's crowded studio. Then I tied my bonnet mechanically, tucked my portfolio under one arm beneath the cloak, and pulled on my gloves.

But when I saw the note on my dressing table, my arms went weak and the portfolio slid to the floor, for the handwriting was Julian's. Joy and apprehension were inextricably mixed as I seized it; impatience to open it vied with the fear of doing so. Did it bode good or ill, happiness or unhappiness?

I hardly remember slitting the envelope, but I shall always remember my joy as I read the message inside:

> Your mother has given me permission to call upon you tomorrow morning at eleven: this morning, Eustacia, for I am writing this as I leave, and the hour is now three. Please do not refuse to see me, for I have something important to ask.

There was a sound behind me. It was Luella—wearing a trailing negligee lavishly ornamented with ostrich feathers and on top of it an old woolen shawl to keep out the morning cold; but to me she looked anything but incongruous; she looked beautiful. Her smile was radiant and her voice gentle.

"You put this here?" I asked breathlessly.

She nodded. "He gave it to me. You were at breakfast with Michelle when I brought it up, so I left it here and then listened for you to come. Naturally, I was not going to hand it to you in front of Michelle. She sees too much."

I refused to think of what Michelle saw, and in the happiness of this moment I had forgotten it anyway. Luella was untying my cloak and casting it aside; she was taking from my wardrobe a becoming morning gown of heliotrope and telling me to discard "that serviceable brown thing" with its accompanying holland smock. As they fell about my feet, she kicked them aside disdainfully, as if kicking aside forever all traces of my old life.

Which, indeed, she was, for I never went back to Joseph Whitehead's studio.

We were in the little morning room on the first floor when Julian rang the front-door bell. Luella, now respectably clad, said, "I do not think it would be unseemly, my love, if you opened the door to him yourself."

I was only vaguely aware of Michelle on her way to do so, and of her abrupt halt on the landing as I forestalled her. I sailed downstairs and opened the door, standing quite still when I saw Julian's tall figure outlined against the gray morning light. We looked at each other, saying not a word; then his steps were behind me as I remounted the stairs.

The morning room was empty. Luella had left it to us.

Julian closed the door, and I turned and looked at him. He was pale and his eyes were shadowed, and at this evidence of the distress our separation had caused him, my love overflowed and I held out my hands in a swift and impassioned gesture. I scarcely heard his formal proposal of marriage; it seemed less important than the fact that he was here, that I had not lost him, that his arms were closing about me and holding me as if he would never let me go.

Later, over his shoulder, I saw the gray skies outside and thought how beautiful the day was. Most beautiful indeed.

We were married quickly and quietly. Julian wanted it that way, and my eagerness matched his own. Only briefly, amidst the whirl of preparation, did I question him about his family. I was anxious for their approval and afraid that a sudden marriage might antagonize them. Julian brushed all that aside.

"My father has been incapacitated for a long time—

the result of a stroke after Gerald, my elder brother died. He is confined to a wheelchair now and spends most of his life in his room at Dragonmede—that's our family estate in Sussex. Aunt Dorcas looks after him. She is his sister and returned to Dragonmede when she was widowed. So neither of them will be able to come."

"But what of your mother? Won't she be anxious to attend her son's wedding?"

"My mother died when I was born, but I have a stepmother, the Lady Miriam, of whom I think highly. Since my father's stroke she has rarely gone anywhere. Two things fill her life now—Dragonmede, which she loves, and Christopher, my young half-brother, whom she loves above everything. He will soon enter Sandhurst and I fear she is going to miss him badly; she has never parted from him. He didn't go to Eton as Gerald and I did, but was educated by tutors at home. Miriam always maintained he was delicate, but Gerald and I thought him pampered—and I think my father did too, because shortly before he had the stroke he insisted that Christopher should have a military career. He said it would make a man of him, and so it will. He's too dreamy by half—always mooning about the place, or painting pictures, or going off for long walks alone."

"Are his paintings good?"

"I haven't the faintest idea. I've never seen them, and am not particularly interested anyway. A man should be a man. Christopher isn't. Hates blood sports. Even the sight of a gun turns him green." Julian laughed. "No man is cut out for country life if he can't handle a gun. That's one thing Sandhurst will teach him, at least."

I felt a sneaking sympathy for Christopher, who disliked blood sports and was forced to live in a world that took them for granted. I hoped I wouldn't be expected to hunt when I became a member of the

Kershaw family. Riding was one thing; killing, another. When I said this, Julian laughed again, and kissed me.

"There speaks your city upbringing, Eustacia. When you have adapted yourself to country life, you'll realize that hunting is a great sport and a necessary one. It helps to keep down the vermin fox, for which the farmers are grateful."

I changed the subject, because I wanted nothing, not even a differing point of view, to cause dissension between us. I inquired about the rest of the family. Had he no other relatives whom he would like to see at our wedding?

"None. I've a cousin, Nicholas Bligh, Aunt Dorcas' son, but I don't see much of him. He visits Dragonmede to see his mother, but of course he isn't really a Kershaw, stemming from the distaff side. And he takes very much after his father. Poor Dorcas blotted the family escutcheon when she married Matthew Bligh."

"Why? What was wrong with him?"

"Only that he was the village doctor, so not of any social standing."

I felt a stab of apprehension.

"Then what will they think of me?—for I have no social standing at all!"

Julian answered lightly that they would adore me, as he did.

"You're young and beautiful and healthy, and that's all you need to be. And remember that Dorcas was of an earlier generation, whose standards were different from ours. She was expected to make a brilliant marriage. I understand she was very good-looking when young and could have had many a man. Choosing a village doctor in the face of parental opposition was a pretty outrageous thing to do, in those days. It would be easier now, since the medical profession has risen in esteem. Even Nicholas is considered acceptable by many county families." Did I imagine that note of dislike—or was it resentment? Julian finished indifferently, "He became a doctor too."

"Your aunt must have loved his father very much."

"Which made it all worthwhile, I suppose."

I almost asked, "As loving me makes it all worthwhile to you?" but checked the words. I could only pray that such deep-dyed social prejudice no longer prevailed in the Kershaw family, for Julian had chosen a bride who was not only penniless but from a background so far removed from his own that if his relatives ever learned the truth about it, his marriage would be far less acceptable that his aunt's had ever been.

My apprehension deepened, but I thrust it aside, concentrating on the thought of how deeply Julian must love me. It was I who was gaining everything from this marriage; he who was gaining nothing. And yet he had set his heart upon me, rushing the wedding because he was impatient to make me his wife and ready to take me back to Dragonmede proudly and happily.

I considered myself the most fortunate young woman in the world.

Only one small thing marred my wedding day: the presence of the man Crowther. Since the ceremony was so quiet and the guests so few, I failed to understand why he was invited, but Luella merely shrugged when I protested.

"Why not, my love? He is uncouth, I grant you, but he is rich and has given you a lavish wedding present. And remember, but for him you would never have met Julian."

This was true, so I made no further protest, nor did I allow myself to speculate upon the friendship between my mother and Crowther. That it was no more than friendship I was well aware. It was a long time since Luella had taken a lover, and if anything of that nature had been impending between them I would have known; the signs were familiar to me. In a way, the mere fact that no sexuality was involved made their friendship even more significant; its roots were buried deeper, in some obscure earth.

Because I had no father to give me away, Joseph Whitehead did so. His celebrated name brought the event to the attention of the *London Gazette,* and because the bridegroom was heir to a baronetcy, my wedding created quite a stir. I had a strong suspicion that Luella had made sure that the *Gazette* was informed, and an even stronger and more unhappy one that Julian was not particularly pleased about it. I wanted to plead with him in her behalf, to point out that a proud mother should be forgiven on such an occasion as this, but there were moments when, despite the depth of feeling between us, Julian could become unapproachable. It was as if a barricade went up, and at such moments he became a stranger to me, chill, aloof, making me very much aware that he was marrying outside his social sphere.

I refused to think of it as "marrying beneath him," for not only had he already brushed that suggestion aside, but I felt in no way inferior to him. My "finishing" at Bedlington, my association with girls from noble families, my visits to their homes, my acceptance as one of them—all this had equipped me well for marriage to Julian Kershaw. So I attributed these moments to nothing but moodiness, and since they always passed quickly I refused to worry about them.

The parish church was surprisingly full, most of Bloomsbury's artistic and bohemian quarter flocking in to watch. Many of them, like myself, had rarely been inside a church; Luella had turned her back on religion when she ran away from the parsonage, and I was therefore surprised when she insisted on a church ceremony and not a civil one. I was glad of this, for to me my marriage was a sacred thing—the dedication of myself and my life to one man. I wanted it to be blessed.

Julian said there had never been so beautiful a bride. Everyone else said the same, but to me it was Luella who looked magnificent. Happiness revitalized her. I alone knew how passionately she had yearned for me to marry well, and now I was doing so. I was justifying all the expense of Bedlington Grange, and all her determination that I should be equipped for a better life than her own. Her obsessive desire that her daughter should achieve the accolade of respectability, which such a marriage as this inevitably brought, was now most wonderfully fulfilled. No wonder she looked radiant, almost triumphant. My heard warmed when I looked at her.

But not when I looked at Michelle. As I returned up the aisle on my husband's arm, I caught sight of her face—white, tense, distraught. I had seen that look once before, when she had come hurrying upstairs and pleaded, "Don't go down there, *chérie*. Don't go down there!"

Hard on that echo, I heard another. "He spells danger, *chérie. Danger!*"

For a stabbing moment, fear touched me, thrusting through the serenity and peace of the church, putting a cold finger upon my happiness. And then I saw Crowther, looking on with a sardonic smile, as if secretly and maliciously amused.

There was time for only a week's honeymoon before Julian had to return to Dragonmede. Since his father's illness he had taken over responsibility for the estate and therefore could not be away for too long, even though he had an able young steward to help him.

Already he had overstayed his holiday in London, extending it from a month to six weeks because of our marriage. It seemed incredible that we had known each other for so short a time. He had become the most important part of my life so swiftly that it was hard to recall what it had been like without him.

I suppose the way in which we spent our honeymoon was unusual, but to us it was the only way, the perfect way. No honeymoon hotel. No bridal suite. No journey abroad. No visit to the south coast or to a country beauty spot. Julian took me back to the apartment he was occupying in Grosvenor Square, and there we shut the door upon the world, waited upon by a discreet manservant whom, Julian told me, he had rented with the place: a man who came and went daily, attending to our needs when required and disappearing when not.

Alone in this private world Julian initiated me into the delights of love, and my body changed from that of a girl into that of a woman. He was a tender and then an increasingly passionate lover, and my response was unstinting.

With his head resting on my bare shoulder and his body at peace, he said one day, "Thank God you're not one of these frigid women that men seem to expect their wives to be nowadays, a symbol of saintly and unappetizing virtue."

It was impossible for me even to pretend to be. I had all my mother's passionate nature, but in one respect I was different: I could never have given myself so freely to more than one man, and the fact that this man was my husband made it all the more lovely and more right. The bonds of matrimony were bonds I welcomed, and now I pitied Luella because she had never married again. That was the root of her unhappiness, her restlessness, and her promiscuity. She had met no man capable of replacing my father.

The thought of losing Julian terrified me, for surely

no man would ever be able to replace him either. I clung to him then, remembering the tragedies in his family to which he had referred not lightly, but with a kind of acceptance, an inevitability: the death of his mother in childbirth, his father's stroke, the loss of his elder brother.

"What is it, Eustacia? You seem frightened."

I admitted that I was.

"Why, my love? Did you have a bad dream? I thought you were sleeping peacefully. You always do, after I have loved you."

"I did, and I had no bad dream." But suddenly I had to tell him. "I am terrified of losing you."

His hands caressed me.

"Is it likely? What put such a thought into your head?"

"I was thinking of your brother Gerald. From the way you talked of him, he sounded alive and vigorous."

"So he was."

"Then how did he die?"

"He was drowned in the lake at Dragonmede."

I shuddered, and he drew my body closer to his.

"Don't think about it, my sweet."

"But how did it happen?"

"Nobody really knows. He was found floating in the lake. His dinghy also, upturned. There's a small island in the middle of the lake with an Italian arbor on it. My grandfather had a passion for landscape gardening and designed the lake and the arbor. We used to row across to it when we were children and have the greatest games. It isn't a big lake, and is sheltered from winds."

"And yet Gerald's boat capsized?"

"Yes. The verdict was accidental death, of course."

His voice shook a little, which told me that despite his attitude of calm acceptance, he still grieved for his brother. I resolved then never to refer to Gerald's death again.

The honeymoon week ended; we had to emerge from our private world. On the morning of departure, Julian received a letter from his stepmother, saying that Smithers the coachman would meet us at Rye and that she looked forward to meeting her daughter-in-law, who she felt sure was as lovely as he declared.

We saw the notice in the *London Gazette*. I was glad your letter preceded it, although by so few hours . . .

I asked what she meant, though there could be only one answer: Julian had not written to his family about our marriage until the last minute, when he knew the announcement was to appear in the *Gazette*. This explained the absence of any greeting from them on our wedding day, a fact which had troubled me, but which I had excused. His father was incapable of writing and his aunt, no doubt, too much occupied with nursing him to have time to do so. As for his stepmother, I had thought she could hardly be expected to be enthusiastic over the marriage of a son who was not really her own, and too busy, in the midst of all her responsibilities, to spare a moment to pen a line of congratulation and good wishes. I had reiterated all these excuses in my mind and suppressed a feeling of uneasiness because it was necessary to do so. But now that uneasiness returned a hundredfold.

"You didn't let them know until the last minute!" I accused. "Why? Were you ashamed of your marriage? Of me?"

"Of course not, but it all happened so quickly."

"You wanted it that way. You set the pace. And even so, there was time to write to your family."

"I did write. Doesn't Miriam's letter prove that?"

"But not until you were forced to, just in time to prevent them from learning the news through another source!"

It was our first quarrel, and mercifully brief. There was one way in which Julian could terminate or forestall any dissension between us. He did it now, eagerly, determinedly, pushing me down upon the bed.

Our bags were packed. Soon the cab would be at the door. *Let it wait, let it wait!* As our senses merged, there were no divisions, no separateness, no demarcation lines between love and sexual desire. I had learned, and was still learning, that in marriage the one sparked the other, and because I had been reared without any hypocritical taboos I was able to give myself with unthinking delight.

But when we finally set out on the journey, something occurred that made me feel I was married to a stranger. As Julian paid off the cab at the rail depot and gave instructions to a porter about our bags, brushing aside others who scrambled to serve us in order to pick up a shilling, I glanced around and was horrified by what I saw. I had heard that prostitutes haunted rail depots in London, even those now being built in the outer suburbs, but my journeys to and from Bedlington Grange had always been early in the day; now it was late afternoon, but they were here in droves, their young-old faces stamped with a kind of universal weariness and a hardness born of desperation. Hunger was in their eyes, despair in their voices as they called bawdily to each other or hurled abuse at the head of one who had managed to snatch a customer from under their noses.

Some were little more than children, with wizened monkey faces, hollow cheeks, dark-ringed eyes. Some actually were children, dragged by the hand of some evil-looking crone and offered blatantly to any passing man. Some were mothers, old before their time, gaunt with starvation, clad in rags, so unappetizing that they were brushed aside like vermin, and when Julian pushed one begging creature out of his way contemptuously, I felt almost stunned with shock.

He took hold of my arm and shepherded me through the crowd. I couldn't look at him, but knew he was looking at me. I knew also that my face had blanched.

He asked gently, "Darling, what's the matter?"

"It's all this."

He nodded indifferently.

"I know. It's about time they cleaned up our rail depots, but I don't suppose they ever will."

"But some are *children,* and others little more! And that poor creature you brushed aside: how *could* you?"

He looked surprised. "You surely didn't expect me to do anything else?"

"She looked half starved. Even a sixpence would have helped."

He said patiently, "My dear Eustacia, there are soup kitchens to help the good poor. Unfortunately, the bad poor outnumber them by thousands."

"Is there a difference between 'good' poor and 'bad' poor?"

I choked with indignation, realizing for the first time the sufferings Michelle must have endured when turned out onto the streets of London, in this day and age the biggest city in the world, and the richest. I was appalled that such poverty could be allowed to exist in the capital of the most extensive empire known to history, with the vaults of the Bank of England stacked with more gold bars than there were in any other country, and its gold sovereigns, more common than the paper pound note, eagerly accepted all over the world.

Evidently my feelings were reflected in my face, for as Julian led me to the ticket barrier he said with a touch of impatience, "If it shocks you, don't look. If you don't like it, don't think about it."

I lacked my husband's ability to dismiss the unpleasant and was silent for the greater part of the journey, distressed by what I had seen and even more by Julian's attitude toward it. Lady Miriam's letter worried me too, and as we traveled through the Sussex Weald I began to think about it again. To me, it had seemed to hold an undercurrent of reproach; to Julian, it had seemed merely affectionate, putting his mind at ease. That fact alone was disturbing.

I asked anxiously, "You weren't worried about your family's reaction to our marriage, were you? You weren't afraid that they would not welcome me?"

"Now, don't start that again, Stacy!"

He went on to asure me that never for a moment had he harbored the slightest doubt, and this seemed to be proved by his increasing eagerness as the journey progressed, so that I knew he was looking forward to presenting me to his family and that all my doubts and apprehensions had been unnecessary. They had been no more than those which any bride feels when faced with the ordeal of meeting her unknown in-laws.

I was bolstered by his pride in me—"They'll adore you the moment they see you, as I did, my darling!"—and by an undercurrent of excitement within him: a gay, almost devilish excitement which seemed to increase the closer we came to Dragonmede.

But my own reaction to the place was one of which I was totally unprepared. I experienced a feeling of unaccountable recognition which was in no way due to Julian's description of my future home. All he had told me was that it had been in his family for generations and that, compared with the house in Bloomsbury, I would no doubt find it rather different, but would soon get used to it. Therefore I knew it was old and, since it was a family home in the country, anticipated that it would be quiet and dignified—but not immense, overpowering, and above all frightening; not a house, but a mansion: gaunt, cold, and forbidding. A mansion encircled by vast acres surrounded by fortresslike walls.

For this I was indeed unprepared, as I was for the uncanny sensation that I had been there before and an instinctive desire to escape as quickly as possible.

Michelle would have had some psychic explanation for it: either that I had visited Dragonmede in an earlier life, or was now fulfilling some long-forgotten premonition that I should do so. At both ideas I would have scoffed.

Nevertheless, as the brougham swept round the broad apex of the drive toward wide stone steps and an impressive pillared entrance, this strange feeling of recognition increased, accompanied by an instinctive fear which I found impossible to suppress. Perhaps I sensed that the chains of Dragonmede were to bind me fast and that was why I hhd the inexplicable urge to flee from the place as it loomed up out of the late-evening mist. Massive walls looked down like grim giants with many faces: gargoyled faces jutting out from ancient stones, growing larger and more menacing the closer we approached.

The brougham halted at the foot of the steps. I glanced up them and saw imposing double doors, closed against the world. Even these seemed vaguely familiar, as if in some forgotten time I had been here before. And yet I knew it could not be true.

What was true was that this immense and intimidating place suddenly seemed like a prison which I was terrified to enter.

Three

THE GREAT DOORS, studded like those of a jail, swung slowly open, and from the shadowy depths beyond them the figure of a woman emerged. For a moment she stood poised at the top of the stone steps, looking down upon us. It was a dramatic appearance, and she held it effectively.

I gazed up at her, somewhat awed, and knew that despite the distance between us she was taking in every detail about me, but whether she approved or not I had no idea, because her calm, well-bred face betrayed absolutely nothing.

I became aware that Smithers had opened the door of the brougham and that Julian had descended and was holding out his hand to me. I lifted my skirts and accepted his help, descending carefully because I was terrified of making a slip before this elegant, poised, good-looking woman who still made no movement but stood waiting for us to approach, like a queen waiting for a new subject to be presented at her throne.

Those steps leading up to the main entrance of Dragonmede seemed endless: two flights of deep treads, twelve in each flight; I counted subconsciously as my husband led me up them. The woman's unblinking scrutiny did nothing to put me at ease.

When we reached the top, Julian exclaimed, "Miriam, you look as handsome as ever!" His voice was kind, coaxing, charming.

So this was his stepmother, of whom he thought so highly. Since I knew that a man of my husband's nature could respond only to warmth in others, there had to be hidden depths in this woman which were not evinced at this moment. I sensed banked-down fires quietly smoldering, and the impression was more unnerving than her icy mask. I stood hesitant, waiting to be greeted, and was thankful for the encouraging clasp of Julian's hand as he drew me forward and said a shade too brightly, "And here is Eustacia. Isn't she lovely?"

"Very."

Miriam Kershaw's voice was exactly as I expected: quiet, cultured, unemotional. Then she leaned very slightly toward me and unsmilingly offered her cheek to be kissed. The gesture was more remote than a handshake. I also sensed patronage in it: a royal gesture, magnanimously proffered. I disliked it, but obeyed. I kissed the cool cheek, then immediately offered my own in return. The reflex action took her by surprise, and it pleased me that she was forced to reciprocate. This immediately placed us on a level footing and established right from the start that I would accept no queen-and-subject attitude.

"Welcome to Dragonmede, Eustacia." The words came from her unwillingly, but they did come, and although I knew there was no welcome in them, I had to be satisfied for the time being.

As we turned and went into the house, Julian slipped one hand beneath his stepmother's elbow and the other beneath mine. His gesture to her was conciliatory and to me encouraging, so I knew he had sensed the tension between us. I felt he was thankful that the first stile had been crossed, and that I had scaled it with dignity. But what else did he expect me to do? Be cowed by the lady of the manor? No one had ever cowed me in my life, or ever would.

I glanced up at him with a touch of defiant pride before being plunged into a situation that was impressive but, to me, almost unnerving, for never before had I seen a whole household of servants lined up to greet a young heir and his bride. Here at Dragonmede they were ranged the full length of a vast and gloomy hall, so that our progress was like a royal inspection. The entire staff was there, from the highest to the lowest. Garfield, the butler, presented the menservants, and Mrs. Levitt, the housekeeper, presented the maids. I could feel the Lady Miriam's cold eyes watching me as I made acknowledgments. I felt she was waiting for me to commit some faux pas, but after an initial twinge of apprehension I realized that all one had to do was be courteous and pleasant, exchange a word with the principal servants and smile at the lesser ones, conveying pleasure in meeting them.

Then my sense of humor asserted itself. I was amused by the solemnity of the occasion, and as we made our slow progress down the long, high, echoing hall I felt that the only thing needed was sacred music. I glanced up. Sure enough, there was a minstrels' gallery. A subdued quartet or an unseen organ would not have been inappropriate, I thought, as one by one stiff male backs bowed, and becapped and aproned women curtsied low, paying homage. For the household of a baronet this retinue was large, almost worthy of an earl.

I heard my mother-in-law saying that she had put us in the yellow room. "Your old room would be overcrowded with a double bed in it, Julian. The yellow room is bigger and much more suitable for a married couple. It also had that beautiful view of the lake. . . ."

Smithers and a boy were carrying our bags upstairs. Miriam asked, in a tone of surprise, if that was all we had, and when Julian failed to answer I looked at him and was startled by the dismay in his face. I said swiftly that our trunks were following by station wagon, added that I would like to change out of my traveling clothes, and drew Julian toward the stairs, where Mrs. Levitt, carrying an ornate silver can-

delabrum, was politely waiting to escort us. At that,
Julian seemed to regain possession of himself.

"The yellow room?" he echoed heartily. "That will
be splendid! Eustacia will love it, I'm sure. By
the way, how is Father?"

"Far from well. I am afraid it will be impossible
for Eustacia to be presented to him tonight. Perhaps
tomorrow. Dorcas will decide."

"He hasn't taken a turn for the worse, I hope?"

"Not exactly worse, but, well, the shock, the
surprise, the unexpectedness of it all . . ."

"You mean our wedding? He should be pleased.
He had been nagging me long enough about marrying
and producing an heir—or was, when he was able to
speak."

Mrs. Levitt was mounting the stairs, her back
ramrod-straight, her full black skirts sweeping behind
her. She was safely out of earshot, but perhaps Miriam
Kershaw was afraid of echoes between these lofty stone
walls, because she dropped her voice as she answered,
"Your father has an heir already. You, Julian."

And after you, my son. . . . The words sprang into
my mind as if breathed into it. Was this the reason
for her cool welcome of me? Was she resentful because now that Julian was married, her own son's
chances of inheriting Dragonmede were lessened?

I took a couple of steps in Mrs. Levitt's wake, but
the Lady Miriam remained at the foot of the stairs,
and so did Julian. I looked back at them, aware that
I was momentarily forgotten, and rather glad because
it gave me an opportunity to study this woman who
had not taken her eyes off me since our arrival. It was
a relief to be rid of her close inspection, and I only
hoped that I would not be subjected to such scrutiny
when meeting the rest of my husband's family.

My mother-in-law's fading blond hair must once
had been beautiful, and her features still retained a
symmetry which must have been exceptional in youth.

Undoubtedly, she was good-looking still, but hers were the kind of looks that one admired in the way one admires a piece of sculpture, without wishing to resemble it or even to touch it. Nevertheless, beneath her icy composure the smoldering remained. I disliked those banked-down fires. I mistrusted them.

Julian seemed about to say something, changed his mind, dropped a kiss lightly on his stepmother's brow, favored her with a vivid smile, and turned back to me. Together we mounted the stairs, our feet echoing on the uncarpeted stone treads. The sound as well as the bareness struck a chill into me. It was like climbing out of an enormous vault into darker regions above. There was no warmth anywhere and scarcely any light, despite fluttering candles in great wall sconces and hugh fires which, looking back, I saw blazing within deep stone hearths at each end of the hall. It was the first time I had noticed them, but now that the staff had respectfully filed away, the whole area of the dimly lit hall lay spread out below, inhabited only by the solitary figure of my mother-in-law, still watching me.

Briefly, our eyes met. She jerked her head away instantly, and I was glad that it was she, not I, who was disconcerted. Still looking over my shoulder, I let myself by guided upstairs by Julian. This enabled me to watch his stepmother's departure, her voluminous skirt swinging gently as she glided across the solid oak floor of the hall toward a distant doorway. The only sounds were the rustle of her stiff petticoats and the almost inaudible whisper of her slippered feet. On carpets, her tread would be unheard. It put me in mind of the soft padding of a cat.

At the top of the stairs Mrs. Levitt paused and, reaching up, drew down a great brass oil lamp by a pulley, applied a flame to it from one of the candles, then returned the lamp to its place beneath the carved stone canopy high above the stairwell. The spread of light revealed corridors running to right and left. The floors up here were mercifully carpeted. The walls were paneled, and from them family portraits looked down. One glance told me that they badly needed restoring.

Joseph Whitehead would never have tolerated such neglect of oil paintings. Varnishes had darkened and surfaces deteriorated through age or damp. My fingers itched to apply a gentle solution of soap and water to remove the initial grime, and then to set to work on the restoration. Many of these portraits were master-pieces, and it would be exciting to reveal what lay beneath, to revive original colors and retouch where necessary—prolonged work, but one that my exacting master had insisted his students learn.

Julian nodded toward the portraits casually. "Mostly Kershaws," he said, "but some Derwents as well—Miriam's people. Her father was Lord Derwent, eldest son of the Earl of Calverley, and of course he inherited the title on the Earl's death. I must say my own father did well to marry into so wealthy a breed. Their money saved this place, and Miriam is justly proud of all she has done for Dragonmede. The fleet of servants were installed by her; the daughter of an earl could hardly be expected to tolerate the depleted staff that was all the Kershaws could afford. Mrs. Levitt will remember those days." He added, to the housekeeper, "Don't you, Mrs. Levitt? You remember the days when Dragonmede was more than half shut up?"

The erect figure stood to attention respectfully, and when Julian continued, "Been here all your life, haven't you, Mrs. Levitt?" she inclined her head.

"I have indeed, Mr. Julian, right from my girlhood, as my mother was before me, and my grandmother before her."

"A fine local family, the Levitts." My husband smiled at the woman with an approval that was almost affection. Somehow I had the feeling that she had more right to be here than I.

"How old is the house?" I asked.

"Late-sixteenth-century—1575, to be exact; built by that elderly gentleman in the center of the wall." Julian gestured toward a heavy gilt frame with an almost indistinguishable portrait within it. "The first Sir Julian, founder of the Kershaw family, made a baronet for reasons long forgotten—and, for reasons long forgotten, never elevated further. In those days even a baronet could afford to build and run a place like this, but times have changed. Now we need wives to rescue us from financial misfortune, don't we, Mrs. Levitt?"

"I wouldn't say that, sir."

"Because you are a worthy, well-mannered servant, very much aware of your place; but I can say it, and do. So thank God for the Derwent fortune."

I thought the Derwent fortune should have been stretched to preserve these valuable paintings, but all I remarked was that I would like to see the portrait of the first Sir Julian cleaned and restored. At this my husband laughed aloud.

"That old thing! It isn't worth the trouble."

"It is very much worth the trouble. It was probably painted by a master. It grieves me to see valuable paintings neglected."

"I had forgotten you are an artist." As he took my arm again and led me down a long corridor to the right, Mrs. Levitt still lighting our way, he continued indifferently, "Personally, I find paintings of little interest. Nothing is more boring to me than an art gallery, and nothing of less interest at Dragonmede than this dreary display of ancestors. Now I am shocking you, aren't I, my love?" He pressed my arm affectionately and added in a teasing voice, "But I am glad too hear these paintings are valuable, although

I would prefer to have the money. Why did artists in those days paint everything so gloomily?"

"But they didn't. Most of them mixed their own pigments, and the vividness of the colors could be restored with careful handling. The portrait of the first Sir Julian, for instance: the film surface grime could be removed, and tests made after that to discover what pigments were used. If resin was included, a mild solvent of alcohol could safely restore the orginal colors. It would be useless on a hardened layer of oil paint, but—"

Julian interrupted, "What a waste of good alcohol! But how fortunate I am to have such a clever wife."

The mockery in his tone hurt me, and I was humiliated when he remarked to the housekeeper, "Isn't she clever, Mrs. Levitt? And would you ever suspect it by looking at her? Beauty and brains: how will I be able to live up to such a combination?"

If the housekeeper saw the sensitive flush on my face, she gave no indication. She merely reached impassively in front of us and opened a door, standing aside for us to enter.

"Ah, the yellow room! The best room in the house, next to those of my parents. The room with the view of the lake. Come and see it, my darling."

He walked to the center of three tall windows, while behind me Mrs. Levitt said, "I will send Lucy to unpack for you, Madam. She will be your personal maid. You will find her a good girl. I trained her myself."

I turned to thank her, and was startled by the piercing scrutiny in eyes that had previously been discreetly blank. I felt she was surveying me more with curiosity than with criticism. I supposed it was natural enough, but it made me feel uncomfortable. Her glance was speculative, but the moment my eyes met hers it became respectful and blank again, betraying nothing.

I watched her set down the candles and move to

the door. I was convinced that before she finally departed I would receive another searching glance, and I was right. It came fleetingly but thoroughly as she was closing the door behind her. I was glad to see embarrassment flicker across her face, although something told me that this stolid, poker-faced woman would never forgive me for it.

Julian said impatiently, "Why are you staring at the door when I am waiting to show you the view?"

"I'm sorry. I didn't care for the housekeeper's scrutiny."

"What did you expect? The servants are bound to be curious about you. You must tolerate their stares until you are accepted at Dragonmede."

"Accepted? Am I on trial, then?"

We were both slightly on edge. I felt that on my part it was hardly surprising, but on Julian's I failed to understand it. He was at home here. I was not.

He retorted impatiently, "Don't be ridiculous, Stacy. Now come here and admire the lake, the beautiful lake that put an end to my brother's life."

The note of unhappiness in his voice communicated so sharply that I went to him and slipped my hand within his, anxious to comfort him. The lake sparkled below like an enormous mirror streaked with shadows. We had arrived late, and now darkness had almost set in. In addition to the gleam of water and the surrounding shapes of trees, I could see the silhouette of an Italian arbor set on a small island. The scene was beautiful, but involuntarily I suppressed a shiver, for in my imagination I saw a body floating there, face down, the water lapping the back of a man's head.

I walked away from the window, untying my bonnet with fingers that were suddenly unsteady. Then I shed my cloak and turned to smooth my hair before the dressing-table mirror. Julian was still standing beside

the window, staring fixedly outside, and I knew he
wasn't even aware that I was near.

The knock on the door was almost like a reprieve
breaking a spell that threatened to separate us. A maid
entered, who I guessed was Lucy. She carried more
candles, and behind her came two undermaids bearing
a steaming tub of water. Lucy bobbed a curtsy.

"I thought Madam would wish to take a bath after
her journey." As she spoke she crossed the room and
drew back a heavy tapestry curtain, revealing an
alcove, rather like a *rouelle* in a French château, containing a hip bath, a screen, a table bearing a pitcher
and bowl, and a wooden rack with towels. While the
maids emptied the hot water into the bath, Lucy set
down the candles, then began to unpack my carpet-
bag.

"Leave that," Julian commanded. "You can unpack
for your mistress when our trunks arrive."

"They are on the way up, sir. Smithers and Bateman
are bringing them now."

"Then return later."

"Yes, sir." She bobbed another curtsy and made
for the door. I picked up a robe which she had
dropped on the bed, and smiled at her reassuringly.
The girl was flustered by Julian's peremptory dismissal, and it was even more peremptory to the menservants who appeared at that moment.

"Put those trunks down and be gone."

They obeyed hurriedly, and I went into the alcove,
drawing the heavy curtain behind me. I heard the
grating of a key as it locked our door and knew that
Julian, in the unpredictable way with which I was
already becoming familiar, had descended into one
of his withdrawn moods. As I undressed, I was already
making excuses for him. He was tired. Presenting me
to his stepmother, not to mention the endless line of
servants, must have been a strain, for no doubt he had
been anxious despite all his pretense.

I thought of plenty of reasons for his change of mood, but knew there was really only one: The view of the lake had reminded him too painfully of his brother's death. That was why he had been shocked into silence on hearing that we had been allotted the yellow room. He didn't want it.

I was about to step into the hip bath when the heavy curtain rings jerked along the rail. Being naked, and startled, I slipped behind the screen, whereupon Julian thrust it aside.

"What's this?" he scoffed. "False modesty all of a sudden?"

"I was startled. I had forgotten the maids had gone. I thought perhaps—"

The words sounded lame, my voice tired. I was tired. I wanted nothing so much as to sit in that hip bath, with the warm water lapping up to my breasts, relaxed and quiet. I didn't want my husband to bring his black mood into this semiprivate place; I didn't want my peace invaded. I wanted to be alone, just for a little while, before I dressed and went downstairs for the late supper which, Miriam had told us, would be served in an hour's time. By then Julian's moroseness would have vanished, probably as quickly as it had arisen, and later we would be happy together in the darkness of the night, and from my mind would be blotted out even the memory of his indifference to human suffering and degradation, which had shocked me so much that even now it lingered in the back of my mind, although I had told myself repeatedly that men had a different attitude toward these things, that they were more practical and less emotional than women, and had to be. I was ready to seek and find excuses for anything that might seem like a fault in this man whom I loved so obsessively.

But Julian had no intention of leaving me alone just now. He looked me up and down, ran his hands over my body, let them roam where they willed, gripped my breasts until they hurt, and when I cried out, he pushed me aside.

"Don't ever protest like that again. I own you. Remember that. I own every inch of you."

The curtain closed behind him, jerked back savagely along the rail. I sank into the steaming water gratefully, and closed my eyes. He was right, of course. My body was all I had brought him. I was no rich bride who could help her husband financially. He had gained nothing by marrying me. The gain was all on my side.

When I emerged from the alcove, I saw my sapphire gown upon the bed and our trunks agape. Julian had unlocked them and apparently selected this gown for me. It was the one Michelle had made, the one I had worn the first evening he had spent at the Bloomsbury house. He had told me several times that it was his favorite, and I was touched that he should think of it now.

Anxious to appease him, I said, "You especially want me to wear this?"

He nodded. "It is becoming and ladylike. It will give a good impression."

Dampened, I said nothing, but sat down before my dressing table and began to brush my hair. In the candlelight it gleamed, dark and glossy as shining new chestnuts, and my complexion, fresh from the warm bath, was glowing and flawless. Usually my husband would come and stand behind me, taking the brush from my hand and running it through my hair. It was something he loved to do, but tonight he seemed to have forgotten. He was back at the window, staring down upon the lake.

I said gently, "Come away from there, Julian. It is time to dress. Your stepmother said supper would be served in an hour."

"The Lady Miriam," he corrected sharply. "The

daughter of earls or dukes who marry men of lesser rank take the same order of precedence as their husbands, but are referred to as they were before marriage. So Miriam isn't just plain Lady Kershaw, but 'The Lady Miriam Kershaw'—referred to in the third person as 'the Lady Miriam,' but addressed personally simply as 'Lady Miriam.' "

My cheeks blazed. So did my anger. I retorted, "I need no instruction. I was educated at Bedlington and made many friends there, apart from which my mother was not an ignorant woman and nor am I. In referring to the Lady Miriam as your stepmother I was not displaying ignorance. I notice you call her by her Christian name only. Will the time come when I shall be so privileged, or am I to address her formally and speak of her formally forever, like an outsider?"

He was sorry immediately. He came across and put his hands on my shoulders, full of contrition. "I'm a brute. Forgive me."

But I was in no forgiving mood. I jerked away and went on brushing my hair. I saw his reflection in the mirror, and was glad to see that it was shamefaced.

"Aren't you going to change?" I asked coolly. "I imagine 'the Lady Miriam' will dislike being kept waiting."

"First say I am forgiven!"

When he spoke like that, when he smiled like that, he was irresistible. I yielded inevitably.

"I ought to be angry."

"You were angry, my love, and with justice. I spoke without thought."

And he had hurt me without thought in the privacy of my toilet alcove. I thrust the memory of that aside and asked him to summon Lucy for me. He crossed to the elaborately embroidered bell rope beside the fireplace, then to the door, which he unlocked. Simultaneously a tap came upon a side door leading from our room, which I had failed to notice. Apparently it led into Julian's dressing room, for a valet appeared and asked if his master was ready to dress. Shortly after the dressing-room door had closed upon them Lucy came hurrying and we embarked upon the elaborate ritual of lacing. I held on to a carved bedpost while she threaded and pulled, remarking with admiration that with such a tiny waist it was scarcely necessary.

"My mother's waist is almost as small, even now," I told her, and was aware of a sudden longing for Luella. I even felt nostalgic for the Bloomsbury house, although I had no desire ever to live there again. One changed in more ways than physically after marriage; one quickly severed one's ties with the past, and I knew that when I revisited my mother's house it would seem more alien now than when I had periodically returned to it from Bedlington.

But, on the other hand, could I ever fit into such a background as this? Could I ever feel at home in this bleak, unfriendly mansion with its thick stone walls and its retinue of servants? A touch of my earlier apprehension returned. If the remaining members of Julian's family were as unwelcoming as his stepmother, I could expect a difficult time.

Lucy was holding out my first petticoat. I stepped into it mechanically, then into the next and the next, until the billowing foundation for my gown was complete. After Lucy had slipped it over my head and fastened the endless hooks and eyes, she stood back admiringly. In the candlelight the blue looked an even deeper sapphire, and somehow the color seemed to be reflected in my eyes.

"You look beautiful, Madam, beautiful!"

I looked at Lucy's round and homely face, liking what I saw. The honesty and simplicity there made me feel oddly comforted.

"Your jewels, Madam?"

"I wear none with this gown. Can you put the finishing touches to my hair?"

But in that respect she was no Michelle, and I knew that I would have to be my own hairdresser at Dragonmede. I struggled to remember the way in which Michelle had coiled the chignon in the nape of my neck, and by the time Julian emerged from his dressing room I had somehow achieved it. From the approving glance he gave me I knew it was to his liking.

He looked very handsome in his formal dinner clothes, and as we turned to leave the room I saw our joint reflection in a long cheval mirror. He was standing slightly behind me, looking down at my bare shoulders, and suddenly he kissed the side of my throat, in the curve between shoulder and neck. As he looked up, his eyes met mine in the mirrored reflection, and desire was there.

He whispered, "Forgive me for hurting you. I don't know what came over me. I swear to God I will never abuse your lovely body again."

I turned and kissed him, and he clung to me, whispering urgently that he wished we could dine alone up here and what a bore it was having to eat with the family.

Memories of our cloistered hours in the Grosvenor Square apartment came flooding back; there had been no restraints between us there, no tensions, no stresses. We had been uninhibited and free in a way that I feared we would never know again, and Julian had been himself in a way that I also feared I would never know again. Since he had crossed the threshold of Dragonmede his personality seemed to have subtly changed. Or perhaps it had started earlier than that: during the journey, when a kind of devilish excitement seemed to stir in him, culminating in the black mood, shot through with cruelty and patronage. Was there something about this sinister place that brought out a different side of his character—and in clinging to me at this moment, was he aware of it, and afraid of it?

Four

SECONDS LATER I was dismissing the idea, for he was smiling at me with his normal charm, and as he led me along the corridor he said happily, "I am proud of you tonight, Eustacia. You look beautiful. Miriam will feel her nose put even more out of joint than when you arrived."

"Surely she didn't—"

"But of course she did. If you were not so modest, you would have been aware of it as acutely as I. Apart from your youth and good looks, you are a threat to her future position. When my father dies you will replace her as mistress here, and poor Miriam will have to retire to the Dower House. After being Queen of Dragonmede and waving a magic wand over the place ever since she married my father, that will be a bitter pill to swallow."

The thing which struck me was that he said this with amusement, and yet he had professed to think highly of his stepmother.

I answered, "I don't want her to feel that way. We must reassure her somehow."

We had reached the top of the stairs. Below us spread the vast hall, a place of flickering candlelight and wavering shadows. I wondered if I would ever get used to it. It seemed like the empty heart of an empty home.

But if the great hall was a barren and echoing place,

the drawing room was not. Double doors opened upon a room tastefully furnished: the rich sheen of rosewood, walnut, and mahogany reflected against mellow paneled walls. Light was everywhere, gleaming from oil lamps and immense candelabra from which massed candles shone down upon the richness of Aubusson carpets and deep red velvet window draperies. A blazing log fire roared in the Gothic hearth, and beside it sat the Lady Miriam, looking extremely elegant in eau de Nile satin with a wide fichu of Brussels lace. Diamonds sparkled at her throat and upon her wrists and fingers. Opposite her sat another woman—older, white-haired, and far less richly dressed. She turned as we entered and focused upon me a frank but not unfriendly stare; then she rose and came to meet me, hand outstretched.

"So you are Eustacia. You must forgive my absence when you arrived, but it happened to coincide with my brother's needs. He retires early, which means that he must dine early, and that means I must be with him for most of the evening hours. No, Julian, no formal introductions. I am sure you have told your wife all about the family, so she must know that I am your Aunt Dorcas." She turned to me and finished, "Dorcas Bligh, my dear. And welcome to Dragonmede."

I felt that here was someone who really meant it. I liked her at once. I liked her open smile and unaffected manners. I liked her brisk handshake and frank way of speaking. So this was the woman who had displeased her parents by marrying a lowly village doctor. Matthew Bligh had been fortunate, I thought.

I was aware of her keen gray eyes studying me, but her scrutiny was uncritical. I felt that she was weighing me up against some mental picture or some preconceived idea of what I would be like, and I wondered how I matched up to it. When I smiled, she gave an apologetic laugh.

"Forgive me, child, but when a woman gets to my age she finds it hard to suppress curiosity. Naturally, we have been wondering what you were like. Julian's eulogy in his hastily written letter was brief, but eloquent. But not eloquent enough. Your wife is lovely, Nephew—and now I promise to stare at her no more."

I joined Miriam upon a sofa. She gave me a cool little smile and drew her skirts aside, although there was more than enough room for both of us; then she picked up a glass of wine and continued to sip it. She had been doing so when I entered, and I had a feeling that this was by no means her first glass; there was a haziness about her eyes as she stared morosely into the fire.

I wondered if I would ever be able to talk to my mother-in-law and what, in the event, we would find to talk about. We came from worlds that were poles apart. If she knew the truth about mine she would undoubtedly be shocked, and if she was shocked, I in turn would be resentful, because it would imply a criticism of my mother and the way in which she had brought me up, and criticism of Luella was something I would never tolerate. She had been the victim of circumstance and a too-responsive heart.

I became aware that Julian had placed a glass beside me, and that Aunt Dorcas had continued to chatter in her amiable fashion; but now she said something which brought Lady Miriam's head up with a jerk, proving that although she appeared to be lost in her own thoughts, her ears were alert.

What Dorcas Bligh said was that Victoria would not be too pleased. Since I did not know who Victoria was or what would displease her, the words meant nothing to me, but they evidently meant a great deal to Miriam, because apart from jerking to attention she commented sharply, "Victoria won't mind in the least. Why should she? A girl as intelligent and accomplished as she won't go into a decline just because the man she was going to marry comes home with a wife."

Startled, I felt my hand jerk and saw wine splash upon my gown. Julian dabbed at the spot with his handkerchief, completely composed, saying smoothly, "May I point out that Victoria and I were never even betrothed?"

"But that didn't prevent her, or her father and everyone else, from expecting that you would be," Aunt Dorcas replied. "But I agree with Miriam. Victoria isn't the type of young woman to go into a decline, and with her looks and accomplishments, not to mention determination, she will soon be looking elsewhere, if she has not done so already. In my opinion, you have made the beter choice, Nephew. I like your Eustacia."

"My dear Dorcas, you may pride yourself on your frankness, but it isn't always tactful." Miriam's voice held repressed irritation. "At times it can be thoroughly disconcerting, as I am sure Julian's wife finds it now."

I assured her that I found it not in the least disconcerting. "How can one feel anything but pleasure on hearing that one is liked? As for Victoria, whoever she may be, I am sorry if she had been displeased or disappointed, but not in the lease sorry that it was I who married Julian."

Miriam held out her glass to be refilled, saying as she did so, "Whoever she may be! My dear Eustacia, Victoria Bellamy is the daughter of a wellborn and influential family. The man who gets her will be lucky."

"And if that isn't more disconcerting than any remark of mine, I would like to hear one!" I felt that Aunt Dorcas wanted to say more, but wisely refrained.

I was grateful to her, for my mother-in-law's words had carried a definite insinuation.

Now she moved restlessly about the room, her gown rustling and swirling about her feet and the wine in her glass rapidly diminishing.

"I wish Christopher would hurry," she fretted between sips. "Once he starts painting he becomes oblivious of time."

"So a painting mood is on him, is it?" My husband's voice was faintly derisive, faintly indulgent— the voice of a layman who couldn't appreciate another person's talents. It perturbed me a little, but I had plenty of time to initiate him into an appreciation of art. I could start with the family portraits, so that he would cease to look on them merely as a row of uninteresting ancestors, and when I had settled down at Dragonmede I intended to start painting again. It was encouraging to hear that one member of the family shared my pleasure in it.

"If he doesn't come soon, Garfield will announce supper. It really is naughty of him to be so late, and I do so dislike delayed meals."

But despite her fretfulness, Miriam's voice was indulgent, and I remembered Julian's telling me that she doted on her son.

Nevertheless, she made me feel guilty about our belated arrival at Dragonmede, and even more guilty when I remembered the cause of it. If I had not yielded to that snatched hour of lovemaking we could have caught an earlier train. We had been selfish, thoughtless, heedless of anyone but ourselves. But from now on perhaps we would have few opportunities to be alone except in the privacy of our room at night, so I felt no regret about the sudden impulse that had made Julian pull me down upon the bed before finally terminating our honeymoon. We had been close then. Far closer than we had been since stepping across the threshold of this ancient house. Even though his good humor had now been restored and he smiled at me fondly across the room, I was still aware of a threatening gulf between us, as if these people and this place were likely to force us apart.

The doors opened abruptly and a youth stood there, one hand on each heavy wrought knob. I knew at once that this was Christopher. Like his mother when she had appeared at the head of the front steps, he held the pose before coming into the room, but not for so long. While he stood there he looked like a portrait in a frame: a portrait of an elegant youth, slightly built, pale, with a lock of corn-colored hair falling over his brow and more growing long and low at the back of his head. Not an outdoor youth, to judge by his pallor. There was also a pampered air about him. His features were almost delicately chiseled and would have been becoming on a girl.

"Forgive my tardiness, Mamma."

He closed the doors behind him and moved gracefully across the room. He too eyed me appraisingly, but without his mother's coldness. There was friendliness there.

"So this is Eustacia." He lifted my hand and kissed it, his long hair swinging forward as he bowed. I sensed rather than saw Julian's irritation as the youth tossed it back. All right, I thought, so he is a bit of a poseur, but why? Because it was one way of combating shyness or self-consciousness, even a feeling of inferiority? I guessed he had been outshone, all his life, by his two very masculine half-brothers.

I wondered what their father had been like. The speculation was in the past tense because now that he was afflicted I knew he must be but a shadow of his former self. I wanted to meet him, and yet was apprehensive—not because meeting an afflicted person was something I dreaded, but because I wondered how he would react to me. Would he be able to conceal his feelings, or would I be met with the plain, unvarnished truth? I felt there would be no glossing over, as with a person in full control of his faculties. The eyes of the sick could be eloquent, and although Julian's father had lost the power of speech, he might well betray himself even more clearly than his self-controlled wife had done. If he liked me, all would be well. If he did not, if anger at his son's whirlwind marriage had prejudiced him against me, I would be grieved for Julian's sake as well as my own.

The Lady Miriam's announcement that I could not be presented to her husband that night was something of a reprieve, for meeting these three, especially my mother-in-law, was strain enough for the time being. She was gracious to me, in her way, during the belated meal, at which she automatically took her place at the head of the table.

"For tonight," she announced, "Eustacia will sit on my right. I am sure Julian won't mind assuming her place on my left, just this once?"

A stickler for etiquette apparently, unbending in my favor only because this was a special occasion. Although the family were so few in number, I guessed that precedence would always be preserved, the heir to Dragonmede normally sitting on the right of its mistress, his wife on her left, then on Julian's right the next heir, with Aunt Dorcas (the poor relation) last of all. And beyond, nothing but a long expanse of table, big enough for a banquet. Things would have been a great deal more cozy and certainly a great deal more friendly if we had seated ourselves round a small table near the fire. Warmer, too. At this distance one could feel little from the deeply recessed hearth at the far end, where a basket grate sent most of the heat up the chimney and little into the room.

I decided that when I eventually became mistress here I would choose a smaller room than this for family occasions. Somewhere in this great house there must be one more suitable and a great deal more intimate than this, with its vaulted ceiling and shadowy corners. Alongside an immense sideboard, impassive servants waited to serve, presenting apparently deaf ears to the conversation.

I caught Aunt Dorcas' eye and had the uncanny feeling that she was reading my thoughts, for a smile flickered about her mouth and for a moment I thought she gave an imperceptible nod, as if to say, "I quite agree, my dear. This isn't what family life should be, at all." But perhaps I was mistaken, for when I gave her a second glance her attention was upon the food.

Throughout the meal I was scarcely aware of what I ate, for I had little appetite. Fatigue was slowly creeping upon me, and I wanted nothing so much as to retire. Lying close to Julian in the great four-poster I would feel safe and secure again.

I heard him inquiring after Dorcas' son. I knew it was mere politeness, for my impression that Julian disliked his cousin remained with me still; but naturally it pleased his aunt, who announced proudly that old Dr. Fothergill had made Nicholas his partner now.

"He has rooms above the Rye surgery. This suits Fothergill well, for he is able to spend more time at his home in Winchelsea, tending his garden, and it pleases Nicholas, who loves nothing as much as his work."

"Even more than women, I think," Miriam remarked, in a tone which implied that this indicated a lot.

Julian laughed. "I find that hard to believe. My worthy cousin's Achilles' heel is his weakness for the opposite sex." He turned a mocking eye upon Christopher and finished, "Which is more than can be said for you, sir."

"Christopher has plenty of time," Miriam interposed in swift defense. "He is only twenty-one."

"In twenty-one years a man reveals his sexual appetite." Julian was impervious to his stepmother's frown and his half-brother's painful flush. I felt a sneaking pity for the Lady Miriam, brought up in a world in which any word pertaining to sex was not only taboo but vulgar and ill bred, and an equal pity for her son, who was plainly hurt by taunts. I cast around in my mind for some change of subject, but the moment was mercifully saved by Aunt Dorcas, who asked me if I enjoyed riding.

I admitted that I had not ridden since leaving Bedlington Grange, but that I was looking forward to doing so again.

"Bedlington!" There was unflattering surprise in my mother-in-law's voice. "So you were finished at Bedlington? I had no idea."

"I have always heard that the place turns out young women of charm and good manners," Dorcas commented. "Now I believe it."

I was grateful both for her words and for her smile; grateful too for the arrival of the next course. After this there would be only one more to sit through. I stifled a yawn and prayed that we would not be expected to linger over coffee, but that the lateness of the hour and the fatigue of our journey would excuse us.

Aunt Dorcas was saying that Ladybird might be a good mount for me. "She is a bay mare, and trained to the sidesaddle."

"But she needs expert handling," Miriam pointed out. "She has white socks on her forelegs, and white socks on a lady's horse often go with speed—sometimes too much."

"Victoria had ridden her often enough."

"But Victoria is an excellent horsewoman."

"As my wife may prove to be," Julian put in.

"London-bred?" His stepmother regarded me skeptically. "Some of the worst riders I have ever seen are those in Rotten Row. They don't ride. They parade. You have to be a countrywoman to be a good rider, brought up to hounds."

I said lightly to Julian, "I doubt if I could match up to your Victoria. I was a competent pupil, but not brilliant."

Why did I call her 'his' Victoria? It was a slip of the tongue, but it worried me. However, he failed to notice it and said reassuringly that by the time he had had me out in the park a few times I would manage Ladybird well enough.

Throughout this conversation Christopher had remained silent. In an attempt to draw him into things I turned the topic to painting, saying I hoped he would let me see his work, but before he had a chance to reply, his mother announced that Christopher allowed no one to see it except herself.

"He is sensitive, this boy of mine." She reached across the table and patted his hand possessively, and when he jerked it away she gave an indulgent laugh. "And he doesn't like being fussed over, do you, my pet?"

Julian told Christopher that there was now a member of the family to whom he really should show his work. "Eustacia is a real artist; she studied under Joseph Whitehead. I have to admit that I had never heard of the fellow until we met; but, as you know, art isn't my cup of tea."

Christopher looked at me almost with awe.

"Whitehead? *The* Joseph Whitehead? You must be very talented!"

"I was fortunate. He had other students, but I was one of the few females lucky enough to be accepted."

"Which proves how good you must be," Dorcas put in. "My son thinks highly of Whitehead's work."

"Nicholas! What does he know about painting—a country doctor?" There was contempt in my husband's voice.

"He has learned a certain appreciation from

Solomon Slocombe. But how little you really know my son. His interests are wide and varied, although medicine, of course, is his passion."

Julian shrugged indifferently, and I said again to Christopher that I would very much like to see his paintings, to which he hesitantly replied that perhaps he would let me, sometime.

"She is a good judge, I do assure you," Julian put in. "Not until this evening did I learn that out dreary collection of ancestral portraits might well be masterpieces."

At this his stepmother bridled. "They are masterpieces. Those painted of my family, at least."

"But neglected, apparently. Neglected and begrimed. Did you realize that? Did any of us realize that? Were we even aware that they are badly in need of restoration? Do we ever bother to glance at them in their tarnished frames? Yet they were the first thing to catch Eustacia's eye as we went upstairs. She was shocked by their condition—weren't you, my love?—and eager to put matters right. And I do believe she could do it. She knows all the technical jargon. You should get her to talk about them, Stepmother. You will be surprised by her knowledge."

The Lady Miriam pushed back her chair, saying pettishly that she resented the suggestion that she, mistress of this house, should have neglected such treasures or allowed them to gather dirt, adding that she always made sure that the staff dusted them properly.

I said pacifically that pictures could darken with age no matter how diligent a domestic staff might be. "In art galleries they have skilled attention, which no ordinary servants can carry out. The care of oil paintings requires special training, special knowledge."

She looked appeased, but suddenly bored, and as we followed her back to the drawing room I reflected that my handsome mother-in-law was overinclined to touchiness and would need careful handling.

The men accompanied us. I felt this was because Julian had no desire to linger over port with Christopher. Whenever he spoke to the youth there was a touch of intolerance in his voice, the intolerance of a masculine man for the effeminate. I found myself feeling even more sorry for the boy, and yet a certain impatience when he rejected Julian's invitation to join him in a brandy because his mother forbade it. "You are too young, my darling. Brandy is a man's drink." And yet he was a year older than I, and I had no doubt that at his age Julian and Gerald had put boyhood well behind them.

Aunt Dorcas was the first to withdraw, saying she must see if her brother needed anything, but that she hoped he would still be asleep. At this, Miriam sighed unhappily.

"My poor husband, that he should linger only to suffer. Life can be so cruel!"

Cruel to whom? I wondered. To Sir Vivian, or to herself? I though I detected a note of self-pity in her voice, and perhaps Dorcas Bligh did too, because she merely said good night and turned away. Before departing, however, she put her hands on my shoulders and kissed my brow.

"As soon as my brother is well enough to see you, Eustacia, I will take you to him. Meanwhile, forgive the delay. It is better that he should recover a little."

"From the shock of our marriage?" Julian challenged. "I have already told Miriam what I think about that. My father should be glad I have a wife, even if it isn't the wife he expected. A man likes to choose his own bride. Tell him that, Aunt Dorcas, as soon as he is fit enough to hear it. Better still, I'll tell him myself."

Dorcas answered calmly, "I am quite sure he is

aware of it, Julian. Your father was a man too, once upon a time."

It wasn't until morning that I realized how beautiful the yellow room was. Tension and tiredness had caused me to pay little attention to it until then. I was quickly in bed that first night, waiting for my husband in the huge four-poster bed and feeling so overpowered by the canopy overhead that I was thankful when he emerged from his dressing room and came to join me.

I had extinguished all candles except those beside the bed, and as Julian plunged the room into final darkness and then reached for me, I went to him thankfully, seeking comfort in his arms. Only then did I realize to the full how difficult this first evening in his home had been. I felt as if I had been on trial and wondered how long the trial would last, with my mother-in-law as both judge and jury.

Aunt Dorcas was a different proposition altogether, perhaps because of her position at Dragonmede. She had a home here in return for nursing her brother; but at least, I reflected, it was a home in which she had been born and brought up. I wondered what it felt like to be readmitted into a wealthy household after rejecting it for a poorer one, and how she had fared when she turned her back on Dragonmede and embarked on a humbler life as the wife of the village doctor. And when she returned here, as an aging widow, to take second place to her brother's second wife, had she felt as I felt now, alien and bewildered? It must have been strange indeed to come back to one's family home and find it ruled by a new mistress.

But all these thoughts slid from my mind as Julian drew me to him. Afterward, I slept almost at once, but during the night I wakened with a feeling of being abandoned. With a sense of panic I stretched out an arm, only to find the bed empty beside me.

I knew instinctively that it had been empty for a long time. Then I became aware of something else. The room was filled with moonlight. I sat up with a jerk and saw that the curtains had been drawn back. Outlined against the window was my husband's figure, standing very still, staring down upon the lake. He did not even hear me move, although the bed creaked loudly. He was like a man mesmerized. A man I did not know.

Five

I HAD BEEN at Dragonmede a week and had still not met my father-in-law. Dorcas told me that the delay was due to his condition, and because I judged her to be an honest woman, I suppressed the feeling that I was being kept away from him.

The fact that even his wife visited him for only a very short time each day—and some days, I suspected, not at all—should have reassured me, but somehow I knew this was from her own choice. Insidiously, a disturbing picture began to build up in my mind: the picture of a man so stricken that he was frightening. I wondered if his illness had been something worse than a stroke, leaving him mentally deranged—violent, perhaps—or whether Miriam was merely a woman easily upset by the sight of illness.

It was obvious that the lady of the house was thoroughly spoiled. I wondered if she had been pampered as a girl—so sheltered from the harsh realities of life that she was unable to face up to them now.

She had been surrounded by luxury always, and still was.

The extent of that luxury was such as I had never dreamed of. In all my visits to wealthy school friends, I had never come across a woman so cosseted or so well endowed with this world's goods, and yet she took them all for granted—the jewels, the clothes, the fleet of carriages, the finely bred horses, the obsequious servants, the costly out-of-season foods which she invariably toyed with and then pushed aside, the humoring and the indulging and the pandering to her vanity to which even my husband contributed.

I began to suspect that her petulance was due to boredom, self-pity, and lack of interest in others with the exception of her son, on whom she lavished wholly possessive affection; but sometimes I did wonder if her discontent might be due to something deeper— something that she kept hidden from the eyes of the world or escaped from by overindulgence. Her fondness for wine was impossible to overlook. Was it a refuge for her? A source of oblivion?

From the morning after our arrival Julian wasted no time in taking up the reins of the estate again, with the result that I now saw little of him except at mealtimes and when we went to bed at night, and even then he was sometimes too tired for conversation and, occasionally, even for lovemaking. There had been no repetition of his nocturnal staring at the lake. He slept through the night and rose early, wasting no time in getting to work.

The estate was vast, comprising not only Dragonmede itself and the immensity of the surrounding park, but further acres divided into large areas of grazing land for deer, cattle, and sheep, with miles of undulating meadow and woodland left untouched. Timber from regularly replenished forest land was another source of revenue; then there were the Home Farm, devoted to dairy produce, and the Little Farm, which reared poultry, and the Meadow Farm, with its flowing fruit orchards and hop fields which rivaled those of nearby Kent. Each farm was run by a resident factor, but all came under Julian's supervision, with the assistance of an able steward named David Foster, a well-set-up young man whom I liked on sight—the son of a lesser Dorset landowner who would one day take over his parents' farms. I felt that such an able young man would be hard to replace.

Then there were the cottages of estate workers, farm laborers, and forestry hands; all demanded maintenance, and Julian was no indifferent landlord. His pride in everything pertaining to Dragonmede was self-evident, as was his gratitude to his stepmother for endowing it so lavishly. Her fortune had been responsible for the rebirth of a place that was his world, his life, his kingdom.

His kingdom . . . the thought sprang unbidden to my mind when, out riding one day, I saw him standing high upon a hill. At this moment he looked a very different person from the man I had met in London. Here he was a man of the country, and his swift transition from the well-tailored man-about-town to the outdoor squire was something that surprised me, although even in country clothes he was immaculately turned out. His tweeds were always of the finest; his riding clothes fitted like a glove, hand-tailored like his town suits; and in the evening the quality of his formal wear would have graced a prince. He was, I knew, his valet's pride. He was also mine.

I looked at him now, standing tall and erect, his splendid figure outlined against the sky, and I reined Ladybird so that she stood to attention obediently. As Julian had predicted, I had quickly become accustomed to handling her, although she certainly had a tendency to be highly strung. I had realized at once that here was a lady of mettle and that to control her it was necessary to make her aware that

I had mettle too. That accomplished, I had achieved supremacy over my white-socked bay mare; we understood and respected each other. So now she stood quietly, awaiting my next command. I could feel her quivering to be off, but I was absorbed in this secret contemplation of my husband. Coming upon him like this, at a moment when he was entirely alone, and unaware he was watched, I saw him without any social mask, and was impressed.

Even now, in breeches and leggings, he had that air of distinction which had impressed me at our very first meeting. At this moment I had a sidewise view of him, with his profile etched against the sky. A gun was slung beneath his arm, and suddenly it occurred to me that I rarely saw him without that gun. He carried it automatically as another man might carry a walking stick. It seemed to be the insigne of a country gentleman.

Ladybird was getting impatient. I quieted her, and as I did so a cock pheasant, startled by something unseen, broke cover with his strange, coughing cry, and went winging in a span of magnificent color across the near horizon. He was a beautiful sight, plumage vivid, his head proud, his wings outspread and long tail feathers streaming. I caught my breath, marveling at the sight of him. Then, without warning, there was a shattering explosion, and the bird's dead body plunged from the sky.

Shock made my body slump in the saddle and my hands slacken. It also sent Ladybird off at a gallop, her hooves thundering. I lost the reins, groped wildly for them and missed, grabbed and missed again. She was racing uphill, so that I was able to thrust my body forward over her neck as I maintained the secure sidesaddle position with my right leg hooked over the pommel and my foot behind the calf of my left leg, firmly planted in the stirrup. Through my startled mind ran the reassuring thought that it was difficult to throw a rider mounted sidesaddle, but on a horse as mettlesome as this, already terrified, anything could happen when we reached the downward plunge.

I saw the hill's crest looming ahead and was aware that as Ladybird stampeded my husband's voice echoed in a shout which came again and again, but it was nothing more than a receding sound beneath the thunder of her hooves. I leaned down to catch the swinging reins, but missed once more, and then suddenly she was storming over the brow of the hill, and I thrust my body backward to brace against the pitch of her back. Far below I saw the winding road leading to Rye across the Romney Marsh. Long before we reached it I would shoot over Ladybird's neck unless I could rein her, but the bit was now slack in her mouth, leather and martingale adrift.

The situation was hopeless. Fear lurched in my stomach as my body began to sway, and my legs ached from maintaining their vital hold.

Before I was thrown, my brain registered two things, their impression stamped in one flashing moment: first, that the final drop of the hillside was so steep that it would send Ladybird hurtling pell-mell down to the road at a speed so uncontrolled that she would go plunging across it toward the dike-ridden marshland unless she could be halted abruptly; and second, that the only living thing in sight was a man riding along that road, his black hair bare to the wind.

Then I leaped, wrenching my foot from the stirrup so that my right leg was released and dragged over the pommel. I felt the pull of my riding skirt as it remained hooked there; then it was free and I was rolling downhill in a scatter of loose stones and a cloud of dust, until my fall was mercifully braked by an outthrusting bush. I could hear Ladybird storming away into the distance as I lay winded.

After a while I moved gingerly and found that I was close to a bridle path which had showered me with dust and stones, and at that moment Julian appeared over the brow of the hill. He came leaping toward me, slithering down the steep lunge. Despite my shock, the anxiety in his face registered sharply; but I also saw the gun still in his hand, and as he reached me I flung out my arm, striking it from his grasp, hating him for what he had done to that wild and beautiful creature in the sky. I babbled senselessly at him until he seized me by the shoulders and shook me hard.

I had no desire to look at him or to listen to him, and apparently he sensed this, for he said not a word until he had examined me. Then he commented briefly that no bones seemed to be broken, but that the sooner he got me home the better; then Dr. Fothergill could be sent for.

"I'll ride over to Winchelsea myself and fetch him. Now try standing. Take a step or two. See if you can walk."

I obeyed shakily, but suggested that I should remain where I was while he went in search of Ladybird. At that, Julian retorted that she could find her own way home.

"She deserves to be abandoned for bolting like that. Anyone would think I had taken a shot at *her!*"

I felt too shaken to argue, and allowed him to help me up the bridle path. At one point I glanced over my shoulder, but there was no sign of Ladybird, or of the dark rider.

"Be thankful for your youth and your strength, young lady. All you have suffered is a bit of a shaking and some bruises."

Old Dr. Fothergill smiled down at me kindly, but I had the feeling that he considered this call unnecessary. To a countryman, any rider should expect to take a toss now and then. Nevertheless, he prescribed a sleeping draft and the rest of the day in bed, then took his leave—anxious to get back to his roses, it seemed, for as Aunt Dorcas led him from the room he murmured something about Nicholas being on duty, not himself.

Dorcas said pacifically that Julian had wanted no other doctor but him—pandering to male vanity, I thought wryly. When she returned I refused the sleeping draft, but she insisted that I take it.

"Shock is a great deal worse than bruising. My son always says that the medical profession doesn't yet heed the effects of shock sufficiently, but that one day it will. Dr. Fothergill, of course, belongs to the old school, as did my husband, but Matthew always encouraged Nicholas to look ahead in the field of medicine, to study every new point of view before discarding it. So I have a feeling that what dear Dr. Fothergill regards as 'a bit of a shaking' should not be lightly dismissed—so swallow this sleeping draft, Eustacia. Rest is what you need."

She stood over me while I obeyed, then drew the curtains and left me.

How long I slept, I have no idea. I was wakened by voices which seemed, at first, to be a long way off, then suddenly close at hand, and as I struggled from sleep I realized that they were the voices of two men. One was Julian's; the other, unknown.

"I recognized her at once from the white socks on her forelegs. Fortunately, I managed to gallop alongside and grab her reins, but I couldn't bring her back to Dragonmede until I'd made my call in Appledore, which was urgent."

I heard my husband expressing thanks, and the other man asking how it came about that Ladybird was running loose like that. I was alert immediately, conscious of relief because the mare had been found. I wanted to thank her rescuer and, somewhat shakily, slid out of bed. My head felt muzzy, but I pulled on a robe and made my way across the room. The three tall windows overlooked not only the lake and the lawn sweeping down to it, but a wide terrace. The voices came from there, directly beneath the central window, which stood open. Outside was a balcony with a broad stone balustrade and carved pilasters.

When I reached the window I paused for a moment, trying to conquer dizziness, and during that pause I heard my huband say that Ladybird was much too easily frightened. "She was startled by the sound of a gun, and bolted."

"But this isn't the shooting season—unless, of course, someone was taking a potshot at a rabbit."

"That must have been it."

But it wasn't. It wasn't: it had been the slaughtering of a beautiful bird at a time when such shooting was forbidden, which meant that the pheasant had been killed for one reason only, the delight of marksmanship. I was shocked by the fact that Julian concealed his guilt. For a moment I held on to the frame of the tall window while he went on talking.

"She's too highly strung for my wife. I must find her another mount. I expect you saw her thrown?"

"I saw nothing until Ladybird came stampeding towards me with an empty saddle."

So it was the lone dark rider. I thanked heaven that he had been alert enough to brake Ladybird's wild flight before she reached the marshes. I opened the window wider, stepped out onto the balcony to thank him, and was just in time to hear Julian say, "Eustacia will learn how to stay in the saddle, with practice."

"Eustacia? Is she as pretty as her name? She must be, to make you jilt Victoria. So whom do I congratulate, you or your wife? Her, I imagine, for I gather she possesses no more than looks, which is unusual in a Kershaw bride. In the circumstances, she has done well for herself and, from the sound of things, hooked you quickly. Did she stage-manage it herself, or did someone help her?"

I had never felt such fury. I wanted to hurl my indignation in the man's face. Instead, I remained quite still, shocked further by my husband's indifferent laugh.

"You can congratulate me, Cousin. Stacy has a great deal more than looks, if you know what I mean."

"Come now, Julian. A man can get the best bedding woman in London without marrying her, so there must have been another reason."

I clutched the stone balustrade, and as I did so I saw the two men below. The dark man's face was high-cheekboned and strongly cut. I hated him.

I also saw my husband's blond head and handsome features as he turned away, laughing uneasily. "You talk a lot of rubbish, Nick. What other reason could I have for marrying Eustacia—other than loving her?"

"That is what I'm wondering. Even getting her pregnant wouldn't be enough. Most men know how to deal with such situations."

I stumbled back to bed, the contempt in that voice echoing in my ears. So this was Nicholas Bligh, the cousin whom my husband disliked. Now I shared his dislike and knew that it would have given me great satisfaction if Julian had done something stronger than dismiss the man's words with a laugh.

Mercifully, sleep claimed me again, and I failed to stir until Julian joined me hours later, when I awakened only briefly before yielding once more to the effects of the sleeping draft. But when I finally awoke, my head was clear, and morning light sliced the curtains.

Julian put his arms about me, inquiring solictiously how I felt. I assured him with truth that I felt completely well again. Indeed, I was so clearheaded that every detail of yesterday's events was etched in my mind. I could see the vivid burst of feathers against the sky and the dead body of the cock pheasant plunging down to earth.

"Why did you do it?" I demanded.

He was lazily kissing my throat, his hands exploring my body. At any other time I would have been responsive, but not now.

Sensing this, he drew away. "Why did I do what?"

"Shoot that pheasant. Out of season, too, when there was no reason or excuse!"

"Why not? Any game or wildfowl on these lands belongs to the Kershaws, in season or out."

He thrust the bedclothes aside, reached for a robe, and continued with some irritation, "Before you start expressing opinions on life in the country, concentrate on getting accustomed to it. If you go around protesting against the killing of wildlife, you will make yourself unpopular."

"With the hunting and shooting set? Do you think I would care?"

"Bear in mind that I would. I don't want a wife who is squeamish."

"It isn't squeamish to hate bloodshed."

"That's a matter of opinion."

"Christopher shares mine."

"Christopher!" He spat the name contemptuously. "He should have been born a girl."

"He is sensitive."

"And impotent, I'll warrant! He wouldn't know what to do if he found a woman in his bed." With a sudden change of mood my husband leaned over me, smiling mischievously. "He couldn't give you the delight that I do, my love. What a pity it is morning and I have work to attend to."

I flung back, "And I such a good bedding woman! Tell me, is that a country expression? I have never heard it before."

His face changed.

"And where have you heard it now?"

"From your companion on the terrace yesterday.

I had been asleep, and your voices wakened me. I gathered the man was your cousin."

"And what else did you hear?"

"That you must have had some reason for marrying me, other than love. That I had done well for myself, 'hooking' you quickly."

Julian put his hand beneath my chin, tilted up my face, and kissed me. Then the teasing note returned. "Well, my darling, that's the truth, isn't it? You did win me quickly, and since I am the right man for you, you did do well for yourself. And so did I."

Against my will, I laughed.

"All the same," I insisted, "I'm not prepared to forgive your cousin's insinuations, and I would have admired you more if you had thrashed him for them."

Julian gave a mock shudder.

"My love, I would never enter into a fight with Cousin Nick. He won a boxing blue at Cambridge and was champion of his medical school. The man's all beef and brawn, and his opinions not worth heeding. Forget him."

But somehow I knew that Nicholas Bligh wasn't the kind of man a woman could forget.

Six

A STRANGE THING happened later that morning. After Lucy had brought my breakfast and the two undermaids had filled the hip bath and left me alone to complete a leisurely toilet, I made my way downstairs, reluctant, even at this hour, to descend into the vast and gloomy hall. But it seemed that wherever one wanted to go in this sprawling mansion, one had to pass through the hall eventually, so common sense told me I had to get used to it, and the sooner the better.

No one was around. Julian was out on the estate, my mother-in-law never rose until midmorning, Christopher might still be in the breakfast room, and Aunt Dorcas would be attending to Sir Vivian. I wondered absently if I might meet him today, but I was growing accustomed to this continued postponement, so I dismissed the idea. When the moment was ready, I would be ready too; until then, the only thing to do was familiarize myself with my new home. There were still parts of it unexplored. I could start with the kitchens. Why not? I wasn't yet mistress here, but saw no reason why Mrs. Levitt shouldn't welcome a visit from the wife of the heir.

As always, a chill seemed to rise from the ancient hall. Although its floor was of solid oak, the walls were of stone, and the fires in each Gothic hearth, which were necessary in all seasons, Dorcas told me, seemed to make little difference. As always, there was no welcome here, no feeling of ease—only the sinister atmosphere that had struck me upon arrival.

I was halfway across the echoing space when I suddenly had a feeling of being watched. I turned slowly, half afraid, only to find that I was quite alone. But the feeling persisted. Unseen eyes were focused on me. The conviction was as strong as one of Michelle's premonitions, and for this reason it disturbed me. Was this sinister place haunted, or was I becoming affected by its horrible atmosphere?

I stood in the middle of the great hall and looked round: at the walls, the stairs, the minstrels' gallery, and the distant rows of ancestral portraits, darkly seen in their tarnished frames. I was absolutely alone. The feeling could be due to nothing but imagination.

Then a sound brought me round with a jerk. From the shadows Mrs. Levitt's black figure glided. Beyond

her, an open door revealed a long passage leading to
the kitchen quarters. The sound had been the opening
of that door, so I doubted whether it had been she
spying upon me.

She inclined her head deferentially and asked if I
wanted anything.

"Yes, Mrs. Levitt. I would like to see the kitchens."

She looked surprised, but answered respectfully,
"Certainly, Madam," and stood aside for me to pro-
cede her down the passage.

I wasn't wholly surprised that my visit caused a
stir. The entire kitchen staff, from Cook to the lowliest
tweeny, stood to attention. From the butler's pantry
Garfield emerged, hastily whisking off his green baize
apron and donning his jacket respectfully.

Now that I was here, I was uncertain what to do
next. To make a tour of inspection might be resented,
since I was not mistress of Dragonmede, and I had
no doubt that if my mother-in-law heard of it she
would take me to task. I had an uncomfortable feeling
that I had overstepped the mark, that I intruded, and
that the sooner I took my leave the better. But I had
to do it with dignity, not hurriedly or betraying embarrassment, so I forced myself to take my time, exchanging a word with Garfield, and then with Cook,
and then, because she looked scared and pathetic in
her mobcap and lowly apron, I smiled spontaneously
at the kitchen maid, whereupon she bobbed a curtsy,
her eyes wide with awe.

Mrs. Levitt explained that Lucy and the rest of
the housemaids were about their duties elsewhere, and
after taking one glance round the sprawling and in-
convenient place I resisted the temptation to glance
into the stillroom, the dairy, and the sculleries and
laundry beyond. I could imagine what they would
be like: a repetition of this stone-flagged room, but
lacking its warmth. The kitchens might be grim and
dark, but the enormous oven range sent out great

heat and appetizing smells. I complimented Cook before leaving, and her gratification was obvious. At least she and the kitchen maid liked me, I thought, as I turned toward the long corridor leading back to the hall, Mrs. Levitt ushering me away like a hostess seeing a guest off the premises.

The passage door closed behind me. I was alone again. I surveyed the wide expanse of hall and was surprised to find that now it held no fears, no atmosphere. I walked the whole length of it and experienced no feeling of watchful eyes. If they had been there at all, they had gone now.

Common sense told me that it had all been a ridiculous flight of fancy, well worthy of Michelle.

At the thought of Michelle, homesickness assailed me and I felt a sudden yearning for the terraced Bloomsbury house. I had left behind my studio, my easel, my palette and brushes. I had also left warmth and affection and kindness, unconventional as the place had been (or shocking, depending upon how one looked at it), and I had left behind a mother of whom everyone here would disapprove except Julian, who knew her. At this moment I would have given anything for Luella's wide and generous smile, her reckless gaiety, her warmth of heart.

Perhaps it was the thought of my mother which brought Nicholas Bligh's insulting words to mind again: *"Did she stage-manage it herself, or did someone help her?"*

I paused with my foot on the stairs, remembering Luella's determination to make Julian propose to me, and against my will uneasiness crept in. Was it possible that she had used more than maternal tactics to make him woo her daughter? I rejected the idea forcibly. My mother had given me sound advice, no more than that, because there was nothing more within her power.

Suddenly happy, I lifted my skirts and began to

mount the stairs, glad to put the gloomy hall behind me, and as I did so a door below opened and a voice called, "Good morning, Cousin Eustacia. I'm glad to see you are up and about again."

It was Christopher, smiling at me from the entrance to the breakfast room.

I answered lightly, "Don't tell me you have only just finished breakfast!"

"Why not? There is nothing to rise early for. Mamma never stirs before eleven, or makes an appearance before midday, so why should I?"

I could think of a dozen reasons, but mentioned only one.

"You could be at your easel."

"Or you at yours," he retorted.

"Alas, I left it behind in London. I must send for it. I'm eager to start work again."

"Then why wait? You can buy anything you want in Rye. There's a good art dealer there. Would you like me to take you?"

The idea pleased me. I hurried upstairs to get ready, and when I descended Christopher was waiting with a carriage and pair, but first I visited the stables to find out if Ladybird was all right after her bolt, and felt reassured when she nuzzled against me as if she, in turn, had been anxious about me.

Christopher told me he had never known her to take to anyone so quickly. "At first she refused to let Victoria Bellamy so much as mount her."

My pleasure was absurd and deserved to be dampened, which Christopher accomplished effectively by adding that Victoria was accustomed to far more fractious horses and didn't think much of Ladybird anyway.

The day was clear and sunny and I enjoyed the drive to Rye. The countryside of valleys, wooded hills, and clustered villages was beautiful, but as we approached the ancient town the sudden flattening out of the land was dramatic, emphasized by the town of Winchelsea set high upon a hill to our right, with Rye similarly placed beyond it. I was puzzled by the escarpment of both hills until Christopher explained that, centuries ago, the sea had lapped directly beneath them.

Ahead I could see the pitched roofs of historic Rye, set above fortress walls. We entered through the great medieval Land Gate, between two bastion towers once closed by portcullis and drawbridge but now leading directly onto a steep, cobblestoned hill curving into the ancient High Street. I was captivated at once by the ambience of the place, with its network of timbered houses, centuries old, spreading through a labyrinth of narrow cobbled streets toward the beautiful twelfth-century church that marked the heart of the town.

Christopher took me straight to the art dealer, whose raftered shop, set beneath jutting eaves, smelled—not unattractively—of the mustiness of age mingled with the aroma of spices from the bakery next door. I purchased all I needed—easel, palette, paints and brushes, canvases, and turpentine—and then asked hopefully for a quantity of pure alcohol, explaining that I wanted to make tests upon a canvas stained by time. For this I had to proceed to the apothecary on the corner of East Street, and while I did so Christopher waited for my goods to be packaged, promising to load them into the carriage and then return to meet me.

I strolled back along the High Street and found the apothecary easily enough. The dispensary beyond the mahogany counter was partially screened by huge globular colored bottles and ancient apothecary's jars. Two men were talking there: an elderly, bespectacled gentleman wearing a holland overall, obviously the apothecary himself, and a younger, broad-shouldered man with dark, crisp hair. They were discussing a prescription, and I waited until the older man came to answer the jangling doorbell. Then the younger one half-turned, and I recognized him at once.

It was absurd to be startled, but I felt it so strongly that for a moment I could not speak. Then I realized that although I recognized Nicholas Bligh, he could have no idea who I was. At that I pulled myself together and made my request, explaining to the apothecary why I wanted the alcohol.

"It will be necessary for me to ask your name, Madam, and for you to sign this book."

"Alcohol is not a poison," I commented, surprised.

"No, Madam. Nevertheless, the supply of pure alcohol is controlled by law."

"I understand." I drew the book toward me, saying as I did so that I was Mrs. Julian Kershaw of Dragonmede.

I was aware that the dark head in the dispensary jerked to attention and that Nicholas Bligh now surveyed me with interest through a gap in the row of apothecary's jars. I ignored him and casually strolled out of view, examining the shop's wares while my order was dealt with. It was ready quickly, and a few minutes later I was handing coins across the counter, then walking out of the shop. The bell jangled merrily behind me.

I met Christopher outside and he asked if I would like to see one of Rye's historic features, the Ypres Tower, which had endured centuries of attack from across the Channel. I agreed with enthusiasm, and we turned up East Street, thence into Pump Street, leading toward the square-towered church. Soon we were at the top of the old cliff face, with the indestructible tower still looking toward the now-distant Channel and England's onetime enemy country, France.

Except for the sound of the wind, it was very quiet up here. Perhaps for this reason, the echo of heavy footsteps reached us before their owner appeared. They were brisk, determined footsteps, obviously male, and I wasn't in the least surprised when a voice said, "Good morning, Christopher. And what brings you to Rye?"

My brother-in-law turned round quickly; I, not at all. I had heard that voice before and had no desire to meet its owner—who, I guessed, had followed me deliberately. But the meeting was unavoidable, for the next moment Christopher was saying, "Have you met Julian's wife, Cousin Nick?"

I felt Christopher's hand upon my arm and was forced to turn, but I did so unhurriedly, as if reluctant to drag my eyes from the view. I acknowledged the introduction politely, liking the man no better at close quarters than at a distance, although against my will I acknowledged that his face was striking: not handsome, but somehow a face one would remember.

Apart from that, he had little to commend him. His clothes were ill chosen, and worn as if he had pulled them on carelessly, his mind on other things. Unlike my husband, so fastidious in his selection of the right neckcloth to wear with the right jacket, I felt that Nicholas Bligh would merely reach for the nearest to hand, scarcely glancing in a mirror as he tied it. Not that he was unkempt or ill groomed: he was merely a man who would consider that time spent in selecting clothes could be better spent in other ways.

In answer to his bow I held out my hand reluctantly and said, "I presume you followed me from the apothecary, having heard my identity."

Christopher looked surprised. "So you have met!"

"Not formally, cousin. And your sister-in-law is right: I did follow for the purpose of gaining an introduction. Why not? One should always make a point of welcoming new relatives—apart from which, I am anxious to know whether she is fully recovered."

"From what?" I asked pleasantly.

"Your riding accident."

"You mean the toss I took from Ladybird?" I gave a negligent shrug. "A mere nothing, I do assure you. I had to take many a fall when learning to ride in my girlhood."

I thought I saw a corner of his mouth twitch in amusement.

"And yet it was necessary for my partner to confine you to bed. That suggests shock, even if you suffered no injury."

"A slight shaking, nothing more. Permit me to thank you for returning my horse."

"So Julian told you?"

"No. It was unnecessary."

And ponder on *that,* arrogant Dr. Bligh, I thought as I turned back to the view. If he wondered how I knew that he had brought Ladybird home, so much the better, and if he recalled the open bedroom window above the terrace and the words he had uttered, better still. Nothing would please me more than to discomfort this man.

Christopher was congratulating his cousin on being made Fothergill's partner. His liking for the man was apparent, but because I still smarted beneath those abominable remarks to my husband, I failed to share it, and made a mental resolution to pay back Nicholas Bligh one day. Meanwhile, it amused me to hide the fact that I was aware of his low opinion of me, and however much his eyes might now express admiration, I was not foolish enough to be deceived. During my first evening at Dragonmede I had learned of his partiality for women, so I knew this to be a practiced glance. I could imagine the ladies of Rye yearning after their eligible doctor—and more fools they, I thought contemptuously.

Moving to my side, he asked, "And what do you think of Rye, Cousin Eustacia?"

I replied coolly that it appeared to be very interesting—which was not the way I felt at all, because I was enchanted by the place, but I was anxious to discourage further conversation. I underestimated this man, however, for he went on to say that he hoped Christopher had brought me to this spot not only to see the Tower, but for the less-appreciated view of Camber Sands and the ruined castle.

"Beyond it, the sea washed over the town once known as Old Winchelsea. It happened during one of the storms that silted up many harbors of the Cinque Ports, changed the courses of rivers, and created much of the Romney Marsh; but long before this happened, the Romans began to reclaim land from the sea during their thousand years' occupation of ancient Britain, and after their departure succeeding generations carried on—and many individual families, too, building dikes for drainage and turning the reclaimed land into admirable grazing for sheep. They grew rich as a result. They also built the seawall that runs from Camber to Dymchurch and beyond, and the canal stretching all the way to Hythe, to discourage Napoleonic invaders. At Dymchurch the level of the marsh is lower than the sea itself."

Despite my determination to resist this man, my interest was caught.

"No one knows this area as well as Cousin Nick," Christopher said admiringly. "He is steeped in its history. You must get him to tell you about it sometime."

"I'm sure it would take far too long," I answered coolly, and was aware of the doctor's speculative glance as I turned to view the landscape again. He had the uncomfortable ability to make me feel that he could read my mind, and to cover a sudden confusion I asked at random for the identity of the long foreshore to the east, hoping my tone conveyed no more than mild interest.

"That is Dungeness. I'm glad you noticed it. Most

people see nothing but a strip of wild shingle slicing the sea and turn away uninterested, but like you, Cousin Eustacia, I find Dungeness fascinating. Don't deny it. Your eyes have turned to it again and again while we've been standing here."

His perception annoyed me. It was true that the wild strip beyond the saltings seemed to hold some strange kind of magnetism, but now that I had discovered that he shared my interest, I was annoyed with myself for revealing it. I wanted no bonds of any kind with this man.

Christopher remarked with a shudder that Dungeness was a horrible place, but Nicholas disagreed.

"Desolate, I admit—even frightening to some people—but to me it is fascinating, and somehow I think Cousin Eustacia would find it equally so. The best time for a first visit is in the spring, when drifts of sea pinks and a multitude of wild flowers thrust their way up through the stones. But at any time of the year Dungeness is unique. The booming of the sea, the rumbling of the stones, the ceaseless winds cutting across from France, the fantastic formation of the shingle bar thrown up over hundreds of years— can't you appreciate the wonder of that, young Christopher, and hasn't it ever occurred to you that it would make a fantastic subject for painting?"

"That sort of thing doesn't appeal to me. I dislike anything wild or savage, and if it appealed to Eustacia I'd be surprised. I'm sure she was taught to seek more interesting subjects."

I said that on the contrary, Joseph Whitehead encouraged his students to paint whatever they wished. "He believed that what we sought to express was basically us, whether drawn from reality or imagination."

I was gratified by the surprise in Nicholas Bligh's voice when he remarked that he had no idea I was an artist, or that I had studied under such a renowned painter. His appreciation of Whitehead's ability made me feel that he had one redeeming characteristic at least.

I turned my back on the view and looked toward Rye church and the cobbled streets running toward the town. He followed my glance and said softly, "Rye, what a place she must once have been! Along with Winchelsea, she helped the original 'five ports'—Hastings, Romney, Hythe, Dover, and Sandwich—to build ships for the Armada, and so became admitted into the confederation of 'The Cinque Ports and the Two Ancient Towns,' Winchelsea and Rye being called the Two Ancient Towns from that moment on. Queen Elizabeth came here in 1573 and dubbed it Rye Royal—either before or after she received a purse of one hundred golden angels!"

He began to walk back slowly, and we went with him. For the moment I had forgotten my dislike of the man, and found myself absorbed as he went on to talk about Rye's smuggling days.

"Four hundred years of it! Smuggling was active all along the south coast as far as Cornwall, but nowhere more prolific than along this stretch. All the way from Deal, through Folkestone and Hythe and Romney and Dymchurch, it was highly organized, vastly profitable, expertly protected. With sailors such as these parts produced, the run to France, under the cover of darkness, was almost child's play."

"And if they were caught?" I asked. "Was it worth going to prison for?"

"Captured smugglers were never sent to prison; they were much too valuable. They were immediately impressed into the Navy, which counted itself lucky to get such sailors. But considering the vast scale of the smuggling trade, captures were few. Every smugglers' band was as good as its leader, and the leaders were superb. Smuggling wasn't an operation confined to a mere hundred-odd kegs of brandy or crates of tea; it was a gigantic business which kept three-quarters of England supplied with goods and luxuries it would never otherwise have known. Everyone was involved in it, from the highest to the lowest, and those who were too timid kept their mouths shut. It was a better choice than being murdered, or having one's house burned down."

There was a light in his eye which made me feel that somewhere in his ancestry ran the blood of these buccaneers, that if he had been transferred back into a former life he would have been one of them.

"There was scarcely a family in these parts that didn't have a finger in the smuggling pie," he went on. "Many made themselves rich within a few years by running tea and brandy—the Kershaws themselves, no doubt. It is rumored that the first Sir Julian earned his baronetcy by supplying his king with the finest kegs from France. Free, of course."

"Is that true?" Christopher demanded with the first real display of interest I had seen in him.

"Who knows? It might well be, since smuggling was a form of gambling, and gambling being strong in the Kershaw blood."

I stumbled. At once Nicholas had his hand beneath my elbow. "These cobbles," I murmured. "I am unaccustomed to them."

But that wasn't the cause of my stumble, and I had the uncomfortable feeling that he knew it. I was startled to learn that my husband came from gambling stock, and was aware that Nicholas Bligh kept his hand on my arm as we proceeded into Watch Bell Street, thence down Traders Passage to Mermaid Street. But Christopher, quite unaware that I was disturbed in any way, said knowingly that he had heard that Grandfather Kershaw had been a notorious gambler.

"Mamma told me that he lost so much at cards that he eventually mortgaged nearly all of Dragonmede's lands, and even sold the leaseholds of some of the farms to yeoman tenants. My father couldn't afford to buy them back. It was her fortune that did so. Grandfather must have been wildly extravagant, for even when heavily in debt he went ahead with creating the lake and the Italian arbor. Have you visited the arbor yet, Eustacia? If not, it will surprise you. It is more like a pavilion than a conventional arbor: a furnished summerhouse, in fact. Charming in its way, but somehow I don't like its atmosphere."

I confessed I had not yet seen it.

"You should get Julian to row you across. I would take you myself, but I'm no good at rowing or any other sport, and anyway I don't like the island any more than the arbor."

We had reached the Mermaid Inn, where Nicholas insisted we join him for luncheon.

He seemed to take it for granted that his invitation would not be refused; nor was it, for Christopher accepted with alacrity, confessing his delight at the chance to miss luncheon at Dragonmede, and since I was dependent upon him for the drive home, I had no choice but to accept also.

The Mermaid Inn was justly famed, and I found myself relaxing in its atmosphere, listening with increased interest to tales of Rye and its environs. From the time of the Romans the story of the wealds of Kent and Sussex had been recorded and remembered, handed down from generation to generation, just as Nicholas was handing it down now, weaving a spell which drew me back into the past. I could be happy in such a town as this, I thought. Happier by far than at Dragonmede.

Suddenly realizing that his deep voice was winning me over into a mood that was both responsive and dangerous, I pulled myself together and said briskly, "Surely you have work to do, patients to attend to? Don't let us keep you from them."

He smiled broadly. "Even a doctor has to eat

sometimes, Cousin Eustacia, but don't let *me* detain *you*. No doubt you are not yet fully recovered from being thrown by Ladybird and are anxious to return home to rest?"

His eyes mocked me. I wanted to strike him.

Driving back through the ancient gateway of the town, Christopher remarked peevishly that I had seemed in a deal of a hurry to terminate an excellent meal.

"We had been there little more than an hour! I had no idea you were such a spoilsport!"

He sulked from then on, and I was willing to let him, for I was still troubled by the information that gambling was in the Kershaw blood.

Had been, I corrected, for surely it had died out with Julian's extravagant grandfather? My husband's mild flutters at Luella's salon had been merely an excuse to see me, and now that he had returned home, his diligence was self-evident. Dragonmede absorbed him; his whole aim in life was to preserve all that his stepmother had restored to the family.

I decided that I could contribute to this by working on the portraits until they were no longer gloomy faces lost in the grime of centuries. Miriam had given her consent somewhat skeptically, saying that if it amused me, and provided I guaranteed to do no harm to any of the canvases, she saw no reason why I shouldn't try. I planned to select one for a start, then display it as proof of my ability before proceeding with the rest.

There would be months of work ahead, for the restoration of paintings was slow and arduous labor, and because each stage had to be left before I could proceed with the next, I would have plenty of time in between for my own work.

So my thoughts roamed as Christopher and I journeyed home through twisting lanes, the wild marshes left behind with their sighing willows, thrashing reeds, flocks of wild duck and graceful heron. Once we were over the high ridge that marked the earlier cliffs of England we were back in the softness of the Sussex Weald, but gradually I became aware that we were taking a different route from the outward journey, and when I saw the turreted walls of a castle that was unfamiliar to me I knew that this was indeed so. As we drew nearer I saw that most of the castle was in ruins, but still beautiful, standing above a shining moat on which water lilies floated in a multitude of color. From this moat meadows spread down to hop fields and orchards and a village of Sussex-tiled cottages.

"Bodiam," Christopher announced. "I chose this way home so that you should see it. I haven't Cousin Nick's passion for history or a quarter of his knowledge, but I can at least tell you that Bodiam Castle was built in 1386 as a defense against French invaders."

He slowed the horses to a walk as we went through the village and over a bridge toward a rising hill. Halfway up, he halted before an immense pair of wrought-iron gates, beyond which a small manor house stood in splendid isolation amidst formal and well-kept grounds. I could see gardeners, clad in leather aprons and leggings, stooping over their work, but it was the house itself that caught my attention. It was a beautiful place—perhaps Elizabethan—and built, as many Sussex manors were, in red bricks which had faded to a soft rose color, its oak timbers bleached by the centuries.

This had never belonged to any yeoman farmer, even in its earliest days, and whoever owned it now was obviously rich, for the place had an air of proud ownership and of money spent with a lavish hand.

Carved into the stone pillars marking the entrance was the name BODIAM HALL, and from the impressive gates to the ancient porch the long approach was of red bricks carefully interwoven into a geometrical design and kept meticulously free of weeds. It was flanked with fine examples of topiary: yew and box clipped into the shapes of peacocks, pheasants, and chessman ranging from King to Queen, Knight to Bishop, finally culminating in two gigantic heads of a lion and a unicorn. From this approach, the manorial wings spread proudly from east to west beneath well-preserved roofs and gables.

I wasn't entirely surprised to see a sedate nanny wheeling an expensive bassinet. She wore an immaculate uniform, and the perambulator was a costly one. Walking behind her came the prettiest young woman I had seen for a long time, her golden head shielded by a parasol covered in the same sprigged muslin as her gown, which was modishly styled with the looped-skirt draped over a bustle, a style that had long since replaced the crinoline. The draperies fell in soft folds, each edged with fine lace, and the parasol was trimmed to match. A capote bonnet was tied beneath her chin with ribbons as delicate as her lace mittens.

She gave the impression of fragility, but what struck me more forcibly was her solitary air. The fact that she walked behind the nurse, instead of ahead or even beside her as a young mistress might, suggested a timidity which I failed to understand in one so young and lovely.

Christopher was watching her. I was struck by his rapt contemplation and aware that he had forgotten me. So I remained silent, although I very much wanted to ask who the young lady was.

The nurse wheeled the bassinet toward an ornamental pond set in a rose garden, and the vision in sprigged muslin followed. In so doing they came near the gates, and as they approached Christopher called, "Penelope!"

The starched nanny halted, and although there was

in her manner the requisite suggestion of deference toward her mistress, there was disapproval too as the girl started forward, a smile breaking across her quiet, withdrawn face. Then suddenly, as if sensing the woman's attitude, she pulled up, merely inclining her head in sedate greeting.

"Good afternoon, Christopher."

The voice was quiet, encouraging no response, and the trio went on at the same measured pace. I felt that this was a daily exercise for the three of them—mother, nurse, and child. I wondered how many times they paraded the area before the child was taken back to its nursery and the young mother retired to her embroidery or, if the weather was fine as today, to sit decorously upon a garden seat.

Christopher called, "And how is Timothy today?"

I looked at the child, a vision of golden ringlets and crisp petticoats, and judged him to be no more than a year or two old, since he had not yet been breeched and was still at the bassinet stage. Despite ringlets and petticoats, however, he had a boyish little face.

"He is extremely well, thank you."

The nurse headed along the path leading to the pond, the child turning and beaming at us over his shoulder.

"He looks splendid," Christopher called, his eyes on the mother and not on the child. "And if I may say so, Penelope, you look splendid too."

She smiled, hesitated, glanced at the nanny's retreating back, and said breathlessly, "I must go. I always share Timothy's walk."

From the look of things, she shared little of it, I thought. It was almost as if she were allowed to join in only by gracious permission of the child's nurse.

"Penelope, wait a minute! I want to introduce you—"

But she had gone, and the trio was now hidden by

a high brick wall. With obvious reluctance Christopher urged the horses forward, and whether through pique or disappointment, he said to me with a meaningful glance, "I expect you noticed the resemblance, Eustacia?"

"You mean between mother and child? That dazzling fairness is an obvious inheritance."

"I didn't mean in coloring. I meant in feature. Kershaw, of course."

"You mean that pretty girl is related to us by marriage?"

"No. The Kershaw features, my dear sister-in-law, can be detected frequently hereabouts—usually amongst the lowly, since village girls consider it an honor to be seduced by one of us."

I was silent, aware of an underlying maliciousness in his voice. Was he wanting to pay me back for curtailing an enjoyable outing?

"Don't you want to know the identity of the child's father?" he taunted.

"No."

"Never mind. You'll find out. But I warn you not to be shocked by things you hear or see. Life in the country isn't always moral."

"Is it anywhere? Don't forget I come from London. Nothing could be more shocking than a certain side of life there."

"But it didn't strike near home, did it?"

I made no answer. My mother's promiscuity was her own affair, and part of her past. I wondered whether this brother-in-law of mine was trying to probe or to alarm me, and decided on the latter. He had deliberately drawn attention to the child's Kershaw features.

"I thought you liked her," I said.

"Penelope? I like her more than anyone I know."

"And yet you wasted no time in hinting about her personal life."

"That's no reflection on her! She was lonely and friendless, brought to that isolated house by her wealthy father and left there while he traveled about his business. I suppose he thought she would be happy and safe there, but of course she was desperately lonely. Still is, I shouldn't wonder. When she arrived she knew no one in or around the village. She came straight from a convent, totally unacquainted with the ways of the world, so was it surprising that before long she succumbed to something more than friendliness? Poor Penelope: she is to be pitied, because now she is socially unacceptable."

I pitied her too. But for an entirely different reason, the enjoyment had gone out of my day.

Seven

CHRISTOPHER TOLD ME there were plenty of unused rooms at Dragonmede and that I would surely find one to use as a studio, so my first task on returning home was to search for one. I was glad of something to occupy my mind, for his insinuations troubled me. Who could have begotten the Kershaw features in that child but my husband—or Gerald? I hoped the latter, although I felt the inference Christopher wanted me to draw was that my husband was the father. I also suspected that he had chosen the route home by way of Bodiam in the hope of confronting me with the child—a hope that had been fulfilled.

I felt he had baited me as punishment for curtailing his enjoyment at the Mermaid, an unendearing characteristic which I refused to think about as I began my exploration of the house. I also refused to think of Julian's possible involvement with the girl, for although the things he had done before he met me were really no concern of mine, it distressed me to think that he would abandon a girl who was expecting his child. Nor could I believe it of him. The worst of my husband's faults was his propensity for sinking into unpredictable moods. Beyond that, I knew him to be a man of honor. If he had been guilty of fathering Penelope's child, he would have been anxious to do the right thing, even if not wholly in love, and it was comforting to reflect that a man didn't go to the lengths of marrying a girl who was virtually penniless, as I was, unless he cared for her deeply.

So my spirits rose as I climbed the stairs leading from our bedroom floor to the one above, and thence to the attics, the obvious place to find disused rooms. Christopher proved to be right: I had my pick of many—cold and cheerless for the most part—and decided upon one with a big northern skylight, ideal for painting. It also had a dormer window overlooking the park. The problem of heating could be worried about later. If I won Garfield over—and I already felt that, unlike Mrs. Levitt, the staid butler was not antagonistic toward me—I had no doubt he would cooperate by supplying logs to feed the empty grate. Meanwhile, summer was upon us, so that problem could be postponed.

I flung open the dormer window, then pulled the skylight ropes, and after many protesting groans the frame opened, letting in welcome fresh air. Afterward I decided to make my way down to the kitchens and, whether I scandalized the staff or not, collect a broom and duster. Once having cleaned the place, I had only to install my equipment and myself, and set to work. The prospect was stimulating.

What I did not anticipate was getting lost on the way down. I began to retrace my steps, and for a while was convinced that I was dong so, but suddenly I became aware that I was in an unfamiliar wing. From a landing window I looked across a three-sided courtyard toward other windows which spread at right angles to the center block. From there I could see a small tower room which was unfamiliar to me because it was not discernible from the front elevation of the house, nor from the park. It huddled in a corner of steeply pitched roofs, with a round projecting wall running up to it, obviously enclosing spiral steps. I resolved to search for them sometime, but at the moment was intent only on finding my way back to the main part of the house.

Again I retraced my steps, and eventually reached a side staircase, but to my consternation it led to a section that was plainly part of the staff sleeping quarters. I had already trespassed into the kitchens today; how would I be received by the ramrod Mrs. Levitt if I were discovered here?

Hurriedly I pushed open a baize-covered door and was relieved to see carpeted floor instead of bare boards. I had found my way back to the private part of the house—but my heart sank at the sight of an endless corridor ahead. I had no means of knowing in which direction it led, and thought ironically that one needed a compass to find one's way about this rambling mansion. This corridor might even be our bedroom one, approached from another angle. One of the endless row of doors might open into the yellow room. There was only one way to find out: open every one and look inside.

I started with the nearest. The room was adequately furnished, but not elaborate like those reserved for the family, and I was about to shut the door when a gentle voice said, "Pray enter, Mrs. Julian. I have been waiting to welcome you."

She was the most diminutive woman I had ever seen, seated within a tall wing chair. Her white hair was crowned with a lace cap, and although the year was now 1875, she still wore the crinoline. Her gown was of plain gray silk of modest quality, well preserved but faded here and there. Five deep flounces bordered with green covered the billowing skirt, and pagoda sleeves trimmed with smaller flounces revealed attached undersleeves of white lace which matched the collar of her tight, high-necked bodice. Her face, which might once have been pretty, was covered in a network of wrinkles, but the eyes were bright. They pierced me with their eager scrutiny.

"You know who I am, of course, Mrs. Julian."

I stammered, "Yes—yes, of course!"—not knowing who in the world she was but anxious not to hurt her feelings.

"So naturally you appreciate how eager I have been to meet you, and how long I seem to have waited." There was reproach in her voice, which I failed to understand. I couldn't believe she was a member of the family, or she would not have been tucked away up here in a modestly furnished room, wearing yesterday's clothes.

She waved graciously toward a shabby horsehair chair. "Pray, do be seated. May I offer you some tea? I have my own appurtenances here. Everyone is kind, so kind! The Lady Miriam herself gave me this silver teapot and spirit kettle. Of course, she could tell I was accustomed only to the best and had been reared as a lady, which, indeed, is what I am. A lady, always a lady—that is Hannah Grant."

She gave me an arch glance as she tripped across the room toward the fireplace. Beneath her swinging crinoline I caught a glimpse of cloth-topped boots, neatly buttoned but shabby. She poked the fire with a long-handled brass poker, shielding her face from the heat like a young lady afraid of spoiling her complexion, then glided toward a table close to her wing chair and lit the spirit lamp beneath an elaborate silver kettle. It was the one luxurious note in drab surroundings.

Hannah Grant. I turned the name over in my mind, but it meant nothing. Julian had never mentioned it, nor had anyone else in the family, and this little old lady had certainly never appeared at meals.

And why so much insistence that she was a lady? Because she wanted to be recognized as such, to feel on a par with the other occupants of the house? What was she: a superior, pensioned-off family retainer?

Interested and rather touched, I accepted the proffered chair, wincing as the springs twanged beneath me, and as she busied herself at the tea tray I glanced surreptitiously about the room, hoping for some indication of her identity. The place was singularly bereft of personal possessions; an ugly whatnot held an array of knickknacks, and there were more on a table which was covered to the floor by a dark green cloth trimmed with a matching fringe—as if it were immodest for even a table to show its legs. Then my eye was caught by a group of miniatures: three children dressed in the fashions of long ago—a girl, and two boys.

"Ah, you are admiring my treasures, Mrs. Julian! My three treasures I always called them, although Miss Dorcas was often naughty and rebellious. I must confess the boys were my favorites. Alas, poor Dorcas, she went the way I expected her to go, which was always her own and never her poor parents'. They had such dreams for her, such ambitions, and she could have fulfilled all of them, like a dutiful daughter, if only she had not been so willful. There, Mrs. Julian, I do hope this tea is to your liking? Not strong, of course. I disapprove of strong drink, whatever it may happen to be." A nurse? A governess? She was obviously one or the other.

As I accepted a teacup of delicate china, she said proudly, "Rockingham. A gift from the late Lady Kershaw to mark twenty-five years with the family. Dear Lady Kershaw, what a saint she was! Even when the children grew up she insisted that I should remain, which, of course, was only my due since I served the family so well in a position to which I was not accustomed, or brought up to expect. But there, you know all that, of course. Dear Julian will have told you."

Dear Julian had told me nothing. I wished wryly that he had; then I would have been spared this embarrassing situation. I sipped the tea, which was little more than tinted hot water, and let the old lady run on. In this way I hoped to learn much and at the same time conceal my own ignorance, plus my husband's regrettable lapse, which I felt old Hannah Grant would find difficult to forgive.

"And then, of course, when dear Vivian married and Gerald and Julian came along, I taught them *their* lessons until they went away to school. Always, when they come home for holidays, they rush upstairs to see dear Hannah. As soon as they arrive, they come racing to me."

I stared. Didn't she realize that Gerald and Julian had long since grown up? Didn't she know poor Gerald was dead? How could she fail to, since she was aware that I was Julian's wife? It was plain that her mind vacillated between past and present.

Unable to think of a suitable answer, I looked about the room, my glance settling on a table stacked with dusty volumes and a small pile of notebooks. The bright eyes followed.

"Ah! You observe my work. It is going to be a great work, Mrs. Julian, and long overdue. Just imagine, no one has ever written a history of the Kershaws! A family like this, and there is nothing to record them for posterity! But Hannah Grant is doing it. Who could be better qualified? A scholar, and the daughter of a scholar, even if she did have to demean herself—through no fault of her own, I do assure you, but due solely to the tragedy of circumstances."

"In what way, Mrs. Grant?"

"Miss Grant," she retorted primly. "I never married, although I had many an opportunity." There was a faint bridling in her one. "The daughter of a gentleman could not marry just anyone—a mere farmer, or a clerk, or a person of a lesser social standing. You can understand that, naturally. So I came to Dragonmede."

"To teach Aunt Dorcas and Sir Vivian?"

"And Simon, of course. But as a superior governess, you understand, and respected as such."

"Of course." I laid aside my teacup. "Tell me about this family history you are writing."

She slipped out of her wing chair, excited as a child.

"My spectacles! Oh dear, oh dear, where are my spectacles?"

"Round your neck, on their ribbon," I told her gently.

She gave a trilling, girlish laugh. "Stupid me! I do declare I am becoming forgetful—a trifle, mind you, only a trifle!" She perched the spectacles on her nose. "There, that is better."

She broke off abruptly, staring at me, all her vivacity gone. She looked nothing more than a very old lady who had just received a severe shock.

"What is it?" I asked, and when she went on staring at me, saying nothing, I began to be disturbed. I was also reminded of Aunt Dorcas' keen interest, and the feeling it had given me that she was mentally comparing me with some picture she already had in mind.

I asked curiously, "Why are you staring at me like that?"

Hannah Grant shook her head, not in denial, but as if to clear her mind of a vision.

"Am I staring? Oh, dear me, I do apologize. For a moment I thought—but I was wrong, of course, quite wrong. I'm afraid I am a little shortsighted without my spectacles. When you came into the room, and when I saw you downstairs, I saw only a very lovely dark-haired girl."

She changed the subject deliberately.

"Do pray come to the table and see these books, Mrs. Julian. Dear Sir Vivian gave me permission to research amongst the family library, and even access to many private papers, but of course I cannot show you those."

"Why not?"

"Because you are not a member of the family."

"But I am. I am Julian's wife."

"Good gracious me, of course you are! For a moment I thought you were someone else. I never liked her, although dear Dorcas did. Foolish Dorcas, she never had much judgment. That dreadful marriage of hers proved it. She married beneath her, you know, and her son is his father all over again. Not a trace of the Kershaws in him: all Bligh. They were orginally a seafaring family, you know. Very humble. Not a title amongst them. And to think of dear Dorcas choosing to become one of them!"

I replied distantly that I was sure Aunt Dorcas' marriage had been very happy. I disliked this discussion of the family and decided to take my leave, laying aside a book I had just picked up, a dusty volume which looked as if it had not been opened for a long time. The remaining books gave the same impression, and I wondered how long this woman had been pretending to write a history of the Kershaws.

Curiosity compelled me to pick up one of the notebooks. The pages were covered in spidery, illegible handwriting, but before I had a chance to read, it was snatched away.

"No one may see my work yet, no one! It is for posterity."

Poor Hannah Grant. If not mad, she was rather more than eccentric.

I surrendered the notebook without protest and asked, "What did you mean when you said you saw me downstairs?"

"Precisely that. I have been watching you. Naturally, I was anxious to see dear Julian's bride, especially since it was not the bride he was expected to choose."

"You've been watching me?"

She said anxiously, "You have no objection, I hope?"

The idea of being spied upon was unpleasant, but I merely asked where, and how, and when.

"Through the peep, of course."

"The peep?"

"All the best houses have them! When the Lord of the Manor retired to the solar, he could keep an eye on his servants by peeping down on them from above."

"Into the great hall?"

"Where else? It was the hub of the establishment when Dragonmede was built. It was used for banqueting and family dining; for meetings with stewards and tenant farmers, and conclaves with neighboring landowners."

"So it was *you!*"

I wanted to laugh, remembering the feeling of threat that I had experienced earlier, the conviction that someone was spying upon me in the vast, echoing, gloomy hall.

"Take me to the solar, Miss Grant."

She clapped her hands in delight, like a little girl, then, putting her finger to her lips, whispered conspiratorially, "Follow me!"

I proceeded in the wake of her floating crinoline. She took tiny little steps, so that the garment seemed to slide across the floor by its own propulsion. She was like some ghost from the past haunting this oppressive place, and somehow, dainty as she was, she made me uneasy. There was a stealthiness in the way she glided ahead of me, and I could imagine her lurking about the house without anyone's knowing she was around.

The passages she led me through seemed as endless as the rest, and confusingly similar. It was fortunate for me that Hannah Grant knew them well, for they were mostly dark, running through the interior of the mansion with rooms leading from either side. The only light admitted was from windows at distant ends; consequently these corridors were also cold, for the sun could never penetrate them. I was thankful when at last she opened a door and ushered me through.

I stood amazed—dazzled not only by sunlight but by the magnificence of the room. The domed roof was entirely of glass, and at either end was an oriel window, with a picture painted on the glass. The room was long, with a great stone fireplace inset into one wall and the Kershaw crest emblazoned on the fireback. Above and on either side of the fireplace were ancient murals painted onto the original stone, and on the wall opposite hung an immense tapestry.

I walked the length of the room, marveling at its furnishings. I paused to touch the keys of a wing spinet, and saw the date 1688 and the maker's name—Stephen Keene of London—skillfully worked into the marquetry decoration. Although the furniture was a jumble of periods and styles—splat-back Queen Anne chairs, piecrust tables by Chippendale, sixteenth-century French armchairs, and serpentine-fronted sideboards of the kind featured by Hepplewhite in his *Cabinet-maker's Guide*—all blended admirably into the splendor of the room.

When I reached the far end, I admired the painting on the oriel window there, and saw Dürer's signature and the date 1518.

I remarked that this must have been created before Dragonmede was built. "My husband told me that the mansion dates from the late sixteenth century, so early sixteenth was obviously too soon for this window to have been designed specially for it."

"You seem to know something about old houses, Mrs. Julian."

"They interest me greatly."

"Then you will be as proud to be here as I am! And I believe you may be right about the window, for the one at the other end is also by Dürer and earlier still in date. The late Lady Kershaw, dear Julian's grandmother, once told me that her husband spared neither time nor money in adding to the glory of Dragonmede."

Grandfather Kershaw the gambler, I thought.

"What was his Christian name?" I asked.

"William. Kershaw sons always bear the names William, Vivian, Gerald, Julian, or Simon."

"What about Christopher?"

"That is a traditional Calverley name, insisted upon by the Lady Miriam. I expect you know that Calverley was the family name of the Derwents. It is sad that it vanished with the death of the late earl, he being the last male in the line, but naturally the Lady Miriam inherited the entire Derwent fortune."

Vague and eccentric Hannah Grant might be, but where family histories were concerned she had every detail at her fingertips and, I had no doubt, correctly, for the woman possessed the snobbishness of those who serve great families. No wonder she was writing a history of the Kershaws. Or trying to. At her age the task must be monumental, and I was therefore not surprised that the stacked volumes on her table were collecting dust.

"You were going to show me the peep," I reminded her.

"Of course, of course! Come here, dear Mrs. Julian.

You wll be amazed, I'm sure, for unless one knew it was there, one would never find it."

She was standing to one side of the fireplace, facing the wall mural—which, though faded, could still be recognized as an ancient hunting scene, at the center of which a stag was being gutted by serfs while bowmen stood proudly by, watching the butchering of their kill. It was a crude painting, its subject repellent, and the spouting blood must have been vividly painted originally, because even now it dominated the scene in great splashes of dark brown. And it was in the center of one of these dark brown patches that Hannah Grant drew back a stone slab so skillfully hinged that it was indiscernible.

In its place was a small, oblong hole, and when I peeped through I was astonished to see that one could view almost the entire hall below, with the exception of a small area immediately beneath—which, I guessed, was one of the Gothic fireplaces sharing the same chimney stack as this one.

From this angle the hall looked even more immense. I could see the whole of the arched roof, and a massive beam which, from far below, I had not observed. Now it stretched before me, a solid block of blackened oak pinioned between two walls. I puzzled over its use, since a stone-built place of such solidity and proportions had no need of additional support.

When I said so, Hannah replied eagerly, "My dear, can't you guess what it was for? It was put there in an earlier and more barbaric age, of course, when honor was regarded in a somewhat different light from today. The Lord of the Manor used that beam to exact recompense when due."

"In what way?" The words jerked out of me, although I really had no desire to have my horrible suspicions confirmed.

"By hanging the miscreants. Hence the great beam. It is known as the hangman's beam. Horrible, was it not? But in those days people were less civilized. They had their own codes of honor, so perhaps we should not judge them. The last time the hangman's beam was used was when a former Sir Julian executed vengeance upon a Gypsy who had seduced his daughter." Sedately, Hannah Grant added, "What a bad girl she must have been!"

I closed the stone slab, blotting out the scene. No wonder I had taken an instant aversion to that gloomy hall.

Anxious to change the subject, I commented that the domed glass above the solar was surprising, since this room, like the hall below, was in the center of the house. I added that surely there must have been rooms above at some time.

"Yes, indeed, but Sir William had them demolished. He had been on a visit to Italy and returned with this wonderful idea for turning this room into a real solarium. Dear Sir William was always full of ideas. The lake, the Italian arbor—there was no end to his schemes. This room became his favorite. Every item here was collected by him, or brought home from visits to Europe. He used to entertain gentlemen friends in this room."

How? Gambling? This was not a question I could put to Hannah Grant.

"Thank you for showing me the peep," I said. "Is it the only one in the house?"

"I have never discovered another, alas. I did so hope that Dragonmede would have its own chapel, as many great houses have, because then there would have been another peep for the use of members of the household too unwell to attend services. Perhaps even a lepers' squint! *Wouldn't* that have been exciting? But no, family prayers here have always been conducted in the great hall. Or were, until Sir Vivian inherited, and decided that the family should attend a local church. A pity, a great pity."

"Why? It seems to me a good idea that the family should not detach itself from local life."

Had she not been so ladylike, I felt that Hannah Grant would have sniffed. As it was, she merely said, "It was a pity indeed, as things turned out."

I didn't ask why. I was anxious to install my easel and art materials in the attic, so I turned toward the door.

She followed, still chattering. "That was how I became acquainted with the peep—through the family services in the great hall. Lady Kershaw allowed me to sit up here when I suffered from colds, to which, alas, I am prone. I was thus able to share the devotions without running the risk of infecting the children. I looked down on the ceremony, joined in the prayers, and listened to Sir William's splendid voice—a voice not unlike dear Julian's, as I recall—and I confess that at moments I was somewhat naughty."

I laughed. "Naughty? You? In what way?"

"By allowing my attention to wander. My imagination has always been most lively, and I would picture that wicked Gypsy swinging from the hangman's beam."

I decided that her imagination was more macabre than lively.

Outside the solar, we turned right. Ahead was the great staircase and, across the landing, the corridor leading to the yellow room. It was at this point that I noticed stone steps spiraling upward from a narrow opening on the left, and guessed that they led to the small tower I had seen across the courtyard. Hannah confirmed this, saying that the tower room was now used only for storage. "A dusty, disused place. I have not visited it for many a year. Of course, this part of the house is a little outside my own territory."

She then thanked me primly for my visit, and hoped I would honor her with another sometime.

"Only Dorcas comes to see me now," she finished

wistfully, "with the exception of Gerald and Julian, of course, when they come home from Eton."

"Julian is a grown man now," I said gently, "and Gerald—"

I broke off, regretting I had gone so far, but the old lady surprised me again when she switched back to the present and said with calm acceptance, "Gerald is dead, of course. It was to be expected."

"Expected? Why?"

"Because of the curse. The Gypsy's curse."

I stared.

The white head in its pretty lace cap nodded emphatically.

"It has always worked, Mrs. Julian, and it always will. He uttered the curse as he was hung from that beam, a curse on the eldest son of the house."

"What sort of a curse?"

"That he would always die tragically. The eldest son of every succeeding generation. And so it has happened ever since."

I didn't believe a word of it. The old woman was mad. I could dismiss her ramblings as I had dismissed Michelle's premonitions.

I pointed out, practically, that it was nonsense. "Sir Vivian is still alive. Doesn't that prove it?"

"Alas, no: he was not the elder. Simon was. He died when the gatehouse was burned down. No one knew he was there. He perished in the flames. And then, of course, there was poor Gerald, drowned in the lake. I was not surprised. I knew it would come. One can go back and back, and the legend of Dragonmede is proved to be true, every time. An earlier eldest son was killed on the hunting field, trampled to death by his favorite horse. Quite savagely, I understand, as if the beast were suddenly possessed of a devil. Always the eldest son dies tragically. Always the second son inherits."

Somehow I forced a light note into my voice as

I replied, "In that case, my husband is safe and I have nothing to worry about."

She nodded happily.

"Dear Julian, I am so glad for him. But not for you, my dear. The first son you have . . ."

I spun away from her. I had had enough of her alarming tongue. I was aware that she curtsied, and that there was no false deference in it. I was a Kershaw, wife of the heir of Dragonmede, and such obsequience was due to me. Hannah Grant would always do the right thing.

But never again would I encourage her chatter.

Something compelled me to walk to the entrance where once a gatehouse must have stood. I had noticed its absence before and wondered what had caused the blackening on the adjoining walls of the estate. Now this evidence that Hannah Grant's story could be true disturbed me more than I cared to admit.

I was turning back to the house when carriage wheels sounded behind me, and through the entrance a pony trap turned in at a spanking pace. I had to jump aside to avoid being run down. The driver immediately reined. I was surprised to see that it was a handsome young woman of about my own age.

She called an apology, then added, "You must be Julian's wife. He described you to me."

Her voice and manner were very self-assured.

"If he had described you to me," I answered, observing her blazing red hair and strong features, "I would be able to identify you."

She laughed, subtly suggesting that she was not surprised by Julian's omission and that he had good reason for it.

"I am Victoria Bellamy. Are you going up to the house? If so, pray do join me. I am on my way to take tea with dear Miriam."

Her tone implied that she was not merely a favorite guest but an accustomed one. I climbed up beside her, saying nothing, and she continued, "You are every bit as lovely as Julian said."

It was a compliment, but I suspected a hint of patronage.

"And you are all I expected too, Miss Bellamy. The family told me about you on my first evening here."

"I expect so. I have always been looked upon as one of them."

I had no answer to that one, so I let it pass, and to make conversation I admired her handling of the reins.

"Julian taught me when I was very young. We have known each other all our lives."

"Which is why you have always been looked upon as one of the family, no doubt. You must have been like sister and brother."

Far from being disconcerted, she looked amused. "There was nothing brotherly in Julian's attitude towards me, I do assure you."

She then inquired how I felt after my fall, adding that it must have shaken me badly.

"Hardly at all, Miss Bellamy."

"But being London-born and London-bred, opportunity must have denied you the chance to become an expert horse-woman."

"You are quite right. I am considered competent, but no expert."

After that there seemed no more to say, and I felt disinclined toward conversation anyway. Perhaps a certain jealousy prompted my dislike of Victoria Bellamy, although it was really she who had the greater cause, since I had married the man she had expected to win—a match, she had subtly reminded me, that the family had also expected.

She drove straight round to the mews, where she tossed the reins to a groom and then descended nimbly. I followed, turning automatically in the direction from which we had come, only to realize that she was walking in another.

She called over her shoulder, "Tea will be on the terrace on such a day as this. I am taking a shortcut. Do let me show you."

She opened a door set in a high wall, and I followed again. We emerged into a kitchen garden, which led in turn to an orchard. The path was narrow, so that I was forced to proceed in her wake, like a visitor. From the orchard we passed beneath a stone arch into an Italian walk leading toward distant lawns; here it was wide enough for two to walk abreast, but she occupied the center of the path, her bustled skirt sweeping ahead of me, so that again I was forced to walk behind.

Not until we reached the lawn could I draw alongside her, and by then I felt disinclined to. If she wished to emphasize her familiarity with Dragonmede and my own unfamiliarity, she had succeeded admirably. I liked her no more because of it.

"There, you see? Ahead is the terrace, with the table already set as I expected, and dear Miriam waiting for me."

Imperceptibly I lengthened my stride so that I walked up the terrace steps ahead of her, happy to reverse our positions, but nothing could shake Victoria Bellamy's aplomb.

"Darling Miriam, I trust I am not late? I paused to pick up Eustacia." She turned to me with a dazzling smile. "I may call you Eustacia, may I not?"

"By all means."

I glanced fleetingly at the tea table. It was set for two. My mother-in-law graciously suggested that I join them. Equally graciously, I declined, saying I had already taken tea with Hannah Grant.

There was a brief silence, broken by a trilling laugh from Victoria.

"Poor Eustacia! That must have been trying for you."

"Not really. She is a little eccentric, perhaps, but I think she enjoyed my visit."

"Did she have the temerity to *invite* you?" Miriam demanded.

"No. I came across her by accident. I was looking for a room to use as a studio, and opened her door."

I disliked having to explain everything I did, and hoped my tone conveyed it. I went on to say that Christopher had driven me into Rye to buy art materials that morning, and that I was eager to start painting again.

"So that was why he didn't appear at luncheon. It was inconsiderate of you to prevent him, my dear. Cook is entitled to know how many to cater for."

"It was entirely unplanned. We had an unexpected meeting with Nicholas Bligh, who invited us to lunch at the Mermaid."

"Indeed." Her tone was distant, but I saw an alert spark in Victoria's eyes which betrayed the fact that Nicholas Bligh's name was certainly of interest to her.

Miriam reached for a little silver bell, and tinkled it with a languid hand. When Garfield appeared she ordered tea for three despite my refusal, and I had no choice but to take my place beside them.

Victoria brought the conversation back to Hannah Grant.

"She is one of the antiquities here. I don't suppose any of us has given her a thought for many years. Certainly not Julian."

"And certainly not I," Miriam confessed.

I thought that rather sad, and said so. "I imagine her whole life revolves around the Kershaws. She is writing a history of the family."

Victoria's laughter rippled. "My dear Eustacia, she

has been doing that since Julian and I were children. I doubt if the work has ever been started."

"Well, she is certainly writing something."

"A romantic novel, I'll be bound. She used to devour them secretly. Gerald found out. They came in plain wrappers from Mudie's. He and Julian used to hunt for them in her room and smuggle them out to the orchard. We laughed ourselves to death. Deep-dyed villains with curling moustaches; reprobate earls seducing village maidens. But never the heroines, of course. They remained triumphantly virginal to the last page, when wedding bells rang and everything was sweet and pure—and the bridegroom in for a disappointing time in bed, I should imagine."

"My dear Victoria!" Miriam's tone was one of gentle reproof, but her laughter belied it. I was aware of a rapport between these two: the intimacy of people who came from the same social background.

It was a surprise to me to discover that women of their kind could indulge in the same kind of frank conversation that I had heard in my mother's drawing room. The difference was that in Luella's circle there had been no false veneer, no pretense. I found myself comparing the two social levels, to the detriment of this one.

"Do you really think Hannah Grant is writing a novel?" Miriam asked, with ill-concealed amusement.

"What else? Of course, she pretends to be a scholar, so perhaps she deludes herself that she is writing a great work." Victoria paused while Garfield hovered again and an immaculate maid set down a silver cake stand, but after they had been waved aside and we were alone again, she asked casually, "I suppose Hannah Grant told you about the curse?"

I nodded. "On the eldest son of each generation."

"You didn't believe it?"

"Of course not. I could see she was eccentric."

"What a kind way of putting it! Hannah Grant is

three parts mad. She read about that curse in a highly
colored novel called *The Dark-eyed Gipsy*. I remember
it well. Julian stole it and read it aloud to me. It was
all about a virgin seduced by a Gypsy horse thief, and
was quite hilarious." Victoria took a minute cucumber
sandwich from a plate Miriam extended, then asked
abruptly, "Was it because of Hannah's story that you
were studying the walls where the gatehouse once
stood?"

For a moment I felt too foolish to reply, and before
I had an opportunity to do so, my mother-in-law
remarked that Hannah could become a nuisance if
I allowed her to.

"Take my advice, Eustacia, and avoid her."

I said thoughtfully, "She must be very lonely,
spending her life up there away from everyone."

Miriam answered with a touch of asperity, "She
should consider herself fortunate. Many old family
retainers are not so well accommodated. Hannah is
fed, cared for, and housed in the only place in the
world where she wants to be. And allowed to use the
courtyard when she needs fresh air."

"Like a privileged prisoner?"

I spoke without thought, and immediately regretted
it, for I saw indignation flicker across my mother-in-
law's face, and pained surprise on Victoria's.

I apologized at once, but knew I was no longer
welcome at this tête-à-tête. I was wondering how to
make my excuses and leave when Victoria said
casually, "Well, at least the privileged prisoner
evidently told you one true thing: Julian's Uncle Simon
did perish in the gatehouse fire—but it was his own
fault and had nothing to do with the Gypsy's curse.
He was whoring there with one of the servant girls."

My throat felt constricted as I asked what had
happened to the girl.

The elegant Miss Bellamy wiped her fingers
delicately on a lace-edged napkin and answered lightly,

"She perished, of course. The gatehouse was unfurnished, but for straw-filled palliasses installed, no doubt, by Simon. An oil lamp must have overturned and set the straw alight. Perhaps the wench was too modest to run naked from the place!"

Her amused indifference sickened me, and at the sound of Miriam's titter I no longer sought an excuse to escape. I turned my back on the pair of them and went indoors.

I spent the next hour cleaning the unused attic, to Mrs. Levitt's disapproval. She failed to understand why I wanted to do such a menial task, and I felt in no mood to explain my need for physical and mental activity. Despite all resolution, I was haunted by the old governess' story, and even more by Victoria's. In my mind's eye I could still see the blackened walls where the gatehouse had once stood, and I knew that every time I passed them I would inwardly shudder; also that when I walked through the great hall I would be forever aware of the hangman's beam from where the Gypsy had swung, choking out his final curse.

But after energetically tackling the room and installing my equipment, I felt a great deal better, and hurried downstairs to change. Soon Julian would be back, and I had no desire to greet him in a dusty dress and with hair disarrayed. His disapproval of my undertaking so menial a task would be as great as Mrs. Levitt's.

A passing glimpse in an ornate wall mirror revealed a sorry sight. I was wiping a smudge of dirt from my face when Aunt Dorcas appeared.

"So there you are, my dear! I've been searching for you. My brother wants to meet you right away."

My heart sank.

"Not like this! I must change."

She glanced at me, then laughed.

"My dear Eustacia, what have you been up to?"

"Cleaning an attic." My hands flew to my hair, which had escaped its bonds. I could feel tendrils trailing down the nape of my neck, and another across one cheek. "Dear Aunt Dorcas, please give me time to make myself presentable!"

"You look very charming as you are, and poor Vivian's eyesight isn't what it was, but if you would feel happier I will wait before taking you to him. Try not to be too long. He hasn't had such a good day as this for some time, and I cannot guarantee that it will last. The least upset, the smallest frustration . . ."

"I'll hurry!"

I sped to my room, and within five minutes was myself again, wearing a light tarlatan dress which had once belonged to Luella and which Michelle had altered and redesigned to suit me. Aunt Dorcas' approving glance when I rejoined her bolstered my morale considerably.

Even so, I felt nervous as we hurried along to my father-in-law's room, and this nervousness seemed to be reflected in the swish of my long skirts and the rustle of Aunt Dorcas' stiff petticoats. I sensed a suppressed agitation about her which was unusual in one so calm, and as she said, "I think I should warn you, my dear, that after an illness such as my brother's a man doesn't look his normal self," I realized that any nervousness or anxiety she felt was on my behalf.

I assured her that I would show neither shock nor distress, for Julian had already told me that his father's stroke had left him with impaired speech and partial paralysis. I knew also that after a severe stroke a person's face could be distorted and even unrecognizable. The distress of such a sight must be far more acute for those who had known him all their lives.

I had waited apprehensively for this meeting, but now that I was faced with it my nervousness vanished.

After all, what was there to be afraid of in meeting a sick old man? But when Aunt Dorcas opened his door and stood aside for me to enter, I hesitated involuntarily, perhaps because the apartment was so vast, and although I had no time to gaze around, the luxury of the master bedroom made a swift impression, even though the curtains were partially drawn and the room shadowy. There was also an uncanny silence about the place: a hushed atmosphere. Not even my footsteps could be heard as I walked across the thick carpet.

It was as if time had stood still in this room, and after taking a few steps I paused, almost afraid to go farther. I heard the soft closing of the door behind me, and Aunt Dorcas' skirts rustled again. Her hand touched my arm, and she led me toward a bed at the far end of the room. It was then that I heard the breathing—heavy, deep, stertorous—and saw the figure of my father-in-law propped against the pillows.

My first thought was that at one time he must have been a powerfully built man, and this realization awakened in me such a profound pity that any lingering trace of nervousness vanished. It was a terrible thing to see the mighty fallen. This was how Sir Vivian appeared to me: a once-handsome, kingly person reduced to a helpless hulk of humanity, dependent upon others for his smallest need.

Aunt Dorcas said brightly, "Here is Eustacia, Brother."

He beckoned rather feebly with his right hand, and I saw that the other lay stiff and paralyzed upon the bedcover. One side of his face was twisted and rigid, but the other struggled to smile. I went forward instantly, hands outstretched. To touch him was an instinctive gesture, and I laid my hands upon both of his.

In the semidarkness, I saw him peering at me with the intense concentration of the shortsighted, and in those weakened eyes I saw unmistakable pleasure. He was welcoming me. If his wife was disappointed in the marriage Julian had made, Sir Vivian, at least, was not. My heart lifted, and I stopped impulsively and kissed his cheek. When I withdrew, I felt the salt taste of tears upon my lips.

He tried to speak then, but I couldn't understand a word. The sound was as unintelligible as that of an animal—but somehow I knew that Aunt Dorcas understood what he was saying and deliberately pretended not to. I was puzzled. If this poor man was trying to welcome me, why shouldn't she say so?

Her silence appeared to frustrate him, and he gestured impatiently with his normal arm, indicating that the curtains should be pulled back so that he could see me more clearly. His sister obeyed with seeming reluctance—withdrawing them only a little, so that the sunlight failed to reach me. At that Sir Vivian became angry, and she had no choice but to open the curtains to their fullest extent.

What happened next took me totally by surprise. The eyes which had been looking at me with gentle warmth suddenly changed, hardening into something I failed to understand. I felt bewildered. Was there something about me that displeased him? I turned to Aunt Dorcas swiftly, and saw such distress upon her face that I could not utter a word.

I knew then that Julian's father had taken a sudden and inexplicable dislike to me. With the petulance of the sick, his mood had changed. I drew away, disappointed and hurt. It was hard to be rejected so abruptly, but one had to accept the unpredictability of an invalid.

What followed was worse. Sir Vivian cried out, struggling forward from his pillows flinging out his arm as if to push me from his sight. When I stood there, too startled to move, his agitation became worse. There was no doubt that he wanted me to go. That flailing arm, accompanied by harsh and inarticulate noises, was eloquent enough.

I backed away, and felt Aunt Dorcas hurry me to the door. As I left the room I was shaking, but far worse was the echo of that terrible voice ringing in my ears.

Eight

JULIAN DID HIS best to comfort me, saying in a matter-of-fact tone that having visitors frequently upset his father and that people in his state were liable to seizures, so all I had to do was forget the incident.

He seemed indifferent about the old man's condition, and this distressed me. For the first time I acknowledged that there was a streak of callousness in my husband. The first demonstration of this, although I had tried to excuse it, had been at the rail depot in London, but the unfeeling way in which he now spoke of his father moved me to instant protest.

At that he demanded impatiently, "What do you expect me to do? Shed tears? I feel sorry for him, of course, but he is well cared for. Fothergill visits him frequently, and Dorcas attends to his every need. Strokes can happen to a man of his years. He is not in any pain, and he lies there surrounded by luxury."

"But frustrated! Frustrated in every way. What sort of existence is that, lying there like a helpless hulk? He may not feel any pain, but he obviously feels very strong emotions. His reaction to me was intense and frightening. Perhaps Nicholas would be a better doctor for him than Fothergill. He is young enough to be more progressive, more interested in the psychology of a patient."

Julian looked at me with raised eyebrows.

"And since when have you been on Christian-name terms with my cousin? I didn't even know the pair of you had met."

I told him then about the morning in Rye and was surprised by the pleasure I experienced at the recollection of it.

Julian shrugged and turned aside, saying that Fothergill was the more experienced man and, since he had always attended his father, should obviously continue to do so. "He has been our family doctor for years. It would be insulting to demand a younger man."

"And yet he has taken that younger man into partnership. I have a feeling he is glad to hand on the torch. Aunt Dorcas was telling me that his father encouraged Nicholas to study everything new in medicine and never to discard a theory until it had been thoroughly tested. Studying a patient's mental state in association with physical illness may be new, but I can't imagine Dr. Fothergill being interested in a patient's emotions. He seems more interested in his garden."

"I can't say I blame him. I've no time for new-fangled nonsense myself. If a man is ill, all he needs is medical attention, and that is precisely what my father gets."

"But Nicholas might be able to explain his violent reaction to me."

"I doubt it." With elaborate patience Julian reiterated, "My dear Eustacia, I've told you to put the incident out of your mind. Since his stroke, my father has been totally unpredictable. Miriam never knows how he is likely to behave when she visits him. She has told me so herself."

"And how does he behave when you visit him?"

"My love, I rarely do. I'm much too busy. Besides, what would be the use? It's impossible to hold a conversation with him, and there's no sense in sitting beside his bed saying nothing. As for the way he reacted to you, perhaps it was only natural since you are a stranger here."

The words were like cold water thrown in my face; but Julian merely yawned, stretched, and added indifferently, "And now, let's stop talking about this dreary subject and go to bed."

For the first time, as I lay close to him in the darkness, I could not respond to my husband, and when he drew away from me angrily I made no attempt to pacify him. For a long time after he slept I lay awake, unable to forget that moment of terror in my father-in-law's bedroom.

But I was disturbed by something else. Julian had called me a stranger here. It had been a slip of the tongue, perhaps, but what troubled me was the fact that it was true, and I wondered if I would ever be anything else in this somber house.

A burst of fine weather during the next few days gave me the opportunity to get out and explore the countryside around Dragonmede. Sometimes Christopher came with me, but for the most part I went alone, for I didn't wholly enjoy the company of my spoiled young brother-in-law. Too often the compassion I felt for him was mingled with impatience, and it was sometimes a relief to get away from the family completely.

I rode for miles. West to Robertsbridge and Etchingham; east to Rolvenden and Tenterden, across the county border in Kent. Once I rode to the village of Bodiam, but caught no glimpse of the pretty girl at the Hall, although I explored the castle as an excuse to linger in the vicinity. I wanted to meet her again because Christopher's hints about her child's parentage remained with me.

These daily rides became a habit of mine, but in between, I set to work on the restoration of the family portraits. I had sent to Joseph Whitehead for tools that were unobtainable in the country, and they arrived quickly, accompanied by a letter showing such interest in my project that I was spurred on.

I decided it would be a good idea to start with a portrait of Sir Vivian: the gesture might please his wife as well as the family; but when I searched the walls of the great hall and of the minstrels' gallery, I was surprised to find that the most recent portrait was of the George IV period, and the subject—a handsome man with unmistakable Kershaw features—I assumed to be Julian's grandfather.

It struck me as odd that nowhere in the house was there a likeness of Sir Vivian when young. Apart from the miniatures of the three children in Hannah Grant's room, there was absolutely nothing to show me what he had been like before illness struck him down. Even Dorcas, devoted as she was to her brother, surprisingly could produce nothing.

"I can remember him as he was, vividly enough." This was all she said when I raised the question.

I was even more surprised when I came across a family album in the drawing room one day, containing an almost complete set of family pictures, but again, none of Sir Vivian. There were sketches and watercolors of Julian and Gerald as boys, and remarkably alike they had been; there were also some of Dorcas as a girl, and even one of her wedding day. I studied that with interest, thinking that Matthew Bligh, her unacceptable bridegroom, looked an extremely likable man, and Nicholas did indeed bear a strong resemblance to him.

There were portrayals of Miriam as a young mother, with Christopher on her knee. Even then he looked an effeminate child, and I wasn't surprised that Julian and Gerald had cared so little for their half brother. There was also daguerreotypes of earlier Kershaws, but amongst this carefully kept record of the family were blank pages from which pictures were missing, and from the contrast in color between the mounts and the backing it seemed apparent that they had only recently been taken out.

I closed the book thoughtfully. I would have had to be very stupid to realize that those blank spaces had once contained likenesses of my father-in-law, and that for some inexplicable reason they had been deliberately removed.

Finally I selected a small portrait painted sometime in the seventeenth century and carried it upstairs to my studio. I removed the initial grime with a mild solution of soap and water, then dabbed the canvas with a soft cloth and set it aside to dry thoroughly before applying chemical tests. As I did so, a tap sounded on the door. To my surprise, it was Hannah Grant. She had lost no time in discovering that I had taken over this room. Again I felt uneasy. Her silent spying was uncanny.

She blinked bright, birdlike eyes at me, and then at every corner of the room.

"How *interesting* it all looks, dear Mrs. Julian. I have never seen an artist's studio before. Naturally, being the daughter of a gentleman, I never moved in bohemian circles."

I echoed in amusement, "Bohemian? What makes you say that?"

"All artist are bohemian, are they not?"

"Not necessarily. I, for one, am a very conventional person."

"Oh, dear, no, one could never say that of a young woman brought up in London. What part of London?" she added, with a negligence which I considered too elaborate to be anything but deliberate. She was an inquisitive old lady. I was not deceived by her guileless manner.

"Bloomsbury," I told her, checking a smile.

"Bloomsbury! But that is the artistic and literary quarter, is it not?"

"To a certain extent; but if by that you imagine it as Bohemia, you are mistaken. The residents of its exclusive squares are highly respectable, I assure you."

Too respectable, I thought, remembering Pru Holford's mother.

"And I suppose you lived in one of the exclusive squares before you became dear Julian's wife?"

I dried my hands and removed my smock. I had intended to start painting, but knew that if I did there would be no getting rid of Hannah. As Miriam had warned me, the woman could become a nuisance, and I was already irritated by her probing. Later, I might be ashamed of this reaction and think of her as a pathetic and lonely old woman, but at this moment I found her presence irksome and was anxious to escape from it.

I moved to the door.

"No, my home was not in an exclusive square. I lived in a tall terraced house which belonged to my mother and is still her home."

"She must miss you sadly. I expect she will come to visit you here?"

I waited for her to follow me, then locked the door behind us. I had nothing to hide, but the thought of this silent-footed little woman creeping about the room, ferreting amongst my things, was distasteful.

"I hope indeed that my mother will come to visit here," I said as I dropped the key into my pocket.

"Has Sir Vivian indicated that she may? And why did you do that, my dear?"

"Do what?"

"Lock the door."

"Just in case any member of the staff enter and accidentally touch the canvas I am restoring. At its present stage it must be allowed to dry without finger marking."

"What a talented young woman you are. I should so very much like to see your paintings sometime."

"I left them in London."

"But you will be doing more?"

"Oh, yes, I will be doing more."

"I should so like to watch you. The countryside around here is admirable for painting. Solomon Slocombe has spent his life painting it in all its moods. Not that I can understand all his work, but I am sure it is very clever. Do you paint landscapes too, Mrs. Julian? If so, I should be happy to accompany you."

The thought of enduring her garrulous company while working held no appeal, so I evaded her offer by asking who Solomon Slocombe was.

She gave a little gasp.

"Do not tell me you have never heard of him! Mr. Slocombe is renowned locally. You are sure to meet him when taking one of those long rides of yours."

So she even knew that I went riding alone. Did nothing escape this woman's watchful eyes?

The mail arrived at midmorning, the postmaster from the village riding out personally with it and emptying the leather mailbag which was kept in the hall and which Garfield solemnly presented to him. Today there were two letters for me—one from Luella and one from Michelle. I seized them eagerly and carried them off to the yellow room to read in private.

Everything appeared to be well with my mother, although, she said, the house seemed empty without me. "But Crowther is proving to be a good friend and helps to fill the cardroom most nights. I am grateful for this, because I lack the zest for gaming that I once had, entertaining tires me, and one has to do so much entertaining in order to entice people to the table."

I felt a sharp concern—not merely because it was uncharacteristic of my mother to tire easily, but because there seemed to be an indication of increasing dependence upon Crowther.

"I know you dislike the man," she went on, "but he is a good friend. And I mean 'friend,' Eustacia. No more than that."

Well, that was something to be thankful for.

The rest of her letter held little news: Bella's rheumatism seemed to be getting worse, and consequently Michelle was undertaking more and more on the domestic side.

I think she is glad to do so, and I am certainly glad for her to be occupied. She fretted continuously after your departure, full of all sorts of gloomy forebodings about your future. But you know that Michelle is fanciful in the extreme. And I daresay her personal devotion to you makes her think that dire misfortune must befall you without her protection.

She finished by reiterating her pride and delight because I had married so well. "I think of you constantly and thank God that you have a husband whose love will cherish you always. Remember me warmly to him, my dearest Eustacia, and God bless you both."

Michelle's was shorter, but more disturbing.

Your dear mamma will not tell you this, but she is far from well. She caught a severe chill recently, from which she recovered to the doctor's satisfaction, but not to mine. She has lost weight and has no appetite. Of course, she misses you, *chérie,* but I feel she consoles herself too much with M. Crow-

ther, whom I dislike, not because he is ungentle-
manly, but because he was instrumental in bringing
about your marriage.

I laughed impatiently. Dear Michelle would always
blame Crowther for bringing Julian to the house, but
it was ridiculous to imply that he had played any
greater part than that in bringing about my marriage.
For introducing me to Julian I should be grateful to
the man, I thought defensively, and remembered with
a rush of warmth my husband's tenderness to me the
night before, and my inevitable response. I could never
be critical of Julian for long, and any slight quarrel
was quickly forgotten in our physical need for each
other. There was nothing more potent than that to
heal a rift between husband and wife, and last night
Julian's love had blotted out the memory of every hurt
and disappointment.

I turned to the rest of Michelle's letter.

Chérie, I must tell you this: Recently I saw you
quite clearly. Something had shocked you. Your
face was uplifted to the sky and there was distress
in your eyes, as if you were unable to believe the
thing you saw. The day was a Wednesday and the
time about noon. Did something happen then to
frighten or hurt you?

I was shocked into stillness. It was at noon on a
Wednesday that a brilliant bird had plunged out of
the sky with a screech of pain and a scattering of
feathers and blood.

I crushed the letter impulsively. I had always refused
to believe in Michelle's second sight, and I refused
to believe in it now. But I was chilled right through.

I didn't want to read on, but I owed it to her, so
I smoothed out the sheet again. Mercifully, the letter
contained nothing more to disturb me; it finished with

the wish to know how I was, to hear from me soon, and the hope that it would not be too long before she saw me again.

I folded the paper and put it with my mother's letter in a drawer of my dressing table, but I was filled with a sudden urge to get out of the room, out of the house, or I would be haunted by Michelle's unnatural perception. If I believed in it, then I would have to believe other demonstrations of her second sight. Her warnings too.

I changed hurriedly into my riding habit and within a matter of minutes was saddling Ladybird, refusing the help of a groom because even a few minutes' idleness would allow memory to creep in, reviving not only Michelle's alarming prediction and her unhappy face at my wedding, but other incidents which had nothing to do with her but which lay disturbingly in my mind: a shrug of indifference at the sight of human degradation; hands roving my body, not with love but sadistically; anger when I shrank away; contempt because I protested at the shooting of a wild bird; impatience because I was distressed by a man reduced to the total dependence of a child . . .

There were too many moments such as these to crowd into my mind, too many echoes of Julian's voice to frighten me with its ruthless overtones. I wanted to remember only the golden moments between us and to ignore the shadows, but sometimes it seemed that the shadows were lengthening. It was from the threat of these that I wanted to escape as I gave Ladybird her head and went racing across the park and into the open countryside.

The day was glorious, the air sparkling, the light miraculously clear: a wonderful day for outdoor painting, I thought, as I reined Ladybird to a halt upon the brow of a hill. No wonder they called this part of the country The Garden of England. The adjoining wealds of Kent and Sussex spread out before me, dappled with fruit orchards and hop fields and spreading farmlands, the Sussex side more undulating than Kent, sweeping in folds to the west. The light was so clear that from this height I could even discern the jutting outthrust of Beachy Head against the sky, towering above the sea and the resort of Eastbourne on its eastern side.

I rested Ladybird awhile, smoothing her silky mane. There was companionship now between the two of us. She turned her head, trying to nuzzle my knee but reaching only the hem of my outspread skirt, which she sniffed affectionately. I laughed and patted her, and when she moved on I let her roam where she willed, which was automatically toward home. I didn't mind. I was ready to return. Fresh air and exercise had banished my uneasiness.

We were within sight of Dragonmede when I noticed a village nestling in a valley. Although so close, it was one I had not yet visited, so I turned Ladybird toward it. A bridle path lay ahead, and I followed it idly. It was very quiet here, the silence broken only by the sound of hooves and a background of birdsong.

We came upon the man suddenly. A turn in the path brought a view of sweeping fields, with fold after fold of rising ground beyond, shadowy blue in the distance. The man was seated at an easel, his back toward us.

I halted Ladybird, hesitated, then went forward, the compulsion to see another artist's work being too strong to resist.

I called, "Good afternoon! May I see?"

The words died in my throat, for the man had turned and, at the sight of me, stumbled to his feet, staring in disbelief.

Then he cried hoarsely, *"Luella!"*

Nine

*H*E WAS AN aging man, bearded, with bright blue eyes behind steel-rimmed spectacles. Those eyes continued to survey me with such incredulity that I could only stare back, equally incredulous. It was impossible that anyone in these parts should know my mother, and yet there was no denying that this man did, for not only was Luella fairly unusual as a name, but I knew well enough that in looks I resembled her.

I dismounted slowly and went toward him, leading Ladybird by the reins. The man removed a shabby, wide-brimmed hat, revealing a thick thatch of untidy gray hair.

I said, "Something tells me you are Solomon Slocombe."

"So you've heard of me? From her? You can't be Luella, of course—you are much too young—but for the moment it seemed . . ."

He removed his spectacles and passed a shaking hand across his eyes, laughing a little apologetically. "My eyesight isn't what it was, alas."

"My mother's name is Luella."

"Then you must be *her* daughter. So close a resemblance. would be impossible otherwise. Has she actually come back?

Come back? My mother, who had never been here?

"My mother lives in London. I am Eustacia Kershaw, wife of Julian Kershaw."

"So you're the young artist he brought back from London! Even my old ears pricked up at that news, despite my being so self-centered and interested only in my work." He seemed to be speaking at random, anxious to cover up some kind of self-betrayal, but then he added with a rush, "You must be Luella Gideon's daughter!"

"That was her maiden name. It became Rochdale when she married."

"Of course. I'd forgotten the name of the man she ran away with."

"Then you knew them both? My father too?"

"No. I only heard of him after it all happened: a soldier from some Kentish regiment."

A *Kentish* regiment? Not the Guards, as I had always imagined?

I took a deep breath.

"Mr. Slocombe, what made you ask if she had come back? How could my mother come back to a place she never knew?"

"But this was her home! Her father was vicar of Saint John's Church, down there in the village. He didn't approve of her match with Rochdale, and after the elopement she never returned. My dear young lady, did she never tell you?"

I leaned weakly against Ladybird's side, the reins slack in my hands. I heard myself saying that all my mother had told me was that she had been brought up in a country parsonage "somewhere in Sussex." And, of course, about the runaway match and parental disapproval.

"And did your father never tell you where it all took place?"

"I never knew him. He was killed when I was a baby."

The man murmured in distress, "Poor Luella. How did she manage?"

"She managed."

"She would, bless her. She always had courage. And pride. Too much pride. She should have turned

to me. She must have known I would have helped
somehow."

I said nothing. Although it seemed ironical to
associate pride with the way of life Luella had adopted,
I knew nevertheless that in her particular fashion this
was true. She would never have begged. She would
never have crawled home penitent, because she never
was penitent. But none of these thoughts seemed important now. Only one loomed large in my mind.

Why had she never told me that she had been born
and brought up in a village so close to Dragonmede?
And why, when I asked her, did she declare that she
had no idea where Julian's home was?

Obviously, she had kept quiet for my sake, unwilling
to chance any revelation that might interfere with my
marriage to a Kershaw, the most notable family in
these parts. No doubt she pathetically believed that
the disowned daughter of a local parson would not
be acceptable as a mother-in-law to the heir of
Dragonmede, and that any rejection of her would have
rebounded onto me.

And after all these years, perhaps it had been easy
to keep silent, easy to say that she had no knowledge
of the locality of Julian's home, admitting only that
his family was prominent in the county and letting
me assume that she had gleaned this fact from
Crowther, who had brough him to the house.

"You are shivering, Mrs. Kershaw."

I heard the old man's voice as if from a distance.
Shivering? No, I was trembling—filled with a vague and
inexplicable alarm. This was an unreasonable moment
to recall Nicholas Bligh's outrageous suggestion that
someone had stage-managed my marriage to Julian,
but the memory of my mother's careful planning was
inescapable. She had confidently assured me that Julian
would be mine only if I left everything to her.

Solomon Slocombe was packing up his equipment,
saying that his cottage was nearby and perhaps I would

care for a cup of tea. I was glad to accept, because questions about Luella's girlhood here teemed in my mind, none of which I was capable of voicing at the moment, for, apart from my recollection of her determined handling of the situation between Julian and me, I was suddenly remembering the long hours he had spent in the cardroom the night before he proposed to me.

I am writing this as I leave, and the hour is now three.

Had she kept him there deliberately, running him so heavily into debt that she was in a bargaining position at the end of it?

I thrust such an idea aside. Julian was not a poor man; I had no doubt that he could have settled any debts and, after discharging them, he could have left my mother's house and never returned had he felt so inclined. But return he had, and for the sole purpose of asking me to be his wife.

The thought should have reassured me, but failed to because other things troubled me—one being his uneasy laughter when Nicholas made his contemptible man-to-man suggestion that somehow he had been trapped into marriage. This had brought no swift defense of me, which should have been the first reaction of a man who loved his wife. There had been nothing but evasive amusement, a mechanical assurance that he had married me from choice. Even more disturbing was the excuse that although I was penniless I had a great deal to offer him in another way, a sexual way.

I felt like a woman whose enticements had been held up for the delectation of another man, and that other man had merely remarked contemptuously that such enticements could be procured from the best bedding woman in London without marrying for them.

The recollection humiliated me. I felt as if I had been stripped in the marketplace.

Solomon Slocombe's voice said gently, "Come, Mrs. Kershaw. It is no more than ten minutes' walk to my cottage." He placed a hand beneath my elbow and turned me round. "I'm afraid I have shocked you in some way, but I had no idea that—"

"—that I had no idea my mother came from these parts?" I gave a shaky little laugh. "Well, it was a surprise, I admit, but please don't blame yourself. I am only shivering because the sun had gone in."

I wasn't really surprised to discover that the old man's cottage was as shabby as himself, nor that it was untidy and overcrowded, the home of a man so obsessed with painting that surroundings were meaningless to him. Canvases were stacked in every available space, and the living room, into which the front door opened, served also as his bedroom, a truckle bed covered with blankets acting as a couch by day.

Apart from that, there were a couple of armchairs badly in need of repair, a table with a hardwood chair drawn up to it, a rather fine old Welsh dresser, and shelves from floor to ceiling stacked haphazardly with books.

An open door revealed a primitive kitchen, and from the living room a staircase disappeared into regions above. The shaggy head nodded upward.

"My studio. I knocked the two rooms up there into one because both had skylights, making it easier for work." He indicated the stacked canvases about us. "The overflow. Unfortunately, I don't sell much."

As he busied himself in the kitchen, I glanced at some of the canvases, and what I saw surprised and interested me. His work was starkly impressionistic, totally out of keeping with Victorian taste. When he returned, bearing a tray with assorted china, I asked why he had failed to go to Paris, where the French impressionists would surely have welcomed him.

"I tried it, but was homesick—stifled amidst chimney pots and crowded streets. It's true that I managed to sell more pictures there than I've ever sold here or ever will, but the only useful purpose that served was to raise my fare home. I'm Sussex-born and Sussex-bred, Mrs. Kershaw, just like your mother, but, unlike her, I have never been able to pull up my roots."

I drew the tray toward me and poured the tea. As I handed his cup across, I said, "She felt stifled in the country. She told me so many times. She could never come back."

"It wasn't the country that stifled her, but her home life. And no wonder. Josiah Gideon would have crushed the spirit of any lesser person. His wife was a subdued shadow of himself. How they produced a daughter so vivid and alive was one of those miracles the world can never explain. Luella was beautiful and irrepressible, and I daresay still is. Has she never married again?"

"Never."

"I'm surprised. Many a man must have wanted her. I wanted her, but was years too old to offer myself as a husband."

"You loved her, then?" I queried gently.

"I always loved her. Still do, in my aging fashion. She should have come back when she was widowed, but I suppose the thought of her disapproving parents discouraged her. Unnatural parents, they were. She was always in trouble with her father. I remember her stealing a horse from the Dragonmede stables one day—a Sunday, too!—and riding all the way to Bodiam and back during Matins. She came flashing down the lane just as her father was standing at the church porch, saying good-bye to his congregation. I wasn't amongst them, couldn't stand old Gideon. I'd been down to the river, painting, and was walking back at the very moment. And there came Luella, hair streaming, riding astride of all things, her skirts pulled up showing her stockings and buttoned boots. And she was laughing. How she was laughing! It was a sight to behold. She waved to everyone, and even the most sedate couldn't help waving back. That laughter of hers was infectious; her gaiety was infectious. Even the Kershaw family, who had started attending Saint John's instead of keeping up the old tradition of services at home, were amused. I remember Sir Vivian laughing uproariously. But not her father. One look at his face and I knew what Luella was in for. I wanted to carry her off to this cottage and lock her inside for safety. She rode back to Dragonmede, restabled the horse, and walked back home quite unashamed."

"And her father, my grandfather, what did he do?"

"Locked her in her room for twenty-four hours without food."

The teacup rattled in my hand.

"There now, I have distressed you this time, Mrs. Kershaw. Forgive me, but remembering your mother and the wild things she did always carries me away. Poor, lovely Luella. She was never meant to have her wings clipped. After she was released from her room, her father took her to Dragonmede to apologize for stealing the horse. Sir Vivian had become master then, and refused to even listen to an apology; said he had never seen a more lovely sight and that the Reverend Gideon should be proud to have such a daughter. I heard he was outraged by the punishment meted out to the girl and declared that he'd have the man deprived of the living of Saint John's if he treated her so harshly again. Gideon never did. He merely became more vigilant in his supervision, more repressive in his discipline. It wasn't surprising that in the end she ran away."

I sipped my tea absently, distressed by the thought of my mother's early sufferings and, because she had never hinted at anything more than a narrow-minded upbringing, I began to understand more fully the extremes of her moral rebellion.

Solomon continued, "I was grieved when she ran away, but glad for her sake. I had nothing to offer her but this cottage and an unappreciated talent as an artist. Not even youth to match her own. But after she went, the place didn't seem the same. I waited for news of her, but none came. Her parents were unapproachable and, in any case, didn't approve of a nonchurchgoer such as myself. Immoral they thought me, which in actual fact I was not, but unconventional by their standards, yes. I stuck it for a few more years; then when I had managed to save enough, I locked up this place and went to Paris. An old woman in the village kept the cottage aired, so when I returned it was at least habitable. By that time the Reverend Gideon had mercifully died, and his wife soon after. What had become of their daughter no one knew. In time, your mother became nothing but a memory in these parts, and I daresay she is remembered now by only a few of the older ones like Sir Vivian and myself, if he is capable of remembering anything now. Perhaps you can understand why I was so startled when you came riding out of nowhere."

I understood more than that: Aunt Dorcas' frank appraisal of me; Hannah Grant's scrutiny; the feeling that I was being compared with someone. These two women, at least, might well remember my wild mother, but not Miriam, who was not a native of these parts. Her scrutiny had been solely that of a woman who saw a threat to her son's possible inheritance.

I asked Solomon if I could see his studio, and he agreed at once, but warned me to take care as we mounted the rickety stairs, which he had fortified from time to time in an amateurish fashion.

"It's the old original staircase, dating back to the fifteenth century. I remember my father saying it needed replacing, even when I was a child. This has been my home all my life, for the place belonged to my parents. I was born here, and apart from my spell in France I've never lived anywhere else." He finished with a wry smile, "Nicholas Bligh says it's unhealthful, but I survive."

"So you know my husband's cousin?"

"Known him since he was born. It was he who told me of Julian's marriage. His father, Matthew Bligh, was a close friend. We used to play chess together. Our fathers before us were also friends. Mine was headmaster of the local school, not that it was much of a position, or we would have had a better home than this. Matthew's father was a seafaring man from Rye. He saved hard so that Matthew could become a doctor, and now Nicholas is as good a medical man as his father was, if not better."

I recalled the touch of the buccaneer about Nicholas and the feeling that somewhere in his ancestry there could have been pirates or smugglers. I found I could recall his face vividly, although I still clung to my first dislike of him.

The staircase led into a room running the width of the cottage, lit by twin skylights which, Solomon told me, he himself had enlarged many years ago, also demolishing the dividing wall between the room once occupied by his parents and the smaller one in which he had slept as a boy. The light was excellent for painting and, together with the smell of oil paint and turpentine, brought a feeling of nostalgia to me.

Something in my expression must have betrayed me, for Solomon said gently, "Please come anytime you wish, Mrs. Kershaw. You will always be welcome."

I told him I would be delighted, adding that I hoped

he would use my Christian name, as he had done with my mother.

"What did she call you?" I asked.

"Sol. Nothing so solemn as Solomon! That would have been uncharacteristic of Luella."

"Then I shall also call you Sol."

A whinnying from Ladybird, tethered outside, suggested she was getting impatient, but when I glanced through a dormer window I realized that it was not impatience but pleasure that prompted it. Nicholas Bligh was fondling her mane and, disloyally to me, the creature was enjoying it.

Over my shoulder Sol said, "Ah, here's Nick! He often rides over to see; seems to imagine it necessary to keep a weather eye on me just because I have a twinge of rheumatism now and then. And, like his father, won't take a penny for his services."

"If you knew his father, then you also knew his mother, Julian's Aunt Dorcas?"

Helping me down the stairs again, Solomon answered, "Of course. And a nice woman, too. She gave up a lot for Matthew's sake, but I daresay it was little loss, Dragonmede being such a stuffy household."

I echoed in surprise, "Stuffy? From all accounts, her father was a gambling man."

"True enough, but the Kershaw men have always had one law for themselves and another for their womenfolk." He glanced at me briefly, then away. "I hope you are going to be happy there, my dear."

I made no answer—partly because I could think of nothing to say, and partly because Nicholas was walking straight into the cottage and seeming to fill it with his great size.

"Ah, Cousin Eustacia! I guessed you were here. I recognized Ladybird."

I smiled, bowed, and turned to take my departure.

"Must you go?" he called swiftly. "We could ride back together."

I said I had already stayed too long and added to Solomon that I hoped I would be able to stay even longer next time. "I would like your opinion of my work. I intend to start painting again."

The old man's gratification pleased me. "Come anytime, my dear, and if I'm out, you've only to lift the latch and walk in. The place is never locked."

I went away feeling a great deal happier—not only because I had found a link with my mother, whom I missed, but also because I felt I had found a refuge, although I didn't pause to wonder why I needed one.

I couldn't possibly return to Dragonmede without first visiting the church where my tyrannical grandfather had ministered and in which my effervescent mother had worshiped as a girl. I also wanted to see the vicarage which had been her home and from which she had escaped through that romantic elopement with her soldier hero, even if his regiment had merely been a Kentish one instead of a distinguished brigade of Guards.

Both the church and the vicarage were easy to find, standing close together in the center of the village. The church was stone-built, with a square Norman tower, but the house appeared to have been constructed at a much later date: a large, ugly structure which the present incumbent must find cold and depressing. I felt sorry for the wife who had to cope with such a place.

Tethering Ladybird beside a lych-gate opening onto a side path, I walked through a wilderness of grass and forgotten gravestones until I emerged at the front of the church, where more recent graves were marked respectfully with cold marble crosses and vacantly smiling angels. Here were tended borders and mown verges, indicating that someone found time to attend to at least part of the church grounds.

As I stepped from the path onto the main walk, the sound of pawing hooves and a man's voice commanding them to be still jerked my head round. Waiting outside the front gates of the church was an impressive carriage and pair, the coachman on the box clad in a matching maroon livery with double-tiered shoulder cape and cockaded hat. The whole turnout was a costly one, but the carriage bore no crest upon the door, so whoever owned it was not of the gentry.

As I turned back to the church, the studded oak door opened and, to my surprise, out stepped the girl from Bodiam Hall. With her was the vicar, wearing his vestments and with prayer book in hand, so that I knew at once he had been conducting a service. A private one, for her alone?

I felt like an intruder and quickly stepped into the shade of some cypress trees. If this lonely girl, branded as socially unacceptable because she was the mother of an illegitimate child, was so ostracized in her own neighborhood that she was forced to attend another church for religious consolation, then I had no wish to embarrass her by confronting her at such a time, but I was touched by the grateful smile she gave the vicar in farewell, and the compassion in his face as he watched her go.

It was then that my attention was caught by sounds from another direction: the creak of a saddle, the clink of stirrups, and the stamping of hooves as a rider mounted. I spun round, thinking it could be Ladybird—then stood still in surprise, for the man I saw was no horse thief. It was David Foster, steward at Dragonmede, who had been quietly waiting out of sight and now mounted his horse, ready to follow the girl.

I watched their departure with interest. Did he admire her from afar, or had they an assignation?

Either way I wished them well, for both seemed extremely likable.

I followed the vicar into the church. He was at the altar, removing the offices of Holy Communion, and at the sound of the heavy door closing behind me he turned, salver and Communion cup in hand. I must have presented a surprising figure, a young woman entering a church in riding habit. When I apologized for this, he smiled, which, I felt sure, my tyrannical grandfather would never have done.

"God makes no rules about the clothes worshipers should wear in His house, young lady."

He descended the steps of the nave, and as I went to meet him I replied, "But the young lady who has just departed was more suitably clad than I. She looked very lovely."

"She always does," he admitted, but beyond that refused to be drawn. Nor did I really wish to pry. If this kindly man was prepared to offer Holy Communion or ordinary Matins to an ostracized member of another parish, it was their private concern and to be respected.

I introduced myself, adding that I had been riding by and entered the church out of curiosity.

"I believe that before my father-in-law's illness, he and the family worshipped here."

"That is true, but alas, it is rare to see any of the Kershaws amongst the congregation now, although their pew is still reserved. Occasionally the Lady Miriam and her son attend, also Mrs. Bligh when ministrations to Sir Vivian permit, but since the death of his brother I am sad to say that I have never seen your husband in the family pew. May I hope that you may use your influence to bring him back?"

I could make no promises for Julian, but apart from that I was not yet sure whether I myself wanted to attend a church that held unhappy associations for my mother, so I murmured something evasive, hurrying on to say that the building appeared to be very old and that its history must therefore be interesting.

I had obviously touched upon a pet love of the vicar's, for he told me enthusiastically that the archives had been kept meticulously by his predecessors and, if I were interested, could be studied at any time. The suggestion appealed, because I was curious to see my grandfather's entries, although I could imagine them being pedantic in the extreme. I was tempted to ask this man whether he knew anything about a forerunner of his, Josiah Gideon, but refrained.

After showing me some of the historic features of the church, including ancient memorial brasses inset into the stone floor many centuries ago, the vicar invited me for tea.

"My wife would be delighted, Mrs. Kershaw, and so would I."

I hadn't the heart to refuse, nor to tell him that I had already had tea with Sol Slocombe, but apart from that, my desire to see my mother's girlhood home was very strong.

While waiting for the man to shed his clerical robes in the vestry, I wandered to the church font, and experienced deep emotion at the thought that here Luella had been baptized, and that as a child and as a girl she must have sat in a pew close to the pulpit, the traditional place for a parson's family. The order of these things was rigid, she had once told me, the front pew on the right of the aisle being reserved for the leading county family, social standings graded therefrom, and, to the left, the local doctor's, with the clergyman's family seated immediately behind. The distinction between the right-hand pews and those on the left had been great, and I thought with pity of poor little Luella, forced to sit quietly beside her subdued mother and patronized by her social superiors. How she must have hated every moment of it!

The right-hand front pew bore Sir Vivian Kershaw's

name engraved on a small brass plate. It also had its own door, as had all the exclusive pews, with bare wooden chairs thereafter for lesser members of the congregation. I sat down in the Kershaw pew, and at that moment the vicar emerged from the vestry, looked at me, and smiled.

"I know what you are thinking, Mrs. Kershaw: that these distinctions should not exist. I can see it in your face—which, if I may say so, is a very expressive one."

"Well, you must admit this is very much like occupying a box at a theater. Are fees charged for these exclusive seats?"

"We prefer to call them voluntary contributions," he admitted ruefully. "A church tradition, I'm afraid."

I opened the door of the pew and stepped out.

"You said just now that God makes no rules about the clothes worshipers should wear. I'm equally sure He makes no rules regarding charges for the best seats."

Humor touched the man's face. "I can see you are a young woman of wit and wisdom. And I agree. The day must come when such distinctions are set aside."

"I'm quite sure your predecessors would be shocked by that statement."

"Fortunately, my predecessors can't hear me," he quipped, and led me out of the church and toward the vicarage.

I fell silent as we approached the house, and found that conversation was an effort for the rest of the afternoon, charming as the vicar and his wife were. They could not know that I was deeply affected by this visit, or guess the reason why. Someday I might tell them, but not yet. This was a voyage into the past for me, to be shared with no one.

The present tenants had obviously done their best to brighten the house, but nothing could overcome the chill of a place that was too gaunt ever to be homelike. The thought of what it must have been like in dour Josiah Gideon's day depressed me so much that I was glad eventually to make my escape, and understood more than ever my mother's reasons for doing so.

Because of my visit to Sol Slocombe's cottage and the ensuing one to the vicarage, I was late in arriving back at Dragonmede. Julian met me with a frown, which I chose to ignore. I was becoming accustomed to his resentment if I was not home when he returned. It was his prerogative to keep me waiting, never the reverse, and when he angrily demanded an explanation, rebellion sparked in me. I swept upstairs, leaving him to follow.

Once our bedroom door was closed, he said icily, "I asked where you had been, and what kept you so long."

Glancing down at my habit, I remarked that surely an explanation was unnecessary.

"If you've been riding since two-thirty this afternoon, you must have covered miles," he retorted.

"And how do you know I left at two-thirty?" I tossed aside my hard hat, then shook my hair free.

"Hannah Grant told me."

My spark of rebellion flared into annoyance. "Nothing I do escapes that old lady's eye, despite the fact that she is supposed to be confined to her own part of the house."

"Supposed to be? Are you implying that she creeps around the place, prying into corners where she has no right, spying on us all?"

Yes, I thought, that is precisely what I am implying—remembering the solar with its peep, and her sudden appearance at my studio, and her knowledge of my solitary rides about the countryside—but all I said was "Since you are unlikely to visit her quarters but have obviously been talking to her, you must be in a position to draw your own conclusions."

"I met her in the courtyard. One can cut across there from the steward's office in the east wing. I'd been looking for Foster, and found him absent."

I said in swift defense, "Even a steward is entitled to some free time."

From the beginning I had liked David Foster, and if he had been playing truant today in order to see the girl from Bodiam Hall, far be it from me to betray him.

Julian answered crisply, "The working hours of the staff are no concern of yours. Just remember that your place is here, at Dragonmede, as my wife."

"But not as your prisoner!" I shed my jacket, stepped out of my riding skirt, and kicked it aside furiously. "Understand this, Julian. I will come and go as I please, without investigation or reports from members of the household. If I want to go riding, I will go riding."

"The Park offers ample opportunities for that. And you can join the Hunt."

"I don't want to join the Hunt. I only want to explore the countryside at my leisure. Why should you object to that? And while we're on the subject of my freedom, if I want to paint out-of-doors, or elsewhere, I will do so, wherever I choose to go and whenever the mood takes me."

He burst out laughing.

"You're enchanting when angry! Do as you please, my love, so long as you return in time to welcome me home. I insist upon that."

But I wasn't appeased. I resented the idea of his questioning Hannah Grant about me, and said so.

He answered, with elaborate patience, "As I've told you, my darling, I met her by chance. When I couldn't find Foster I decided to spend the rest of the afternoon with my devoted wife, took the shortcut across the courtyard, and there was Hannah, sitting in the sun. She is allowed to use the courtyard, and it does command a view of the south approach to the stables, so it was natural that she should see you go. As for the time of your departure, she remembered that because the clock above the coach house struck the half hour as you went riding away."

The matter seemed so unimportant that I let it pass. Flinging myself into a chair, I held out one leg and then the other for my husband to pull off my long boots, but as he stooped I saw a frown on his handsome face.

"Do you really think Hannah prowls about the house?"

I answered lightly, "Of course not. Why should she? And even if she did, where would be the harm? What could she see, or find out?"

"The family's private affairs, perhaps."

It seemed to me that he was unnecessarily concerned, and as I drew on a robe and rang for Lucy I said indifferently, "All our private affairs are conducted behind closed doors," at which he laughed again and pulled me to him. I felt his hands beneath my robe.

"As they are to be conducted now," he whispered. "Get rid of Lucy when she comes. I've been impatient for you all afternoon."

The ormolu clock upon our bedroom mantelpiece chimed at that moment, and my gladness at its intervention made me feel guilty.

"Darling, we have to dress for dinner."

He put me aside abruptly.

"In other words, you can't even spare me half an hour upon the bed. I remember an occasion when you were more than willing to let a train depart without us."

"We were honeymooners then."

The tactless words were spoken without thought. I bit my lip in regret.

"And now, I suppose, the familiarity of marriage has reduced a wifely duty to monotony."

His tone was biting. His dressing-room door slammed behind him. Simultaneously, Lucy's discreet tap came in answer to my summons. It was too late to call him back, too late to atone. But I would do so tonight, that I vowed. I was learning fast that it was essential to humor my husband in all things.

What I didn't anticipate was that I should have no opportunity. Victoria Bellamy and her widower father were guests at dinner; also, to my surprise, Nicholas Bligh. I knew that he came to Dragonmede regularly to visit his mother, but this was the first time I had known him to be included in a family gathering. Somehow I always had the feeling that he was not regarded as one of them, and the even stronger feeling that he had no wish to be.

He looked distinguished in his formal dinner clothes, which rather surprised me because he was not a handsome man. That craggy face, all planes and angles, was impressive even if it failed to compare with my husband's blond good looks.

Apparently Victoria noticed this too, for after the women had withdrawn and left the men to their port, she remarked in an aside to Dorcas that if ever her son became master here he would fit the role well.

"My son, master of Dragonmede! That is most unlikely." There was amusement in the older woman's voice.

"But not impossible—if anything happened to Julian and he left no heir."

"Victoria, please! You will distress Eustacia."

"I am sure Eustacia is sensible enough to face up to facts."

She cast a glance toward the door, which Miriam had left slightly ajar when, as was her custom after dining, she went to her boudoir to repair any marring of her makeup so that when the men reappeared she would be perfection again. Even so, Victoria lowered her voice—not for my benefit, but in case my mother-in-law might be returning and so overhear whatever she was about to add. And this was frank indeed.

"As I was saying, if anything happened to Julian and he left no heir, Christopher would inherit, and he is most unlikely to leave any progeny! Apart from that, he would be totally inefficient in other ways too. The estate would deteriorate."

"Not with David Foster as steward. That young man is very competent, very well educated."

"And very ambitious. He has his eye elsewhere. He is patently in love with that foolish young woman from Bodiam Hall who, in the circumstances, would obviously be glad to get herself a husband. For his part, taking on the responsibility of another man's bastard would hardly be onerous since her father is so wealthy, and she an only child who will inherit all. What a catch she would have been, had she not been so stupid as to put herself beyond the social pale."

I was interested to have confirmation that David Foster, who was undoubtedly twice the man poor Christopher would ever be, was in love with the girl from Bodiam. Much of Victoria's prattle might be based on gossip, but I also had the evidence of my own eyes that afternoon.

Even so, I wanted to hear no more. I disliked Victoria's capacity for expressing ill-considered opinions.

Somehow I knew that Dorcas shared my reaction, but Victoria was completely oblivious and continued, "In the event of ambitious young David bettering himself by such a marriage, Dragonmede would suffer badly if left in Christopher's hands. The place needs a man, not an effeminate youth who spends his time painting pictures which no one but his dear mamma is allowed to see. I can anticipate so well what Christopher would do once the place became his: run away from responsibility and dissipate his time and inheritance amidst some artistic and useless circle in Paris or Florence, amongst a pack of spongers only too glad to flatter him in order to live off him. Persuasion should be brought upon Christopher to relinquish his rights in your son's favor. His doting mamma's wealth would ensure that even without Dragonmede he would live in luxury for the rest of his life. Surely you would be proud to see Nicholas as master here?"

"His ambitions lie elsewhere."

"In medicine? He is wasted as a country doctor!"

"That is neither my opinion nor his. He finds the work as worthwhile as his father did." Dorcas' firm tone put an end to the conversation.

Victoria's effrontery in discussing the future of a family to which she was totally unrelated staggered me, but failed to upset me, for nothing was likely to happen to a man as healthy as my husband, and I would undoubtedly bear children. As for her hypothetical picture of the way Christopher's life would go—well, perhaps she was right. Sorry as I felt for my young borther-in-law, and much as he liked the lovely Penelope, I knew he would be incapable of satisfying a young woman who had had a Kershaw for a lover. Faults the Kershaw men might have, but at least they had been real men, whereas Christopher was too mother-dominated to become anything but a timid and unsatisfactory lover to any woman. Cruel as my husband's comments about him had once seemed, inwardly I knew them to be justified.

Victoria welcomed the men back to the drawing room with her vivid and self-assured smile. She looked magnificent tonight in emerald green, against which her Titian hair, expertly dressed, shone vividly. I suppressed a swift longing for Michelle's talent.

As it turned out, I was obliged to suppress more than that, for throughout the evening my husband paid marked attention to Victoria, applauding enthusiastically when she sang, praising her accompaniment on the piano, and finally persuading her yawning old father to take his departure, while promising to bring his daughter safely home.

"I will drive her myself, sir. It is only nine o'clock and I know it is your habit to retire early, but you cannot be so cruel as to deprive us of your daughter's sparkling company!"

I heard Nicholas remark that he would be more than willing to save Julian the trouble by escorting Victoria himself; his own carriage was here. Both men seemed eager to dance attendance on this young woman whom, try as I might, I could not like. I felt the stabbing edge of jealousy, and it was not unjustified, with Julian's attention turned away from me and focused entirely upon the girl everyone had expected him to marry.

I don't know which was the most intolerable: my mother-in-law's ill-concealed amusement at the situation, my husband's deliberate ignoring of me, Christopher's bored disgust, Aunt Dorcas' patent endeavor to pretend that nothing untoward was happening, or Nicholas Bligh's intelligent eyes witnessing my humiliation. Finally I terminated things by saying I had had a long day, and begged to be excused.

By that time Dorcas had departed to attend Sir Vivian, Christopher had slouched out of the room without an apology, and Miriam was making steady inroads into a bottle of wine which Julian had judiciously placed at her elbow. I saw her smiling fatuously upon Victoria, who was still trilling away at the piano with Julian turning the music for her, and Nicholas sitting in an easy chair observing them both.

I went to bed feeling troubled in more ways than

one, resolving that when Julian joined me I would suggest that his stepmother should not be encouraged in her fondness for wine, unhappy and lonely as her husband's illness had obviously made her. But I waited so long that I eventually fell asleep.

How soon I wakened I had no idea, but the sound that roused me was unmistakable. It was the rhythmic splash of oars. I rose and went to the window. Moonlight spilled a silver path across the lake, outlining a boat heading toward the island, but before I could identify its occupant the vessel drifted into shadow.

At that moment something else caught my eye: a movement by the edge of the water. A man had stepped from the cover of nearby trees and was watching the departing boat—a figure wearing a greatcoat with an upstanding collar hiding the lower part of his face, the upper being shadowed by the curling brim of a tall-crowned beaver. I caught a glimpse of silver hair between collar and hat brim, but it was impossible to discern his features. The stature of the man was totally unfamiliar.

The thought of some unknown person lurking in the grounds was alarming, but the next moment my attention was diverted by a light moving on the island. In its rays I saw the Italian arbor with its dome-shaped roof, then the pillared entrance. Whoever had been in the boat had now moored and was carrying a lamp up the steps. For a moment I imagined there were two figures enveloped beneath a spreading cloak.

Seconds later, the light was still, and I knew then that it was shining from within the building. Finally, it dimmed as curtains were drawn and, shortly afterward, was extinguished.

I looked back toward the garden below. The watching figure had gone.

That night, Julian didn't come to me.

Ten

"*M* AY I TALK with you, Aunt Dorcas?" Smiling, she looked up from her needlework.

"My dear Eustacia, for me it is always a pleasure to talk to you."

I closed the door of her sewing room and then chose a seat opposite her. From this point I could see her face in full.

I wasted no time in coming to the point.

"You remember my mother, don't you? That was why you studied me so carefully on arrival. You were mentally comparing me with her."

The flying needle stopped, and the fading gray eyes met mine frankly. There had been no need for me to choose a vantage point from which to study her expression. She had nothing to hide.

"I remember her well, child, and was glad to see that you resembled her so closely."

"And yet you said nothing."

"Because Julian didn't. Neither did you. And since returning to Dragonmede I have learned to reserve comments unless asked for them."

"I said nothing because I had no idea she came from these parts."

At that, Dorcas was obviously surprised.

"You mean she never told you?"

"Never. All I knew was that she had been born and brought up somewhere in Sussex, and since it is one of the largest counties in England, that could have meant anywhere within a vast area. Even on my marriage certificate she merely put the county of her birth, not the actual place, and the priest who conducted the ceremony evidently didn't notice. He was rather a vague old man, I remember, making a great fuss of Julian and me while the register was signed."

"So Julian didn't know that she once lived locally?"

"No."

Nor did he now. I had meant to tell him of my encounter with Sol Slocombe yesterday and of all I had learned from him, but the ensuing scene in our bedroom had forestalled that, and later . . .

I refused to think of what had happened later: his treatment of me during the evening, his desertion that night. Nor had he appeared at breakfast this morning. Had he had it in the Italian arbor, that place which, according to Christopher, was like a miniature house? I couldn't imagine Julian preparing breakfast for himself in any circumstances, and jerked my mind away from the thought that perhaps someone else had prepared it for him. Had they taken food across, or was a supply kept there? The implication of that was unpleasant. I had never visited the arbor or the island. Perhaps I should.

Forcing my mind away from such ideas, I poured out to Dorcas all I had learned from Sol Slocombe.

"I knew, of course, of my mother's elopement and her escape from an unhappy home. I knew her father was a clergyman, and very strict, but no more than that. I presume she kept silent when I married Julian because she believed that the granddaughter of a local parson would be considered socially unacceptable as a Kershaw bride. Poor Luella: all my life she has wanted nothing but the best for me."

Dorcas put out a compassionate hand.

"My dear Eustacia, you are the nicest Kershaw bride to come to Dragonmede for many a year. I meant it when I told Julian he had chosen well."

I said nothing of my suspicion that he was now beginning to doubt it. His attentions to Victoria the night before clearly indicated this, unless they had been intended as punishment for me. I now knew my husband sufficiently to realize that he could be vindictive when he felt so inclined.

"Did you know my mother well, Aunt Dorcas?"

"Only by sight. When I was a child, family services were conducted here at Dragonmede. It wasn't until my brother inherited the title that he changed all that and took his wife to worship at Saint John's. Gerald was then about five, and she, poor soul, died at Julian's birth. I am older than my brother by two years, and had married before he did and gone to live in Rye, so my only encounters with Luella Gideon had been occasional ones in the village when we were children, and when she came with her parents and the church choir to sing carols at Dragonmede. It was a custom in those days, held in the great hall, with mince pies and hot toddy to follow."

Annual bounty from the rich, I thought with a touch of bitterness. That must have been one of the early scars on my mother's heart.

"So you didn't really know her?"

"Unfortunately not. I remember her only as a spirited child who, from all accounts, grew up even more so."

I said thoughtfully, "And yet you recalled her so vividly that you searched for a likeness between us when I arrived here. How did you know who I was?"

For the first time, I sensed a touch of evasion.

"Curiosity, I suppose. Luella wasn't the sort of girl one could forget, even from childhood. As for knowing your identity, we saw the wedding announcement in the *London Gazette*. Julian's letter merely said he had married a lovely girl called Eustacia, but of course the marriage announcement named you as the daughter of Mrs. Luella Rochdale and the late Eustace Rochdale. I recalled the names."

"Your brother too? Was his reaction to me due to my resemblance to my mother? Did he realize who I was and think me undesirable as a daughter-in-law compared with the more acceptable Victoria Bellamy?"

"What ever put such an idea into your head? My brother couldn't possibly remember your mother; he can remember little, poor man, and more often than not doesn't even know his own wife. So how could he remember a girl from the dim and distant past who left the village in her teens? Their paths never crossed; they moved in different worlds."

"But he might recall one memorable incident, when she stole a horse from the Dragonmede stables and went galloping through the village just when her father's congregation was coming out of church. Sol Slocombe told me about it. He said your brother was highly amused and, later, when she was brought to him to apologize, took my grandfather to task for punishing her."

Dorcas laughed in genuine amusement. "Now you mention it, I do recall hearing of the incident, but good gracious, girl, your mother could have been no more than fifteen at the time, and my brother long married. It was years ago! Poor Vivian cannot remember the immediate past, let alone the dim and distant one. Julian can confirm this. On the rare occasions he visits his father, communication between them is impossible because my brother's comprehension of things has gone. When Julian tries to talk about estate affairs, they are meaningless to him. When poor Miriam tries to make him aware of her, she cannot get through. Only I can understand his needs and wishes, and those, believe me, are concerned solely with the immediate moment."

With that I had to be satisfied, because Mrs. Levitt appeared, announcing that Sir Vivian needed her, whereupon Dorcas laid aside her needlework and rose, but after the housekeeper's departure she lingered for a final word.

"Eustacia, you must rid your mind of the idea that a country clergyman's granddaughter isn't good enough to be a Kershaw bride. If my own husband had considered himself socially beneath me, our marriage would have been unhappy indeed. As it was, my escape from Dragonmede was as merciful to me as was your mother's from that dreary parsonage."

I answered swiftly, "I don't consider myself an unsuitable bride. I merely though that others might."

"Miriam, perhaps, and Victoria naturally, because she herself expected to marry Julian, but not I, my child." She stooped and kissed me. "I'm glad we had this talk, because now you can put the whole matter out of your head and concentrate only on being happy here."

Happy? After my husband's behavior last night, and other disturbing incidents? My uneasiness was little appeased when Julian, arrived for luncheon with a bright and breezy smile, kissed me affectionately, for all the world as if nothing had happened. I found it hard to respond, but for the sake of appearances before the family I made a pretense of doing so. When we were alone I fully expected him to explain last night's desertion, or at least apologize, but he did neither. Even when we were in bed at the end of the day he made no reference to it, but took me in his arms automatically, in a "taking-for-granted" way. At that, something within me froze.

In the darkness I asked abruptly, "Was it you out there on the lake last night, going to the arbor?"

I felt him stiffen. "I? My dear love, have you ever known me to go out on that damned lake? Do you think I'd even want to, after what it did to Gerald?"

I remembered then our first night at Dragonmede, when I had wakened to see him staring out the window in distress. I felt contrite immediately.

"If you want to know where I slept, it was in my dressing room next door. Ask Hobson if you don't believe me. The man's the soul of discretion, but I knew he was concerned when he found me there this morning and guessed there had been a marital tiff."

I had no intention of discussing the situation with his valet. My jealousy and suspicions now shamed me, but I couldn't let the matter rest.

"Someone was out there. The sound of oars wakened me and curiosity drew me to the window. Then I saw a lamp moving towards the arbor, and whoever carried it went inside."

"And you actually thought it was me?"

"Well, I wondered."

"Then never do so again. I hate that lake. I hate all it stands for—my grandfather's extravagance, but for which Dragonmede would never have had to rely on my stepmother's bounty, and even worse, my brother's death. Ornamental the lake may be, but it is also treacherous. Keep away from it, my love, as I do.

Despite his words, the nocturnal visitor to the island haunted me. The figure had been too tangible to be a ghost, and those strong strokes of the oars had been wielded by a man.

Christopher, perhaps? But he had professed a dislike of the island and of the arbor and had admitted that he was not much of an oarsman, so was it likely that he would venture there at night? Or was his lack of physical prowess merely a pose because he liked to dramatize himself as a person of artistic ability, sensitive into the bargain? I remembered his leaving the drawing room in an ill-tempered mood; had he sought isolation from the family entirely? I doubted it. Besides, I was convinced that the nocturnal oarsman had not been alone and that it was a man and a woman who sought refuge in the arbor, like trysting lovers.

So, upon reflection, I was left with only one choice:

to believe that Julian had spent the night in his dressing room, or to believe that he lied. For my own peace of mind, I had to choose the former.

Then Julian himself supplied an answer that had not occurred to me. "I'll tell you who it would be: Cousin Nick. Being on the premises last night, he no doubt made the most of his opportunities before returning home. A moonlit night, a lake, a convenient and private place, and a boat all ready to take them there. Who can blame him? He's a bachelor, and free."

"But who was with him?"

"Surely you can guess? Didn't you notice his determination to oust me when I offered to drive Victoria home? Didn't you see him watching jealously as I turned the music for her? Long after you had gone to bed and Victoria had solicitiously handed my stepmother over to Mrs. Levitt, Nicholas lingered, as I knew he would."

"So you didn't drive her home, after all?"

"Of course not. With my cousin's carriage ready and waiting and her home lying just ouside Rye, it was only natural that he should take her. But before doing so, they must have slipped away to the island."

"I didn't know he was in love with her."

"A man doesn't have to be in love with a woman to want to spend the night with her, and Victoria is very attractive, you'll have to admit."

I did admit it, but said that I would never have expected her to take as a lover a man with whom she wasn't in love.

"And how do you know she isn't?"

I wanted to say, "Because she is in love with you, and for this reason resents your marriage to me." But the words remained unspoken, and in the silence my husband said drowsily, "Think no more about it. It doesn't concern us. If Cousin Nick and Victoria choose to have an affair, it is no one's business but their own, and provided she is discreet about it, her reputation will be unscathed."

"That is the important thing, of course, her reputation!"

"Naturally."

Julian sounded bored, but I felt the reverse. Disgust with the hypocrisy of the social level I had married into vied with emotions I couldn't totally analyze, but dominant above all was the recollection of Victoria's insistence that Nicholas would make a good master of Dragonmede. She was ambitious. Was she also unscrupulous? *"If anything happened to Julian and he left no heir . . ."*

Love him or not, was she capable of plotting against him to further her ambitions, with Nicholas as her ally? But surely it would be better still if something happened to me, leaving Julian free again?

I shuddered involuntarily and, mistaking it for a shiver, my husband drew me closer. "Cold, my love?" His voice promised more than warmth to replace it.

That was the moment when tranquillity could have been restored to my marriage, had I allowed it. That was the moment when I could have atoned to my husband for rejecting his lovemaking when desire was impatient within him. But I was unready.

I said, "Some person knows who went across to the arbor. Someone watched from the edge of the lake. A man. A stranger. I saw him."

"A stranger in the grounds! You must be mistaken."

"No. I am sure."

"Then it must have been someone from the household. Or David Foster, perhaps, taking a midnight stroll."

"It didn't look like David. The figure was taller, and older."

"How could you see so closely?"

"I couldn't. It was an impression. Something about

the man's stance, which wasn't that of a young man. Besides, I glimpsed silver hair."

"Only Garfield is white-haired, and the servants aren't allowed in the grounds except when serving us. Garfield values his job too much to jeopardize it. How long did this stranger remain?"

"I don't know. When I looked back, he was gone."

"I'm still convinced you imagined it. Moonlight plays tricks with shadows."

He yawned, dismissing the whole thing, but I still had more to tell him. I revealed then all I had learned about my mother's association with the village. I thought it would interest him, but for a while he said nothing. Then I realized he was shaking with silent laughter.

"Luella, daughter of the local parson," he choked. "And to think of what she became!"

I couldn't speak. If I uttered a word it would be in angry defense of her, and another quarrel would ensue, so I lay there, listening to his laughter and hating him for it, just as once, long ago, I had hated Pru Holford in the dusty garden of a Bloomsbury square.

Between gusts of laughter Julian gasped, "My love, it's hilarious, but for God's sake don't spread it around."

"Why not? What is there to be ashamed of in having a clergyman's daughter for a mother?"

"It's having her for a mother-in-law that I'm concerned about, and not because she was a clergyman's daughter."

I knew what he was implying, and my hatred increased. I fought to suppress it, but even when his laughter subsided and he came closer, claiming my body, our union was no more than submission on my part and, on his, an animal mating in the dark.

That was the point at which I knew that love had gone out of my marriage, but not the point at which fear replaced it. That was to come later. For the present, all that disturbed me was the realization that the cruel streak in my husband's nature, which I had struggled to ignore, could not be ignored any longer. There was a sadistic side to Julian which made him capable of killing a wild bird for sheer enjoyment, or of hurting his wife by making it plain that he was ashamed of her mother and wanted no acknowledgment of the relationship. This fact he drove home one afternoon a few days later, when I announced that I wanted to invite Luella to stay at Dragonmede because she had been unwell.

"Never," he announced calmly. "I will never receive Luella Rochdale in this house. You must accept my ruling on this matter."

Shocked, I burst out, "But why? You must have a reason! You were amiable enough to her when you visited us at Bloomsbury."

"Naturally. One is always amiable to one's hostess. But Dragonmede isn't Bloomsbury, and your mother would not fit in here. Everone would see at a glance the type of woman she had become." He touched my cheek with a conciliatory hand. "There, now, my little love, I've upset you, but it is your own fault. You must reject everything connected with your life before our marriage."

I jerked away.

"I can never reject Luella. She's my mother!"

"Alas, I am aware of that."

"You were also aware of it when you married me."

"Unfortunately, yes, but I had no intention of allowing the relationship to encroach upon my life."

"Then why did you marry me? I had nothing to offer you, no advantage to bring you!"

"Ah, but you had. Marrying you was very much

D.—G

worth my while. And you can't complain. You've done well out of the bargain."

"Bargain? I never considered our marriage a bargain."

"But your mother did. A clever woman, your mother, but one who had better keep out of my way."

A chill ran through me. I remembered Nicholas Bligh's voice asking whether Julian had been compelled to marry me for some reason. His guess was right. I could delude myself no longer, for truth stared me in the face. Somehow Luella had forced Julian's hand, and there was only one method she could have used.

Painfully, I asked the all-important question: "Did you owe her money?"

"I did, to the tune of several thousands. The stakes were high that night. She saw to that and kept me at the tables until three in the morning. She trapped me skillfully, running me so heavily into debt that it was impossible for me to discharge it except on her terms."

"Marriage with me," I said dully.

"Precisely." He gave a contemptuous laugh. "Why else do you think I married the daughter of a whore?"

Eleven

So now I knew; but this time there was no striking back, as when the truth had first been thrust upon me. Shock was like a physical pain from which I wanted only to escape. All I could do was fling myself away from him and go racing off to my one sure place of refuge; Sol's cottage.

I rode blindly, too sick and shaken to do anything but allow Ladybird her head, and because my visits to the cottage had become more and more frequent I turned her automatically in that direction, so she knew instinctively where to take me. When I arrived, I was so emotionally spent that I clung to the pommel before sliding limply from the saddle.

An arm came out and held me.

"You've had a shock. What has happened?"

It was Nicholas. I stared up at him in a dazed sort of way, tried to speak, and failed. I saw his strong face look down at me with such penetration and compassion that I wanted to lean against him and feel his arms hold me closely, protectively; but I could not move. Without another word he led me indoors and, sweeping some books from an armchair, gently placed me within it. Then he stooped and put a light to the fire.

"Solomon's out," he said in a matter-of-fact voice. "I'll make some tea."

I sat inertly, incapable of moving until he came back and, lifting my hand, placed a cup within it. There was no saucer. He took hold of the fingers of both my hands, encircling the cup so that warmth ran into me. "And now drink up," he ordered. "Gently does it."

I was grateful because he said no more; grateful for the hot tea which ran in a comforting tide through me. When I had finished, he took the cup away and I let my head fall back against the chair. I heard him moving in the primitive kitchen, rinsing the tea things beneath the pump which was Solomon's only water supply. Then he returned and, leaning one elbow upon the mantelpiece, stood looking down at me.

"It's Julian, isn't it? He has hurt you. I've been afraid of this."

Slowly, I lifted my head.

"And yet you asked him why he married me. You

asked if he had been forced to. I heard you, out there on the terrace."

His answering glance held regret, but he made no denial.

"I hadn't met you then," he said gently, and switched the subject. "Was the trouble over Victoria? Were you upset by Julian's attentions to her the other night? Perhaps he was trying to make you jealous. Have you thought of that?"

I laughed. "Don't try to comfort me that way, Nicholas."

He looked at me keenly, then said, "Very well, but if talking would help?"

"It wouldn't."

I was sorry about the abrupt rejection, but he accepted it with equanimity, changing the subject by saying that Solomon was probably out painting somewhere and would no doubt return soon. "I dropped in to see how he was. He is apt to neglect himself, and this damp place is no good for him. I've tried to persuade him to move, without success."

"His roots are here."

"I know, but the day may come when he is so crippled that painting will be impossible, and that would be a living death to him. He finds it difficult enough already."

I was aware of that. On several occasions I had noticed how painfully he held the brushes.

"If he left here, where would he go?" I asked.

"I could find him a place in Rye. In my work I meet many people, visit many houses. I hear when rooms become available. If he were nearer, I could then keep a closer eye on him."

It seemed to me that he kept a close eye on Sol already. So often, when I came here to paint, he dropped in. I was glad to have my thoughts turned from myself to the old man, and as we talked and I felt the warmth of the fire spreading through the

tiny room, my tension began to ease. I was conscious
of Nick's satisfied glance and realized he had been
talking for this very purpose. He was a good doctor,
I reflected wryly. His interest was solely professional:
not the personal concern of a man for a woman. I was
Cousin Eustacia, temporarily distressed by a quarrel
with his Cousin Julian. No more than that.

I looked up, and for a moment each of our glances
imprisoned the other. I forced my eyes away from
his, but found it impossible to reject his face, lean and
dark under a high, proud forehead from which black
hair swept back, curling thickly in the nape of his neck.
Beneath vigorous brows his eyes were compelling—so
compelling that I continued to avoid them. Then I
looked at his mouth, chiseled with such perfection
that I knew how it would look when smiling with
love.

But it held no smile now. It was tight and controlled, somehow suggesting suppressed emotion. My
glance went from the mouth to the chin, which was
strong and had a cleft in it, as if impressed by a
sculptor's hand. All these features should have added
up to handsomeness; instead, they totaled something
unforgettable. I was disturbed by it, by him, and failed
to understand why, especially at a time when Julian
had rocked the very foundations of our marriage,
leaving me bereft of all feeling.

"I must go."

I half-rose, but Nicholas said, "Not yet. You've
ridden that mare of yours hard and she deserves a
rest. So do you." He glanced down at my bombazine
dress, which betrayed the fact that I had fled in too
much of a hurry to think of changing. "Solomon would
be sorry to miss you," he added, "so while you wait
for him, I'll give Ladybird a rubdown."

I hadnt been aware that my horse was sweating,
or even that I had ridden so hard, but I let Nicholas
go without protest. When alone, I realized that I had

no desire to see Sol after all. His wise old eyes would see too much. He would wonder, and speculate, and perhaps question. Besides my need for comfort had somehow been assuaged, although Nicholas had offered none.

When I went outside, he had finished wiping Ladybird down and was giving her a handful of oats. He swung me up into the saddle, his hands falling away quickly once I was there. Then he looked up at me for a long moment.

"Don't worry about things, Eustacia. Leave them to time. Let life take over."

Then he was walking back into the cottage, Ladybird was heading for home, and I was thinking that it was the first time he had not called me Cousin, as if he were no longer thinking of me as a relative, even by marriage.

In a way it was fortunate that my mare cast a shoe when we were in the center of the village; in another it was not, for the cobblestones were of flint, and but for the proximity of the blacksmith she would have gone lame. An even worse disaster could have befallen me, for her stumble nearly threw me, and only a reflex action on my part saved me from pitching over her head and cracking my skull on the iron-hard ground.

Somehow I pulled myself upright, steadied her, and dismounted. She limped unhappily as I led her over the few remaining yards to the forge, situated opposite the village inn. There she had to wait while the smith finished shoeing another horse, brought in, he told me, by a gentleman who had arrived at the inn a few days before.

I wasn't wholly sorry about the delay—not only because the jolt had shaken me, but because I had no desire to return to Dragonmede yet, no desire to face Julian. I was glad to take the smith's advice to adjourn to the inn parlor and "rest awhiles."

"Old Jem, the landlord, do make good coffee by all accounts, Ma'am. Not that I can vouch for it like, bein' an ale-drinkin' man meself."

It was when I was seated in the bow window of the inn's parlor, sipping coffee and reflecting that the smith's recommendation had been good, that I realized I was not alone. A man was sitting beside the inglenook, legs out-thrust, and his gaze was fixed on me with undisguised interest. I turned away, disliking his scrutiny, but not before my mind registered a swift impression of silver hair, middle age, tanned skin, dissolute good looks, shabby elegance, and an instinctive mistrust. I assumed this was the stranger whose horse was being shod, but even when the blacksmith arrived to report that the job was done, the man lingered, and so did his bold assessment of me.

I laid aside my cup, paid the innkeeper, and went across to the forge to wait while Ladybird was fitted with a new shoe. Better the company of the smith than that of an inquisitive stranger.

The atmosphere within the forge quickly made me forget the man; flying sparks, the clang of the anvil, and the skill of a craftsman who loved his work were soothing and stimulating at the same time. It wasn't until my mare was finally led outside and I remounted that I saw the stranger watching me from the window of the inn. Somehow I knew he had been waiting to see me emerge, and with resentment and a vague alarm I rode away without waiting for the blacksmith's change for my crown piece, or heeding his remark that from the look of things there was no reason why my mare should have cast a shoe.

"Seemed to have been loosened like, Ma'am. Not worn, nor come adrift natural."

It was only later that I remembered those words.

What made me look back before turning the bend in the village street I shall never know, but I was annoyed with myself for doing so because the stranger had come out of the inn and now stood on the pavement, watching me. Even more annoyingly, he bowed. Whoever he was, he was not lacking in insolence.

"I've been searching for you everywhere, Cousin."

It was Christopher, looking pettish. His mother, he said, was in bed with one of her migraines, and Julian had gone off with Victoria. So she was here again, I thought. Her visits seemed to be becoming very frequent.

"She said she had called to see you," Christopher went on, "but of course I didn't believe her. She and Julian went wandering off into the Park. I daresay we may find them."

I had no desire to. Nor had I any real desire for Christopher's company. I wanted nothing so much as to be alone, to think, to come to terms with a situation which, whether I liked it or not, I had to accept. I was Julian's wife and had to remain so. Discovering that I had been married for expediency and not for love was no grounds for divorce, quite apart from the fact that such a social stigma would never be acceptable to the Kershaw family. In such circles an appearance of conjugal respectability was an essential, even where there was no conjugal bliss. I had no illusions now about the morals of county society; they differed in no way from those of London society. In both the only commandment to be heeded was "Thou shalt not be found out."

In any case, in my marriage there was nothing to be found out, except my personal humiliation. In time, I prayed, even that would be dulled and I would come to accept a loveless bargain. There would be children to console me, and I would find joy in them, even though conceived merely through wifely duty. I had a warm-blooded husband who would expect his rights, and would have no hesitation in taking them by force if necessary. I would submit because I had no choice— no lover to run away with, as Luella had once had.

The thought of my mother brought her into the foreground of my mind, and I realized that I had been stubbornly refusing to think about her because the anger I felt over her behavior was dangerous. I could not think of it dispassionately. She had trapped Julian into marrying me, and concealed the fact. To put it crudely, she had sold me.

But to put it more honestly, she had fought to get me my heart's desire. I had to remember that. "Do you wish to be Julian Kershaw's wife?" she had asked, and I had admitted that I wanted nothing more passionately. I had also agreed to leave everything to her, so I could hardly protest now over the methods she had used.

"If you like," Christopher was saying, "I'll have a horse saddled and ride with you across the Park, but don't you want to change out of that dress?"

"No, I'm riding no more today. I'll stable Ladybird and then go up to my studio. I want to get on with the restoration of the portrait."

He answered, in spoiled tones, "I did think that you, of all people, would be sociable! Julian and Victoria made it plain that they didn't want me, and even David Foster didn't welcome me when I strolled into his office."

"I expect he was busy."

"Oh, he was. He always is. My half brother is absorbed with the great outdoors and our steward with his ledgers. It's all very boring."

"You could paint," I suggested, as I led the mare into the stableyard.

"I've been painting!"

Sometimes Christopher's petulance was difficult to tolerate, but I said pacifically, "Then let me see what you've done. You have never yet shown me your paintings."

"Nor will I, until I feel so inclined."

I shrugged, handed Ladybird over to a groom, and walked away. Christopher followed. I took the path through the orchard that Victoria had first shown me, then crossed the lawn below the terrace. On my left, the lake glistened, and I could see the arbor standing upon a little knoll on the island. Christopher was right: it was more like a small house than an arbor—a miniature house where lovers could be alone together.

I turned away from it abruptly and faced the broad west wing of Dragonmede. I could see the windows of our bedroom and, to the left, the even more impressive ones of my father-in-law's room.

And his face looking down at me: twisted, paralyzed, and watchful. Something inside me went very still, as if my heart were trapped by fear, but I continued to walk until I reached the terrace and mounted the balustraded steps, and all the time I could feel the old man's eyes boring through the crown of my head with the stabbing, suspicious glare of the unbalanced. Was his mind really unhinged, or was the tragic distortion of his face solely responsible for the impression? I forced myself not to look up again, but within the radius of his sight my spine prickled and every nerve in my body tightened defensively.

"I see my father is sitting by his window this afternoon. This must be one of his good days."

Christopher's voice made me jump. I had been so lost in thought that I was unaware of him still beside me.

"Then why don't you visit him?" I asked, entering the house.

"Because I don't want to. I can't stand the sight of anyone sick, and besides, I get on his nerves. I always did. He was always comparing me with Julian and Gerald, and I daresay still is, behind that gruesome mask."

"Don't talk about him like that."

"But it's true. He never considered me manly because I hate shooting and every other boring country sport. If he still imagines I'm going to Sandhurst, I only hope he's sufficiently deranged to go on deluding himself, because I haven't the slightest intention of even playing at being a soldier. I'll quit Dragonmede first!"

"And risk losing your inheritance?"

"It isn't likely to come to me, particularly now Julian has married."

"And you don't care?"

"Not in the least. The place would be a millstone round my neck."

Victoria would be pleased to hear him say that, I thought as I mounted the stairs. Christopher would need little persuasion to abdicate in favor of Nicholas.

And would Nicholas be pleased too? Was he really Victoria's ally? Anything was possible, I thought unhappily—anything at all; but at this moment I was in no mood to care about people's secret ambitions. All I felt was a desperate need to be occupied, and without pausing I went straight up to my studio, with Christopher at my heels.

"May I stay and watch?" he asked, as I took my holland smock from its hook behind the door and crossed to the portrait.

I told him he could, provided he didn't disturb me— at which he perched himself upon the windowsill and glowered. I lacked the heart to ask him to leave, although this stage of my work demanded total concentration. One wrong move could cause damage. I mixed a solution carefully.

"What are you doing now?" he asked curiously.

I told him I was mixing a mild solvent to treat the

surface coating, which the varnishing had made brittle and discolored. For a while he watched with interest, but his attention soon wandered. I was glad when he stared moodily out the window, but not so glad when he opened it, admitting a strong current of air which blew my hair across my eyes at a moment when I was watching every movement of my fingers, every stroke of my brush. I halted immediately, and was about to protest when a sound came up to us from below, carried sharply on the wind.

It was the screech of an animal in pain, and at once Christopher was leaning out the window, shouting, "Stop it! Stop it!" The words were carried back to him on the wind, but he went on shouting as I laid aside my brush and moved the solvent to a safe place, by which time he had turned back to the room, white-faced.

"Eustacia, look!"

I was cowardly enough not to wish to, but Christopher seized my arm and dragged me across. From this height, a wide stretch of the Park could be seen, and on the edge of it, close to the house, stood Victoria and Julian, watching a ferret with its teeth in the belly of a rabbit. Both carried guns.

Christopher sobbed wildly, "Oh, my God, how can they stand there and watch!"

I was out of the room and racing downstairs, sick in the pit of my stomach. By the time I reached them, the rabbit was in its death throes, but conscious enough to continue screaming intermittently. The grass beneath its mutilated body was stained a bright red.

In one fleeting glance I saw the fascination on my husband's face and the gun beneath his arm, and I did something I had never done in my life. I snatched the gun, focused blindly, and fired. The ferret dashed away. The rabbit quivered and was still, all pain gone. Then the gun fell nervelessly from my hands as the ferret came racing back and fell avidly on its prey.

Then a second shot rang out, and the ferret was dead.

Julian was staring at Victoria in amazement.

"What on earth made you do that?" he demanded.

"The sport was over," she said calmly. "Watching an animal kill its prey is fascinating, but once the creature is dead there's no more fun in it. Besides, I don't like ferrets much."

I turned abruptly and walked away. I wanted to put as much distance as possible between myself and the pair of them. I heard Julian's voice call after me, "That was an unnecessary thing to do, my dear wife. A waste of a good bullet. The ferret would have finished the job."

At that, I ran. I heard laughter behind me and, from above, inarticulate sounds as I drew near to the house, and there was my father-in-law, still seated at his open window, watching me. Was he protesting too? Was he trying to declare that I had behaved like a squeamish fool? I stopped in my tracks and looked up at him, watching his twisted face mouthing incoherently. I knew he was trying to say something to me, and that whatever it was he felt it strongly, but the wind carried the inarticulate sounds away, and a moment later, Aunt Dorcas appeared and gently put her arms about her brother, drawing him back into the room.

I went on into the house, glancing to neither right nor left because I didn't want to look at this place from which I now wanted most passionately to escape.

Christopher was still in my studio, seated with his back to the window.

He said, "This house is evil. You know that, don't you?"

Twelve

I MADE NO answer. I went across to the portrait and covered it, for in my present state I could no longer work.

At that he cried, "I tell you it's evil, and so are its inhabitants. That is what Dragonmede does to people. Every cruelty committed in its history lives on, self-perpetuating, infecting every generation."

"I don't believe it. You didn't enjoy that scene just now any more than I did."

"No, but I'm afraid. I am a Kershaw too, you see, and the Kershaws have always been cruel, especially to their women. Julian was cruel to you the other night, the way he ignored you and lavished attention on Victoria. You were humiliated and hurt. I saw it. He could at least have let Cousin Nick take her home instead of adding the final insult."

"Nicholas did take her home."

"Oh, no, he didn't. I saw Nick leave shortly after you had gone to bed and poor Mamma had been taken care of by her maid. I heard you come upstairs, and then Victoria bringing Mamma up too and handing her over to Mrs. Levitt in the corridor outside my room." He sighed. "It often happens nowadays. Mamma drinks too much wine, and then starts crying in that maudlin way and demanding to see her darling son, but when Mrs. Levitt knocked on my door I pretended to be asleep. I wasn't, of course. I was sitting by the window, wishing I could have my inheritance now and get away from Dragonmede, but Mamma takes good care not to let me have enough money, so I can't escape. She still has control of her fortune because her father was wily enough to tie it up in her behalf, to prevent its passing into the hands of her husband when she married, whoever he might be. But I mustn't really grumble; she's been generous to me in her way, which is why I haven't the courage to face penury. I haven't been brought up to it."

I was unbuttoning my smock with fingers that were unsteady and yet stiff. I didn't want to listen to Christopher's conversation, but was driven by a desire to learn the truth.

"It was Nicholas who drove Victoria home," I insisted.

"If Julian told you that, he was lying. I saw Nick leave. I was at my window and watched him drive away, alone. I heard him say good night to Garfield, and even in the distance I could see his carriage lamps heading towards Rye. So I knew then that Julian and Victoria were alone downstairs, but at what time he took her home I have no idea because suddenly I was tired and went to bed."

And suddenly I was tired too. Quite desperately. Perhaps Christopher sensed this, and that was why he took his departure.

After he had gone I sat down, and remained so until the afternoon light began to fade; then I moved to the window and closed it, for there was an autumnal nip in the air. Summer was over.

So was the summer of my girlhood, and the wondrous enchantment of my marriage.

That evening I waited until dinner was halfway through before announcing that I was going to visit my mother, leaving next morning. That gave Julian no chance to oppose me, because to do so he would have to explain why, and the last thing he was likely to tell his family (especially in front of the servants) was that he had forbidden his wife to associate with his mother-in-law because he considered her to be a whore.

I looked across at him, challenging him, and the cold fury in his eyes left me unmoved. He knew then that I was no longer amenable and easy to manipulate, and that something must have happened to bring about this sudden change. He was intelligent enough to guess that only one thing could be responsible: I had found out the truth about him and Victoria, and one word besmirching unhappy Luella would bring accusations hurling back.

That he and Victoria had spent the night on the island I now had no doubt at all, and in order to convey this to him I said serenely, over coffee in the drawing room, what a pity it was that the evening was chill, because I would have enjoyed a sail across the lake.

"I have never seen the arbor, and it looks so pretty. I understand it is like a little house, fully furnished and equipped. Isn't that what you said, Christopher?"

My brother-in-law nodded.

"I wonder why it was designed that way," I mused idly.

Christopher laughed. "Why do you think? My illustrious grandfather created it for his own diversion. He was a notorious rake. I've even heard that he used to take the maids across there, if he fancied them."

"Christopher, darling!" his mother reproached. "There has never been any scandal in the Kershaw family."

I saw Aunt Dorcas' eyes flicker momentarily.

I murmured to my husband, so that he alone could hear, "And there never will be any scandal, will there? At all costs, the good name of Kershaw must be preserved."

Conversation hummed around us. We joined in, maintaining a false display of affability. Christopher, bored by all this family talk, wandered over to the piano and began to play loudly to drown it. He was in that sort of mood, and nothing could have suited me better. Beneath his strumming I was able to continue unheard, except by Julian beside me.

"So we'll go on pretending that it was Nicholas who took his mistress there the other night, even though he left alone long before I saw the boat crossing the lake, and both Christopher and Garfield can testify to that."

I yawned delicately, stretched languidly. I was tormenting my husband, and felt no shame. I was also making a stand against him, flouting his orders, and wasn't in the least ashamed.

I went to bed ahead of everyone, saying I must get Lucy to pack a bag for me, although I had already done so myself and hidden it in the *rouelle*. Miriam, perhaps because she was pleased to have me out of the way for a while, ordered her personal coach to take me to Rye immediately after breakfast, and Christopher offered to accompany me and put me on the train. Julian drawled his thanks and added his regrets that the demands of work would prevent him from taking me personally. Aunt Dorcas smiled and asked me to convey her kind regards to my mother. I said good night to them all and went upstairs, locking the bedroom door behind me, and then the communicating door into Julian's dressing room. I had no desire to see him again before I left.

I might have known that no locks would keep him out. He entered by the simple expedient of forcing his dressing-room door. I heard the violent wrenching of the lock as I lay in darkness, sensed the viciousness behind it, and felt the sharp edge of fear run through me.

Our sleeping quarters were well away from the rest of the family, and a swift attack upon an inner door could cause no more than a brief and distant disturbance. And in the morning a discreet Hobson would quietly have the lock repaired.

All this ran through my mind as swiftly as the realization that my defiance had been foolhardy and I was about to be punished for it.

I was. It was my first experience of sex accompanied by viciousness.

In the morning Julian came through from his dressing room and looked down at me. I could feel the pallor of my face and the hollows beneath my eyes, due to a night without sleep. When he had finally left me I had lain exhausted, eventually dragging myself to the window, opening it wide, and stepping out onto the balcony to cleanse myself in the night air. The fatigue that even now seemed smothering had been worse then—so much so that as I clung to the stone balustrade my dazed mind had conjured up fancies. I could recall the confused impression of a man's face looking up from the garden below, and the glint of silver hair as moonlight touched him.

I heard my husband say smoothly, "Well, my love, do you still intend to visit your whoring mother?"

My body was exhausted, but not my spirit. "Even more so. And you can't stop me because you can give no acceptable reason to your family. Miriam has put her coach at my disposal. What excuse would you give for rejecting her offer? If you say I am unwell, I will prove otherwise by coming downstairs ready to travel. Dragonmede depends largely on your step-mother's bounty; that is why you pander to her and why she is the last person you would wish to know the truth about our marriage—and please observe that I say our marriage, not my mother, who is not and never has been a whore. A whore takes money for her services. My mother has had lovers, yes, but the only thing she has ever taken, and given, has been love. That puts her above the women of your world, because in so-called 'society' a man's mistress is paid in jewels and furs and luxuries, like a high-class prostitute. But secretly, of course, never openly and honestly. I won't ask what you gave Victoria in return for your night on the island. . . ."

His hand shot out and struck me across the face.

"That is to show you who is master here. And I'll still be master when you return. Remember that."

If I return, I thought. *If* I return.

The terraced house looked shabby, badly in need of redecorating. The net curtains were clean, but becoming threadbare. Bella's footsteps beyond the front door seemed to drag more tiredly than before, and when she opened it she seemed older than I remembered her. And yet I had been gone for such a short time.

She peered at me as if unable to believe her eyes, and not until I said her name did she realize who I was. Promptly, she burst into tears.

"Thank God, Miss Stacy! Oh, thank God you've come!"

And there was Michelle, running downstairs, arms outspread. It was the sight of her that made me feel that I had not entered a strange house after all, and when she embraced me I felt at last that I had come home.

But only briefly. After the first onrush of affection, I detached myself and looked around. The same hall, the same stairs, the same furnishings and decorations, yet not the same. The place had a desolate air which struck a chill into me. It was like a house that had once been alive and was now slowly dying.

"Mother," I demanded. "Where is my mother?"

I knew, before Michelle told me, that she was ill.

"I wrote a few weeks ago, *chérie,* hoping you would come."

"But you said she had recovered. A chill, you said."

"Which developed into pleurisy. But the danger is now over, thanks to M'sieur Crowther, who insisted on her having the best possible treatment and paid for it himself. But with your coming, she will recover completely. It is all she needs to regain her spirits."

But the change in Luella shocked me. I knelt beside her bed and took her thin hands in mine. She must have recognized my touch, for her eyelids, blue-veined and unrecognizable without their once-skillful make-up, opened slowly and with disbelief. I gathered her to me, cradling her, fighting tears. The room was dimmed by partially drawn curtains, and for this I was thankful because we could neither of us see the other clearly, and neither of us was ready to be seen.

All the way from Rye I had felt the sting of Julian's blow upon my cheek and knew that by the time I arrived in Bloomsbury its mark would be self-evident. I could explain it away by saying that the carriage door had struck me as the train jerked, and no doubt I would be believed, but at this precise moment my mother was my only real concern. She clung to me as if she would never let me go.

In the days that followed I learned a lot: that Luella could no longer run her card salon owing to ill health, and consequently life was difficult. Michelle was taking in dressmaking to help make ends meet.

"And I have to admit, *chérie,* that M'sieur Crowther has been both generous and kind. There is no relationship of any kind between him and your mother. Alas, poor Madame: those days are gone for her now, and nothing is more guaranteed to make her feel old that *that* realization! But there is a bond between them of some kind. I confess I have never been able to understand it, he so uncouth and she so fastidious, but there it is. He is about the only real friend she has now."

"Except yourself, Michelle. And Bella. Both so loyal to her always."

"But naturally! Even so, she cannot afford us. She could certainly do with one less mouth to feed." Michelle put out a pleading hand. "Please, *chérie*, take me back to Dragonmede with you."

What could I say? That I had no intention of returning, that I had run away from what was now a loveless marriage? Admit that all her forebodings had been justified? The time was not yet ripe for such admissions; there were problems in this house which had to be faced first. Had I sufficient income of my own, I could stay and look after us all, accept no charity from Crowther, and live a quiet and placid life with a mother who no longer yearned for gaiety and romance. But I had no income, and if I left my husband I could hope for none. I would be another mouth to feed, another burden. The most I could earn would be a meager salary as a teacher of art, which would be inadequate to meet the mortage which, Luella told me, she had been forced to raise on the house. The more I thought about it, the more I realized that it was impossible to pick up the threads of a life one had snapped.

Nevertheless, I stayed on, and within a few days Luella was able to get up for longer and longer periods. I wrote to my mother-in-law explaining my extended absence, but not so much as a line to Julian. I had yet to decide what to do about my marriage.

To discuss it with my mother was out of the question. At the back of my mind I think I had had some intention of reproaching her for concealing things from me, but now that I was face to face with her it was impossible. She was too frail to face any emotional scene, and I loved her too much to inflict it on her.

Not until three weeks after my return did I meet Crowther. He had been north to his mills, and when he called I found him as rough-mannered as ever.

Michelle, I could see, felt the same way about him, despite the fact that she was now ready to admit his generosity, but the accusation she had once made about the part he played in bringing about my marriage now troubled me as it had never done before. She had blamed him solely because he had brought Julian to the house in the first place, but now I wondered just how much he knew about Luella's scheming. Had he been present on that fateful night when she trapped Julian so heavily into debt? I remembered his cynical smile at my wedding, which now seemed to indicate a lot.

When we met he stooped over my hand clumsily, saying he was glad to see that I had been able to tear myself away from the delights of high society and that he hoped all was well with me and my charming husband. To all appearances he meant every word, and yet I knew that he mocked.

"And how long are you staying, Mrs. Kershaw? Long enough to see your mother over this unhappy patch, I hope. Until she is well enough to travel back with thee to Dragonmede, and recover in the peace of the countryside?"

I was glad we were alone, for his shrewd eyes were assessing me. Beneath his glance, my own fell. He saw too much, guessed too much. When I heard him say, "Or won't your snobbish in-laws accept her?" it was impossible for me to answer. I looked back at him unhappily and was surprised to see compassion there.

"So you don't want to talk about things. Very well, Mrs. Kershaw. But if tha ever do, I'm not the ruthless bastard you take me for. Rough, I grant you, uneducated. But I have a heart. Remember that."

"I know it. Michelle has told me of all you have done for Luella. More, I think, than my mother even suspects. Someday I will repay you, Mr. Crowther."

He answered gruffly, "I want no repayment."

"The doctor's bills, at least. You engaged the best for her, not that odious man who came to this house the night we brought Michelle here, and who, I gather, still practices locally."

"So you remember him, lass? I heard the story from your mother some time ago. I was glad to get someone else. Not all doctors are inhuman."

"I know that." The hewn face of Nicholas Bligh came suddenly into my mind, and to my surprise, I experienced a homesickness for Rye and the Romney Marsh; for the sweeping Sussex countryside and the feel of Ladybird galloping into the wind; for Sol Slocombe's cottage, and the smell of canvas and oil paint, and Nick's long legs outthrust beside the fire as the three of us drank tea out of thick mugs. I had a longing to be back there. But not at Dragonmede. Never again at Dragonmede, with its imprisoning walls and its underlying feeling of menace.

Later, when he took his leave, Crowther remarked, "Remember what I said, next time we meet. And we will meet, Mrs. Kershaw, though it won't be here."

He was gone before I had the chance to ask what he meant.

A few evenings later, Luella and I were dining at a small table beside the fire. I knew the opportunity had come to ask why she had concealed her birthplace from me.

She smiled and said a little sadly, "Surely it is obvious? The Kershaws are the leading family in those parts. I was afraid they might not accept the granddaughter of a local parson, a humble position in those days, and it still is, I expect. I wanted nothing to come in the way of your happiness with Julian, and I don't regret keeping silent. The greatest joy in my life is the knowledge that you are married to the man you love."

I was unable to speak. The fish that Michelle had

cooked so delectably, Bella being unable to do what she called "any of that fancy stuff," I found suddenly unappetizing.

As if from a distance I heard Luella ask how I discovered that she came from the area.

"Sol Slocombe told me. When we first met, he mistook me for you."

"Sol, dear Sol! He is still alive, then?"

"Very much so. I visit his cottage frequently."

"The same old place?" For the first time since my return there was real animation in my mother's face. "Don't tell me he is still living in his parents' cottage?"

"He is, but Nicholas says he shouldn't."

"Nicholas?"

"Dorcas Bligh's son. She remembers you and sends her kind regards."

Luella's face softened.

"Dorcas Kershaw? Who married against her parents' wishes?"

I nodded, and was soon telling her about Dorcas' return to Dragonmede after her widowhood, of her son's qualifying as a doctor, even of my meeting with the present vicar of St. John's and of taking tea with him and his wife.

"And is the vicarage as gloomy as ever, Stacy?"

"They have done their best to improve it, but obviously lack means. I gather they tackle the church garden single-handed. I often wish my father-in-law could help them, but now he is an invalid I imagine he is unaware of the situation."

"And how is your father-in-law?" she asked politely.

I told her, but found I had little desire to talk about the inhabitants of Dragonmede, because it brought back the problem of my marriage. Somehow I had to reach a solution; somehow I had to confide in Luella, confess my unhappiness and my desire never to go back. And somehow I couldn't do it. Sitting there in the firelight she looked contented and at peace, as if all were at last right with her world.

"My dear Stacy, you are not eating."

I looked at the food on my plate, and pushed it aside distastefully.

"I'm not hungry," I answered, attributing my reaction to an inability to face up to problems and a reluctance to shatter my mother's dreams.

As it happened, I was forced to do neither, for matters were resolved for me. A week later I knew the reason for my recurrent nausea, and Luella, of course, was overjoyed.

"A child! My darling Stacy, I couldn't be happier for you! This is the most wonderful news, the thing I've been praying for. You must hurry home at once. Julian will be delighted when he hears you are to give him an heir, an heir to Dragonmede. Could anything be more wonderful than that?"

Thirteen

"YOU HAVE BEEN away five weeks," said the Lady Miriam.

"It was unavoidable, Stepmother."

It was the first time I had used my husband's familiar name for her. I thought I detected raised eyebrows, but was uncaring. I had a trump card up my sleeve and knew it.

When I had first learned of my pregnancy I had felt trapped, rebelling against a fate that forced me back into a marriage which had only humiliated me. But I had no choice. I had to return to Dragonmede whether I wanted to or not, for there was no place for me elsewhere. Not only had I grown away from the Bloomsbury background, but I knew full well that even if I begged to remain, Luella would remind me that a Kershaw should be born in his rightful home and that it would be wrong to cheat a child of its heritage. I also knew that if I left my husband, he could take the child away from me.

My next feeling had been one that every woman experiences when discovering that she is to have a baby: a sense of wonderment, as if she had been selected for a miracle. It was significant that this reaction came second, but now it had taken hold of me and given me joy plus confidence, so my mother-in-law's raised eyebrows left me unperturbed.

"It was unwise to leave a man like Julian alone for so long," she admonished.

"What are you trying to tell me? That he has been unfaithful in my absence? But men do console themselves, do they not?"

"You sound uncaring!"

"His wife is back. Isn't that sufficient?"

"I hope indeed that it will be."

"But if not, I am to look the other way? That is the social code, I understand. And I suppose you are hoping that I shall ask for my rival's identity. Would it surprise you to learn that I know it already? Who else but Victoria?"

She looked at me in such surprise that I laughed.

"You must have thought me very naive not to realize that in your eyes she would have been much more acceptable as Julian's wife. The fact remains that *I* am that. Also, I am home. And that puts an end to this discussion, don't you agree?"

I had never before taken the wind out of Miriam's sails. I enjoyed doing so now. At least I had returned to Dragonmede with a feeling of greater importance.

There was a sound from behind me. I turned and saw my husband lounging in the doorway.

"So you're back?" he drawled, "And I see you have brought that French maid. Why, may I ask?"

"She wanted to come, and I want her with me."

"You have a maid already."

"Michelle will not replace Lucy. She will be a companion to me. Dress my hair, look after my clothes. She is an expert needlewoman."

He turned to Miriam and asked, with exaggerated boredom, "Do we need an expert needlewoman in this household, Stepmother?"

Before she had a chance to reply, I cut in, "I need one. Michelle is to make our child's layette."

The change that came over my husband was instant and miraculous. He swung me off my feet, kissing me rapturously, beside himself with joy.

"Did you hear that, Miriam? A son! We're to have a son, a new heir for Dragonmede!"

Miriam was very still, very silent. There had been a smile on her face and it remained there, as if she had been struck and died with it frozen on her lips. Then the lips moved and said, "Congratulations. But don't overlook the possibility that it might be a daughter."

At that he scoffed. "The Kershaws always breed sons."

"What about Dorcas?"

He made a gesture of dismissal. "She was the only girl in three generations, or was it four? Of course it will be a son."

"Let us hope your confidence will be justified." Miriam kissed him on both cheeks. She did the same to me. Her lips felt cold.

"I am happy for you, my dear. We must all take good care of you."

Julian said, with a great show of tenderness, "I will take care of her. Eustacia, my darling, you've made me proud and happy."

He was the man I had fallen in love with, radiating

charm. With him like this, it was impossible to recall him as I had last known him—sadistic, brutal—but the moment his stepmother left us he changed again, laughing and slapping his thigh with malicious glee.

"Poor Miriam, that's shaken her! Her precious son is now one step further away from possessing Dragonmede."

"Which he doesn't want. He told me so."

"But she wants it for him. I've been the stumbling block in her path ever since Gerald was drowned, and now there's another."

I shivered slightly. "Don't frighten me, Julian."

"Oh, good Lord, there's nothing to be frightened about. She's not going to try to get rid of you, or harm you. She wouldn't have the guts or the brains. She'll comfort herself with wine and smolder with resentment, but that's all." He brushed his stepmother aside with a shrug.

"I thought you were fond of her," I accused.

"It's wise to pretend to be. Or it was. Now I'm in a more powerful position and can afford to ignore her. Her throne is imperiled and she knows it. When my father dies I will be master here, with my son, not hers, next in line. She will have to retire to the Dower House, and by God, she'll hate that. Even more, she'll hate Christopher's nose being put out of joint."

He seized my hand.

"Come, we must tell my father. This is news that he must surely grasp, and Dorcas tells me he has been more lucid lately, even asking in his incoherent fashion where you were, and why he didn't see you in the garden. I'll guarantee he won't banish you from his room this time!"

I marveled at the way in which Julian could switch from one personality to another within the space of minutes. I wished I could do the same, but happy as I now was about the child, I knew it was the prospect of motherhood that made me so, not the fact that the child I was carrying was his. My husband's affections might vacillate, but not mine, and the hurts he had dealt me had gone too deep to be wiped out as quickly as his own memory of them. As he led me upstairs, I knew that our last night together was something he had totally forgotten.

But not I. I had returned to Dragonmede haunted by the recollection of it and dreading any repetition. Now I knew that dread to be unnecessary. My news had reinstated me in his esteem. I only prayed I would remain there, so that our marriage would become tolerable and, perhaps, with time, even happy; but I knew in my heart that I would never regain my earlier feelings for him. It was I who had changed, and changed permanently.

When Aunt Dorcas opened the door of Sir Vivian's room, Julian led me inside, saying proudly, "Doesn't she look lovely? I've always heard that approaching motherhood adds bloom to a woman. Is my father well enough to hear the glad news?"

Once again I was face to face with this wreck of a man. This time he was not in bed but propped in an armchair, a rug over his knees. Slowly and carefully Julian made his announcement, and slowly but surely comprehension dawned in the stricken eyes. Sir Vivian's one good hand came out to me. I took hold of it, and felt the bones grasp my hand with surprising strength. It was then that I realized the vigor which must once have been his. For a while he clung to me, staring into my face. Then he dropped my hand abruptly and turned away, but this time I knew his action was prompted by emotion, not aversion.

It was decided at dinner that night that the news should be announced at the Christmas Ball, held annually in the great hall and attended by everyone for miles around.

"It's the event of the season," Julian told me, "and this will make it the most memorable in years."

I disliked the idea of anything so personal being announced publicly, but apparently it was the tradition at Dragonmede, and whether I liked it or not, tradition had to be maintained.

The child was due in May and Christmas was a month ahead, so I would still be able to wear something elegant. Michelle set to work with a will, determined that I should outshine every woman present. I knew that my mother-in-law was curious to see what my nimble-fingered Frenchwoman was creating, but Michelle discouraged curiosity by the simple expedient of locking the door of the sewing room when she was absent and, when she was not, covering her work if anyone should enter by chance. It was of course beneath Miriam's dignity to wander into the workroom of a servant, which was the level at which she classed Michelle.

But to me, Michelle's presence in the house was more like that of an elder sister, and it was her company I sought in preference to anyone else's. We lapsed into French as naturally as before. Sometimes, when I was working in my studio, she would bring her sewing there and sit quietly while I concentrated upon the portrait. It was coming along well. Since my return the November weather had been cold and damp, preventing me from riding about the countryside even if my husband had not expressly forbidden it. This was one command that I was prepared to obey, but so that Ladybird should not miss me I visited her daily in the stables, giving her her feed, fondling her, and assuring her that we would ride together after my baby was born, and I could have sworn that she understood.

Michelle settled down more easily than I had expected, although her expressive glance at the forbidding walls of my new home had betrayed her reaction on arrival. She kept out of Julian's way as much as possible and I knew her feelings about him remained unchanged, but she no longer made dire predictions about my marriage. She accepted it as a fait accompli, and kept her own counsel.

It was a joy to have her dressing my hair again. Every evening before dinner she came to my room, and my now-indulgent husband watched approvingly while she brushed and combed and twisted and coiled, so that every evening I presented a new appearance, according to my gown. I would see Miriam's eyes surveying me swiftly the moment I appeared. Her own maid could not match Michelle's skill, and when Miriam grudgingly admitted so one night, I suggested she might give Michelle the chance to dress her own hair occasionally. I knew this was what my mother-in-law wanted and that she was too proud to ask, but when I told Michelle, I had to use all my persuasion to make her agree.

"She is spoiled, that one. Vain and spoiled. She will be impossible to please."

"But try, for my sake," I pleaded. "When one has to live with one's in-laws, as I do, it is as well to keep on good terms with them."

So for my sake she gave in the following evening but I was totally unprepared for what happened later. Miriam was well satisfied and suggested that Michelle be paid for the additional service of dressing her hair regularly, but to my astonishment, Michelle declined at once. Never again, she declared, would she go into that room.

"You mean my mother-in-law's bedroom? But why not?"

"Because I do not choose to." She added negligently, "Have you ever been in there, *chérie?*"

I admitted I had not. I was not on sufficiently familiar terms with my mother-in-law to be invited to her room for cozy chats.

"What is wrong with the room, and why do you dislike it?" I asked.

"Nothing is wrong. In fact, it is very beautiful." At which, with characteristic stubbornness, Michelle closed her lips.

That was the most I could get out of her, but the incident marked a change in Michelle. From then on she became guarded and uncommunicative, except when we sat alone together in my studio and reminisced about the past.

"You are nostalgic for Bloomsbury," I told her one day. "Would you like to go back?"

"Not unless you do. Wherever you are, there I must be too, to look after you."

"I don't need a nursemaid," I chided with a laugh.

"No, but you do need protection. I can feel it."

Her premonitions were back. I sighed, and dismissed them as I had always done. And that was the greatest mistake I could have made.

One person at Dragonmede particularly resented Michelle's coming, and that, surprisingly, was Hannah Grant; and because of her long residence in the house, she evidently felt privileged to say so.

"You talk secretly together, don't you, Mrs. Julian? That is why you converse in French."

I replied indignantly that she had no right to say such a thing, and that Michelle and I had talked to each other in French always.

"That was why my mother originally engaged her: to teach me to speak the language fluently." I added pointedly that anyone who understood French really well would know how innocent our conversations were. "Although, of course, eavesdropping is not an innocent pastime."

My answer had the desired effect, and sent Hannah away in a huff. She stopped visiting my studio, to my relief, and kept to her own quarters more rigidly, although sometimes when I passed through the great hall I would experience again the uncanny sensation of being watched, and would promptly look up in the direction of the peep, which was too small to be seen from this distance despite the radius it covered. At such moments I hoped that my stare embarrassed her.

After my return I saw nothing of Victoria Bellamy, and guessed that Julian, in his new burst of husbandly devotion, had broken with her. He even admitted it when I remarked one night that presumably Victoria and her father would be invited to the ball.

"I'm afraid so, my love; the Bellamys have always been amongst the guests of honor. But you need feel no embarrassment. There is nothing between myself and Victoria now."

"I have no need to be embarrassed. I just thought she might be."

He laughed. "You don't know Victoria. It takes a lot to embarrass her. She was brought up to be superbly self-confident, and of course her aging father dotes on her. He believes she can do no wrong."

It seemed an unfortunate turn of phrase, but I let it pass. I knew that Julian was grateful for a forgiving wife, but the truth was that I no longer cared. Infidelities hurt only when you loved a person. I wondered with a touch of sadness if I would ever love again, and hoped not, for I was tied forever to this man.

"Sometimes I wonder why you didn't marry Victoria. You would have had a rich wife then."

"But not one who would discharge my debts," he answered candidly. "Victoria is as shrewd as her father where money is concerned, and that old skinflint most certainly wouldn't have cleared them. He would have clamped down on our marriage if he so much as suspected that I gambled."

Well, at least he was honest with me now. Unfortunately, his honesty had come too late and too brutally for me to forget the shock of it, or the pretense he had maintained. For once he was sensitive enough to guess my thoughts, for he put his arms about me and said, "If you're imagining that I never loved you, you're wrong. I wanted you passionately, and I still do. We can be happy together, you and I, despite everything."

He was anxious to prove this to me as often as possible, and I yielded as often as I could bear. Because I was young and healthy my body responded physically, even though I no longer loved him with my heart; Julian was content, because he didn't recognize the difference.

But I wondered what would happen when my pregnancy advanced and the intimate side of our marriage would have to cease. He wasn't the kind of man to do without a woman, even temporarily.

It was early one morning that I looked from our bedroom window and stared at a man striding across the outer perimeter of the park, the Kershaw beagles at his heels. His silver hair shone in the wintry sun, and even at this distance I could see the dissolute, aging handsomeness of him.

It was the stranger I had seen at the inn, and for some reason apprehension ran through me.

I called to Julian, asking who the man was. He strolled to the window and glanced over my shoulder.

"That's Ballard, the new kennelman. I engaged him while you were away. Seems good at his job. Knows how to handle dogs. He's had a' lot of experience with animals abroad, I gather. Why, what's wrong?"

I answered slowly, "That is the man I saw standing at the edge of the lake the night you took Victoria to the arbor."

My husband wasn't in the least embarrassed. He merely answered practically, "It can't be. He wasn't employed here then."

"Nevertheless, it is he. I'm positive. He was lodging in the village at the time. I saw him at the inn one day while Ladybird was being shod."

"Our horses are shod here. Why the village blacksmith?"

"She had cast a shoe." I repeated the smith's remark that it appeared to have been loosened, but agreed with my husband when he said the man must have made a mistake.

"Who would deliberately loosen a horse's shoe?" he demanded. "And why? An accident like that, slight as it seems, could injure a rider."

It could have done more than that to me, occurring as it did against cobblestones hard enough to shatter my skull had I been thrown.

"What day was this?" Julian asked.

Untruthfully, I told him I had forgotten. The accident had occurred on the day he had revealed how he had been trapped into marrying me. For my own peace of mind I wanted never to refer to that day again; but now I remembered the hatred that had flared between us, and the loathing in his voice, as if he had wanted to be rid of me. Had his hatred been strong enough to make him try? I was forced to dismiss this notion, for time had been against him. I had whirled away instantly, too wild with distress even to bother to change my clothes, so if anyone had loosened that shoe, it couldn't have been my husband. It had to be someone given both time and opportunity.

Only one person had had that. Nicholas Bligh.

For some reason the thought was painful, but could not be avoided. He could have loosened the shoe when he made the excuse to wipe down Ladybird after her frantic gallop. I had lingered in the cottage long enough for him to do whatever he wished—long enough for him to feed her a handful of oats as a cover-up when I emerged. And obscure as his motive might seem, it was there. If I were killed I would never bear my husband an heir, and that would bring him one step closer to inheriting Dragonmede, as Victoria had outlined.

Logical planning between this man and woman hit me like a blow. On her part, she had always expected to become mistress here; and on his, smoldering resentment against a family that had despised his father, and to which his mother had been forced to return merely as a nurse to her brother, could well spark determination to wrest Dragonmede from them. Nicholas Bligh was no lily-livered parasite, willing to hang on to the fringe of his mother's family. His fighting buccaneer's face told its own story, and I would be wise not to underestimate it. Wiser still to forget that moment in the cottage when our glances had imprisoned each other's.

After Julian had gone into his dressing room I remained at the window, watching the stranger walk away into the distance, but the sight of him had reawakened another memory: the hazy memory of a man's face seen through mists of pain as I clung to the balcony rail after Julian's sadistic onslaught on my body; a face staring up at me, crowned by silver hair, witnessing my distress and experienced enough to guess the reason for it. I had thought later that the face had been an illusion. Now I knew it was not. For some reason this man had lingered in the grounds on more than one occasion, and now he was part of the household.

I withdrew from the window, but the atmosphere of the room was suddenly thick with unease. There was something significant about the coming of this stranger. Something impending, something alarming, so real and tangible that it seemed to close about me, dark with threat.

Now that I was forbidden to ride, I went by carriage to visit Sol, but it was irksome to have a driver waiting and horses become restive. It meant that our painting sessions together had to terminate earlier, and when Nicholas realized this he offered to teach me how to handle a pony trap and brought one over on his next visit.

I mastered the reins in an afternoon's lesson and resolved thereafter to use a trap from Dragonmede. "Take it easily and you'll meet with no mishap to harm the child," he said, when the lesson was over.

"So you know."

"Of course. Fothergill told me."

But he couldn't have known on the day of my wild gallop to the cottage. I myself had not known then. So any attempt to destroy me could only have been to prevent such a contingency.

I was not really surprised to hear now that he knew about the coming child. Julian had insisted on Fothergill's attentions from the moment I gave him the news.

Nicholas said quietly, "Didn't you want me to know?"

His eyes moved over my face with a gentleness that made a jumbled heap of my emotions, and at once all my neat tabulations about possible intrigue between this man and Victoria seemed wild and improbable.

"Are you glad about the child?" he asked.

"I am glad to be becoming a mother."

He looked at me hard, made no answer, and drove me back to Sol's cottage without another word. He left almost at once, and I was sorry. I wanted him to stay because somehow, during that afternoon together, I seemed to have glimpsed a smoother, happier road than the one I had embarked upon when I married Julian. I smiled as we said goodbye, but saw no answering smile in return, and as he drove away I felt as if a wall had risen between us.

Beside me, Sol said gently, "Poor Nicholas. It is sad when a man falls in love with a woman he cannot have."

My heart seemed to stumble, although I knew the old man could not be referring to me. There would be plenty of women in the life of a man like Nicholas, and as Julian had pointed out, he was a bachelor, free to do what he liked, live as he liked.

I went upstairs with Sol to the studio and for the next hour concentrated on painting, but before I left, something compelled me to ask, "Who is the woman Nicholas loves and cannot have?"

"A married woman, alas. It is always a waste of time to love another man's wife."

"In some levels of society they compromise."

"Nicholas isn't a man to be content with compromise."

During the drive home I couldn't decide which were the most confused—my emotions, my thoughts, or my powers of reasoning. I had heard that expectant mothers sometimes developed illogical fancies, and decided I must be doing so, for surely wise old Sol could not possibly have meant that Nicholas had fallen in love with me.

The next day I had a trap harnessed and took a trial run through the park. The pony was gentle, obedient, and a light stepper. As a substitute for riding, this form of transport was highly acceptable and gave me the independence I enjoyed. There was also a tranquillity about it, so that when I returned I was in a serene frame of mind and quite unprepared for what was to come.

It happened within five minutes' drive of the coach house, close to which stood the beagler's cottage, with its wide backyard surrounded by walls, in which the animals were allowed to run free when not being exercised. Over the wall I saw the kennelman filling drinking troughs, and at the sound of my approach he looked up. Perhaps I was becoming accustomed to his lean dark face, which contrasted so startlingly with his silver hair, for I experienced less mistrust of it now, but no lessening of my usual discomfort beneath his scrutiny. Whenever I was within range of him I was conscious of his watchful eyes, but apart from the encounter in the inn, this was the first time I had come near him when alone.

The carriageway skirted the cottage. He had only to open the gate from the yard and step outside to waylay me. I had a conviction that he was going to do so, and I was right. By the time I was level with the cottage he was standing on the verge, waiting for me.

At close quarters, I realized that despite his age he had strength and vigor. As obvious as the dissipation in his once-handsome face were the signs that he had led a tough and hardening life, and despite his rough workaday clothes, he gave the impression of being a gentleman. This was confirmed when he spoke. His voice was cultured.

"Good morning, Mrs. Kershaw."

Not "Madam," as any other estate worker would have said. Subservience in any degree would not come naturally to this man.

"Good morning, Ballard."

At that, he smiled. It was a smile of genuine amusement and made me feel uncomfortable. With a cool inclination of my head I continued on my way. If he hoped that I would pause for a chat, he was to be disappointed.

To my astonishment, he stepped forward, seized the pony's bridle, and brought him to a halt.

Then he said smoothly, "Now, you wouldn't do that, would you, Eustacia? You wouldn't drive by and ignore your own father?"

Fourteen

1 WAS UNABLE to speak. I saw him watching me with the intent gaze of a gambler who had thrown a die and is waiting to see which way it lands.

Somehow I managed to hold on to one small piece of logic, and I heard myself say, "My father's name was Rochdale, and he is dead."

"Eustace Ballard Rochdale. And I can't blame Luella for letting you think I was dead. I brought her nothing but trouble, and she was generous and loyal to me—although, on second thoughts, it isn't very loyal to tell a man's daughter he is dead, even if he did agree to go out of her life forever. Luella's, I mean."

Though his expression was bland, under the surface I sensed uncertainty, as if he were doubtful what kind of reception he would have, and this had the merciful effect of giving me confidence.

"I would need proof before I believed you. Anyone could have found out my father's names, although for what reason . . ."

"I have plenty of reasons. A desire to see you, to meet a daughter who was a baby when I had to go away. I also have plenty of proof. My Army papers, for instance. Ex-Army, I'm afraid. I was cashiered. Gambling dishonestly in the mess. Poor Luella, she had a bad time; but I'd taught her a lot, so I'm sure she survived."

"Never blame your father for leaving me unprovided for. He died young and he did his best. He also . . . taught me a lot. . . ." I could hear Luella's words, and see her fingers handling the cards like lightning, and all the pity I had ever felt for her increased a

226

hundredfold. Her romantic elopement had given her plenty of cause for regret; instead, she had accepted the inevitable and put a brave front on life, her one mistake being to devise a hero-father for a child to respect.

On the other hand, how would I have grown up had I known that he had been a cardsharper, exposed and disgraced?

I tried to speak and failed, for suddenly words were inadequate in a situation that seemed too preposterous and melodramatic to be true; but at last I jerked out, "If what you say is true, and you did promise to go out of her life, then I beg you, don't come back into it. Leave her alone."

"My dear daughter, I have every intention of leaving her alone. I know where she lives. I've known for years. There was an episode once. It was reported in the press. I read about it months later when I picked up a back number of a newspaper in a Johannesburg club. Had I wanted to break my promise, I could have written to her at any time during my years of voluntary exile, and I could have rung her front-door bell as soon as I arrived in England months ago. In my rolling-stone existence it took me years to save enough money to return, but in any case it would have been folly to do so earlier, because, for other reasons besides being kicked out of the Army, which I scarcely regretted, I had to stay out of this country. I'll spare you those details, because I can see that Luella has kept them from you. Bless her, she was always generous, so I hope she didn't paint too black a picture of your dead father."

"Far from it. I think the one she painted was kinder than you deserve."

"That sounds typical of her. Besides having a generous heart she also had a kind one. She gave me all the money she possessed to get me out of the country and keep me out of jail, and I appreciated that. And I loved her, in my fashion." He held up a hand. It bore a signet ring with the initials E.B.R. engraved upon it. "She gave me this ring when we married, and I've never parted with it. A man doesn't break a promise to a woman who means that much to him. And I wasn't wholly bad, nor am I now. I understood her reason for striking terms, and I understand it even better now. She wanted her daughter to grow up ignorant of her father's character and free of his influence." He sighed. "That hurts—but, as I say, I can't blame her."

"Then why are you here?"

His glance came up, struck mine, held it in a gaze so level and intent that I couldn't flinch away, but I wondered whether he was giving me the whole truth when he said, "I've already told you: I wanted to see you. I think the idea first sparked when I read the announcement of your marriage in the *London Gazette*. I thought what a triumph that was for Luella, her daughter marrying the heir to Dragonmede, the house that had ruled her native village. I enjoyed reading that marriage announcement almost as much as she must have enjoyed inserting it, even though you were described as the daughter of the 'late' Eustace Rochdale. That was how I knew I was supposed to be dead. Of course, in a way I should be grateful for that; letting it get around that I was dead, after bribing the skipper of a fishing vessel in Folkestone harbor to smuggle me across to France, protected me, I have no doubt. From which you will gather that your regrettable father is a bad lot."

I caught a wicked flash of deviltry that drew me like a magnet: the unfailing fascination exerted by the bold and the experienced. Then his tone changed.

"Don't be angry, my dear, and don't be afraid. I promise that no one here shall ever find out who I am. That is why I gave my name as Ballard, Edwin

Ballard. And just as I have kept my promise to your mother, I shall keep my promise to my daughter. All I want is to stay here for a while. To watch over you, perhaps. Call it the belated instincts of a father, if you like."

For a moment I glimpsed the man my mother had fallen in love with. Dissolute he might have become and dishonest he might always have been, but deep at the core of him I sensed a streak of kindness.

"And I promise I won't embarrass you," he went on. "Nor will I approach you again, if that is your wish. In any case, if that husband of yours saw me pestering you I imagine I'd be out on my ear in no time. So please, for my sake as well as your own, pretend you don't know me. I am not ready to leave here yet."

He released the bridle and was gone. I jerked the reins and drove on toward the mews, surprised that my hands were so steady when I was inwardly shaken.

I went straight upstairs and lay down upon the bed. Light struck harshly through the windows and I rose, went across to draw the curtains, and paused as recollection struck me. The sight of the balcony outside, and the stretch of lawn below, brought sharply back into my mind the memory of this man's figure seen twice out there in the darkness: first by the edge of the lake, watching my husband take his mistress across to the island and, later, looking directly up at me as I clung to the balcony rail in dazed distress.

"All I want is to stay here . . . To watch over you, perhaps. . . ."

His words did not necessarily mean that, like Michelle, this man who claimed to be my father wanted to stand guard, but the suggestion was there. I tried to reject it, for the necessity to be guarded was not a thing to dwell upon, or to wonder about, much less to be believed; but the thought worried me like an insistent, jabbing pain.

Remembering Dr. Fothergill's advice to rest every afternoon, I lay down again, but sleep refused to come to a mind alerted by shock. The face, the voice, the words of a man whom I had believed to be dead gave me no peace, and I had no doubt at all that everything he said was true, and that all these years he had known where we lived. Across continents the information had traveled to him in a newspaper report of what he called an "episode," but which had been a great deal more than that. A shooting in a woman's house would be covered in detail: the date, the time, the address, the people. Across the years I heard again the shout of a newsboy in the street, and Michelle's footsteps running out to him, and my mother's voice crying, "Acquitted? He's been *acquitted?*" But the line drawing of the man's face was hard to recall—smudged out of my mind like obliterated print on a newssheet.

And then I remembered another picture which had had nothing to do with the shooting, and of which I had scarcely caught a glimpse. It had been amongst a batch of scattered bills, snatched from my hands. Some old picture torn from a periodical. Since the sight of unpaid bills never worried my mother, it must have been the picture that upset her. I groped down the dark channels of memory to relive that moment, but they yielded nothing. I hadn't the faintest recollection of what that picture featured.

Hannah Grant clapped her little hands like an excited child.

"A ball! A ball at Dragonmede again! I shall watch from the peep. I have spent the whole of today there, watching the decorations being put up. That strong new kennelman has hung foliage in great clusters from the hangman's beam. They had to bring in the tallest ladder on the estate to reach it, and he climbed up with ease, a stock of holly and evergreens and hops on his back. It is the custom in the wealds to use hops as Christmas decorations, and very lovely they look with their dry, bunchy little clusters of flowers. Did you see him, dear Mrs. Julian? He scaled that ladder with tremendous agility for a man of his years; but I hear he has done all sorts of things abroad—lumberjacking, gold mining, cattle herding—so no wonder he is strong!"

I made a noncommittal sound and continued with my work on the portrait, now almost completed. By the night of the ball it would be ready to rehang, and I knew it would stand out against its drab, neglected neighbors.

Never had I been more thankful of an occupation than during these last few days. The weather had been too cold and damp for me to drive over to Sol's cottage, so I had concentrated on finishing this work, retreating to my studio daily despite Michelle's insistence that I should rest. I was bored with resting, and could never relax, because my thoughts ran around in circles with my newly discovered father at the center of them, my mind swinging between credulity and incredulity, belief and disbelief, coupled with the conviction that fate had brought him into my life for some specific reason other than mere curiosity.

He was a rake, a ne'er-do-well, but something told me that he possessed that strange code of honor which made such people keep their word to those who, like his wife, had helped them. I even felt that his particular brand of love for my mother had been genuine, and that she had recognized it for the quality it was: abiding in its fashion, but not exclusive or necessarily irreplaceable in his life. He had gone his way and she had gone hers.

Belief in his identity was further substantiated by the fact that my mother had never married again: not, as I always imagined, because she had failed to find someone to replace an irreplaceable husband, but because she had never been free to do so. All the time she had known that somewhere in the world her husband was still alive; hence the succession of lovers, the increasing loneliness, and the gathering edges of despair.

To bring my parents together again was, of course, out of the question. Not only had their lives diverged too widely, but a man like Ballard—and as yet I could think of him only as Ballard—would never be anything but an encumbrance in my mother's life: a rolling stone by his own admission, a makeshift, an opportunist, and a liability. His coming had placed a burden of secrecy upon me.

Vaguely, I was aware of Hannah's flow of chatter as I stooped above the canvas. I had trained my ears to shut out her voice, but her reference to the new kennelman riveted my attention.

"How do you know so much about him?" I asked, apparently intent on my brushstrokes. The colors were reviving beautifully, but beneath my satisfaction over this lay apprehension as I waited for her reply.

She answered with a touch of smug self-satisfaction that Mr. Ballard talked to her a lot. "Sometimes he sits with me in the courtyard. He is such an interesting man and has me quite spellbound with his stories. He is delightful to listen to and so easy to talk to, and even though I am an old lady, he pays the utmost attention to everything I tell him. Particularly about Dragonmede and the family. He is the only person I have ever known who doesn't scorn the legend. In fact, when I told him about it he listened very seriously indeed, and seemed so interested that I have let him read some chapters of my history of the Kershaws."

So she was at work at something more serious than a romantic novel. I wondered how Victoria would react to that.

Hannah prattled on, "Life is stranger than fiction, Mr. Ballard says, and his stories prove it."

"What kind of stories?"

"Fantastic ones! Tales of voodoo and tribal magic, and all of them true, so the legend of the firstborn sons of Dragonmede is not one he rejects."

"You seem to have found yourself a very gullible audience," I said unkindly. It was the only way to fight the sickening uprush of fear that I never failed to experience now at any reminder of the legend.

Fifteen

THE COMING BALL was the sole subject of discussion during the ensuing days. The excitement of it even spread to the village, as I learned from the vicar's wife. I had taken to calling upon her—partly because I liked her, and partly because I felt a link with the vicarage. Every time I visited the place I felt closer to Luella's girlhood, and now that I had met the man she eloped with I was able to picture even more vividly her desperate escape from restriction, her furtive meetings with the dashing soldier, her secret journeys from this house to rendezvous with him. I now thought of Ballard as the man my mother had eloped with, not yet as my father—perhaps because all my life he had had no real identity, or any association with myself.

I noticed that he was becoming more and more useful at Dragonmede, assuming duties well beyond those of an ordinary kennelman. Julian liked him. I often saw them laughing and joking together in a man-to-man fashion, in a way that my husband never adopted with servants. David Foster was the only estate employee who had any kind of social standing;

but evidently Julian recognized in his new kennelman a quality also above that of an ordinary servant, as others on the estate did. The man's speech and education placed him on a higher plane, and he occupied it well.

The shooting season had begun, and naturally, as kennelman, he accompanied the shoot, controlling the dogs so well that he was soon accepted by members of the party on an affable and informal footing. Nothing established a bond between members of a shoot so much as skill and knowledge, and this my father most certainly possessed. I saw at work the charm of this man and his ability to make himself liked and trusted, to worm his way into the center of things. My uneasiness developed. He had commanded me to secrecy; but at the rate at which he was ingratiating himself here, how long would he maintain secrecy himself?

Inevitably, Michelle noticed him. "He is bursting with confidence, that one, and far too curious about everyone. He has poor Hannah Grant twisted round his little finger, but really he is not in the least interested in her, only in the information he can charm out of her."

"What sort of information?"

Michelle shrugged eloquently. "How should I know? *I* have never been allowed to see that diary of hers."

"I didn't know she kept a diary, but if she does, it can't be very interesting to a man of the world."

"M'sieur Ballard seems to find it so."

I remembered the stack of notebooks on Hannah's table and the flurry she had flown into when I opened one. I told Michelle about the incident, and her expressive face spoke volumes.

"Well, *chérie,* whatever she is writing is obviously kept secret from everyone else, but not from our charming kennelman. He can wheedle anything out of her, and out of a great many people, I suspect. He puts me in mind of many a gambler who came to your mother's salon in the old days."

There wasn't much that escaped Michelle—such as my mother-in-law's fondness for wine, and Victoria Bellamy's proprietorial attitude toward my husband, which she still maintained despite the fact that the intimacy of their relationship was at an end. Somehow a wife always knew when such was the case. This was a sad lesson I had learned all too soon, and I knew equally that Michelle had guessed about the affair even though it had preceded her own arrival here, and that she would be no more surprised than I if it were renewed.

I was well aware that Michelle disliked Julian as much as ever, but he was my husband, and a child was coming, and in this particular social sphere circumstances had to be accepted, so she never referred to her dire predictions about my marriage, or to her pleas for me not to enter into it. We lived in the present, not the past; but I was aware that she was now more watchful than she had ever been, more uneasy, more given to psychic reactions which she never revealed. I could feel them like shadows about me.

More and more we talked to each other in her native tongue, although for the most part our conversations were innocuous enough except when we discussed Luella and life in Bloomsbury. I would see Julian watching us assessingly and knew that he disliked our use of French, because it made him suspicious. The moment he appeared we would turn the conversation to trivialities: clothes, hair styles, feminine topics—anything that could give him no cause for speculation or doubt. His knowledge of French, although rusty through disuse since he had left the university, was quite sufficient to permit him to follow the gist of a conversation, as was my mother-in-law's, unless we talked quickly, which we always did. Miriam would be particularly peeved when she heard us chattering at speed in a language that most English people followed only slowly.

She was also offended because Michelle refused to dress her hair again, making the excuse that she was too busy with my ball gown to spare time for anything else. And there was nothing Miriam could do about it, no protest she could make, because Michelle had been brought to Dragonmede by me and her wages were paid by me. From the outset Michelle made it quite clear that she served no other mistress.

But on the day of the ball I persuaded Michelle to humor my mother-in-law. "Just this once, Michelle. Why not? She is an unhappy woman, remember that."

It was something which I had learned to remember myself—so much so that my mother-in-law's barbed tongue no longer disturbed me, much less her patronage. This had diminished since she had learned of my coming child, which, whether she resented it or not, had increased my importance in the household. I was more deferred to by the servants, particularly by the unlikable Mrs. Levitt, and one day Christopher congratulated me heartily on what he called my "achievement."

"It knocks us all into a cocked hat, Cousin Eustacia. There'll be no competing for the Dragonmede throne now the succession is so well assured."

He had strolled into Michelle's sewing room without invitation and was lolling indolently in a chair. "I am unaware of any competition," I fenced, at which he laughed and told me to stop pretending.

"You know full well that Mamma's greatest ambition is for me to inherit, and I wouldn't put it past Aunt Dorcas to nurse the same ambition for Cousin Nick."

"And Nicholas himself? What of him?"

I don't know what made me ask that question, except that I was always aware of, and frequently puzzled by, Nicholas Bligh. Sometimes friendly, sometimes guarded, often unapproachable, this enigmatic man occupied my mind too much.

In answer, Christopher merely shrugged. "Oh, one never knows what Cousin Nick is up to, what he thinks, or where his real ambitions lie. He keeps all that to himself."

"Which is wise of Dr. Nicholas," Michelle remarked cryptically after my brother-in-law departed. "And now, *chérie*, please try on this gown. I swear it is the finest thing I have ever made, and that no one will ever suspect that you are four months pregnant!"

She was right. It was so skillfully cut and designed that the coming birth would be a surprise when the news was announced. The gown was made of peacock blue taffeta shot through with emerald, and on the night of the ball Julian insisted upon my wearing an emerald necklace and earrings which had belonged to his mother and which had remained locked up in his father's room ever since. Dorcas fetched them willingly, and both were unstinting in their praise of Michelle's skill, Dorcas declaring that the woman was a genius and that I well deserved her.

"You look beautiful, Eustacia. Absolutely beautiful." She kissed me warmly on both cheeks. "You will be proud of your wife tonight, Nephew."

"I am always proud of her," Julian retorted, forgetful that he had ever made me feel inferior and called me the daughter of a whore. The days when his flattery could go to my head had passed, and I knew in this moment that all he wanted of me was that I do him vast credit that night.

I heard Aunt Dorcas saying that she would like Sir Vivian to see me, and Julian agreeing, but before going to his room I turned to thank Michelle, standing silently in the background. I fully expected to see nothing but pride in her face, but instead I saw the tense mask which had met me the night she opened the door of the Bloomsbury house to my future husband, the expression which told me that a sudden foreboding had fallen upon her; and this time I could not dismiss it. I felt icy tentacles of fear reaching out to me, a feeling of threat and impending doom. I began to tremble, and groped for a chair.

Instantly, Julian was beside me, and Dorcas was saying that perhaps all this excitement had been too much for me in my condition, and that after tonight they must all make sure that I took life quietly. "We wouldn't want anything to go wrong," she finished, at which Julian remarked tersely that he would take good care that nothing should, for the sake of his son and heir.

I pleaded for no further fuss, reminded Michelle that she could now go along to the Lady Miriam's room to dress her hair, and finished, "And I do beg you, Julian, not to count on my giving you a son. You place too much responsibility on me in that direction."

"I do not. It is your duty to give me a son—if not this first time, then the next, or the next. You are young and healthy. You can have plenty of children."

I retorted with some annoyance that he made me sound like a brood mare, and went on my way to Sir Vivian's room, Michelle following reluctantly. On the way we passed my mother-in-law's room. The door was open, revealing a lavish interior and Miriam sitting at her dressing table, impatiently awaiting Michelle while her own maid stood by, sulking. Miriam was scolding her, complaining that she was useless, and commanding her to refill her empty champagne glass. I heard Julian mutter wryly to Dorcas that apparently his stepmother was at it already.

"It is her only comfort, Nephew."

I heard the door of Miriam's room close behind Michelle and found myself reflecting that that was the first glimpse I had ever had of my mother-in-law's private apartments, although I knew that Victoria Bellamy visited them frequently, usually to comfort Miriam when she was suffering from one of her migraines, which I had long since realized were caused by overindulgence.

But I forgot all that when I was face to face with my father-in-law. He sat very still, just looking at me, not even trying to speak, so I was spared the inarticulate noises which only Dorcas could interpret. But I needed no signs or sounds to make me aware that there was more than his approval of my appearance; something about me moved him profoundly. It could only be the emeralds. He was remembering times long distant when his first wife had worn them.

The great hall looked magnificent—lit by a thousand candles, the ancient floor beeswaxed for dancing, a stringed orchestra ready and waiting in the minstrels' gallery, and great fires sending out a welcoming blaze from the enormous Gothic fireplaces. I scarcely recognized the place. Bedecked with holly, ivy, mistletoe, and great clusters of hops, plus banks of hothouse blooms from the estate's greenhouses, it was completely transformed.

We stood ready to receive our guests. Footmen bearing silver trays laden with champagne glasses also stood waiting in the background under the eagle eye of Garfield. Opening from the great hall successive rooms were prepared for supper, on which, I suspected, my husband had lavished more money than was justified. He had prepared for a banquet, something that would outdo anything served at Dragonmede before, a feast that people would never forget; and if, as I suspected, his stepmother was left to meet the bill, she would have the gratification of knowing that the night's festivities were on a par with those of an earl's house and therefore worthy of her. I knew my husband so well now that I also knew how he would answer any criticism or protest about extravagance.

As always, Julian looked very handsome in his immaculate evening clothes. There was a suppressed air of excitement about him, for this was to be a great occasion in his life: the great occasion when county society would hear an announcement not made within these walls since before the birth of his elder brother. "Let us herald the start of another generation of Kershaws! Pray God the first will be a male child, a son and heir for Dragonmede." That, he had told me, was the traditional wording, although he would hold God in no way responsible if the prayer came true. Only me, if it did not.

Beside us, bored and rather sullen, stood Christopher, the epitome of spoiled and aristocratic youth, and then came Dorcas, the swish of her gray silk train echoing behind her on the great staircase. Nicholas had already arrived. He had taken one glance at me, stooped over my hand, murmured a conventional greeting, then looked away. I was acutely aware that he had not glanced at me since, and conscious of disappointment. I wanted his admiration; I wanted him to notice me, even to tell me, as the others had done, that I looked beautiful. Instead, he studiously ignored me, and I felt a touch of bleakness in my heart.

I heard Julian asking where Miriam was. "She should be here, ready and waiting. Our guests will be arriving soon."

"I am here, dear Julian."

She was descending the stairs, resplendent in peach-colored satin lavishly embroidered with pearls, her hair piled high and crowned with a diamond tiara. More diamonds sparkled at wrists and throat and ears. She carried them well, and herself well, although it was plain that she had to hold on to the ancient carved banister to do so.

Julian signaled to the orchestra, who promptly started playing, drowning the ensuing conversation from any ears but ours.

"Nicholas, do something quickly, or she will disgrace us." Miriam was close enough to overhear. "Nonsense, my dear Julian! If you think I have drunk too much champagne already, let me assure you I haven't yet even begun. And tonight is a celebration, is it not? The greatest night of your life, when this charming wife of yours is to be lauded to the skies because she is carrying your child. Well, I have made sure that you will be equally proud of your devoted stepmother. Not even your wife's splendid emeralds can outshine the Calverley diamonds."

She looked at us all with a mocking smile which seemed to be focused particularly on me.

"Congratulations, my dear Eustacia. Not because you are to have a child—after all, it isn't born yet, and to offer premature congratulations is tempting Providence—but because you are allowed to wear the Kershaw emeralds, which my husband refused to allow me to wear, or to be sold even in times of financial need, and those times were frequent enough, God knows. Which is why he married me, of course."

Julian said urgently, "Miriam, you don't know what you are saying. Go to your room and lie down for a while. I'll make your excuses, tell our guests that you are unwell but hope to join us later."

She rapped him on the arm with the handle of a long, bejeweled fan.

"I'll do no such thing! My place is here. I am hostess at Dragonmede, kindly remember. You haven't inherited yet. You would do well to remember that; also that perhaps you never will. Neither you, nor your clever young wife."

"Mamma, please!"

She leaned forward and kissed Christopher's cheek.

"Darling boy, remember this: nothing can ever be guaranteed until it is accomplished. Eustacia may wear the emeralds now because, according to the Kershaw tradition, they can only be worn by the wife of the heir apparent, but inheritances can change overnight. An heir can die, and another never be born."

I felt myself tremble, and was conscious that Nicholas moved unobtrusively to my side.

Julian hissed, *"Go to your room and lie down, Stepmother."*

"And spoil my coiffure? This elegant coiffure which your wife's unwilling French companion created for me? To do the woman justice, I must admit that she was unstinting in her efforts, even though she hated every moment of it. I knew full well she was eager to get out of my room. There is something about it she dislikes. A strange creature, Michelle Dubois, full of peculiar fancies. I could swear she is psychic. Does she predict the future, Eustacia? Has she made any predictions about this coming child? I wonder what she would foretell for me: if the future holds anything for me in this house."

Her voice trailed away on a tearful, self-pitying note, and Christoper groaned, "Oh, Lord, now she's going to have one of her crying fits!"

Beside us, there was a discreet cough, Miriam spun round, then gave a sparkling, artificial laugh.

"Ah, Ballard! The indispensable kennelman who appeared from nowhere overnight and is now so much a part of the household. You look very splendid, my man! Tell me, are you here as a waiter or as a guest?"

I stared in disbelief, for there was the man who claimed to be my father, resplendent in formal dress.

"Ballard is here in an official capacity to help supervise arrangements, at my express wish," Julian said calmly. "He has had considerable experience in such matters at a consulate overseas."

"And what about Garfield?"

"You could say I am here merely to assist him, my lady."

"Then a footman's uniform would have been more appropriate."

My husband rasped, "Not for a Master of Ceremonies, Stepmother."

"Is there no end to your talents, my good Ballard?" She looked at him with a mocking coquetry which was almost grotesque from behind her mask of makeup.

Ballard lowered his eyes with apparent respect, saying nothing, and suddenly I had a wild desire to laugh. It came rising up in me hysterically, for the whole situation had such a farcical aspect that I felt I would start making introductions at any minute: "Julian, my love, you already know my mother, whom you call a whore; do let me present my father, a disgraced cardsharper who I am quite sure never set foot inside any overseas consulate lest he be arrested and shipped back to England as a wanted man!"

The words shrieked for utterance in a silent frenzy of mirth even while my glance passed calmly from one face to another, seeing them only as masks with artificial smiles; faces concealing hatreds and suspicions and resentments and jealousies. And dear God, I was one of them, trapped in a puppet world, a marionette bedecked in taffeta and emeralds, a creature I neither knew nor wanted to be.

Then briefly Ballard's eyes met mine and looked away again. They were reassuringly blank, and I knew that not only had he no intention of claiming acquaintance with me, but if I attempted to identify him, he would deny it.

I moved forward and took hold of Miriam's arm, turning her toward the stairs. "Your coiffure is beautiful, Stepmother, but unhappily, a few strands have come astray. Let me take you upstairs and tidy them for you."

I touched the back of her head, which was immaculate, dislodging some hair which could easily be replaced. The important thing was to get her to her room and calm her down, although calming Miriam in her present state was something at which her maid was more experienced than I. However, she yielded willingly, appalled at the thought that her appearance held the slightest flaw and accusing Michelle of having done it deliberately.

"That woman hates me, I know. Everybody hates me!" She rambled incoherently all the way to her room, where she seated herself sulkily before her mirror.

I picked up a hairbrush and began to use it slowly: anything to prolong the moment, to give her time to sober even slightly; but she twisted and turned her head petulantly, accusing Michelle of maliciousness, of cheating, of pretending to do her best while ruining the effect at the back. I felt guilty, but not sorry, for Miriam in her present state would have created acute embarrassment as guests arrived—and still might, if I allowed her to go downstairs too soon. The question was, how to handle her? What did Mrs. Levitt do when one of these "attacks" threatened? Surely something was kept in the house to deal with the situation?

My mind ran on feverishly as I continued to smooth and resmooth the back of her hair, and as I did so I saw a man's face reflected over my shoulder in the mirror. Nicholas.

He said quietly, "Drink this, Miriam. It will make you feel much better."

"I don't feel ill!"

"I know, but you have a long and strenuous night

ahead. It can be hard on a hostess unless she has something to fortify her."

I felt I would be eternally grateful to him for coming to my aid so providentially.

Miriam said pettishly, "You mean it will help me to endure all these boring people and all this pantomime about heralding a new generation of Kershaws?"

He assured her impassively that it would.

She took the medicine glass and eyed me mockingly over the rim. "Of course, you don't need anything to help you through the evening, do you, Eustacia, because all the honor and the glory is to be yours. Isn't she wonderful, Nicholas? So clever and talented! Have you seen the portrait she has restored? It is hanging in the hall downstairs; do take a look at it. The girl's a genius, besides having other qualities so essential in a wife, even to becoming pregnant within the first year. And I'm sure she'll have lots more children. Lots of charming Kershaw sons to oust my darling Christopher."

"Drink up," he said firmly, not looking at me.

She obeyed, grimaced, and said at once that she knew what it was. "Mrs. Levitt gives me that stuff when I feel unwell."

He nodded. "And when you have rested awhile, you will no longer feel unwell. And thank you for telling me about the portrait. I shall certainly take a look at it."

"And be filled with admiration for Eustacia, like everyone else." She frowned into the mirror. "Have you really tidied my hair properly?" she asked, and ran a slightly shaking hand over the back of her head to make sure. "What I need is that jeweled hair clasp which your irritating Frenchwoman declined to use. She said it would be too much with a tiara, when all the time she was merely being spiteful, making sure that straying hair would spoil the effect."

I answered stonily, "Michelle is not like that."

Nicholas said, "Half an hour upon your bed, Miriam; as a doctor, I insist."

"And as a woman I insist on finding my jeweled clasp! It was right here, on my dressing table, beside my gold-framed pictures . . ." She broke off with a little shriek. "They're, they're gone!"

Her hands searched feverishly amongst her toilet accessories, scattering perfume bottles and rouge pots, jars of face creams and silver-backed brushes and combs. Costly accouterments went flying to the floor with discarded jewels, tumbling in a heap which she kicked aside furiously. When I stooped to gather up the debris, she screamed, "Leave them! *Leave them!* Nothing there means a thing to me compared with my pictures, my husband and I when we were young, and Christopher as a baby, beautiful pictures in beautiful frames. That is why she stole them, of course—for the frames. They were presents from my father: gold, studded with diamonds. That French-woman is a thief, a common thief!"

Nicholas seized her shoulders and shook her. She sobered instantly, but her eyes on me were malevolent.

"You brought her into this house, but I will send her away!"

A bracelet I had picked up fell nervelessly from my fingers.

"If you are accusing Michelle . . ."

"I am accusing her! She was alone here after I left the room. She said she would put away my brushes and combs, but did she? *Did she?* She put nothing away, as you can see. She stole, instead. What sort of woman have you brought to this house? What is her background? Notorious, I'll be bound!"

The mirror seemed to spin in front of me, showing a vision of my white face floating . . . floating . . .

I heard Nicholas saying something about Miriam being beside herself and that obviously the matter would be cleared up, and myself answering through stiff lips, "Michelle is not and never has been notorious," but even as I spoke I was remembering the story she had told us years ago about her dismissal from Lady Shalford's house, and her expulsion from the convent. Could history repeat itself so many years later? Temptation had never been put in her way in Luella's household, and besides, while there she had been aware of all she owed to my mother, but here, with this lavish carelessness spread out before her and an overindulged and careless woman to whom she owed no debt at all . . .

Fiercely, my mind rejected the idea. I suggested calmly that Mrs. Levitt should be sent for to tidy up here. "And I have no doubt that in all this mess your jeweled hair clasp will be found. As for your pictures, no doubt Mrs. Levitt has put them somewhere. She looks after you, not Michelle, and so long as I remain at Dragonmede, Michelle remains too."

From the door, Julian's voice demanded, "What is going on here? For goodness' sake, Eustacia, come downstairs at once; the first guests are arriving!"

He seized my arm and almost pulled me from the room, rapping over his shoulder, "And for God's sake, Cousin Nick, don't let my stepmother come downstairs until she's stone-cold sober."

"She is," Nicholas answered curtly. "Shock has done that to her."

I felt that she was on Miriam's side, not mine, and as we descended the great staircase I heard them coming behind. I could imagine his hand beneath her elbow, solicitously. I lifted my head and forced a smile, too proud to reveal any hurt, but the effort was so great that I scarcely heard my husband quietly scolding me for bothering about Miriam. "You should have left her to Aunt Dorcas and Cousin Nick. Your place is beside me, and don't you forget it."

That was the beginning of the evening. The end was much worse. And between the beginning and the end, events rocketed.

Sixteen

AFTER THE ENDLESS line of guests had been received, Julian and I led the dancing. The immense hall was a whirl of glitter and color, filled with faces unknown to me, but here and there one or two stood out. Victoria Bellamy, very striking in a low-cut black velvet gown from which her shoulders rose whitely, framed by cascading ringlets of her vivid red hair. She had kissed me effusively on both cheeks, but had not deceived me: I was the wife of a lover who had rejected her, and for that she hated me, but her blazing self-confidence would carry her triumphantly through the evening and she was assured of attracting male homage.

I saw David Foster standing on the outskirts and scanning the crowd as if looking for someone. If he hoped to see the girl from Bodiam Hall he would be disappointed, for I knew that no invitation had been sent to her.

As we danced, Julian asked what the scene had been about in his stepmother's bedroom.

"You will hear," I answered indifferently, well aware that Miriam had no intention of letting the incident pass, and telling myself that I would be triumphant when her precious pictures turned up, as they surely must.

I saw her dancing by with Nicholas, a brilliant smile

fixed upon her face. He had been right in saying that shock had sobered her, but I knew that beneath her composure she was seething with fury, and when her eyes met mine there was ice between us.

The vicar and his wife went waltzing past. Both were obviously enjoying themselves, and I guessed that an occasion like this was a rarity in their lives, and that it was a long time since her old-fashioned dimity gown had been worn. I saw amusement flicker across my husband's face and heard him murmur beneath his breath that one could almost smell the mothballs, but my reaction to this unkind remark was eclipsed by joy at the sight of Solomon Slocombe, a late arrival. It seemed that he too was wearing clothes that he had not worn for many a year, for his old-fashioned suit hung on him loosely, making him appear more frail than ever. I told Julian how glad I was that the old man had been invited, to which he replied indifferently that even local "characters" were included, out of charity.

"But not the pretty girl from Bodiam Hall," I said without thinking.

"And what do you know about her?" The amiable smile on his face didn't waver, and I hoped it was matched by my own. We were the personification of a happy couple tonight. This was my role and I had to play it well.

"Nothing, except that she is extremely pretty and has a child, reputedly by a Kershaw."

"Meaning me or my brother Gerald? I see you've been listening to gossip."

"No. I have seen the child. He bears a remarkable resemblance to this family."

"But not through me, my love. And what Gerald did in his lifetime died with him."

The music stopped, and with his hand beneath my elbow my husband led me from the floor, where I paused to greet Solomon. Julian waited politely, but

I was glad that after taking Miriam back to her chair Nicholas joined us, accompanied by his mother. I was also pleased when he pointed out the portrait I had restored, and gratified by Sol's praise.

I knew that even Julian appreciated my work and that he now looked upon the family collection as being something worth treasuring. He asked which picture I had decided to restore next, and I said the idea of working on one of his father appealed to me. "But strangely enough, I can find none of him."

Julian replied that there was nothing strange about that; they had all been put away. "Didn't you tell me it was by Miriam's choice, Aunt Dorcas?"

She nodded. "Your stepmother found it unbearable to be faced with a constant comparison between the man he had once been and the man he has become."

Dorcas' face was inscrutable, and remained so when Julian remarked that oddly enough, he himself had never noticed their absence until after our arrival from London.

"That is hardly surprising, Nephew. One becomes so accustomed to family portraits that they merge into the walls." She changed the subject adroitly. "My dear Solomon, it is good to see you. Nicholas reports that your health hasn't been too good and that you would do well to move from that cottage of yours."

"You son, my dear Dorcas, is a fusser."

Their conversation ran on, scarcely heeded by me. I was wondering if Julian realized that every picture of his father had been removed not only from the walls of Dragonmede, but from family albums, which made it seem illogical that his stepmother should keep a reminder of a young husband in the intimacy of her bedroom, if comparison with him now was so unbearable. Which did she value more, the pictures or their bejeweled frames?

But I had little chance for further speculation, for the next minute I was catapulted into surprise by the arrival of the girl from Bodiam Hall, accompanied by her father. As their names were announced I spun round in astonishment, but it was no mistake, no coincidence, and the name was no error. The man whose arm Penelope held was none other than Crowther.

"Who invited them?" Miriam demanded furiously.

We were back in the family group. David Foster had already claimed Penelope for a dance, and Crowther, after bowing formally to us, had moved on and now stood at the far end of the hall, almost out of sight.

"I did, Mamma. I stole an invitation from your desk and mailed it personally."

"Christopher, why did you do such a thing?"

"Because I like Penelope and feel sorry for her."

"She must be the only girl you've ever been aware of, but it doesn't seem that she reciprocates," Julian remarked cruelly.

He was as angry as Miriam, but for a different reason It was Crowther's presence that he resented, not Penelope's, and I was well aware that he avoided my eyes because he knew I must be wondering why he had never told me that Crowther was a neighbor. I was also wondering why Crowther had never mentioned it either.

Speculation and suspicion ran riot in my mind. It could be no more of a coincidence that Crowther had introduced us than my contrived marriage to Julian had been, or the fact that my mother had lived near Dragonmede as a girl and hidden the fact from me. Coincidence didn't stalk through life so outrageously. I felt as if I were in the center of an uncompleted jigsaw puzzle of which I could not even glimpse the final picture.

Christopher muttered resentfully that David Foster had an impudence to dance with Penelope before he himself had a chance to. "After all, I am a Kershaw, not he."

I was tempted to remark that being a Kershaw was something he claimed not to value, but was far too concerned with my own speculations to bother. As soon as I could get Julian alone I would ask him outright why he had maintained a secrecy about Crowther's residence here. Perhaps he guessed this determination, for he dodged it by asking his stepmother to dance, and the next moment my mind was distracted by Nicholas' claiming me.

He danced well, so it was ridiculous for me to stumble slightly as he placed his arm about my waist, but after that we moved smoothly and rhythmically, dancing in a silence which united us more closely than conversation could have done. I was most potently aware of him, but refused to face the reason for it. I wanted this waltz never to end. Apart from the moment when he had lifted me into Ladybird's saddle and let his hands fall away quickly, too quickly, I could recall no other time at which Nicholas had held me, and this proximity was so disturbing that I avoided meeting his glance in case he should see my reaction; but even without looking at him I knew that throughout the dance his eyes never left my face.

There are some moments in life that seem timeless, yet all too short. This was one of them. When the music ceased he held me for a moment longer, then released me, proffering his arm to lead me back to my chair.

It was then that I came face to face with Crowther. I halted immediately and said that I was sorry not to have been able to greet him more fully on arrival. His sardonic smile spoke for itself.

"Thank you, Mrs. Kershaw, but I expected neither you nor your in-laws to have any particular greeting for me, or for my lass."

"Then you were mistaken. Apart from the fact that

you are my mother's friend, and therefore mine, I am delighted that you brought your daughter, whom I think charming. I would like to know her better. Pray tell her so, and that I will take the opportunity of calling if she will let me know her At Home days."

"She has none, Ma'am. She knows the ways of society but has no opportunity to exercise them in these parts. As for where we come from, folk don't stand on ceremony there."

"Not all of us do here," Nicholas put in easily, "so I hope my cousin's wife will be welcome at Bodiam Hall whenever she cares to drop in."

I was grateful to him for easing the moment. Perhaps Crowther was too, for his slightly aggressive tone softened as he aswered, "I'm sure Mrs. Kershaw is aware of that, Doctor."

"Then I shall call tomorrow," I told him, "and I hope that before the evening is out you will ask me to dance."

"Nay, lass, in your position you must dance with the nobs, as we say up North."

I smiled. "I hope I may fulfill all duty dances and dance with a friend of my mother's." I turned to Nicholas. "I suppose you are unaware that my mother was born and brought up nearby."

"I am well aware of it. Not only has Solomon told me, but my mother too. I hear she was very beautiful, and I must say the fact doesn't surprise me."

It was absurd to let a remark like that make me feel so happy. The orchestra struck up again and I said to Crowther spontaneously, "There is no time like the present, and I'm sure you would never be so ungallant as to refuse a lady who wishes to dance with you."

As we moved onto the floor I knew full well that the family would be aghast. So did Crowther, for he remarked that I was asking for trouble. "This snobbish family you've wed into won't approve of thee dancing with the likes of me. They'll consider it cheek on my part, for asking."

"But you didn't ask me. I had to persuade you, and I'm not in the least afraid of admitting it if I have to. Meanwhile, there are one or two thing I would like to know."

"Which is why you 'persuaded' me. I guessed that, of course."

"Then you make things easier for me. Why have you never mentioned that you live nearby?"

"I scarcely do. I'm hardly ever here. My business is up North."

"Which must make things very lonely for your daughter."

He answered gruffly, "She's better off here, away from the mill background."

"The whole of Lancashire isn't devoted to mills, surely?"

"No, but our folks are. Crowthers have always been millowners, working up from the looms years back, gathering lots of brass but no culture. I made sure my lass had both: sent her away to be educated, finished in Paris, taught elocution and deportment—and placed her miles above the lot of us. Bring her back to Lancashire after all that? She'd be like a fish out of water. She came on a visit once and couldn't understand a word of the dialect. Found us all uncouth, I daresay. She'd never have found the right kind of husband back home."

I refrained from pointing out that she had failed to find the right kind of husband here.

"Aye, I know what you're thinking, Mrs. Kershaw: that she isn't much better off in her present position; and you're right. Maybe I made a mistake, but I didn't think so at the time. And but for being drowned the way he was, she's still convinced that Gerald Kershaw would have married her. Me, I don't know. Maybe he would, maybe he wouldn't, but I've no more love for the Kershaws because of it."

"Then what made you come tonight?"

He gave a wry smile. "Couldn't resist it. And besides, my lass was overjoyed when the invitation came for the pair of us. We've you to thank for that, I daresay."

"How could I send an invitation to the pair of you when I didn't even know you were related? I've only known her as Penelope, or thought of her as the girl from Bodiam Hall. It was Christopher who sent the invitation, not I, but I'm very glad he did. My young brother-in-law has a soft corner in his heart for your daughter."

"Him?" There was typical masculine contempt in his voice. "Well, I'm glad he likes the girl, but he's no sort of a man. The one she's dancing with is. There's nothing wrong with that one."

"Penelope shares your opinion, that much is obvious. And now I'll repeat my question. Why have you never mentioned, either when I married or when we met again in London recently, that you own a house so close to Dragonmede?"

His mouth curved bitterly. "Don't you know it's the dream of every self-made man from the North to own a country mansion in the South, plus a luxury apartment in London? I should have thought that husband of yours would have told you. Or maybe he liked to pretend it was his own?"

I stopped dancing abruptly.

"That place in Grosvenor Square, was it yours?"

"Still is. And people are staring, Mrs. Kershaw, including your husband. Don't you think we'd best get on with the dance?"

I moved mechanically, and through my bewilderment I realized that another piece of the jigsaw had fallen into place. A small piece, but the key to others.

"Was it by accident or design that you brought

Julian to my mother's house in Bloomsbury, and were you there the night she . . ."

The music whirled to a halt. He bowed and released me, and Julian was at my side, leading me away, saying that the time had come for the announcement to be made, after which supper would be served. He was amiable, polite, but his voice was edged with steel. He led me to the dais at the far end of the hall, and I heard the Master of Ceremonies—my own father, I thought with wild and ironic humor—calling for silence. I stood beside my husband, my hand in his, while behind us the family were grouped. I heard Julian make the announcement and the ring in his voice, not of pride in me, but of triumph for what was to be accomplished through me. I heard the applause, the toasts, the congratulations. A glass of champagne was in my hand and Julian clinked his own against it.

"To our child, my love. And by God, it had better be a son. I'm not having Dragonmede pass on to either Christopher or Nick, much as they both covet it."

Only I could hear his words beneath the bright chatter around us. Only he could hear mine as I asked coolly, "Why didn't you tell me that our honeymoon was by courtesy of Crowther?"

"What the devil d'you mean?"

"You know perfectly well. He lent you that apartment in Grosvenor Square, and don't pretend otherwise. I now know when you are lying, Julian."

He stooped and kissed me, and people smiled indulgently, whereupon he made a great display of this sign of devotion, whispering in my ear so that everyone thought he was murmuring words of love.

"What odds does it make, darling? We were happy there, and we'll be happy in the same way again. I still want you, still find you desirable. Pregnancy can be a nuisance, but only temporarily. When it's over

I'll be able to make love to you without the restraint I have to exercise now. Without any restraint at all."

"As you did one memorable night?" I answered in a low, shaking voice.

"Why not? As I told you when we arrived here, I own every inch of you, by which I mean your body. By God, I paid well for it. Remember that."

That was the moment when I realized that to tolerate this man was something that would grow more unbearable with the years, corroding my life. I turned away from him, and a chink of light high up near the ceiling at the far end of the hall caught my eye: Hannah Grant, of course, watching through the peep in the solar. I was filled with a sudden pity for the lonely little woman and promptly went in search of her.

To my astonishment, she was on her knees. I stood at the entrance of the flamboyant room in which the wild Sir William had entertained his gentlemen friends, gambling away the family fortune. Hannah's eyes were closed, her hands clasped. She didn't even hear me enter.

"Hannah, why are you praying?"

She opened her eyes and looked at me.

"I have just heard the announcement, Mrs. Julian, so naturally I am praying for you. And for your first-born. May it not be a son."

I spun away from her, forgetful of my concern for her loneliness. I hurried back to the ballroom, and came face to face with Victoria Bellamy at the foot of the great stairs. She smiled at me radiantly.

"Congratulations, Eustacia. I know everyone has been showering them on you, so I won't bore you by being over-effusive." She looked at me sharply. "You look tired. Come in here and sit down awhile."

She opened a door and I walked through, glad to escape from the noise and the crowd. It opened into a small gun room: warm, rather austere, but thickly carpeted and with deep armchairs on either side of the fireplace. I sank into one and let my head fall back. It was absurd to let Hannah's words upset me, but upset me they had, because in the deep recesses of my heart I too was praying that my firstborn should not be a son—not so much because of the legend, which would apply to the first son I gave birth to whether he was my firstborn child or not, but because he might resemble his father.

I heard the door close, but Victoria had not left me. She was sauntering about the room, examining cases of guns, commenting on them knowledgeably, pointing out dueling pistols and double-barreled sporting guns, quoting technical details like an expert.

"But all this bores you, doesn't it, Eustacia? Guns, killing wildlife, enjoying blood sports: you just don't begin to comprehend the thrill of it, do you?"

She opened a glazed door and took down a small pistol, handling it with familiarity and ease. "Do you know what this is? A derringer, point-twenty-two caliber: the sort a man can carry in his pocket because it only measures four inches—and for the same reason, a woman can handle it with ease, like this."

She leveled it, cocked it, and laughed. "Don't worry, it isn't loaded; and much as I dislike you, it isn't you I want to kill. It's Julian. He was my lover, and he jilted me, which no man has ever done before." Idly, she opened a box, took out some bullets, and loaded the gun, saying negligently, "Easy, isn't it? One touch of the trigger, and . . ." She put the pistol down. "Am I frightening you?"

"Well, I can hardly say I'm enjoying it."

I rose and went to the door. Strains of music echoed beyond, but I was in no mood for dancing. The tension of the evening was taking its toll; Victoria had been right when she said I looked tired. Now her voice came to me again. It was meant to be mocking, but all I heard was the desperate unhappiness in it.

"I could kill Julian, you know, and he'd be no loss to either of us, but I love him, sadist though he is. A touch of savagery in a man has always appealed to me, and Julian has more than a touch."

I looked back at her with compassion. I remembered the potency of my husband's attraction, even though he could no longer exercise it over me.

"And it would be you to have his child," she went on bitterly. "I'd been hoping and praying it would be me, even though it wouldn't make him my husband. Divorce in our circle is taboo; it means social ostracism and never again to be admitted into the Royal Enclosure at Ascot. I must confess I could never face up to that, and certainly the Kershaws couldn't. But to have a child by Julian would have been a permanent tie between us, even if I married someone else."

"Such as Nicholas?"

"Not if he remained a country doctor."

"But as master of Dragonmede? I seem to recall your pointing out to Aunt Dorcas the advantage of manipulating things."

"But that was only in the event of anything happening to Julian."

"Whom you say you would like to kill."

"So I would, but what would it avail me now he has made sure of the succession through you? Nicholas is further away from possession than ever before, which is a pity because he is a very attractive man—and I like attractive men, but to me he does lack Julian's special quality."

"You mean his 'touch of savagery'?"

"Yes. Nicholas would be passionate and very masculine, and I wouldn't hesitate to marry such a man if he achieved a position better than the one he now holds, but I doubt if he would turn a blind eye on any postmarital relationship, and I would require that in a husband. Then Julian and I could continue to be lovers, because that is all right so long as one is never found out. Everybody does it, which is why I am confident he will come back to me when the novelty of being a father wears off. Meanwhile, I'm leaving for Marienbad tomorrow, with Papa to provide the right note of propriety—and money, of course. He makes an ideal escort: retiring to bed conveniently early and fondly imagining I do the same. I hear Marienbad is very gay and patronized by the most eligible members of some of Europe's most noble families."

"Then it will be a happy hunting ground for you, Victoria." It was Julian's voice from the door. "But don't assume too much about the renewal of our relationship when you return. And now, go back to the ball. I want to talk to my wife."

She flung him a look of hatred so vicious that a chill ran through me, and walked out of the room so quietly that even her step seemed to hold menace. I was glad when the door closed, but even then the anger didn't leave my husband's face, and I realized it was also leveled against me.

"What now?" I asked wearily.

"Miriam has just told me about the theft from her room. I've given instructions for Michelle's room to be searched after the ball."

"I'll allow no such thing!"

"You cannot prevent it. You pay her wages out of your allowance, but I can reduce that anytime I choose, or stop it altogether."

I was in no mood for threats, and retorted, contemptuously, that his stepmother had scarcely known what she was saying. "Her dressing table was all muddle and confusion. She was probably unaware of what was there and what was not."

"Mrs. Levitt reports that everything has been tidied and the item is still missing."

"Item? Only one? Miriam claimed there were two—a jeweled hair clasp and a triple picture frame made of gold. So one article has turned up, I presume. The other will do so too."

"When that Frenchwoman hands it over. You had no right to bring her here without my permission, but I humored you and let her stay. But no longer. I won't have a thief harbored in this house."

"Michelle is not a thief!"

"But she used to be. I've known all along. I had it from Letitia Shalford, a long-standing acquaintance. She told me about Michelle Dubois when she learned that I was visiting your mother's establishment in Bloomsbury. But Letitia was always a bore, and I paid little heed to her prattle. And whoever your mother employed was no concern of mine. Who is employed here is a different matter."

I answered furiously that from the day Michelle had entered our Bloomsbury home her entire life had changed. "So is she likely to revert to her unhappy past now? And talking about unhappiness, I actually find myself feeling sorry for Victoria. You've hurt her."

He shrugged. "She has known what to expect, or should have done, when I started indulging her again after my marriage to you."

"Is that what you call it: 'indulging' a woman?" The small room echoed with the disgust in my voice.

"What else? She wanted to renew our liaison, so she had to accept the terms."

"You had a liaison with her before we married?"

"My darling Eustacia, I've amused myself with Victoria for years. She must have been fourteen when I seduced her."

"In the arbor? Was it always a trysting place?"

"Of course, from my reprobate grandfather downwards. I'm not so sure about my own father, though. Aunt Dorcas always claims that he was the most moral

Kershaw of us all. But none of this matters, and you needn't think you can divert me from the far more important matter of your thieving French companion. Her room will be searched, and out she goes first thing in the morning."

"Even if proved innocent?" I demanded furiously.

"She won't be. Once a thief, always a thief."

"That's not true! Have you no heart?"

My voice cracked on a high, taut note; and at that precise moment the door opened and the man who claimed to be my father stood there. I saw his eyes flicker from one to the other of us. I was leaning against the table, supporting myself tiredly on my arms, and I knew that he observed this as he observed everything else. All this passed in the fraction of a second before he announced that supper was ready to be served, the guests waiting.

In the tension of the moment, it didn't occur to either of us that it was Garfield who should have come to fetch us. Julian answered curtly that we would come at once, but I begged to be excused. "I could eat nothing. I am very tired. I am sure people will understand."

My husband's eyes raked me, studying my face to see if I was speaking the truth. He was thinking of the child, and that fatigue was bad for an expectant mother, and apparently I showed traces of it, for he nodded agreement and told me to go to bed at once. The man calling himself Ballard stood aside as we left the room, but I was aware of his perceptive eyes—eyes that missed nothing. I felt that not the smallest detail in that room escaped him. Nor the smallest detail about me and my husband.

I went straight to my mother-in-law's room. It was empty and immaculate, her bed turned down and costly nightwear laid out. No matter how late she came to bed, she would ring for Mrs. Levitt to undress her.

I thought of the woman yawning wearily in her room, awaiting the summons; she wasn't likely to intrude until then, so I could search at leisure, and did so. Everything on the dressing table was in its place; crystal and silver shone in the lamplight; the jeweled hair clasp sparkled on a silver tray. But there was no sign of any triple picture frame, diamond-studded or otherwise, nor in any drawer or cupboard, and after a systematic search I hurried to Michelle's room.

She was in bed, but not asleep. I wasted no time in telling her why I had come.

"You are innocent, I know, but my husband is convinced otherwise and is intent on sending you away at once." I added reluctantly that he knew of her unhappy past through Lady Shalford.

She clung to me so desperately that I could feel fear running from her mind into my own.

"*Chérie,* don't let him part us!"

"Then help me to prove your innocence. If we do that, he must retract. I protested when I heard that your room is to be searched, but on second thought it would be wise to agree. Nothing could clear you more effectively."

Panic showed in her face. "But I cannot leave you alone in this place. Whatever the price, I must stay beside you. You need protection here. I know it, feel it!"

" 'Whatever the price'?" I echoed. "What do you mean?"

She closed her lips stubbornly, avoiding my eyes, and I realized that she was not denying the theft. My vehement defense of her had been a mistake.

Shocked, I whispered, "So you did!" Then I burst out, "Why, in God's name, why?"

With an air of despairing resignation she slipped out of bed, crossed to her wardrobe, and unlocked the long drawer at the bottom. The next moment, the little jeweled triptych was in her hands, the two sides closed over the center, concealing the pictures.

"I will replace it at once," she said, making for the door.

"No. I will." When she tried to resist, I took it with authority. She watched mutely as I opened the frames. The pictures to right and left scarcely registered. Only the center one, from which the past came leaping out at me.

I was looking again at Lucky Jack and his bride.

Seventeen

"So she did take it, as I guessed. And, as I guessed, you came to warn her. Your excuses about being tired didn't deceive me for a moment. I gave you permission to go to bed only because I knew exactly what you would do. That was why I followed you."

Julian's hand reached out and took the jeweled frames from my nerveless hands.

"Thank you, my love; you've saved the time and trouble of a search. But don't imagine I shall forgive you for what you planned to do now. You were going to put it back in my stepmother's room, shielding this common thief of whom you are so inordinately fond." His voice held a knife edge of steel. "If it weren't for the fact that you are carrying my child, I would turn you out with her."

"And I would gladly go!"

His hands clenched. I saw his throat muscles become strained and rigid. Violence was never far below the surface of my husband's smooth exterior.

Michelle burst into a torrent of French abuse. For answer, he turned the back of his hand toward her and struck it hard against one cheek and back across the other. Her head jerked like a puppet's about to snap. She sagged in a small heap onto the floor.

I felt him dragging me out of the room.

"I've made your excuses to tthe assembly, Eustacia, so go to bed you will. And when that Frenchwoman is out of this house, you will toe the line, my line. I'll make a worthy mistress for Dragonmede out of you yet."

Opening the door of our bedroom, he pushed me inside, cast me one final glance, and laughed. "And don't try to look as if you've had a shock, my love. There's been nothing to shock you tonight, and I've every right to be angry. And now I'll return this thing to Miriam's room and rejoin our guests, or everyone will be imagining I have no respect for your condition and have followed you to bed."

His laughter echoed in the room even after he had gone. I waited until his footsteps had disappeared down the corridor, allowed time for him to visit his stepmother's room and then rejoin the ball, then hurried back to Michelle. She had dragged herself from the floor to her bed and now sat in a forlorn huddle, red weals sharp upon her face. It was the sight of those weals that hardened my determination.

"I am coming away with you," I said. "I can no longer live in this house."

"Your mother will insist on your coming back. You don't know how much it means to her that you should become mistress of Dragonmede."

"I am beginning to. You were afraid I would recognize that picture, weren't you? That was why you once asked if I had ever visited my mother-in-law's room. If I had said yes, you would have known that I had seen the picture and that it meant nothing to me, but when you learned I had not, you decided to take no chances. Now I know why you were shocked the first time you went into that room."

"Not shocked, frightened. I knew who she was and who your husband was before I came, but it was plain that you didn't, and your mamma took good care that you shouldn't. She never referred to Lucky Jack after— after it was all over. But she never forgot him, either. She loved him more than she ever loved any man. She fully expected him to return to her. Instead . . ."

"Instead, he married someone else, and you were afraid I would remember the wedding picture even after all these years. It was an artist's impression, but a superb likeness, as was the line portrait published after his trial."

We were talking in whispers, sitting close upon the bed. I had taken the precaution of locking the door, although I knew it was unnecessary. Confident that he had dealt effectively with both of us, Julian would now devote himself lightheartedly to his guests, playing the host to perfection, the proud father-to-be.

"Children can remember things," Michelle said. "The risk was too great. I didn't want you to suspect anything."

"Meaning my mother's triumph in marrying me to Sir Vivian's son? I know how she did it, but not until tonight did I realize why."

"*Chérie,* you must understand and be fair to her. However she arranged it—and I do not know that she did, mind you, because she never took me into her confidence about it—but however she did it, it was mainly because you had set your heart on him; otherwise not even for revenge would she have done so. Not your mamma. Her heart is too tender. That is why the hurt went deep when Sir Vivian never came back to her. It seems strange to me to hear him called Sir Vivian. He was always known by his second name, John, which everyone shortened to Jack. Your poor mamma—I suppose she hoped he would marry her."

"That was impossible. My father was alive, and still is."

Michelle uttered a long drawn out, "So-o! That explains much."

I nodded, but there was no more time to talk about the past.

"Tomorrow, after you have left, I will have the trap harnessed and follow you. I will bring no clothes, so it will appear that I am only going for a drive, but I will bring all the money I have."

"You know your poor mamma will be beside herself. She was always improvident, uncaring about the future, which is why her position is so difficult now. I can make money by dressmaking, but do not expect her to be happy at the idea of your becoming a poorly paid art teacher, *chérie,* which is about all you can hope for. And then there is the child; it will be taken from you."

"If it is a boy, yes, in which case I will fight to keep him. I doubt if my husband will be interested in a daughter; he wants only sons, as an extension of himself, but he can be vindictive. I may have to fight to keep my child, whatever its sex. But I can do more than teach art. I can restore paintings, and such work is well paid."

"But only men do it! Who would employ a woman?"

"Stop trying to discourage me, Michelle. Listen instead. We will not go back to Luella. I have already realized that my life there can never be picked up again. When you leave this house, go to Solomon Slocombe; tell him what has happened. I will follow you. Sol is wise and understanding; he will think of something, or he and I will think of something together. And now, bathe your poor face and go to bed."

I kissed the inflamed cheek, and was about to return to my room when she startled me by saying, "I think it would be a better idea to go to Dr. Bligh. He is wise and understanding too. More so than an old man in failing health, I think."

But such a step I would not contemplate. There

was still an unanswered question in my mind about Nicholas. What thoughts went on behind his buccaneer's face I could never really guess, and too frequently of late, he made turmoil of my emotions. Besides, buccaneers were dangerous because they were plunderers.

I lay in bed and thought about the tragic hulk of a man lying upstairs, unable to believe that he had once been the handsome Lucky Jack. But another piece of the jigsaw fell into place, for now I understood his first violent reaction to me. I resembled Luella, and the sight had been a shock.

From then on he had watched me from his window whenever possible, his unwavering stare sending chills through me, like cold shivers of hatred directed from his mind into my own. I wondered if the ordeal of a sensational court trial had turned his love for her into antipathy, causing him to marry another woman on the rebound, or whether, as Miriam had pathetically declared when her guard was down, he had indeed married her solely for her money. He too must have been a gambler. That was why he had visited my mother's house in the first instance, although he had obviously continued to because he had become her lover. Across the years a child's voice in a dusty Bloomsbury garden echoed in my ears. ". . . *two men fought over her, and one was shot.*" I wondered now whether such an incident could turn a man's love into hatred, or whether the sight of me had been too poignant a reminder of the love they had shared and its terrible culmination.

Now I understood the long delay in being presented to him when I first came to Dragonmede. Dorcas had chosen the time and the moment, not only because she knew who I was, but because of the effect the meeting might have upon him. Everyone in the house must have known my identity; the announcement in the *London Gazette* had named me as the daughter of Mrs. Luella Rochdale. Dorcas would remember my mother not merely from girlhood but from the scandalous affair involving her brother, and for this reason Miriam must have recalled her name too, although they had never met.

Now I understood Miriam's cold welcome and her burning resentment that I should push her adored son further down the line of succession. She had restored Dragonmede to all its glory, and even this threatened to be taken from her by the daughter of the woman she had most cause to hate.

Was it Dorcas who had removed all pictures of her brother prior to my arrival, in case I should recognize him, even though I had been the merest child when the trial took place? But how was she to know that I wasn't already aware of his identity?

A more logical explanation seemed to be that Julian had no knowledge of the affair—or, at least, of my mother's part in it—and that Dorcas considered it wiser that he remain in ignorance. Any chance recognition of "Lucky Jack" on my part would have revealed things best forgotten. Julian and Gerald had been away at school when their father featured so dramatically in the public eye, and scandal sheets would be kept severely away from pupils in sheltered establishments for the sons of gentlemen. The more I thought about it, the more convinced I became that Julian was totally unaware of the part my mother had played in his father's life, because, knowing him as I now did, I was fully aware that he would have taunted me cruelly with the fact.

But not all the jigsaw pieces had fallen into place, even though I now understood Dorcas' scruniy of me on arrival, and even Hannah Grant's reaction, which, at the time, had been so mystifying—so much so that I had been forced to ask if I reminded her of someone, and been bewildered by her remark that she had "never liked her, although dear Dorcas did."

And prior to that she had been watching me secretly from the peep in the solarium, perhaps hurrying back to her room to record the event in her history of the Kershaws.

Mistrust seemed to creep toward me from every corner of the room—mistrust of every person in this house, including the knowing Mrs. Levitt, who would most certainly remember the wild girl from the vicarage and the shooting incident years later involving Sir Vivian, and be scandalized by the arrival of the woman's daughter as the wife of his son. And then there was unhappy Miriam, tormented by the knowledge that she had been married to avert financial disaster, and perhaps by the realization that her son was not only effeminate but ineffectual.

My thoughts reverted to Dorcas again. She was always amiable, calm, and seemingly friendly, but not only had she ample reason for resenting the rejection of her husband and every right to feel that there would be poetic justice in recompense being achieved for her son, but her devotion to her brother might well prompt a feeling of outrage at the thought of Luella Rochdale's daughter becoming mistress here. Did she too wear a mask?

I felt like an innocent fly who had wandered into a spider's web and that all around me the spiders were gathering, ready to strangle me with strands of that web. To remain in this house for the sake of the coming child no longer seemed a sane thing to do, for how would the child grow up in such an atmosphere, with a father initiating him into attitudes of mind that I deplored, setting him examples of arrogance and bullying and the divine right to kill for the pleasure of it? Stay at Dragonmede, and I would be held a prisoner of his will forever. So, too, would my child until he became a replica of him.

Reaching a decision brought a measure of relief from the fears and bitter disappointment of my marriage.

It was as if my mind and body slowly unclenched, and it was then that I must have fallen asleep.

So the sound of the shot could only have been in a dream—a dream recapturing the echo of an incident in childhood which Michelle had explained away as a door banging in the wind. But I was awake and sitting up in bed, and there was no wind to slam any door throughout the great house, and I was no longer a child but the wife of Julian Kershaw, heir of Dragonmede, who was still downstairs entertaining guests at the ball.

But the music had ceased, and the vast house was silent, and dawn was faintly slicing the curtains like the ghostly edges of fog.

I was relieved that Julian had not come to join me. Perhaps he was asleep in his dressing room; perhaps with another woman. The thought left me unmoved. I tried to sleep again, drowsed, slipped back into the past, and saw a picture being snatched out of my hand by my mother's long, well-manicured fingers. A picture torn from a periodical. A picture of a house. A large, impressive country house from which grim gargoyles with many faces looked down upon spreading acres . . . and then I was driving up to that house with a feeling of unaccountable recognition. . .

I awakened sharply. At last I understood the uncanny sensation I had experienced on arriving at Dragonmede. That picture, briefly glimpsed, had been stamped upon my mind by my mother's sharp reaction, lying dormant ever since. For how long had Luella secretly treasured a picture of this place—the home of Sir Vivian Kershaw, whom she had loved since she was a girl at the local parsonage and he a married man, way beyond her? My childish hands had stumbled upon her secret at a time when he awaited trial for shooting a man because of her, and to her the reminder had been unbearable.

It was strange that only then did a vitally important question leap into my mind.

Who was the man he had shot?

There was a stirring in the house. Not of people, and unaccompanied by any sound. It was more like a message coming to me through the atmosphere, but there was nothing supernatural about it. I wasn't afraid, but I was curious. Any stirring in the atmosphere had to be caused by movement of some sort, and movement was usually physical, but I could hear neither footsteps nor voices. Nor was it close at hand, so it couldn't be Julian in his dressing room, retiring at long last.

I sat up again, and listened. The silence all around me was so heavy that it seemed to have density, like an imprisoning wall, but deep at the heart of it something communicated like an urgent whisper. And yet I experienced no feeling of threat. I merely felt that something was happening and had to find out what it was.

I groped for a candle, lit it, pulled on a robe, and went barefoot out into the corridor. My feet were soundless on the carpeted floor, and shadows cast by the candle flame danced up the walls, lurked amongst the carved ceilings, lay in wait in the spreading darkness ahead. Apprehension touched me, but unnecessarily. Any house could seem sinister when shrouded in darkness, especially one so vast as this. Behind closed doors the household slept.

The sprawling blackness of the great hall held no more than its usual feeling of discomfort when I reached the head of the stairs. The smell of a thousand extinguished candles came up to me, the only reminder that a few hours ago the place had been aglitter and awhirl.

What made me descend I have no idea: some vague intention of finding Julian, perhaps, who might be sprawling asleep in an armchair somewhere, befogged by wine and the intoxication of being an admired and flattered host. His vanity fed upon such things, just as his ego fed upon cruelty. What would I do if I found him? Wake him and urge him to bed? *But not to mine, not to mine.* I had no desire to share my last night in this house with my husband, so if I found him asleep somewhere I would leave him there. I decided this quite calmly as I went step by step down the stairs.

But the creaking I began to hear was strange. The stairs were of stone, ice-cold to my feet, and steps made of stone made no sound. I halted, listened, and heard it continue, regular and rhythmic, like the creak of a rocking chair.

Or footsteps on the oak floor below?

The calmness in me wavered, although I reminded myself that the sound could be a door gently moving in a draft from an open window, or curtain rings creaking upon their wooden rods from the same cause. But there was no draft, no penetration of air, nothing to create that whispering sound which also had a grating sharpness about it.

I turned and looked back up the stairs. The landing above was as empty as I had left it, and so was the minstrels' gallery, now bare of its musicians.

My ears alert, I continued down the stairs until I reached the hall itself. The floor was no longer cold beneath my feet; invisible servants had replaced Persian rugs upon polished wood, restoring the house to order after the ball so that when the family descended next day everything would be normal again. Briefly I stood still, wondering where to go, which doors to open, which rooms to search, and what I was searching for. As I did so, I became aware that the creaking was somehow louder, nearer, and came from overhead.

I lifted the candle high, and as I did so my foot stubbed against something hard. To my surprise, it was the great ladder that had been used for putting up decorations. It lay abandoned on the floor, and I thought absently that after such meticulous tidying it had been careless of the servants to leave it lying around. And why take down the decorations before Christmas had even arrived?

I looked up, and saw the great clusters of holly and ivy, mistletoe and hops still adorning the hangman's beam. Then the pale gleam from the candle focused on something else. A rope dangling tautly . . . creaking, creaking, creaking . . . with my husband's body swinging gently on the end of it.

Eighteen

SOMEONE WAS STOOPING over me. I saw my father's face swim into focus and fade again. There was a sensation of being lifted, darkness ebbing and flowing, a feeling that I had slipped away from the world and had no desire to return. But my eyes opened, heavy, reluctant, and there was a softness under me as I had been laid upon something protective and warm.

It was the first time in my life that I had fainted. I emerged to the realization that I was on my bed and that in my father's face there was concern. He put an arm beneath my head and lifted it, tilting a flask to his hip pocket, laying my head back gently with the other hand. He was talking, saying something about not intending that I should be the one to discover the body, that he had expected one of the servants to find it in the morning.

His words made no sense, because they were submerged by shock and the dawning recollection that Julian had hanged himself.

I murmured, "Please—get Michelle—" but he made no move, and through my stupefied senses I realized that he didn't want to leave me, torn between anxiety in my behalf and anxiety to keep everyone away.

My head began to clear, to reason, to think. I said, "You carried me up here?"

He nodded, and I mumbled unintelligibly, "Why are you in the house? And what do you mean, that you didn't, didn't want me to be the one to . . ."

Dizziness took over. I closed my eyes, trying to force myself back to coherent thought, but this was impossible because of the stunned realization that my husband was dead. Hanged, in the manner of legendary forebears, from the massive hangman's beam, and at a time when he had everything he most wanted: the prospect of a son and future mastery of Dragonmede. He couldn't have done it himself. It was out of character. But there was the massive ladder, kicked aside, to prove that he had.

I asked for Michelle again. In a reeling world I wanted to cling to her—not to this stranger who called himself my father, despite his concern for me.

I begged, "Please, fetch Michelle. Her room is the third on the left, the floor above this."

I saw anxiety sharpen in his eyes and knew that he was fearing the effect of shock upon my condition. I saw hesitation, a final yielding; but before going he said, "Eustacia, say nothing, not even to Michelle. Leave things to me and I'll get you away somehow."

I had no idea what he meant, and when he finished beneath his breath, "Pray God you'll be fit to travel," I was only confused the more, wondering how he knew that I was planning to leave this house.

Then he was saying urgently, "Eustacia, if anything should go wrong and you really cannot travel, answer no questions. Say you know of no reason why he should have done it."

"There is no reason!"

"You're wrong, but as soon as they examine his body they'll find out he didn't do it anyway. You realize that, don't you? That is why I must get you away; but slinging him up there gives us time."

I stared in bewilderment. "I don't know what you mean."

He stated with quiet deliberation, "I mean that I saw everything in the gun room. The pistol on the table, the scene between you and that man you married. I know you had every cause to want him dead, but try not to give yourself away. I've covered for you, temporarily at least."

His words were still meaningless. He began to look at me almost in desperation, as if wondering how to get through to me.

"Listen, listen carefully, Eustacia. There's no evidence pointing to you, I've seen to that, so on second thoughts, helping you to escape may not be a good idea. It would arouse suspicion, pinpointing you. So I'll summon the Frenchwoman and then be gone. She'll wonder how it is that I am fetching her, but tell her as little as you can. You were sleepwalking, and I was clearing up downstairs and found you. Tell her anything, but not what you saw. Let someone else find him in the morning. You know nothing, understand? Nothing. It must come as a complete surprise to you, and in your shocked condition that should be convincing enough so long as you keep you head."

I felt his hand touch my cheek briefly, almost like a gesture of farewell; then the door closed and, shortly after, opened again. Michelle was beside me. In flickering candlelight she took one look at me and cried, "I'll fetch Dr. Nicholas!"

I murmured stupidly, "You can't, all the way to Rye."

"He isn't in Rye. He's here. Lie still, *chérie,* lie still!"

She was gone, and I was glad to obey. I wanted nothing so much as to slip into oblivion and forget that body swinging gently on the end of a creaking rope; but reason has a way of penetrating even when one's mind is bent on retreat, and reason argued that only a recently hanged body goes on swinging after it has kicked the ladder away, so I must have arrived on the scene very soon. Perhaps, even now, Julian's life might not have entirely ebbed.

But my father had said he was dead.

How did he know?

In my bemused state I was grateful for the gentleness of Nick's examination. I had often noticed the size of his hands and the strength of them, but never before realized that they could be more tender in their touch than Julian's had been even in the early days of our love, before his baser instincts took over.

I heard him say reassuringly that everything was all right, and ask what had happened. Michelle explained that I had fainted.

"And what caused the faint?"

She stammered that she had no idea.

"It was lucky I stayed overnight." His hand touched my brow reassuringly. "You'll be all right, Eustacia, but you must rest. I'll tell Julian you must on no account be disturbed." He added casually, "Where is he, by the way?"

Neither Michelle nor I could answer that: she because she didn't know, and I because I found it impossible to say that he was hanging by the neck in the great hall. I swallowed, tried to speak, and failed, whereupon Nicholas urged, "Don't try, Eustacia. I'll fetch a sleeping draft for you." In the flickering candlelight I saw speculation in his eyes. "It was lucky indeed that Michelle happened to come along to your room."

"I, I sent for her. I didn't feel well. I managed to get to the bell rope by the fireplace and rang. One of the servants answered; I can't remember which one."

Why was I lying? Something had to be done, and

quickly. I couldn't leave Julian hanging there just because some urgency had communicated from my father's mind into my own, commanding me to silence. I opened my mouth to speak, but was forestalled by Nicholas' telling Michelle to stay with me, and then he was gone.

Michelle held my hands tightly, asking what had happened and how it was that the man called Ballard had come to fetch her.

"He didn't tell you?"

"All he said was that you had fainted, and needed me. 'Go to her quickly,' he said, and off he went very quickly himself! A strange man, but I could see he was anxious about you." When I made no answer she continued, *"Chérie,* something serious has happened. You can't hide things from me. It is your husband, is it not? That is why he is not here."

The door opened. "You can go to bed now, Michelle. I'll stay until she sleeps."

It was Nicholas, and as soon as we were alone I said, "There is something I must tell you."

He answered firmly, "That can wait."

"No, now." I took a deep breath. "Julian is downstairs—the hangman's beam——I saw him swinging there."

He paused only to hold a glass to my lips, and after I had swallowed the draft, he left at once. And almost at once, I slept.

I learned next day that Julian was indeed dead, but not by hanging. He had been shot through the back of the neck, near the base of his skull, very precisely. The bullet was gone, and no weapon had been left lying around. The entrance hole was the size made by a .22-caliber pistol, of which there were many in the gun room.

A derringer, I thought. I knew. Victoria had shown it to me and made great play of leveling it at me as she talked about killing Julian. She had loaded it, demonstrating how easy it was to handle, then left it there on the table. I could see her, even now, walking out of the room with angry menace in her step after Julian had ordered her away. The whole scene came back to me as Dorcas sat beside my bed and told me that my husband was dead, reluctantly at first and then quite factually as she realized that I was calm enough to listen.

I let her run on, thankful that all I had to do was listen and make no answers, but suddenly my mind was alert and my memory sharp. Everything my father has said came back to me, and I understood it all.

He believed I had shot Julian, used the derringer that had been lying on the gun-room table when he intruded on the scene between us. He believed that sometime later I had used the pistol to kill my husband, and in a bungling attempt to cover up for me he had removed the bullet, cleaned the gun, and put it away amongst the others. He had dragged the body from wherever he had found it, fetched the ladder and some rope, and hauled Julian up to the hangman's beam, leaving the ladder on the floor to look as if it had been kicked away.

That had been the stirring in the night, the communication which had penetrated my sleep and sent me groping through the darkness of the house; and hearing me come, he must have hidden, because he expected no one to arrive on the scene so quickly, with the body still swinging. That was why he had been there, near at hand, watching from the shadows, and seen me faint.

It was amazing how coolly my mind could reason and follow the workings of his. His actions had been mistaken, perhaps foolish, but he had never been expert enough to avoid pitfalls. This time he had taken the wildest gamble of all, hoping to pull the wool over official eyes and lead to a confusion that would not only give me time to escape, but protect me by the logical conclusion that a woman would not have the strength to drag a man's body up a great ladder and sling it through a noose. If a woman had shot a man, she would leave him lying there.

And that was precisely what Dorcas was saying now. "Whoever did it was either trying to cover up for someone or carrying out an enormous bluff to give themselves time to get away. So it had to be someone strong enough to haul a man's body up that ladder, which means another man, of course."

I saw her looking at me carefully. I found it impossible to read the expression in her eyes. Life had taught her to hide her reactions, her thoughts, even her feelings perhaps. She did indeed wear a mask, and she wore it well. It was there now, although she looked at me so kindly. She was hiding a lot. Suspicion of me? Perhaps even sympathetic suspicion, but wondering whom I had enlisted to stage the fake hanging?

"Nicholas will be along to see you after you have drunk this." I saw then that she had brought me a bowl of broth. "If you are well enough, he will let you get up, but at the moment he must wait for the police and make his report on the body. One of the grooms had been dispatched to the nearest petty constable, who will then have to ride over to Rye to fetch an officer. It will take some time for them to get here."

I replied truthfully that there was no need for Nicholas to spare any time for me; I felt quite well. In fact, I felt amazingly calm and clearheaded, aware of miraculous relief because the threatened chains of a lifetime had suddenly slid away. I was free. Free of Julian and his cruelties, free of his corroding influence on my life, free of the fear that he would turn our child into a replica of himself.

Then Dorcas said softly, "But we must take very

great care of you, Eustacia. Do your realize that your coming child will now be the direct heir to Dragonmede?"

It was as if she had laid an ice-cold bandage on my heart, numbing it.

"Only if it is a son," I managed to say, and to avoid looking at her I began to sip the broth.

"Of course; but my poor brother cannot live long in his present condition, which means that your child may inherit sooner than you expect."

I managed to ask if Sir Vivian had yet been told of Julian's death. She looked aghast and said of course not; the shock would undoubtedly shorten his life.

She left me then, telling me to rest when I had finished the broth, but as soon as she had gone I put it aside and slid out of bed. My legs felt stronger than I had expected; the fainting fit had left me unharmed. All I wanted now was to get out of this room, out of this house, out into the fresh air which always seemed so much sweeter after the atmosphere of Dragonmede.

There was cold water in a pitcher in the *rouelle,* and I welcomed its sharp revival against my face and neck and arms. It seemed to be the final trick in clearing my head too, so that I was able to dress quite quickly. Then, wrapping a cloak about me, I slipped out of my room. I now knew the way to the green baize door leading from the private apartments to the servants' quarters. I had used it several times as a shortcut down to the mews, but today, with the shock of my husband's death paralyzing the household, I hoped I would meet no one, for the sight of his widow leaving the premises when she was expected to be prostrate with grief in her room would undoubtedly arouse comment

I was passing Hannah Grant's door when it opened abruptly. She seemed to possess some hidden antennae which picked up silent footfalls; how else had she known I was coming along the carpeted corridor?

She looked at me with grief-stricken eyes. "My poor Mrs. Julian! Should you not be abed?"

"I need fresh air, Hannah. Isolation in my room is unbearable."

"Of course, of course. I know how unbearable loneliness can be, but no one else would understand, would they? So you are slipping out unobserved? Do you intend to take a walk or a drive? Rest assured I shall tell no one, or they would hurry after you to bring you back, or worse."

"What do you mean, worse?"

"Merely that your child will now be heir in place of his poor dear father, so we wouldn't want anything to happen to you, would we?"

I drew my cloak closer and went on my way. Her voice followed me. There was a plaintive, injured note about it.

"A strange thing has happened, Mrs. Julian. Someone has stolen my final chapter." When I looked back, she said, "My history, you know. The history of this family on which I have worked for so many years. All recorded so neatly in my notebooks, and now the final one is missing!"

"I am sure it will turn up," I said, and closed the green baize door behind me.

I met no one on my way to the mews. Not even a stableboy was about. There seemed to be a strange, unearthly hush about Dragonmede, in which the sound of the pony's hooves, as I backed it into the shafts and harnessed it, seemed so loud on the cobblestones that I was sure someone would come hurrying to find out the cause, but no one did.

As I drove away, something made me look back. I was skirting the three-sided courtyard, and my glance fell directly on the window of the tower room. It had its usual empty, disused look, and yet I thought I detected a fleeting movement, as of someone withdrawing hastily. Hannah, perhaps, searching for her mislaid manuscript, or at her spying again?

I gave a mental shrug, dismissing her, and headed swiftly for Victoria's home, a mile or two outside Rye. When I reached the gates—tall, impressive wrought-iron affairs—the lodge keeper was fastening them back, as if preparing for an arrival or departure.

A departure, of course. I remembered, as I drove straight through, that Victoria was leaving for Marienbad this very day, so I wasn't surprised to see a carriage drawn up at the front door, and another behind it on which dome-lidded basket trunks were being loaded. I had timed my arrival well.

The house was of Queen Anne style, with a porticoed entrance opening straight onto the drive. It had a decided air of wealth and prosperity. As I reined to a halt, Victoria emerged, preceded by a footman carrying her personal grip. She looked elegant as always, but in the harsh light of day I saw shadows beneath her eyes and tight lines about her mouth which I had never noticed before.

She stopped dead at the sight of me.

"Don't tell me you have come to wish me bon voyage, Eustacia!"

I ignored the mockery in her voice; I could ignore many things about Victoria now. But before I could answer, she said, "You look dreadful. So pale! Are you ill?"

I told her quietly that Julian was dead, shot through the back of the neck, and that on examination Nicholas believed the wound to have been caused by a .22-caliber weapon.

She fought for control, and found it. "Come inside. We can't talk here." She beckoned authoritatively, and a coachman took the reins from me and helped

D.–K

me down, his face inscrutable; but I was beyond caring whether he had overheard, because the news would be all over the neighborhood very soon, if it wasn't already.

In a salon off the hall, Victoria closed the door and leaned against it weakly. Then she rallied and asked, "Was the bullet from the derringer?"

"We don't know yet. The murder weapon hasn't been found. Nor has the bullet."

I told her how I had awakened in the night with the feeling that something was happening in the house and that in a dream I thought I heard a shot. "But it couldn't have been a dream, I realize that now."

"And do you mean to tell me that no one else heard it?"

"Apparently not. My father-in-law is given something every night to make him sleep soundly. My mother-in-law . . ."

". . . was probably sleeping equally soundly, thanks to the champagne. But what about Dorcas? And the rest of the household?"

I hadn't thought about Dorcas, who slept in the room next to her brother's. Upon reflection, it seemed odd that nothing had disturbed her, but I said, "She is getting on in years and was probably very tired. And the rest of the household sleeps on the floor above, well away from the family's rooms. The servants' wing, of course, is far removed."

"And the gun room off a remote corner of the great hall," she finished reflectively.

"If he was shot there . . ."

She echoed sharply, *"If?* Weren't you accusing me just now of going back to that room to do just that?"

"Not accusing. Wondering. You declared your intention to kill him, so can you blame me?"

She said bitterly, "Don't tell me you came to warn

me! I can't believe you could have so much concern for your husband's ex-mistress."

I said truthfully that I was not sure why I had come; that all I had wanted was to get away from the oppressiveness of Dragonmede. At that she looked almost shocked.

"Oppressive? The place is magnificent! You've never appreciated it, but others have, others do . . ." She broke off, then finished slowly, "Do you realize what a powerful position you are now in?"

"Powerful?" I echoed.

"Or dangerous, whichever way you care to look at it. That child you are having will be next in line."

"I know."

"And you're not afraid?"

I tried not to show it, but against my will fear licked my heart.

Victoria sat down, unpinned an enormous hat with sweeping brim and magnificent ostrich feathers, and said with helpless self-pity, "I can't believe that I shall never see him again!" There was a bleak note which I had never expected to hear in her self-confident voice.

If she was guilty, she was a superb actress.

"Who found him?" she asked dully. "And what did you mean when you said 'if he was shot' in that room?"

I was forced then to tell her how I had discovered the body swinging from the hangman's beam.

"You mean that after he was shot someone actually tried to pretend that Julian had hanged himself?" She jerked to life then. "Doesn't that prove my innocence? Do you imagine I could have the physical strength for that?"

I shook my head. "No woman could. The police will realize that, of course."

"So they will suspect an accomplice; that is what you are implying, isn't it?"

"Dorcas has already thought of that."

Victoria had passed through shock and bewilderment; now anger took over. In one furious movement she crossed to the fireplace, tugged the bell rope repeatedly until a servant came running, and ordered that the baggage be unloaded and taken back upstairs. "At once! And tell my father we are not going to Marienbad."

When the door closed, she looked at me almost contemptuously. "And don't ask me why I did that, Eustacia. I'm not fool enough to leave at a time like this and give the impression that I'm running away. Is that what you expected me to do? Did you come here to make sure that I did, because nothing would point to my guilt more effectively? Tell them I loaded that pistol if you like, but try to prove that I used it! My coachman will vouch that he brought me home long before the ball was over, and everyone who saw me leave will be able to confirm that Julian was very much alive when I did so. And not only the servants here can testify to when I returned, but my father too. I went to his room to say good night. He never really settles until I do." Her mouth curved maliciously. "Sorry Eustacia, I didn't kill your husband, and the police aren't likely to suspect that I did. They are much more likely to suspect you. You both put up a great pretense of marital bliss last night, but it didn't fool me, and I shan't have the slighest hesitation in confessing—oh, so reluctantly!—that alas, all was not ideal in your marriage. No one knows that better than the woman a man really loves."

Two things haunted me as I drove away: the underlying viciousness which even grief could not overcome in her, and the feeling of impending danger which she and Dorcas and Hannah Grant had all made me aware of. Whoever killed Julian would want to kill me next because of the child I was bearing. I was in a most vulnerable and perilous position. Within the imprisoning walls of Dragonmede fear would stalk behind me like a shadow, and if I attempted to leave I would become the prime suspect for my husband's death.

It now seemed to me that in the whole of that great house there was only one person I could trust: Michelle, who would urge me to leave as quickly as possible because her prediction about evil influences had most certainly been fulfilled, as had her predictions about my marriage and the danger Julian spelled in my life. I had scorned them all, but I could scorn nothing now, not even my doubts about Julian's relatives. Miriam might sometimes drink too much, but not enough to make her careless should she plan to dispose of me. Beneath her unhappiness lay a ruthless ambition which could well refuse to be thwarted. Had she taken the first step already toward achieving it? Was it she who had found the loaded derringer, small and neat enough for a woman to handle? Had she removed the current heir as the first step toward removing his successor? When both were dead, her adored Christopher would come into his own.

Or Dorcas? What about Dorcas, who had made no appearance last night even though the shot must have echoed up the stairs to her room as well as my own? Nor had she referred to it when we talked this morning. But she had to take one more step than Miriam if she hoped to win Dragonmede for her own son—which meant that after me, Christopher would be the next victim.

And last of all, Nicholas. Would he aid and abet his mother, or even act independently? Every instinct cried out in protest, struggling to reject such ideas, because I loved this man and could no longer deny it. It was as if Julian's sudden death had just as suddenly ripped away the shutters with which I had deliberately covered my eyes. Imprinted on my mind was a picture of Nicholas as he lifted me onto Ladybird's saddle, a shadow from a tree branch casting triangles of shade beneath high cheekbones, emphasizing the deep cleft in his chin, the lines running from nose to mouth, the well-cut jaw, the sensuous lips—sensuous in a way that Julian's had never resembled. I knew the difference between lasciviousness and tenderness now. And then, in contrast, I saw the buccaneer's face, proud and ruthless and unyielding. I could not equate the two images. All my intuition grasped was my ability to love both.

All these thoughts absorbed me as I drove away from Victoria's home, and soon I saw the wide stretch of the Romney Marsh far below. I halted and looked down upon the dike-strewn land, with its patches of grazing sheep and tall reeds growing in the swampy areas stretching toward the sea. The winds that always cut across from France brushed my face, my hair, my brow. I took deep breaths of it, more reluctant than ever to return to the vast house of which—incredibly, it now seemed—my mother had cherished a picture.

I began the descent toward the marshes. In the distance I could see the wild stretch of shingle that was Dungeness; it was the outermost rim of land, the farthermost point to which I could travel away from Dragonmede. I had a longing to stand there with my face toward France and my back toward everything that menaced me. Fear might then slip away into the sea.

But when I reached it, the wild desolation of this thrusting spit of shingle was hardly reassuring, although the solitude was oddly comforting. No one could reach me here, I thought. No one touch me. I tethered the pony beside a fisherman's hut, then walked along the seemingly endless beach, which was marked with occasional fishing boats and tarred huts and goats nibbling wild plants that thrust upward through the shingle.

The tinkle of goat bells seemed incongruous against the background noise of the sea, until I realized that these solitary huts were inhabited by solitary fisherfolk whose only supply of milk came from the goats they bred.

Mist came drifting inland. By the time I reached the water's edge it had obscured the whole of the coastline curving from Rye to distant Hythe. I knew that soon I would have to go back, but still hesitated. As I stood there on an isolated stretch of beach with not a soul in sight, my solitude was complete.

Or so I thought until footsteps sounded behind me, growing louder, nearer, crunching the stones. There was a deliberation about them which made me jerk round in alarm. A figure was coming toward me: a woman, holding a cloak about her, her mist-enshrouded face not yet discernible. She approached relentlessly, and gathering fear rendered me incapable of moving. I saw the cloak billowing from beneath her folded arms, like the wings of a bat.

She stopped within a yard of me.

"At last," she said, "I have caught up with you."

It was Dorcas.

Nineteen

CHILL, APPREHENSION, EVEN terror ran through me before she said, "You must come with me at once. This is a most dangerous place when mist rises."

"Come with you to where?" I asked without moving.

"Home, of course. I could be angry with you for leaving Dragonmede without telling anyone, if it were not for the fact that something worse has happened."

I saw then that her face was haggard—not the face of the woman I knew.

I took a reluctant step toward her, asking what she meant.

"I mean that my brother is dead."

The words seemed to shout on the wind, striking me dumb. She reached out then and took hold of my arm, and I went with her like an automaton. Lucky Jack was dead. The throne of Dragonmede vacated so soon, waiting for my unborn son! *Dear God, dear God, let it be a daughter* . . . But whoever coveted the throne would take no chances on that.

Dorcas led me back across the shingle—back to the wilderness where goats strayed and tarred huts loomed up like black sentinels out of the mist. I saw fishermen folding their nets, felt their curious glances as we passed, and in the terrified corners of my mind ran the detached, incongruous thought that this fantastic stretch of earth could hold a strange beauty. Someone had told me that. Nicholas, this woman's son, whom I loved, and with whom I would like to return, to see the place through his eyes, if I ever lived to.

But there ahead of us was the pony and trap, and close beside it one of the horses from the Dragonmede stables, a mount that I had seen Dorcas use. If she attempted anything now, I had only to make a dash for the vehicle, untie it quickly, and drive away at speed. Despite a lifetime in the saddle, age was against Dorcas; a canter was the most she could manage now, and my high-stepping young pony could gallop well.

I jerked out, "You came alone in search of me?"

"Naturally. Nicholas left Garfield to wait for the police when the groom returned with the news that the petty constable was out after a poacher, so the message to the Rye constabulary was delayed. Smithers has gone directly to them now. We will be home long before they arrive. Nicholas organized search parties to look for you, and is out himself. The man Ballard couldn't be found when we looked for him to join in." She was tethering her horse behind the trap as she spoke. "The dogs hadn't even been fed. Their hungry barking could be heard all over the place. The man had no right to take French leave like that. Gone off for the day to Hastings or somewhere, I'll be bound. I can't bear animals to be neglected, and I shall reprimand him sharply when he returns."

But he wouldn't return. By now he would be safely on a cross-Channel steamer out of Dover or Folkestone, on the way to France and beyond. I felt a certain gladness, because at least he had tried to protect me, or believed he had. I knew I would never see him again.

"Fortunately, I caught sight of you in the distance, looking down on the marsh, but I failed to catch up with you, although I kept you in sight." She was handing me firmly into the trap, taking the reins in her own hands as she mounted beside me, determined to leave no chance of my escaping again. Apprehension expanded once more. Where was she taking me? What was she planning to do? Stage an accident somewhere—not necessarily to kill me, but to make me lose my child? Had all trust left me, that I could now suspect a woman whom I had previously liked and respected?

As she urged the pony forward, she went on, "It was thoughtless of you to frighten us like this, Eustacia. As if there hasn't been enough to shock us on this distressing day!" She caught at self-control and finished more gently, "Forgive me. I have no doubt it was shock that made you run away."

She gave the reins another jerk, heading inland along the rough track leading back to the marsh—but evidently knowing of a better route, because in far less time than it had taken me we were on the road home.

I asked what had caused her brother's sudden death.

"The very thing I feared: the shock about Julian."

"But you said he was not to be told yet."

"I did indeed, but Christopher acted without thought and went to console his father when I was not present. I know the boy meant well, and that he didn't realize the news had been kept from him, but if only I had been there I could have prevented it. You know I take my brother's tray to him personally. When I entered, there was Christopher, standing beside the bed with poor Jack—as I always call him, because he preferred it to Vivian—gasping and clinging to him. Of course, the boy was terrified. He thought his father was having another stroke, and didn't realize it was much worse." Her voice trembled. "He died very quickly, and perhaps after all it was better that he should, for there was no hope of recovery for him —none at all. He could have lingered in that terrible state for years, but to suffer a shock like that was something I would have spared him if I could. We were close, my brother and I. He was the only member of my family who stood by me when I married, and of course I stood by him when—"

She clipped off the words, and I finished quietly, "—when he was arrested for shooting someone in my mother's house."

Her haggard face jerked round at me. "So you did know!"

"Not until last night. It all happened when I was very small."

"For that reason I hoped you knew nothing of it, or had forgotten."

"But just in case any reminder might make me recall it and tell Julian, you removed every picture of his father before I arrived. But for restoring the family portraits, I would never have noticed, or wondered why."

She sighed. When she answered, her voice sounded very tired. "He never wanted his sons to know about the affair, and I don't think they ever did. They probably learned that their father had been involved in a scandal of some sort, but that was nothing new in Kershaw history and would pass unheeded. Of course, it was a shock when we heard whom Julian had married, and I kept your true identity from my brother."

"Hence his reaction when he saw me."

"I'm afraid so. For that, I blame myself. I didn't know whether to prepare him, or keep silent. I decided to keep silent, because since the days of the trial we had never referred to it, and I hoped his memory might have totally rejected the past and that not even the sight of you, so very like your mother, would revive it. I tried to choose what I judged to be a good moment to present you and failed. For that, you must forgive me."

I asked painfully, "Was he anything like Julian, when a young man?"

"Only in looks. Julian was more like his grandfather in character; they say that characteristics skip a generation. Certainly my own father was not a man to be proud of, and I have always been thankful that Nicholas so closely resembles my husband."

So she did know what Julian had been like.

"All the same," I said, "your brother hurt my mother. She loved him. Really loved him."

"It may surprise you to know that he loved her too. After his first wife's death he met Luella again in London. I remember him telling me about it. He had come over to Rye to visit Matthew and me, and suddenly he asked if I remembered that wild young girl from the ficarage. 'She's grown into one most beautiful women I've ever known,' he said; 'beautiful in every way.' I knew then that he had fallen in love with her. Later, he told me more, about the things that had happened to her: her runaway husband, the way she was forced to earn a living —and about the little girl she wanted so passionately to protect. I knew then that he did indeed love her."

"Yet he never went back to her."

"And for that you blame him. It is easy to criticize others, Eustacia, especially when people we care about are involved. I suppose that is why I can see Jack's side of things. The Kershaws were on the verge of bankruptcy; the estate was overwhelmingly in debt; he had two sons, still to be educated and their futures planned for. And then there was the cost of the trial. Miriam paid for it, as she paid for everything else, without his knowledge. That placed him under an obligation he could never discharge. Say if you like that Miriam bought him; it is as easy to sit in judgment on people as it is to criticize them. But she could never buy his love, poor soul, and since you came she has seen him watching you from his window and recognized, as I have, his yearning for the past. He didn't see you—he saw Luella. He wasn't hating you; he was crying out for what he had lost."

We rode in silence after that, until Dorcas broke it by saying, "I've often wondered how you and Julian met. He told us nothing, but that was typical of my nephew. He was always secretive. As far as your marriage was concerned, it seemed obvious that his real reason for silence was that he really had been on the verge of marrying Victoria. He spoke the truth when he said that they were never formally betrothed, but it was to have been announced on his return from London. Then he met you and jilted her without even letting her know. There was a cruel streak in him, as I'm sure you found out. Do tell me how you met him, Eustacia."

"Crowther brought him to my mother's house."

"*Crowther!*" The reins fell limply into her lap. The pony faltered, and her hands tightened at once, but the gesture was entirely mechanical, for she was staring at me with an astonishment I failed to understand.

I said, "You seem shocked. Why? How was Crowther to know that Julian's father and my mother had been acquainted in the past?"

"He knew well enough. His brother was the man whom Jack shot accidentally."

Another piece for the jigsaw, filling an unsuspected gap. The inference was obvious, and Dorcas confirmed it.

"Crowther has good reason to hate the Kershaws. First because of his brother, a hotheaded gambler from all accounts, but his brother all the same. And then his daughter, seduced by Gerald and left with an illegitimate child. I have always had a lurking fear that one day Crowther would exact venegance if he could. It seems he has achieved it. He entered Dragonmede for the first time in his life last night."

"And murdered Julian? Is that what you believe?"

"He could have done it. An eye for an eye."

I had a picture of the rough, bluff Northerner sitting in my mother's drawing room that first night, sardonic, watchful, calculating, frightening me a little with his shrewd assessment of us all. It seemed in character that such a man might wait years to avenge his brother's death, scheming as he amassed enough money to meet the Kershaws on a social footing, worming his way in, then finding himself up against the stiff, crusted snobbishness of county society, all doors barred and his daughter used for their pleasure as any village wench might be.

Small wonder if he decided to use Julian as his pawn in the first move of the game, offering him hospitality in his splendid London flat and good gambling at a card salon he knew of. Events after that might have been unpredictable, for Crowther had no means of knowing that Julian would be attracted to Luella Rochdale's daughter, but he might well have calculated that Luella would be only too pleased to make Sir Vivian's son lose heavily at her tables.

What he had not known was that maliciousness was never part of Luella's nature. She had accepted the buffetings of fate with a stoicism not untinged with bitterness, but her delight in having Lucky Jack's son brought unexpectedly into her house had been prompted solely by ambition for me. What she had missed, I might achieve. To her, it was a vicarious triumph to place me in shoes that she had never occupied, and to Crowther it was enjoyable to aid and abet her, a successful ploy in hitting back at the Kershaws. But the idea of his killing a Kershaw son to avenge his brother's death was more difficult to accept, for I could imagine no man being willing to leave an unhappy daughter to face the additional burden of being branded as the offspring of a murderer.

As we turned through the entrance of Dragonmede, passing the scarred walls of the burned-out lodge, I experienced even more sharply that sense of imprisonment which the place gave out. The feeling of threat intensified. These walls had never welcomed me. I had never been wanted here. I was wanted even less now. Dorcas could be dragging Crowther before me as a red herring to divert suspicion.

I gave her a sidewise glance, and saw her face staring straight ahead. It told me nothing.

Nicholas was in the hall, shedding his greatcoat. The relief in his face was reassuring and, I felt, genuine, but I was afraid now to trust my emotions, afraid to trust anyone. Yet I was glad of his nearness, and of the feeling of strength and reliability he gave out. I was ready to seize on any hint of support in a world that was fraught with fear.

He said, "Sol will be as relieved as I to know you are back safe and unharmed. I'll send a message to him. He has been out searching too. I came back to find out if there was any news."

I answered tautly, "Why shouldn't I be safe and unharmed?"

"Because you are suffering from the aftereffects of shock, and I suspect my mother has told you about my uncle, which has shocked you more. I can see it in your face. There is little you can hide from me, Eustacia."

He could put an intimate note into his voice that wrapped itself around the heart. I had to mistrust that too. I walked toward the stairs, not looking at him, struggling to untie my cloak with fingers that were suddenly unsteady. He followed, and when we reached the quiet corridor leading to my room, he halted and untied the strings for me. I felt his fingers accidentally touch my skin, but when I jerked away, he took my face between his hands and held it gently.

"You have no need to be afraid of me, Eustacia. I love you, and if you haven't realized it, you have been deliberately blinding yourself. I've loved you almost from the moment I first saw you, and if I'm being premature in telling you this so soon after your husband's death, I don't give a damn. All I want is that you should believe it, and remember it."

He stooped and kissed me. Beneath his lips my own grew warm, and when he held me close I experienced something that I had never felt in Julian's arms. Something more than passion. Deeper, and more abiding. The passion was there, but linked now with a sense of protection.

When he put me aside, he said with authority, "I told Michelle that if you returned before I did, she was to take some food to your room, see that you ate it, and make you rest after that. I'll find her at once."

I went to my room in a daze, almost afraid to believe what had happened and the things he had said, but suddenly in an insecure world I felt at peace. Not even the yellow room disturbed me with its memories of cruelty and disillusion.

There was a tap on the door, and Christopher's voice calling my name softly. He looked bereft, standing outside with the helpless bewilderment of a child.

"Cousin Eustacia, please let me talk to you. Everyone is blaming me. Mamma is prostrate on her bed. But how was I to know that Papa didn't know about Julian?"

I felt in no mood for talking or sympathizing, but his grief reached out to me and refused to be rejected.

"We can't talk here," I said.

"Of course not. How about the tower room? No one ever goes up there. You'll find the steps leading up to it at the far end of this corridor on the other side of the main landing."

I nodded. "Very well. I'll join you in a few minutes."

"Promise?" he begged.

"I promise."

When he had gone I shed my cloak, tidied my hair, then walked along the corridor. On the way I met Michelle, carrying my tray. I told her to leave it in my room and went on my way, crossing the landing to the opposite extension.

The stone steps spiraled upward steeper than I expected, and the tower room was larger than it appeared from outside. I looked around curiously, surprised to find that although the floor was of stone the place was comparatively warm, owing to heavy curtains of velour which covered the walls. I had expected a lumber room, but it was unexpectedly tidy, well furnished, and over by a leaded window stood an easel with a black canvas on it.

"So this is where you paint?"

Christopher nodded absently, saying he had been

about to start something but wasn't in the mood anymore.

"What were you planning?" I asked, hoping to lure him away from self-pity.

"Something I thought of last night at the ball—plenty of color and life and movement; but now death has taken over, I can't recapture it. All I can remember is Papa's face when I told him Julian had hanged himself. It will haunt me forever, I know it will!"

He finished on a hysterical note, and I said sternly that he should have told his father no such thing, because it was untrue. "Surely you knew? Nicholas discovered he had been shot as soon as he examined the body."

Christopher nodded, tears blinding him. "I do know, but how could I tell Papa that his son had been murdered? His favorite son, too. Gerald and Julian were always his favorites."

I moved impatiently. If he was going to start whining about that again, I was not staying to listen.

"Don't go! Please, don't go!" He rose and drew me over to a chair near his own, urging me into it. "I—I know I'm irritating and ineffectual and stupid. I know I'm not a man like Gerald and Julian were, but I do feel things more than they did. The wouldn't have paused to think about the best way to comfort Papa, but I did. I wanted him to know that he still had one son who cared about him, and then I just seemed to blurt things out badly, because when face to face with him I was always terrified. It was bad enough before he had the stroke, but afterwards it was worse because his eyes became so staring. They seemed to look right into you. You can't imagine how it felt."

"I can. I do."

"Dear Cousin." He reached forward and clung to me. "You are the only person in this house I can talk to. I've been waiting so desperately for you to come home. I tried to tell Aunt Dorcas, but she wouldn't listen, and of course Mamma had hysterics, and Cousin Nick was only concerned about what could have happened to you. No one had time for me, no one at all. The way he *clung* to me, Eustacia!—Papa, I mean." He shuddered at the recollection. "All I said was that it must have been an accident, Julian hanging himself like that. He had probably been fooling around after the ball. He had drunk too much."

"He wasn't drunk when I last saw him. Getting drunk was one thing Julian never did."

"But he did other things, didn't he? Like being unfaithful to you."

I rose and made for the door.

"I didn't come up here to talk about the past."

"Forgive me! I'm so distraught I really don't know what I'm saying. Don't go!"

He shot in front of me, barring my way, insisting that he had to make someone understand that he had acted without thought.

I said tiredly, "I'm sure everyone realizes you acted without thought." Fatigue was claiming me. I wanted nothing so much as to get back to my room, but the wretchedness in Christopher's eyes held me.

"But they are all blaming me, and they will blame me forever. They'll say I killed my own father!"

"They'll say nothing of the sort. Shock killed him."

"But I was responsible. I can't forgive myself."

He broke down then. I was helpless in the face of his grief. I touched his bowed head, and he caught at my hand, clinging to it tightly.

"I wanted to tell him that he could rely on me to take Julian's place and run Dragonmede, and do all the things he and Gerald had done. Well, some of the things. Not the hunting and killing, of course—I couldn't face up to that—but maintaining Dragonmede as it should be. After all, that was why he married my mother, for the money the Kershaws needed. That is probably why he never loved me."

The self-pity was back. With infinite kindness and patience I might be able to teach him to harness that self-pity someday, but I was incapable of starting just now. I tried to free my hand, but failed.

"Let me go," I said. "I'm very tired."

He looked up with stricken eyes.

"Do you think I'll be able to do it, Eustacia? Do you think I'll be able to run Dragonmede well? With a new steward, of course, because David Foster will have to go. I shall tell him myself, of course." He straightened his shoulders and smiled. "I shall enjoy that."

"I don't follow you. Why should David go?"

"Because of what Julian told me last night." There were tears on his cheeks. I found myself watching them dry. I was confused, puzzled.

"What did Julian tell you?"

Christopher's voice choked again, but this time with anger, not grief.

"That David was going to marry Penelope. He taunted me with it. He actually laughed and said, 'How does that make you feel, sir?' He sneered when he called me 'sir,' as if I wasn't masculine enough to deserve the title. And now, after all, it is mine."

I said gently, "Not yet. As far as I am concerned, you are welcome to it, but if I have a son. . . ."

"You won't have a son."

"One can't be sure of these things, though personally I hope for a daughter."

"I can understand that. What woman would want to bear a son like Julian? And I do hope we can persuade the police that he really did hang himself. Suicide is unpleasant, but not nearly so unpleasant as murder, and I couldn't bear to think of you being suspected."

With one swift wrench, I freed my hand. "I can't be suspected of a crime I didn't commit."

"But people have been. History is full of such cases. Innocent people have even been hanged."

I had had enough. I made for the door, but again he was before me. This time he was smiling and holding something out to me.

"It's a present, Eustacia. I painted it specially for you. It was to be a surprise. Please, take it."

I accepted it tiredly, not bothering to unwrap it, and his voice went on, "We really must try to make the police believe that Julian hanged himself."

"That will be impossible. For one thing, there is the wound."

"Which might not have killed him. That would have to be proved. The shot might only have scathed him."

"Nicholas can certify that death was due to shooting."

"Perhaps we could persuade him to say otherwise."

"I can't imagine Nicholas agreeing to that, unless it was true. Besides, there would have to be a motive for Julian's hanging himself."

"But there was," Christopher answered softly. "He killed Gerald."

Twenty

THE ROOM WAS spinning. I put out a hand to steady myself, realized that Christopher was about to take hold of it again, and thrust him away.

"It's true, Cousin Eustacia. I have proof." From behind the blank canvas on the easel he whipped out a notebook and held it up. "It's all recorded here.

We have an historian in this house—quite an archivist, in fact. Hannah Grant has kept meticulous records for years. Poor dear, she's in a fret about the loss of her final manuscript, but she's not going to have it back, because she wrote down everything she saw the night Gerald was drowned.

"Where did you get that?"

"From the kennelman's cottage, of all places. He'd been twisting that silly old woman round his little finger, flattering her so much that she let him read her precious history of the Kershaws, the one nobody really believed she was writing. I used to see them from this window, sitting down there in the courtyard together. One day she showed him some notebooks, and he seemed to find them so interesting that I wondered if they might be worth looking at. Until then I'd paid no attention to the woman's boastings. She even let the man borrow the books, and when he gave them back to her a few days ago, she handed him one more. The last one. This one. The next time I saw her safely in the courtyard I went along to her room and found the rest. I borrowed one at a time after that, because she would have missed them if I'd taken the lot. I learned all sorts of things; about my father being brought to trial for shooting a man in the house of a woman named Luella Rochdale, for instance. That made me sit up, I can tell you, because that was the name in your wedding announcement. 'Eustacia Rochdale, daughter of Mrs. Luella Rochdale.' It couldn't be coincidence, I thought. No wonder poor Mamma was in such a state about it! And of course, it won't look well for you if it comes out."

I answered stonily, "That is all in the past."

"But the past links up with the present. There's no escaping it. That was what I told Julian last night, but not until he goaded me. Until then, I'd kept everything to myself. When I'd finished reading old Hannah's little pile of notebooks, I went to Ballard's cottage and found this one. He was safely out of the way, hanging decorations for the ball. It's a pity there isn't time for you to read this book, Eustacia, because it makes the most fascinating reading! Julian tampered with the boat. Hannah saw him from her window. He was boring a hole through the bottom and then left the boat high and dry on the bank for Gerald to use. He must have known his brother was going to the arbor later. Hannah records that Gerald came at dusk and dragged the boat down to the water and pushed off. I can guess why he was going. When either of my two dear half brothers had a tryst in the arbor he would go across to see that everything was in readiness—Julian for Victoria, Gerald for Penelope. That was the situation then, but of course there were others as far as Julian was concerned, very often the servant girls. Gerald was different. He really *was* in love with Penelope and, I think, wanted to marry her. Only this time he didn't come back to meet her and ferry her across. And although it has always been maintained that the boat capsized, it isn't true. It shipped water gradually until, right out there in the middle of the lake, it sank like a stone."

"If Hannah Grant really knew all this, I cannot imagine why she kept silent."

"I can. To reveal the truth would have meant an end to her living here. Where could she have gone? Only to the workhouse, for she hasn't a penny of her own. She would do anything not to sacrifice her home at Dragonmede, but luckily she couldn't resist keeping a sort of diary." Christopher gave a high, excited giggle. "Such an athlete Gerald was, but he couldn't swim! Julian knew that, of course. He would never have become heir of Dragonmede if he hadn't got rid of his older brother."

Remotely, I saw Julian staring down upon the lake, like a man mesmerized or haunted.

Christopher raced on, "He didn't like it last night

when I retaliated by telling him what I knew. I meant to keep it a secret awhile longer, but taunting me like that, about David Foster being a man and me being only half of one, I had to hit back somehow." He finished at a tangent: "By the way, I promised to show you my paintings, didn't I?"

I managed to say, as I edged to the door, "Some other time—" but my words were cut off by the sound of heavy curtains being wrenched aside, and staring at me from the walls, all around me, every way I looked, were pictures of such savagery and violence that I recoiled.

In the small corner of my mind not blanked out by shock something cried, *"A maniac . . . a maniac . . . you're dealing with a maniac . . ."*

Christopher was babbling now. "Of course, Mamma didn't want you to see them. She has always stopped me from showing my paintings to people, because she doesn't like them. That's why she has a key to this room and why she put up these heavy curtains to hide them. I can't think why. They're really very good. I started when I was quite young, painting all the things Gerald and Julian made me want to do to them, and it was wonderful. On paper I could do them all, and more besides; things I could never do in real life. And yet, last night, it was so easy. I'd spent the evening watching Penelope and that man dancing together; she looked so pretty and they both looked so happy that I hated them for it. I knew there was something between them which I could never experience. And afterwards, when everyone was gone, Julian called me into the gun room. He said he wanted to have a word with me. He told me then that Penelope and David were going to be married, and how well suited they were. 'Don't you agree, young Chris? Every woman needs a real man to make her happy. Half a man, like you, is no good to the opposite sex!' Then he laughed and went on laughing, so I flung in his face all I knew about Gerald's death. He stopped laughing then.''

Christopher made a slicing gesture with his hand. "His laughter cut off just like that! I could see every word I'd uttered was true, although he pretended it wasn't and said I'd have to produce proof, so I taunted him even more by telling him that I could not only do that but produce a witness as well—Hannah Grant, so respectable that she's never told a lie in her life!"

I was reaching the door. A few more steps and I'd be there . . .

Christopher's voice continued boastfully, "I'm not the stupid fool everyone thinks! Julian found that out. When he ordered me to hand over any proof I had, I refused. I wouldn't even tell him where I'd hidden it, which was up here, of course. He shouted, "I'll make you hand it over, you lily-livered . . ." The voice choked again. "I won't tell you the name he called me, because I hate it, *hate it!* That was when he reached for the pistol on the table; but I was quicker, because I was standing right beside it, and snatched it first. Then he started laughing again and told me to stop playacting. 'You don't even know how to fire the thing! You've never handled a gun in your life!'

"I can hear him saying that now, sneering and going on laughing as he turned to walk out of the room. Then suddenly there was a neat little hole in the nape of his neck. I didn't realize it could be so tidy. I just dropped the pistol and stepped over him and went to bed, and someone kindly slung him from the hangman's beam, just like in the legend of Dragonmede."

I had reached the door now, but so had he. To my surprise, he reached behind and opened it for me.

"But I've kept you too long, Cousin. I can see you are anxious to go. And of course you must go, but I really am sorry, because I was so fond of you. But do look at my present first. I painted it specially for you and you haven't even unwrapped it. Allow me."

I heard the rustle of paper, and then in one swift movement he held the picture up. There was a leaping nausea in my stomach, a dizziness behind my eyes, a roaring sound in my ears through which I seemed to hear Nicholas calling my name a long way off. I felt my body jerk back in swift recoil and my hands fly out to shut from my sight the picture of a dead baby. I staggered in retreat, and Christopher came after me relentlessly, thrusting the picture before my eyes.

"Dear Eustacia, take a look at your child. This is the only way you will ever see him, if you see him at all. I've never really wanted to kill you, but you do understand, don't you, that the possibility of another heir superseding me is out of the question? I've always pretended not to want Dragonmede, but it isn't true. Mamma has every right to feel that I deserve to inherit, but her reasons aren't mine. I want to prove that I'm more worthy as a successor than Gerald or Julian would ever have been. When Gerald drowned, I was glad. That left only Julian, although how to get rid of him was another matter."

He waved a graceful hand toward the violent paintings on the walls. "Any one of these methods, perhaps, except that they would have been impossible to cover up or make appear to be accidental, and somehow I lacked the courage except on canvas. But when he married you, things became urgent. If you had a child, a son, I would be further away then ever. That was why I loosened Ladybird's shoe one day, hoping that the next time you rode her an accident would happen and prevent you from ever having a child. Many a woman rider has been injured that way and motherhood ruled out forever."

Through the tightness in my throat I jerked out, "And what if he had married Victoria?"

"I would have done the same thing, of course. Only I do admire you so much more than Victoria that I didn't like the idea of hurting you. I don't now. I don't really want to kill you, because you've been kind to me ever since you came. But it will be over quickly, I promise, and the important thing is that it will look like a genuine accident."

As if from a distance I heard footsteps echoing from below—hurrying, urgent—but they could not have been real, because Christopher didn't hear them at all. He was smiling, giggling, excited and elated as he came closer and closer. I took a violent step backward and felt my heel pitch over the top step at the precise moment that he thrust hard against me and sent me hurtling down. My body bumped and spiraled heavily in a blinding whirl of pain, bouncing, jarring, vicious with every impact until I was miraculously halted caught up, held.

But the searing pain remained, consuming me.

Epilogue

I LEARNED LATER that after waiting for me to return to my room, Michelle went in search of Nicholas, telling him how she had seen me go up to the tower room and because this was part of the family's private apartments she didn't like to intrude.

He was in time to save me, but not my child.

I have recovered from the mixed sadness of that now. There is always a tragic sense of loss when an expectant mother miscarries, but looking back, I think it was perhaps a good thing that Julian's seed was not perpetuated.

And looking back, it all seems so long ago, for I

have had three children since becoming Mrs. Nicholas Bligh, and they fill our house in Rye with perpetual noise and my days with perpetual work, but occasionally I find time to escape to the top floor, which Nicholas converted into a studio for me so that I could paint undisturbed. It looks out across the marshes, for the house stands close to the Ypres Tower, looking over and beyond the spot where we talked together for the first time, with the wild strip of Dungeness slicing the sea, and the coast of distant France sometimes emerging on the horizon.

I love this house, for there is happiness in it. It is nothing so grand as Dragonmede, but neither Nicholas nor I ever want a house like Dragonmede. I learned before I married him that he had renounced any future claim to the place long before I was brought there as Julian's bride, and that he had kept the fact secret even from his mother in case she should be disappointed. Dorcas wasn't. She was glad. She wanted her son to tread in her husband's footsteps and live his kind of life.

And that is what he did, and still does, but more extensively, for since Fothergill's retirement the practice has grown, and it is because of my husband's ability that it has. When he took it over exclusively we were able to move out of the rooms above the surgery and find a place that would house a family, and then move Sol out of his crumbling cottage and install him over the surgery instead.

But Nicholas did more than that. He went to London and insisted upon my mother's disposing of the lease of the Bloomsbury house while I found one in Rye to replace it. She lives here now, with Bella, in an Elizabethan cottage in the square surrounding the church, midway between our house and the surgery, so that she is able to visit us whenever she wishes and also keep an eye on old Sol, as well as on Bella, for although ostensibly it is Bella who looks after her, in reality the positions are reversed, since Bella is now too old to do much more than shuffle round the house. All this has given my mother a new lease on life, and age, perhaps, has mellowed her. Caring for others has imparted a serenity she never had before.

We never talk about the past, Luella and I. What is gone is gone, and what she did, well, but for that I would never have met Nicholas eventually, so I can bless her for it now.

But there was one moment when she realized that I knew the truth about my father. That was when a man called one day, a seafaring man who had put in at Dover and journeyed from there to Dragonmede in quest of me, and learned my whereabouts from Garfield. He brought a ring—a man's signet ring which I recognized at once. It bore the engraved initials E.B.R., and as the man placed it in my palm I knew that even after all these years Luella recognized it too.

She had come to take tea with me, so it was impossible to conceal anything from her or to prevent the man from explaining his call. The owner of the ring, Eustace Ballard Rochdale, had died of some sickness on the Gold Coast, but before doing so he had asked the sailor to deliver this ring to his daughter with the message that it was all a gambler had to leave, except his blessing.

When he had gone, Luella sat quietly, looking at me. Neither of us spoke. Then she asked if she might have the ring, and I gave it to her. She folded her fingers about it gently. At one time it had meant something to her; now it meant only that she was free at last, but too late.

She wrapped the ring carefully in a handkerchief and put it away. We have never referred to it since.

Penelope Crowther went to live in Dorset after she married, where her husband manages his parents' farms. Occasionally we hear of her through her father, who writes that the marriage is happy and successful, but after she went he returned to his mills in the North and sold Bodiam Hall to Dorcas, who was well provided for under her brother's will. Like me, she was glad to leave Dragonmede when Christopher was certified and taken away, but Miriam remains there in splendor and proud ownership. I visit her occasionally, and her attitude had softened toward me since I married Nicholas and went out of her life. Sometimes, too, I see Victoria, who still seems to be looking for the illustrious husband she hankers after.

I talked with Crowther only once before he left. Dorcas was present.

"I want you to know, Ma'am," he said to her, "that I've borne your brother no hatred for the accident which involved mine. He was a wild, hotheaded wastrel, that lad, forever causing trouble. Apparently he drew a gun on Lucky Jack, so what could the man do but defend himself? Gerald Kershaw's treatment of my daughter was another matter. I'd have had his scalp for that if I could, and I must admit I got a satisfaction out of taking Julian to be fleeced at the card tables, and a certain pleasure at seeing Eustacia installed as a bride at Dragonmede. It made me laugh up my sleeve. I never bothered to think whether it was fair to Eustacia, but I didn't know then the kind of chap she was really marrying. Nor did her mother. I can guess now, but I doubt if Luella does."

"She must never guess," I told him, closing a door on the past once and for all.

"Aye," he agreed. "And you can put it well behind you now, lass. You've got yourself a better man by far."

Who knows that better than I? I can hear him now, coming into the house and shouting greetings to the children as they rush to meet him, and Michelle ordering them to make less noise because their mamma is painting and must not be disturbed, and I smile and lay aside my brushes, for my husband's footsteps are coming up the stairs, two at a time, impatient and eager, knowing that whatever I am doing I am always ready to put it aside for him.

All Futura Books are available at your bookshop or newsagent, or can be ordered from the following address:
Futura Books, Cash Sales Department,
P.O. Box 11, Falmouth, Cornwall.

Please send cheque or postal order (no currency), and allow 30p for postage and packing for the first book plus 15p for the second book and 12p for each additional book ordered up to a maximum charge of £1.29 in U.K.

Customers in Eire and B.F.P.O. please allow 30p for the first book, 15p for the second book plus 12p per copy for the next 7 books, thereafter 6p per book.

Overseas customers please allow 50p for postage and packing for the first book and 10p per copy for each additional book.